LOSERS in SPACE

BOOKS BY
John Barnes

•••••·•●

The Man Who Pulled Down the Sky

Sin of Origin ♦ *Orbital Resonance*

Wartide ♦ *Battlecry*

Union Fires ♦ *A Million Open Doors*

Mother of Storms ♦ *Kaleidoscope Century*

One for the Morning Glory ♦ *Encounter with Tiber* (with Buzz Aldrin)

Patton's Spaceship ♦ *Washington's Dirigible*

Caesar's Bicycle ♦ *Apostrophes and Apocalypses* (stories)

Earth Made of Glass ♦ *Finity*

Candle ♦ *The Return* (with Buzz Aldrin)

The Merchants of Souls ♦ *The Duke of Uranium*

The Sky So Big and Black ♦ *A Princess of the Aerie*

In the Hall of the Martian King ♦ *Gaudeamus*

The Armies of Memory ♦ *Tales of the Madman Underground*

Directive 51 ♦ *Daybreak Zero*

The Last President ♦ *Losers in Space*

John Barnes

LOSERS in SPACE

VIKING
an imprint of Penguin Group (USA) Inc.

VIKING

Published by Penguin Group

Penguin Group (USA) Inc., 345 Hudson Street, New York, New York 10014, U.S.A.

Penguin Group (Canada), 90 Eglinton Avenue East, Suite 700, Toronto, Ontario, Canada M4P 2Y3 (a division of Pearson Penguin Canada Inc.)

Penguin Books Ltd, 80 Strand, London WC2R 0RL, England

Penguin Ireland, 25 St Stephen's Green, Dublin 2, Ireland (a division of Penguin Books Ltd)

Penguin Group (Australia), 250 Camberwell Road, Camberwell, Victoria 3124, Australia (a division of Pearson Australia Group Pty Ltd)

Penguin Books India Pvt Ltd, 11 Community Centre, Panchsheel Park, New Delhi – 110 017, India

Penguin Group (NZ), 67 Apollo Drive, Rosedale, Auckland 0632, New Zealand (a division of Pearson New Zealand Ltd.)

Penguin Books (South Africa) (Pty) Ltd, 24 Sturdee Avenue, Rosebank, Johannesburg 2196, South Africa

Penguin Books Ltd, Registered Offices: 80 Strand, London WC2R 0RL, England

First published in 2012 by Viking, a member of Penguin Group (USA) Inc.

1   3   5   7   9   10   8   6   4   2

Copyright © John Barnes, 2012

All rights reserved

LIBRARY OF CONGRESS CATALOGING-IN-PUBLICATION DATA IS AVAILABLE

ISBN 978-0-670-06156-3

Printed in U.S.A.   Set in Melior   Book design by Nancy Brennan

For Diane Talbot,
because I've got some catching up to do,
and because, with her around, I want to do it.

CONTENTS

Notes for the Interested, #0

Please skip this and every other Note for the Interested if you're not interested

Most science fiction fans nowadays come to SF from gaming, movies, television, and other media, rather than from reading. If you haven't seen much written science fiction, you might not be familiar with "hard" science fiction (hard SF).

Hard SF is science fiction where the science is as true and correct as the writer can make it in the light of current science; George Scithers, a great editor (and one of the first ones I worked with), used to say it was hard science fiction if, when Superman leaped a tall building at a single bound, he kicked a hole in the sidewalk.

Media SF is rarely hard SF. Film, television, games, and comics have always favored stories like *Firefly, Doom,* and *Star Trek* (where science is mostly invented by screenwriters), and *Star Wars, Doctor Who,* and *Spider-Man* (where the science is really old-fashioned magic, just given scientific-sounding names).

Hard SF is found mostly in literature; it's an elite club, where the elite geeks insist that writers respect facts, such as:

- explosions are silent in the vacuum of space
- there are fewer than 120 chemical elements and their properties are known; no one discovers new antigravity metals

- "force field" refers to gravity or magnetism, not to magic glass shields
- an invisible man would be blind because his invisible corneas would not focus light and his invisible retinas wouldn't receive it
- a human being is more closely related to a clam than to any being from another planet, and would be less likely to have children with an extraterrestrial than to pollinate a rosebush.
- the physics of spaceflight requires so much energy to lift even a small object off Earth that a spaceship has to be a thin shell connected to a mountain of explosives.

Hard SF fans like accuracy, they like to learn things, and they like to know what's real and what isn't. So written hard SF uses one form or another of what we called **infodumps**: lectures about the science, the imaginary world, and so on, either directly or by having characters explain things to each other. (How many characters does it take to change a lightbulb in a hard SF story? One to do it, and one to say, "As you know, Bob, a lightbulb consists of a tungsten filament in an inert-gas-filled glass enclosure . . .")

People who geek on just knowing stuff, either about the real science or the fictional future, *love* infodumps, but infodumps are boring obstacles for readers who just want to get on with the story.

I'm trying out a compromise: information that would go into infodumps is in short sections called *Notes for the Interested*.

In the main text, I'll explain only as much as a reader needs to follow the story; if it's just more cool science upon which you may wish to geek, I'll package it in a *Note for the Interested*. You can read the whole book and follow the story without reading a single *Note for the Interested* (if you're *not* interested). On the other hand, if you *are* interested, they're easy to find.

FROM
EARTH
TO
BEYOND
THE
MOON

MARCH 13–APRIL 23, 2129

POSITIONS OF MARS, EARTH, AND SPACESHIP VIRGO—MARCH 13-APRIL 23, 2129

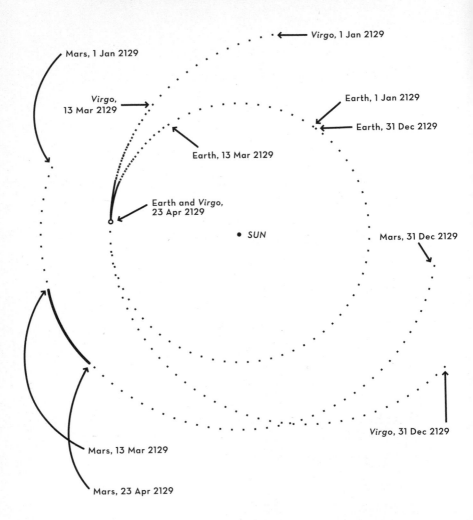

Virgo, 1 Jan 2129

Mars, 1 Jan 2129

Virgo, 13 Mar 2129

Earth, 1 Jan 2129

Earth, 31 Dec 2129

Earth, 13 Mar 2129

Earth and Virgo, 23 Apr 2129

SUN

Mars, 31 Dec 2129

Virgo, 31 Dec 2129

Mars, 13 Mar 2129

Mars, 23 Apr 2129

We're looking down on the solar system from directly above the north pole of the sun. The solid dark lines show the movements of the planets and *Virgo*; dots show the position of the sun (at center) and some reference positions of where the planets and ship are during the rest of 2129. From this perspective, the planets and Virgo go around the sun counterclockwise.

EENIE MEANIE MINEY MOE

March 13, 2129. Baker Lounge, Excellence Shop, District of Oregon/Idaho, Earth.

"THIS COLLECTION OF losers and misfits will now come to order for a report from your activities chairman." We look at the stairs and see Derlock's descending feet. "Or in other words, shut up, all you moes, I got the stuff!"

"What stuff?" Bari's voice aches with hope that "the stuff" will be some new drug. Sheeyeffinit. My shortly-to-be-ex-boyfriend hasn't even noticed how hard I've been ignoring him, but mention drugs and he's *awake.* "What stuff?"

"The stuff we are about to discuss."

Wychee whines, "Do we have to discuss anything? Can't we just relax for once?"

Derlock looks around Baker Lounge at the bodies draped over the crappy, gaudy, squishy hundred-year-old 2020s-style furniture. Just the usual Baker Lounge evening crowd, known to ourselves as "the moes." My gaze follows his; *he's the only one in the room,* I think, *who is seeing people the way they really are.* It's like his eyes are the mirror of truth. *They're also gorgeous and I would enjoy drowning in them.*

We're in two bunches and two singletons. The first bunch has most of the girls and my X2B Bari, who looks like a used-to-be-handsome version of his famous mother. He's so blasted on all the drugs he takes that he doesn't even notice that he's sitting next to Fleeta, who is painfully gorgeous—her parents had her geneered for a perfect-for-media body and hair, eyes, and skin colors that were perfectly palette-balanced. They also bought her a genius level IQ, but that didn't last: she took happistuf two years ago, and nobody caught her in time, so now she's joyful and stupid. Bari likes morose smart girls, so I don't worry about her poaching him, even though she's still ultra beautiful and sitting very close to him.

Fleeta used to be my best friend. I guess she still thinks I'm hers, with whatever she has left to think with. I just feel weird around her since she transformed herself from the friend who I most wanted to be into the friend who most resembles a golden retriever.

The rest of that clump, who have all been chattering about celeb news and flipping around on a screen to see which meeds are trending, is the pair of friends I usually think of as the Dissatisfied Duo. Emerald's mom just barely qualified to get her into this place, and she doesn't fit in; she's awkward at parties, loud, sulky, whiny, and opinionated, but she could get away with that if she didn't look like a fire hydrant wearing a frog mask. She was born before her mother's big break, so she didn't get geneered, and she's a spineless coward about the surgery she needs to lengthen her thick legs, round off her wide flat ass, and add definition to her squidgy face. All the expensive smartcomb- and coswand-styling in the world just can't help. Her best friend, Wychee, sits beside her; she's got ten times the looks and twenty times the attitude: deep-brown skin and bright green eyes and strawberry blonde hair (very like mine, that look was ultra fashionable the year we were born), and she could probably draw some camera time and gossip, but puts her life into outwhining Emerald.

I know Derlock and I are thinking the same thing about the girl-clump of moes: *nobody we need to take into account, ever.*

The boy-clump would be even more moe and even more no-account if that were possible. King is Bari's drug buddy, another geneered guy with all the genes to be gorgeous and all the habits to be haggard, only interested in what he can put in his bloodstream. (*At least he hasn't done happistuf, though*, I think, looking away from Fleeta.) F.B. should have been gorgeous, with the look of an actor or model who gets cast as the "short but tough" sidekick. He has nice muscles, a cute slightly crooked nose, and perfect black curls. His dad geneered him super-sexy retroLatin, except he's so out of it socially that his security blanket wouldn't want to be seen with him, and he could be outwitted by a young brick. He has this obsession with astronomy and has memorized reams and reams of names of asteroids and stars, astronomers who discovered things, all kinds of sheeyeffinit, but I can tell he doesn't understand much of it. Whenever he's nervous he'll start spouting all these astronomical non sequiturs, and even though it makes no sense, he tells everyone he wants to be a famous astronomer. Nowadays that's like being a famous stamp collector or a famous knitter; all the astronomers are mineys who just do it for fun. Nobody seems to be able to reason with him about it; if you bring it up he just lays the memorized facts on thicker.

Stack is gorgeous—muscles like a Renaissance statue, classic East Afro features. Those were ultra out of fashion when he was born, but a tradition in his family, which includes more pro athletes than most people have relatives. But Stack is a waste of all those jock genes: he's been cut from every team because he won't practice or do what the coach asks, so he's never competed in anything. The athletes won't let him hang out with them, because they hate constant critiques from a guy who never plays. His major physical skill is bullying.

The fourth guy is Glisters, Stack's favorite victim. Glisters is a pulpy white-skinned stringy-haired throwback Caucasian (I'd throw him back, anyway, if anyone knew what sewer he was caught in) with a giant head and a scrawny little body. He's really brainy and all that sheeyeffinit, and he uses all those brains to splycter porn meeds into tiny little segments and reassemble them into porn that goes by too fast for anyone to follow. I would regard him as the creepiest person here at the school except he seems to have a huge crush on me, so I regard him as the creepiest person in the solar system.

Glisters, F.B., Stack, and King are gathered around four-handed chess, like little boys playing their little gamey-game. I don't know why they play when the outcome is guaranteed: King, who is too drugged to follow the game, will be eliminated, quickly followed by F.B., who is stupid. Then Stack will fix that *I'm gonna kill you* glare on Glisters, who will let Stack win out of pure terror. Besides, Glisters isn't thinking about the game nearly as much as he's staring at me.

Yuck, by the way.

Then there are two of us sitting by ourselves. Marioschke is sitting cross-legged, hands resting on her knees, palms up, styling Mysterious Profound Mystic—not convincingly. She's fat, even though you can cure that with a shot, and pretentious, because apparently you can't cure that even with constant mockery. Her room is this ultra weird jungle of mats on the floor and plants in pots; every so often she starts crying and says everyone is hurting her feelings, and goes into her room for a few days. Maybe we'll be lucky and she'll get her feelings hurt soon, by someone.

Maybe me.

I've been sitting by myself re-brushing my face with the coswand and my hair with the smartcomb, getting perfect, waiting for Derlock. Now that he's here, he's the only thing that is. He eclipses Baker Lounge, and the school, and the whole planet—and when he arrives, for me, the other moes in Baker Lounge just cease to exist.

||||||||||||||||||||||||||||||||||||||||||||||||||||||||||||||||||||||||

Notes for the Interested, #1

MOES: *an extremely common nickname for the loser clique at the most expensive schools*

In 2057 the global economy, environment, and society were in complete, irrecoverable collapse, even though with fully robotic production, the entire global population could have lived like the millionaires of a few generations before. No physical reason existed for the fighting, starvation, random destruction, and shortages of every necessity all over the planet, and yet that misery had persisted for more than a decade.

The United Nations, pushed to the brink by the Rich Man's Famine in 2056, decreed Permanent Peace and Prosperity—commonly known as PermaPaxPerity—in which everyone on the planet would receive a "social minimum" for which they would do no work, and robots would produce nearly all goods and provide nearly all services.

From then on, humans would do only labor in which human beings were irreplaceable and had to be paid to do it. The short list of these occupations included:

- high-level work in the arts and competitive athletics
- human-relations-intensive fields like nursing and teaching
- roles that people wanted to watch, such as being a celebrity.

One job that only humans could do still had to be restricted because too many people wanted to do it: making babies. Every baby registered for the social minimum is given a lifetime sterilizing implant, which can be switched on and off; switchoff permission is granted for three children per registered pair of people, or two per single.

Seventy years later, at the time of this story, it has turned out that the slight extra effort required to have a child (the application process for a switchoff takes about a month on the calendar and about ten hours of interviews and filling out forms, and is good for only three months) has caused the birth rate to fall far below replacement. For three generations, the population has rapidly dwindled and the average age increased; by the time of this story the world population is at about 3 billion, less than half its 2010 level, and only about 7% of it is children and teenagers (in 2010, that percentage was 19%). It's a world of very comfortable middle-aged and older people who mostly watch entertainment all day.

PermaPaxPerity decrees that more than 96% of the global population are **mineys**—people who live on the social minimum, an income roughly comparable to two million dollars a year in 2010 dollars. Some mineys practice very elaborate hobbies that occupy nearly all their time (almost all scientists, scholars, and artists are mineys). Regardless of how they spend their time, they are not permitted to earn more than the social minimum.

Most mineys, however, just consume entertainment for their entire lives, with a few years spent raising one or two children. About three-quarters of mineys elect at one time or another to switch their sterilization off and have a child; though most mineys have one, almost no one has more.

Just over 3% of the population have the EE prefix,

standing for *eligible for employment*, on their social minimum number. Over time EEnies became Eenies and finally just **eenies**. Eenies are celebrities whose image can be sold (celeb-eenies), or people who perform jobs that only people can do (talent-eenies), and earn incomes about 100 times as large as the mineys earn. Free training to qualify as a talent-eenie is restricted to the very small part of the population that achieves a very high score on the PotEvals (Potential Evaluation Examinations).

Because only a small part of the population actually needs training beyond basic literacy, the colleges and universities are gone (just as, since there is almost no war, there are no real armies, just police forces for suppressing riots and terrorism). Many mineys are highly educated, but they teach themselves the things they want to know (using the net or finding mentors), learning it whenever they care to during their adult lives, and since there is no need to prove they learned it, there are no exams, degrees, or diplomas (except, again, for the specialists among the talent-eenies).

Less than 1% of global population are **meanies**—violent chronic offenders, uncontrolled sociopaths, and various other people who must be locked up for public safety.

It is a stated, sacred principle of PermaPaxPerity that everyone should have the same chance to qualify as an eenie. Children of eenies who do not qualify in their own right become mineys at twenty-one and cannot inherit money or property from their parents. As a practical matter, however, this law is enforceable only on the talent-eenies; celebrity babies, children, and families are popular in the news, and so celeb-eenies are very often able to make their children famous before the age of twenty-one.

Thus elite schools, such as Excellence Shop, are in the business of helping eenie children qualify for permanent, adult eenie status. For the children with unusual talent and ability—the kind who would be at the very top of a gifted and talented program in 2010—this means preparing for the PotEvals, because a passing score on the PotEvals is required for admission to accredited professional training in any EE-class, paid occupation. For the children of celebrities, this means pretending to study for the PotEvals while actually networking and trying to draw media attention.

In every elite school, some kids just give up. They know their talent is insufficient, they don't want to work, their appearance is out of fashion, maybe they just have no confidence. Although in a few years they will stop living on their parents' eenie-level salaries and have to live as mineys, they stop making the effort to become eenies. Since they are not incurably criminally insane, they won't become meanies either. At every elite school, all over Earth, the moon, and Mars, these permanently defeated children make the same bitter joke; since they are not yet eenies, meanies, or mineys, they call themselves moes. It sounds better than "losers."

▌▌▌

Derlock is staring right at me. God, he has eyes and a smile. I style a pose, letting him be my camera.

He says, "Susan, it was really your idea."

"Oh, that." I don't know what he is talking about.

"That day in the library when you were talking about being a *real* eenie, a celeb-eenie—"

I sit up straight and shake my hair loose; he rewards me with a little smile, seeing that now we're in this together.

It's amazing and wonderful how much of a lie that boy can pack into so few words. We *did* talk about it and it *is* something I think about a lot. But it wasn't in the library; we had cut class and sneaked off for sex in his room.

Derlock looks around the room, being gorgeous, styling charisma and leadership till it drips off that perfect cleft chin. "Every year some loser bastard who's been sweating some art or sport for decades, just as a hobby, with no success, gets recognition somehow, and goes straight from miney to eenie." He looks right at Marioschke. "Say people start reading her poetry." Then at F.B. "Or he makes a major astronomical discovery. That's one road to being an eenie that doesn't involve passing the stupid PotEval exam, doing all that advanced training, and qualifying as a talent-eenie. Make it into enough popular meeds and you're a celeb-eenie, no boring work—except for doing your art—required. Right?"

"Hey, most of us aren't stupid"—Stack focuses on F.B.—"we all know that."

Derlock rides right over him. "But teaching yourself to do great art or great science is even harder than passing the PotEvals to qualify for training. There's a better way to get eenie."

Now, I'm listening. Derlock isn't just any guy named

Derlock, like so many guys are because the main guy on *Always Sexy Vampires* a couple generations ago was named Derlock. He's Derlock *Slabilis*—son of Sir Penn Slabilis, the lawyer who pioneered the overriding media interest defense, which is one of a half dozen reasons why celeb-eenie is the only kind of eenie to be. His father could buy Excellence Shop out of his petty cash and make them declare Derlock the Most Popular and God-for-a-Month.

Derlock winks at me. I puddle, and nod, as if he's conducting me with a baton.

The room is silent; we know something big is coming.

He explains, "You have to *start* from being famous. Then whatever you do, people will *want* to see it, and *that* means you're an eenie, it's the way the *rules* work. Remember last year when Reynold Wells took a power saw and cut up his girlfriend? Till then he was like n-nillion other miney songwriters, ultra dark, ultra grim, ultra predictable, ultra just a hobby. But after he dropped the pieces of her off his balcony, people got *interested* in his songs. He became an eenie *months* before he was convicted." He pauses to let the thought sink in. "Well, that's the way you do it. Us moes only need to become famous for something, kick our recognition indexes up, and then people would want *whatever* we did afterward. Images or poetry or finger painting."

"Or astronomy," F.B. says. "I'm going to be the most famous astronomer ever. Herschel was so famous after he found Uranus that—"

"I *bet* what's-his-name found Uranus. And used it

too," Stack says, in his *you-be-scared-now* tone.

"The trick is," Derlock says, "it's hard to get famous just for *being* an astronomer, but people will want to hear about your astronomy *if you're famous*. If you have too much style and class to crawl around being a goody-goody, 'maximizing your opportunities,' always networking and 'personally developing' and studying all the time for the PotEvals like the pathetic scared little talenty-kids here at school, then the way to get to eenie—is to get famous. Then if you *want* to be a scientist, you're an *eenie* scientist."

Scientists are usually happy being mineys; they do what they love and don't worry about being famous. I learned that when Fleeta and I were sent around to visit dozens of scientists, back when we were best friends, and I was Crazy Science Girl. Fleeta and I had so much fun when we were twelve, winning science competitions, fast-tracked for elite science schools, all that sheeyeffinit. And those scientists just doing research because they loved it were probably the happiest people I've ever seen—except for Fleeta, now, since she has decided to be a happy moron forever.

As for me, I grew boobs and an attitude and found out about boys and drugs, and I decided to get real about the way things work: Happy is nice; famous is what counts. That whole year I was running around being Crazy Science Girl with my best friend, I was only mentioned—not even splyctered into a hook, just mentioned—exactly four times in meeds that year.

‖‖

Notes for the Interested, #2

MEEDS: *the only art form that matters in 2129*

The word *meed* back-formed sometime after 2080 from the plural media. A **meed** is an arrangement of audio and visual tracks intended to be seen together. Television commercials, music videos, film scenes, and news segments would all be described, in 2129, as meeds—very old, slow meeds. Most people watch meeds on any available screen most of the time.

A stream of meeds coming from a single source is called a **face**, probably short for *interface*; a face for meeds is what a URL is for Web content, a channel is for television, a station is for radio, or a magazine is for articles.

Most meeds are made up of shots and images sampled from other meeds. The really popular parts of a 5-minute meed might be a few 1-second shots; these little very-popular shots are called **hooks**. When a creator pulls hooks out of a meed to use in a new meed, he **splycters** the original meed.

For example, when making his porn meeds, Glisters takes a dozen porn scenes, which are each a few minutes long, and extracts and separates (splycters) his favorite little one- or two-second bursts (the hooks). Then he puts the hooks together into a meed of his own, which runs through dozens of hooks at very high speed.

All over the world, hundreds of millions of hobbyists (and a few thousand professionals) splycter meeds into hooks and assemble new meeds out of the hooks. Then they upload their new meeds to the net. The overall system tracks every frame and sound back to its origin, counting every viewing of every one, so the more people who watch meeds that contain hooks that contain you, the more popular you are.

A very small number of meeds account for almost all the hooks (just as only a small fraction of songs account for almost all the airplay, or 1% of actors make 95% of the money in Hollywood).

Theoretically everyone is paid for every appearance in a hook on every screen, but the payments are tiny, and anyway they are deducted from your social minimum, so your social minimum payment is the same every week regardless of how popular you are—up to the magic tipping point that Susan, Derlock, and their friends are dreaming about.

If 2 or more out of every 10,000 hooks that are splyctered within one month, by everyone worldwide, contain you, you are so popular that you are declared a celebrity and automatically upgraded to the EE prefix—you are famous enough to receive an eenie stipend, and your hook fees are paid on top of that, not deducted.

Being splyctered into hooks is the only way to become either rich or famous under PermaPaxPerity. In the obsolete terminology of the 2010s, you are "being paid to entertain everyone else by appearing in very fast sampled clips pulled from your media appearances."

- Average length of a meed: less than 10 minutes.
- Average original content in a meed: less than 2%.
- Average length of a hook: about 1.5 seconds.

- Hooks splyctered out of any one meed: almost none, usually

So in my guise as Crazy Science Girl I was splyctered into four hooks in one year. That's the same as not existing.

The next year, just after I turned thirteen and got my chick-body, a whole eight-second meed of me was splyctered like crazy.

The original meed ran on Ed Teach, which has the highest recognition score of any pirate face. Within a day, every single frame had been splyctered into five thousand other meeds. That eight-second hook hit number 45 in the top 100 for the Hot-Underage category. The two-second hook where you could see both boobs bouncing and one of my nipples stayed between number 26 and number 18 for 64 hours, and ran on over 300 different faces.

Unfortunately it didn't last long enough to get me my EE. You have to be that popular for at least a month. And you don't stay popular if your hook is a joke, which mine turned into.

Whoever put it up on Ed Teach clipped the original eight-second hook out of the Lunatic Club's face, one of those club faces that's nothing but camera feed from the dance floor. That eight-second hook that got splyctered so much showed me dancing, holding a drink, and kind of spilling it on my silk dress for some cling on one boob.

Ed Teach's synthesized voice-over said, "Susan Tervaille, daughter of classical actor Robert Tervaille, shows the values she learned at *Restore the Family!* rallies with her father." People thought that was funny.

It ultra destroyed any serious hotness, and turned the hook into just an excuse to embarrass Pop.

He called me up and lectured me for a solid hour about how this was *beneath* me, my little titty show was *unworthy*. Like there is anything more unworthy than being stuck as a miney for life.

When I came to Excellence Shop a month after that, I stayed in the advanced science and math classes because, well, why not, but I am *not* Crazy Science Girl anymore. Someday I'll be seriously splyctered; hooks of me get splyctered every year, just nothing so far hits the levels I need.

Till then, I'm a moe, looking to be an eenie.

Which is why, aside from being hot, Derlock is taking my breath away. He's so *right*. There's a way. First be famous; then you can be a famous whatever-you-want.

"Look," Derlock says. "None of us has studied at all. We can't possibly pass the PotEvals. But I have come up with a way that we can get famous, so it won't *matter* that we can't pass the PotEvals," Derlock says, his perfect grin widening like a curtain coming up on a show. "It won't *matter* that we don't know shit."

His gaze on me is more intense than it was when he was pulling down my pants. *Scary*. People have left school because of things Derlock did. It would be so *zoomed* to have a boyfriend that scared me. If necessary, I can just dump Bari with no ceremony at all.

Derlock explains, "For 78 more days—till we flunk the PotEvals and get expelled—we can just ask the Resource Office for go-anywhere-do-anything-as-long-as-it's-a-learning-experience permissions. Now how do you suppose we can become famous with a learning-experience permission?" He is looking straight at me when he says, softly, "Let me give you a big hint . . *Virgo* is starting an Earthpass right now." He lets them all digest that for a breath. "Susan," he says, and my name sounds like his hand sliding up my thigh, "don't you have an aunt on *Virgo*?"

"My aunt Destiny. She's an evalist."

"Why is she the evilest person?" Fleeta asks. "Being evil is bad."

Everyone laughs at her, which makes her happy and me sick. And it's not like all of them know, either; they're just enjoying laughing at Fleeta. So I explain: "*E-v-a-l-i-s-t,* not *e-v-i-l-e-s-t.* Aunt Destiny's an expert at evas, which is what they call operations outside the ship. I'm not sure why they call it that, I think it used to be an abbreviation like scuba or laser, but an eva is a spacewalk, and Destiny's a spacewalker."

Derlock's smile makes everyone look at me differently than they ever have before, and that is ultra zoomed.

His plan is to go up in a cap and visit *Virgo* during Earthpass, duck out of the return cap, and stow away to Mars. Since *Virgo* is an Aldrin cycler, it can't turn around or even change course much more than the little precession it has to do in each cycle; *Virgo* will *have* to take us to Mars.

To send us home, they'll have to wait for *Leo*, the last down-cycler for this opposition, and that will give us almost three weeks on Mars.

"This is so stupid I can't believe we're talking about it," Emerald says, "but whatever. When we come out of hiding they'll just charge our parents a big pile of money to cover the cost, then turn the ship around and bring us home. We'll never even get close to Mars."

"That's the beauty of it," Derlock says. "They can't do that."

Glisters is nodding enthusiastically. "Derlock is right. That option is not available at any price."

"Don't be stupid," Emerald says. "Nothing really costs anything at *all* anymore, with PermaPaxPerity the Scarcity Age is *over.* They tell us that all the time. They might charge a ridiculous amount of money, but money is supposed to just keep people from using too much resources for stupid crappy reasons, it doesn't ration things the way it did. That's what they've said in every economics class I took. Turning a spaceship around is just one more thing you can buy, no matter how expensive it is."

"That's what they *say.*" Wychee sounds like they say it just to hurt her feelings. "Why won't they just spend the money to turn the ship around and bring us back to Earth?"

"They *can't* turn *Virgo* around," Glisters repeats, "no matter how much money they spend. Physics beats economics every time."

Derlock gives him a little mock round of applause. "Right on target. I checked this, but I want Glisters and Susan to recheck it for me. *Virgo*'s engines are only big enough to do course corrections, and they only take on enough reaction mass at Earth for the delta-v to put them close to Mars at the other end."

"I never heard of delta-v," Emerald says, as if that means it can't affect her.

|||||||||||||||||||||||||||||||||||||||||||||||||||||||||||||||||||||||||||||

Notes for the Interested, #3

ALDRIN CYCLERS: *the bus line to Mars, but the bus can't turn around*

Earth goes around the sun in one year; Mars goes around the sun in 1.88 years. The result of this is that Earth passes Mars every 26 months. The point where one planet passes another in orbit is called an **opposition** (because at that point, from the viewpoint of the Earth, the sun is on one side of the Earth and Mars is exactly opposite it, on the other side). At opposition, the distance between two planets is the smallest it can be, so that's a good time to cross.

Up and *high* refer to moving away from the source of the gravity, and *down* and *low* to moving toward it. Within the solar system the main source of gravity is the sun, so when spaceships travel inside the solar system, they go up (away from the sun) or down (toward the sun); Mars is higher than the Earth (orbits farther from the sun). In 2129, those terms have mostly replaced the ones we use today, *inner* and *outer*, which tend to see the solar system as a territory with the sun as its capital, rather than the more accurate image of a gravity field around the sun.

Buzz Aldrin, the second man to land on the moon, developed the idea of putting a spaceship or station in a 26-month orbit around the sun, with the low side of the orbit at the same distance from the sun as Earth, timing it so that it would hit that low point 4 months before an opposition. Thus the ship would pass very close to Earth, and then its orbit would carry it up to Mars in only about 4 months, a very fast trip. If the ship did not land on Mars (instead sending crew and cargo down to Mars in smaller spacecraft, called *caps* in this story), then the ship would continue on, and 26 months later, it would cross Earth's orbit again, 4 months before another Mars opposition.

So once you have the ship up and running, it's a fast free ride from Earth to Mars every 26 months. To be in a 26-month orbit, a ship must spend as much time going away from the sun (the 13-month up-leg) as it does coming down (the down-leg). Because of the shape and position of the orbits (see diagram p. 58), even though obviously every cycler goes up and down, only the up-leg or the down-leg, not both, can be in the right position to give a fast 4-month ride between the planets. On *Virgo*, it's the up-leg, so *Virgo* is an up-cycler.

There are also down-cyclers, like *Leo*, which are set up to pass Mars at opposition on their down-leg, and then Earth 4 months later; down-cyclers are a fast free ride back. No ship can be both an up- and a down-cycler; if it has a leg in the right position at opposition, then its other leg will be 13 months away from opposition, and not go near either planet.

So the price of the "fast free ride" is that you also have to take a long ride that is not free at all. For 22 months out of 26, the cycler is just coming back to its starting point and is not good for anything. Out of its 26-month orbit, a cycler is only hauling stuff and people between planets for 4; if the 4 are when it's upbound (Earth–Mars) it's an up-cycler, if they are when it's downbound, it's a down-cycler.

Because the timing is tied to opposition, up-cyclers and down-cyclers all pass Mars within a few weeks of each other—those few months are an extremely busy time for Martian settlers, as the caps bring in new immigrants and imports from the up-cyclers, and take people and goods to the down-cyclers for return to Earth.

If Earth and Mars came into opposition at the exact same part of their orbits every time, you would never need any fuel at all. But, in fact, the position where they come into opposition changes each time through the cycle, moving about two months forward on each orbit each time. So it's necessary to change the course a little bit on every trip. A change in course, in rocket science, is called a **delta-v**; *delta* is the math symbol for "change in" and *v* stands for "velocity," which technically is a speed and a direction. (Ten miles an hour is a speed, north is a direction, and ten miles an hour going north is a velocity.)

To change velocity, a ship in space must use some kind of rocket. The material that goes out the back of the rocket is called "reaction mass." Aldrin proposed that for reaction mass, the ship could use ice mined from the moon.

It took a huge amount of reaction mass to put six ships into

Aldrin cycler orbits, but that was 30 years before the time of this story. Once the ships were in their correct orbits, since they no longer needed the gigantic engine arrays and fuel tanks, they melted them down and used them as material for other parts of the ship; the Aldrin cyclers were literally "built on the fly."

Now, in 2129, as they pass by the Earth and Moon, they take on only enough reaction mass to tweak the orbit with just enough delta-v to stay close to Mars—much, much less delta-v than it took to launch the ship in the first place.

Of course, since each ship is carrying passengers and cargo for only 4 months, and it's in a 26-month orbit, for 22 months it carries no cargo and passengers as it runs through empty space. After passing Mars, an up-cycler keeps rising away from the sun for 9 more months, and then takes 13 months to fall back to Earth. This will come up later.

▌▌▌

The Dissatisfied Duo keeps right on whining, and Glisters and Derlock keep right on explaining, and I seriously consider exploding. After a while I can't resist trying to get it across, myself. "To change to an orbit that came directly back to Earth, they'd need a hundred times or more their own mass in lunar ice—"

Emerald styles an expression like a cat trying to figure out what stinks. "Well, sheeyeffinit, so *what*? I *mean*, that's my *point* and *you're* not *list*ening, but whatever. I don't see why they won't just buy more lunar ice."

Derlock says, "Because they have nothing but vacuum ahead for the next sixty or seventy million kilometers. There will be no one there to sell it to them, with no way to deliver it, no matter how much anyone spends."

"That seems kind of unfair," Fleeta says. "People should be able to buy what they want."

Fleeta takes Fendrisol, the best therapy there is, but it doesn't fix the damage already done, and it only slows the brain's deterioration. Emerald is struck temporarily dumb by the thought that she might sound as if she's agreeing with Fleeta. She stops and actually seems to think, a miracle right there.

"Not enough ice to turn around with," Emerald says.

"Right."

"And nowhere to buy it, no matter how much they pay." Emerald seems very proud of having understood.

Wychee adds, "All right, now I've got it. Why didn't you say so?"

Derlock bravely tries to work his way back to his plan. "So if we take one of the last caps up to *Virgo*, which is the last up-cycler to pass Earth on this opposition, and stow away, and don't come out till we're out of cap range of Earth, they have no way to send us back. *Virgo* has to go to Mars, and they have to take us. And at Mars, all they can do is send us back on *Leo*, which is the last down-cycler for this opposition."

"So we get back—then what?" Glisters asks. "The foamhouse?"

"It'd be fun to have you in the foamhouse with me," Stack says, leering at Glisters. "I'd ultra make you my ultra bitch, Glissy."

Derlock says, "Shut up, Stack. No one will do any time."

"I don't see why not," Emerald says, "when your plan involves like n-nillion anti-PermaPaxPerity felonies."

Derlock grins. "This is where I'm so glad I have the father I do. We'll have the most famous celeb-law and overriding-media-interest lawyer in the solar system on our side. Dad will eat this one up for an appetizer, and then chew up the Martian Settlement Authority, the Space Patrol, the PermaPaxPerity Authority, and the whole UN for a main course. We probably won't do even one hour in the foamhouse. We'll tour Mars like *royalty*." He hammers his point till you'd think it would break. "Just think about the publicity—oh, god, *god, god*! the publicity. *Children of celeb-eenies—stowaways to Mars!*" He writes it in the air in about 150-point type. "And once we're in a few million meeds, whatever we do will *sell*—Glisters's porn, Marioschke's philosophopoems—"

That's what Marioschke calls that shit that takes her three days to write one lousy screen of (and half that screen is white space—the good half). I guess "philosophopoems" *is* better marketing than "drippy little insipidities from a dippy fat chickie who can't punctuate."

Derlock rolls on. "F.B. not only gets to be famous, but being on *Virgo*, with access to the external instruments, he'll even have time to work up a couple brilliant discoveries." *And maybe,* I think to myself, remembering one

of Pop's biggest roles, *the Wizard will give him a brain!*
"Whatever any of us want to do, it will be famous *because
it was done by a famous stowaway to Mars.*"

After all the eyes and attention from Derlock, what I
want to do does not require going to Mars; a short walk
down the hall would take care of it very nicely.

What he's doing to me is basically what he's doing to
all the moes: offering everything we want deep inside in
his cupped hands. But as nice and supported and cradled
as that feels, he also has a long sharp fingernail dug into
our soft little dreams, and he's gently pulling; we can let
him drag us along, or he'll pop our dreams like garden
slugs. He ticks off points with one extended index finger like he's smearing boogers on a mirror. "Celeb family.
Massive media coverage. Popular story meeting the public
need for entertainment. That adds up to all punishment
suspended—don't you people ever watch crime meeds?"

"Actually we won't hurt anybody, either," Glisters says.
"Will we?"

"There might be a tiny bit of property damage if we do
it the way I think we will," Derlock says, "but you're right
that 'no harm to persons and minimal harm to property'
will help our case. It isn't necessary, though."

That little *isn't necessary, though* makes me shudder. I
see Emerald and Wychee also notice.

Derlock looks around the room. "I guess maybe you all
don't watch many crime meeds. What do you think 'sentence suspended on grounds of overriding media interest'
means?"

Creepier and creepier. Penn Slabilis's famous case that established that principle was *Munshi v. Slabilis*— in which he successfully pleaded guilty to a rape charge but received no punishment. Since then he's helped a half dozen celeb-eenies literally get away with murder, and he very nearly won the case for Chiang, the man who invented happistuf. Maybe we aren't going to hurt anyone, but it wouldn't matter to Derlock if we *were*.

"Is media, like, lots of meeds?" Fleet asks. "So that's like lots of the meeds are interesting when people ride over things?"

"Close enough," Derlock says, with a warm smile.

She glows like a beautiful saint at having gotten something right. I miss her so badly.

"Susan," Emerald says, "this only works if you're willing to lie to your aunt—so, do you *really* want to?"

I style Bold Pout just like my coach taught me. "Well, you know, Aunt Destiny loves me, and in her heart, she'll *like* that spunk and initiative in her niece."

That was zoomed: great speech, likeable content but styled all bratty-sexy. Glisters winks and flashes me a thumbs-up; he recorded it, because he's always got a camera running someplace just in case one of us reveals a boob or styles a pose. That'll pop up in some meed. I could almost hug the giant-headed albino freak, if we both wore pressure suits and I wiped mine down real good just after.

SOLID GOLD TURD

March 13, 2129. Later that night, Susan's bedroom, Achiever Dormitory, Excellence Shop, Oregon-Idaho District, Earth.

LATER THAT EVENING, all comfy-nakies with Derlock on my bed, I raise my head from his nice pecs, doing the hair-across-my-face thing that I know will work if anything will. "I want a big favor from you."

"Within reason." Derlock kisses the top of my head, which feels exactly like lips on the top of my head. Why do guys think that's romantic? "We'll be splyctered all over if we declare when we come out of hiding on *Virgo*. Want to do that then?"

"Oh, yeah. But that's not the favor. It's more complicated. Bari and King aren't going along to *Virgo* because they're planning to take the laughing dive. That's the real reason I'm breaking up with Bari; I already went through losing Fleeta to happistuf, and I'm not going to watch that happen all over again. Especially not when he's planning to take it all the way to death. And since what one takes, the other takes, if I want to save Bari, I'll have to save King as well. Don't bother telling me you can't help; you're the main supplier here, and if you decide Bari and King don't get any happistuf, they don't."

"It's their choice."

"*Choice? Like Fleeta?* She used to be a genius. Now she's competing to get titty shots splyctered into ultra nasty meeds."

"But till she got caught, her world was a paradise, and she'll still never be sad again."

"And if she ever goes off Fendrisol, she'll lose the rest of her brain function and die in a few months; she's a happy idiot with the same name and face that used to be occupied by a great person." I can feel myself tearing up and I want to punch him, great eyes and chin and charisma notwithstanding. "And Bari and King are planning to take the fast laughing dive straight to the bottom—check into a hotel room on the moon, order auto renew, cancel all maid service, and gasp happistuf every few hours till they don't have the mental capacity to operate the inhaler."

"It's what Bari's always wanted. His whole life has been leading up to it." Derlock freezes. I must be styling something ultra scary. He mutters, "Besides, they'll get caught."

"Bari's mother doesn't want to admit he exists; it'll take them longer to find her than it'll take him to die. King's father is a ground explorer on the Titan expedition. By the time anyone signs a permission for the Moon Marshals to go into the room, Bari and King will either be dead or happy vegetables."

"Strange, isn't it? You want me to save those guys, who

don't want to be saved; and not saving Chiang, who fought every step of the way to live, is my dad's greatest regret."

‖‖

Notes for the Interested, #4

HAPPISTUF: *the drug that keeps on giving, and the most popular execution of the century*

There really are prions. A prion is a twisted, reshaped protein that, when it encounters a protein like the one it was made from, reshapes it into another prion—sort of a contagious distortion. The composition of the molecule does not change, but the change in shape changes its behavior, the way a wadded-up necklace won't go through a narrow hole but the same necklace pulled out straight will go easily.

In effect, a prion reshapes its target protein into more copies of itself, and sometimes those copies do bad things. Common prions found in nature cause mad cow disease, scrapie in sheep, wasting disease in elk, and kuru in humans. It is not clear yet why so many of the known disease prions attack the brain and nervous system.

Engineers in the 2010s are already very close to being able to reshape proteins and other large molecules on cue in the laboratory; computational scientists are closing in on predicting what a molecule will do from its shape. Once both abilities are fully in place, instead of testing natural substances to see what they do, we will be able to decide what we want a molecule to do, and make and shape the molecule to do it.

By the time of this story, more than 100 years in the future, designing and building a particular molecule to do a particular thing may be something anyone can do at home with a simple, cheap kit.

Thus in this future, in May 2117, Chiang Shau-Lu, a miney who had never passed the PotEvals because of poor verbal skills, invented happistuf. Until his arrest in December 2118, he sold it, and the "gaspers" that shot it deep into users' lungs in quarter-gram doses, for just enough to cover costs. By the time he was caught, he had distributed over 40 kilograms of it in the 300 largest cities on Earth, sometimes working 18-hour days to cover as much territory as possible.

His arrest triggered a booby-trap program, which instantly put up hundreds of different meeds, on dozens of faces, telling everyone how to make happistuf by geneering 11 simple changes into a prion that could be extracted from many rodent brains; the original prion was harmless even to the rodents.

Over 300 million people downloaded those meeds before they were all taken down; anyone could make happistuf after that.

Happistuf alters a protein found in human brain cells into a form that locks the pleasure centers into a full-on state that literally feels better than a mother's hug, a massive orgasm, a standing ovation, and a hot fudge sundae all at once. It blocks the receptors you need to feel sadness, fear, anger, or anxiety. And it kills the happistuf-infected brain cells—releasing more happistuf to infect more cells—a few weeks after infection, thus slowly destroying the brain.

On just one dose of happistuf, a person is enjoying things more intensely within five minutes; incapable of sadness within a week; clumsy and noticeably dimmer within three months; and three years later, irreversibly severely retarded. Death comes when a vital function shuts down, typically five years after the first dose. But since there's a big rush right after a gasp, most people don't take it once; they take it repeatedly. Once-a-week serious gaspers, if untreated, die within a year; those who take the laughing dive, gasping every few hours until they are too mentally incapacitated to operate the inhaler, can die within two weeks.

Fendrisol slows happistuf down by a factor of about ten, if the user doesn't take any more. It is not a reversal or a cure; the patient progresses in exactly the same way into joyful idiocy, merely taking much longer to do it.

Sir Penn Slabilis was unable to save Chiang from execution because Chiang said on the stand that he wanted to "wipe out the celebutards and the dolebirds and put the world back to work," and stressed the fact that the eenies he wanted to exterminate were of extremely mixed race, "betraying the traditional human birth lines."

He was found guilty of 48 separate capital felony counts under PermaPaxPerity, including intentional genocide with racist motivation, aggravated bioterrorism, addictive-drug creation, and distributing an illegal substance with intent to cause a fatal injury. All of Sir Penn Slabilis's appeals failed; on October 19, 2122, Chiang was strapped into an execution chair, and a railgun fired a cryofluorine pellet at Mach 12 through the base of his skull, vaporizing and combusting his head. By then it was far too late.

▐▌▌▌▐

In the laughing dive, you take dose after dose of happistuf, so that the phosphoproteins in your neurons convert into happistuf prions very rapidly. After a week or so, you're getting more from the internal conversion than you are from what you're gasping. Within a two weeks to a month either the process reaches the cells that run your heart or breathing or something else vital, or you stop being able to feed yourself or drink when you are thirsty. Then it's lights out, giggling all the way, and they have to cremate you so other people won't dig up your body and crack your skull to get at the happistuf in there. (There are social circles where gasping desiccated brains is extra-high-status.)

Fendrisol has to be taken twice a day, and the most it does is slow happistuf down enough to give you a couple of decades as a joyful moron like Fleeta, followed by a fifteen-year progression to ecstatic vegetable.

And the guy I'm so eager to be declared with sells happistuff. That thought comes to me along with another one: *Shut up, Pop, it's my life, my career, my chance in the world.*

To shut out the internal monologue, I ask Derlock, "So can you do anything about Bari and King?"

"I'll have to think about it. If I give them something that's not happistuf, they'll just find another supplier. So I need a trick that sticks, and I'm not sure what that would be." Derlock's arms fold tight around me. I wonder whether it's really happistuf, or just feeling way too good, that makes you stupid.

— — —

I'm almost asleep when my screen chimes. "Message from Destiny Tervaille."

I extricate myself from Derlock. "This one is from Aunt Destiny; it's probably what we've been waiting for. Cue message up please!"

She's grinning at me and waving like a goofy miney in the crowd behind a popular meed. "Susan! What an absolutely delightful idea! And don't feel bad about not having thought of it sooner; at least you thought of it soon enough. Yes, of course, we'd be delighted to have you and a group of school friends come up. I'll probably reserve *you* just for myself, since you'll only be able to be here for about a day, but we'll get a good guide for your friends and they'll have fun, too. Oh, but thank you! That's what I really wanted to say. Yes, yes, come right up, and thank you for thinking of your poor old crazy Anny Dezzy!"

"Anny Dezzy?" Derlock asks.

"A little trouble talking when you're three years old, and they remind you of it forever. That's what families are all about."

I dress and send an equally enthusiastic message back. Afterward, I say to Derlock, "I feel like a solid gold turd."

"Just another paving stone on the road to fame and success. It'll stop bothering you in a bit."

"Does anything *ever* bother you?"

"I don't do anything I don't think is fun, even if most of the fun is anticipating more fun." He stretches; I admire his body, and he enjoys being admired. "This afternoon Stack and I pinned Glisters down in the bathroom like we were going to put his head in the toilet. I could see him bracing himself and shutting his eyes and trying not to throw up or cry; once I knew he felt like that, of course we let him go and pretended we'd just been teasing all along. But it was fun to scare him that way, fun to know he'll do what I say because he's scared, fun to look forward to the day when I find an excuse to do it for real. Solid gold, yeah, turd, hell no." He deliberately, slowly, looks me up and down, as if deciding to buy a side of beef. "Take off your clothes while I watch."

I say no, he reaches for me, and I show him some of the jiu-jutsu Pop made me learn. A minute later he's outside, banging on the door, asking me to at least throw his clothes out to him. I tell him he's got his thumbprint and his voiceprint and that's all he really needs, because his room will let him in, but if he keeps making noise, someone will come out and see him. He runs off like his ass is on fire.

I still feel like a turd; it's still the solid gold I have doubts about. I console myself that Pop would be pleased that my time with Sensei Kronstadt wasn't wasted, and that Derlock is probably not going to try to shove me around in that particular way again.

I'm almost asleep when he calls to apologize. I tell him three things: that he can have his clothes back tomorrow morning; that I'll still declare with him during the trip to Mars because the added splycterage is to our mutual advantage, even if he's really not that great a boyfriend; and the thing I heard Mom say just before she left Pop: "You can fuck me, if I feel like it, but if you fuck *with* me, you won't like what you feel."

By all reasonable standards, it's a triumph. If I haven't completely tamed Satan, I've made him think again, and I'm going to be his next girlfriend, not his next victim.

As I'm drifting off, my gaze keeps returning to my parents' and Destiny's pictures on the opposite wall. I still feel like a solid gold turd. Nothing I can do about that.

March 24, 2129. Bari's room, Apogee Dorm, Excellence Shop, Oregon/Idaho District, Earth.

Two weeks before departure day, I haven't officially had the closursation with Bari. That won't do. We've been declared for nineteen weeks, and I've only been cheating on Bari with Derlock for six, so I've *got* to style this. Pop always says always style everything like there's a cam.

Bari's door irises. I take two little steps inside, not too far, using the door to frame me, cock a hip, reach up the wall, tilt the head—Meed Classic! "So I thought we should at least say good-bye and it's been fun."

"Meed Classic," Bari says. "You're so good at that."

"Identifying the styling. Sheeyeffinit. Pomo's been over for what, a hundred years? *Ultra* ultra loser. Got any brain cells left?"

"Right now," Bari says, "I have plenty. I just took my first gasp four days ago. So far it puts a peak in my mood and barely puts a dent in my thinking." He beams with joy.

Kind, sweet, sad Bari is still kind and sweet but he'll never be sad again. I'm already too late.

He's pleased enough to pop. "So, now you're Derlock's girl. Don't forget Clytie Ambridge put her whole life into him and then tried to kill herself."

"Twelve-year-olds can be stupid. And that was last year. He's more mature."

"Fifteen-year-olds can be evil, and if he's matured it's just into a more mature evil."

"Don't call him evil. We're declaring as soon as we come out of hiding."

"Wow, perfect publicity." He laughs like it's the best idea he's ever heard.

I put on my best stony *nobody gives sheeyeffinit what you say* expression, and style Hepburn Defiant.

Still giggling, Bari rolls off the bed and hugs me, rumpling my velvet jacket and my hair. *Ultra* degrading. I push him away. "Doesn't Derlock sell you most of the stuff you use?"

"Yeah, so what? I don't have anything he can take from me."

"Your money. Your mind. Your life."

"The money's not mine, it's Mom's, she gets it for having photogenic tits. As for the mind and the life, I wasn't using them anyway."

I have nothing to say to that; I just blurt out, "I wish you'd get treated and come to Mars with me."

"And with Derlock."

"It's better than being dead!"

"Oh, well, that's where we have a difference of opinion."

I close the door on his storm of giggles. I'm Pop's daughter and you don't style *me* out of a curtain line—but somehow I can't think of one.

Derlock's hand is on my shoulder; *so he was listening at the door.* "Tough closursation?"

I slip my arm around his waist. "I wish I knew why he wants to die."

"He's going to die happier than you and I will ever live."

"You know what I mean. He's already started the laughing dive."

"I'll load the first gasp he'll take after we go with a hibernifacient. The dorm's monitor will sense his body temperature falling and call the cops because it won't be able to wake him. That should get him rescued way before he hits Fleeta's level of stupid, let alone dies."

"Perfect," I say, and hug his arm. I'm thinking, *Sometimes, when you need a really good thing done, the best person to do it for you is someone who's pure evil.*

||||||||||||||||||||||||||||||||||||||||||||||||||||||||||||||||||||||

Notes for the Interested, #5

STYLING: *performing everything you do because there's always a camera*

Children of eenies, and mineys who try to become eenies, are always intensely aware that any moment of their lives might be splyctered into hooks and, if the hooks became popular, could raise their recognition scores high enough for an EE. It's particularly important to look good at key times in your life that might become a story in someone's meed.

Nothing so important can be left to improvisation or to chance. Ambitious parents enroll their children early in classes in **styling**: acting to maximize attention in everyday life. There are whole trademarked systems and genres for styling; Classic Meed, for example, is a way of performing every action as if in a pre-1980 movie. There are bits that people master; Susan is particularly good at Bold Pout, a snotty, superior, commanding expression. But even when it's just a matter of expressing an ordinary emotion like anger or pleasure, there might be a camera watching you, the moment might turn out more important than it looks, and you've got to *style* it.

||||||||||||||||||||||||||||||||||||||||||||||||||||||||||||||||||||||

April 3, 2129. A storage shed on the grounds of Excellence Shop, Oregon/Idaho District, Earth.

While Fleeta and I are putting together the special bags that Stack and Derlock are going to smuggle aboard, she says, "I am very worried about Bari."

"He's a big boy."

"He is not. He's a very little boy and a scared one, and so afraid of being a loser that he gives up before he has a chance to lose." She is laughing as she grabs my arm. "No, don't ignore me." She giggles like I'm cracking her up. "I think he wants to be like me, and he doesn't understand how much I wish I weren't."

She makes me so mad. We were apart for one long summer vacation, so I could go to the moon and party, when I was thirteen, and I came back and my best friend had been replaced by an idiot. Now a tiny bit of her old self is peeking out at me again, as if teasing me. So I do something mean. "Wish you weren't what?"

Asking Fleeta to remember what she's just said always throws her. That's why I did it. Now she can't, and she doesn't get to tell me what she wanted to, and she knows her best friend deliberately did that to her.

She giggles uncontrollably at how angry she wishes she could be, wiping her eyes with frustration that makes her feel as happy and relaxed as a drunk on a binge, and when she can't stand it any longer she flees down the hall.

It is faster to pack these bags by myself anyway. It's easier to endure how much I miss her when she's not there.

It was still a mean thing to do.

April 7, 2129. Commons Cafeteria, Excellence Shop, Oregon/Idaho District, Earth.

When I get up there's nothing I'm supposed to do except what I would do anyway. Derlock said if they were going to watch anyone it would be me or him, so he and I have nothing to do but act all natural and innocent.

I go down to breakfast. Nobody sits with me. Of all the weird things, Bari is there. A guy with his habits is never at breakfast, but there he is, beaming with serene happiness, trying to style that he is not watching me.

I finish up breakfast, look around at the Excellence Shop Commons Room for the last time, and make sure my scootsack has my cleanstick, smartcomb, and coswand, plus a change of clothes—that's all Pop ever packs for a whole tour. The inside of my scootsack looks empty and lonely.

When I look up, Bari is standing directly in front of me. I step into his arms.

"Have a good trip," he says. "Be careful."

"You too." I wrap my arms around his neck and whisper, "Don't gasp any more happistuf. Get started on Fendrisol. Today. Please."

He kisses my cheek, gentle and soft and shy the way he always was. "I'll think about it, while I still can. I haven't taken any since we talked, because I wanted to feel as much as I still could when you left." But then he spoils it by smiling like it's Christmas in heaven.

I hug him hard to shut out that awful smile. It's ultra

more of a closursation than what we had in his room, even if it's unsplycterable.

April 7, 2129. Vandenberg Spaceport, Golden Gate District, Earth.

The PersKab wakes me just as we're passing Bakersfield Ruin. I use the cleanstick, smartcomb, and coswand; Glisters will have his cameras out. Funny how once Glisters had a function in life—hacking the systems, prepping for our stowaway, shooting splycterables of the girls—that boy became half as creepy and ten times as competent. He's still a pink-skinned giant-head pervert, of course.

My PersKab zips past maybe a hundred launch pads. Directly ahead of me, the cap is a big white ceramic cone, as tall as a three-storey building. The PersKab floats into the parking slot and clanks as it docks to the cap's main entrance. I grab my scootsack, say "PersKab, I'm done," and walk out.

Another *clank* behind me. The PersKab slams away, its acceleration no longer limited by my comfort.

In the main common space of the cap, I check to see that my two bags are in the pile of luggage. Stack is already there and answers my raised eyebrow with a nod. So the unofficial additional luggage is already aboard, too; it's just a few bags with some burglary tools, enough drugs and liquor to fuel a lot of parties, some of Glisters's purpose-built hacking gear, and extra clothes that might make the crew on *Virgo* wonder why we brought so many showing-off outfits, but that stuff will be essential once we emerge from hiding and into the meeds. We could still do the plan without what's in those bags, but as Pop always says, there's no such thing as overprepared.

Swish. Thrum. Clank. Another PersKab docks. The cap hatch opens and admits Wychee, Marioschke, Fleeta, and Emerald. Emerald and Wychee have Plexaks, like mine, which is this month's brand of scootsack. Marioschke has some soggy miney-handmade canvas thing, and Fleeta is actually carrying a Hobag, last November's brand, because she can't remember to update.

"So what was that, the girl wagon?" Stack asks.

"Wit. Wit. I am pierced by the wit," Emerald says, her voice perfectly flat. Sometimes I kind of like her—sarcastic, dumpy little body and flat face, won't get the surgery she needs, can't dress for shit, unsplycterable, blames everyone else for the way she hasn't just had everything fixed like a sensible girl—but if you squint hard enough you'd swear she has some kind of style all her own.

Stack stomps over into the corner and ostentatiously stares at the console, running his hands over the locked keyboards. They don't *let* passengers mess with anything. Robots are tougher and have better judgment and far faster reflexes than humans. Stack is just styling important guy with something to do.

Meanwhile Marioschke sits, singing a soft "ahhh" in the lotus position. It's the same game Stack is playing; he pretends he could fly the ship, she pretends she could levitate it.

She seems to be even angrier than he is, and I don't

know why. Some strange compulsion makes me sit next to her. "Are you okay?"

"Oh, just . . . it took me so long to find some people that said they'd tend my plants for me. I thought that was really nice, and I gave them some of my best flowers. So I just got a bunch of pictures from one of them on my phone; they waited till I was here and then threw all the plants out the window onto the sidewalk, and sent me pictures with a note that said nobody likes me." Her lower lip is trembling.

I can't help myself; I put an arm around her, and let her cry. After a while she says, "At least I'm going to space with people who treat me better than that. At least I'm not still back there with *them*."

I can think of at least three of my fellow moes that might be just as mean to her, but it doesn't seem like the time to disagree. I hug her again, and try to think of something to say. I'm relieved when Glisters and F.B. come in.

F.B. has a big stupid smile because he had something important to do and it made him feel not-worthless for once, I guess. The truth is, Glisters was the one who set up the sleeper programs that will help conceal our tracks once the cap starts on its way back down. He could have done the whole job in half the time if he hadn't carefully guided F.B. through "helping," so that F.B. feels like he contributed. I can't help thinking that Glisters may be a giant-headed throwback pink geek, but he's a *kind* giant-headed throwback pink geek.

It was clever, too, because it gave Glisters an excuse to

be right there to make sure F.B. got into a PersKab headed to Vandenberg—F.B. is Captain for Life of the Awkward Squad, and if anyone might have missed the launch and then accidentally blurted the truth, it would be F.B.

Derlock is the only one that's late. Maybe he's ratting, right now, and we're about to be arrested. Things like that happen around Satan. Who would know better than his almost-declared girlfriend? But I can't think of any way it's in his self-interest, and this is definitely a splycterworthy escapade. I'm glad Glisters is good with a camera, and I only hope we can override his weird taste in editing—he likes to cut so fast you never quite know what you saw, only what you felt—so people can see the good parts of his work. And the best parts of me, of course.

Another *swish-thrum-clank.* The door irises. Derlock walks in like a general inspecting his troops, and his eyes wander up and down me. That is so zoomed.

We drop our bags into lockers. Nets reach out, cover them, tighten. We strap into our barely needed acceleration hammocks like good little obedient students—max acceleration upbound is 1.5 g, which just means instead of weighing 50 kilos, I'll feel like I weigh 75. Lots of people weigh more than that, all the time. But we all do it anyway—*no troublemakers here, no sir.*

With a hum and a swing, the crane lifts us to the top of the launcher, which is a thirty-storey tower of ice in an aluminum tube. The robots clamp us into place and back away.

‖‖

Notes for the Interested, #6

CAP: *short for* capsule. *An spacecraft shaped like a rounded cone. The easiest structure for going up or coming down in the atmosphere.*

A cap is highly stable; when going up, the pointed nose keeps it faced into the wind, and when coming down, without the rocket under it, it naturally rolls into a position where the heat-shielded rounded bottom faces into the wind, and provides plenty of drag to slow it down.

A cap requires much less guidance and is much more stable than a winged spacecraft like the twentieth-century space shuttle; if it is aimed correctly, it can land just as precisely, if not more so. By 2050, design engineers gave up on winged spacecraft, just as earlier generations of designers gave up on sailing ships, dirigibles, steam-powered cars, and ornithopters.

A cap is launched from Earth on top of an ice rocket, which is simply an aluminum tube, about as tall as a really big office building, filled with ice. (In our real world NASA began looking at this idea before 1980; we just don't have powerful enough lasers to make it work—yet). A laser from the ground is focused into the beam port, turning the ice to superheated plasma; the plasma ejects from ports on the side, creating a rocket exhaust that pushes the rocket at very high speeds. By shaping the beam port, body, and exhaust ports correctly, it is possible to build a rocket that naturally stays on the beam, so that the lasers can guide it to orbit as well as propel it. The laser can deliver much more energy than could be generated from fuel carried on board, allowing more boost for the same sized rocket, and removing any need for carrying volatile, possibly explosive fuel on the flight itself.

▌▌

When I was little, and we'd go to the tourist hotels in orbit, or to the moon for skiing or surfing, Pop always let me put the audio on so I could listen to the countdown. I want to now, but I'm sure Glisters has a camera running and I don't want to style this moment all childish. Luckily Fleeta says, "Countdown, please."

"—three, two, one, laser on." The cap starts moving upward, smooth as an elevator but gaining speed steadily. Under us, the laser from the ground flows into the beam port at the bottom of that ice-filled aluminum skyscraper. Ice vaporizes, molecules tear apart, electrons strip off the atoms.

Fourteen thousand tonnes of ice go out the exhaust ports as oxygen-hydrogen plasma in the next half hour. Since it's a beam rider, the rocket always stays centered with its beam port right on the beam—we studied how that works in math class—and the plasma jets fan out around the beam without blocking it, leaving a 500-meter doughnut of flame about a kilometer behind the ship (where the hydrogen cools down enough to burn back into water). As you go up they switch your rocket from beam to beam so you're finally on exactly the right trajectory.

Sheeyeffinit. I am not thinking celeb-eenie thoughts, even at a career-defining moment. *Gah.* Crazy Science Girl is always inside me, waiting to pop out.

The last beam switches off. There're just a few tonnes of ice rattling around inside the rocket.

Before I can think about my dignity, Fleeta and I release our tie-downs and airswim to the tail-end window; we nearly collide with Glisters coming from the other side. The metal wall facing us through the window backs away from us on its positioning jets.

In minutes, the rocket is far away, a glinting cylinder against the curve of shining ocean wrapped in a thin band of deep blue air. As the remaining ice inside boils from the frictional heat of the thin remaining atmosphere, the nose jet flares in a soundless glowing white wisp. For a moment the empty rocket flashes in the sun, rushing ass-first away before we lose its brilliant glare against the vast Earth.

"What are you all looking at?" Emerald demands.

"You always watch the rocket fall away," Fleeta says, firmly. "It's great."

"The rocket falls away? Where does it go?" Marioschke asks.

"They drop it off at the end of boosting. Then its nose jet shoves it down into the atmosphere so it will fall into one of the catching ranges to be recycled," Glisters says. "When I was little, Mom and I used to sit outside in Hawaii just after sunset and watch the boosters come down over the Pacific. They make these big white trails that aren't like anything else, because they tumble as they come down, and get hot, and the steam from the leftover ice pours out through the ports and kind of makes them pinwheel."

"I used to watch that with my parents," I say.

"It's what you *do*," Fleeta says. "It's so beautiful. Big white scribbles across the sky like angels doing graffiti."

I notice Stack and Derlock smirking. Fury rises in me; Fleeta is *right*, it's *what you do*. Glisters catches my eye and his eyebrows twitch, as if saying, *What idiots. They don't know, do they?* I can't help myself. I smile. He's still a creepy pornographer, but he's my favorite creepy pornographer. I'd watch rockets come in with him, anytime.

"We're already out of gravity," Wychee says, tumbling awkwardly.

Here we are halfway through the second century of space travel, and idiots still talk about the cap "leaving Earth's gravity" because they mix up weight with gravity. We're just going into a very high, lopsided orbit around the Earth, and by definition, if you're orbiting, you're in the gravity.

At the high end of the cap's orbit—seven times farther from Earth than the moon—when *Virgo* grabs us, we will still be *in the gravity*; we just won't have any weight.

Definitely, Crazy Science Girl has returned. Maybe I'm regressing because I'm going to see Aunt Destiny again.

April 7–23, 2129. In a highly elliptical Earth orbit, rising from the top of Earth's atmosphere (160 kilometers up) to intercept with *Virgo* (about 2 million kilometers from Earth, around five times as far as the moon).

Sixteen days in a cap is a long time, but at least that's all it is, going up; because the cap needs to be going more slowly and less steeply when it re-enters the atmosphere, and it's starting from moving away instead of a standing start, the return trip will be more than a month. I'm glad I'm not going to be on it; it might have been so dull that we really would have started studying for PotEvals, like we promised.

The moes are all good at hanging around pointlessly— it's about all we've ever done. We gossip a lot about people back at Excellence Shop, who aren't here to defend themselves. We plug into meeds—we're featured in a quick little pop-up meed on Ed Teach about "celebubrats go to space." Admittedly it's pretty much straight botflog.

Excellence Shop, already milking the fame, is the sponsor. At least we all look good in it, though Pop and Sir Penn Slabilis and all the other celeb-eenie parents actually get more screen space than we do. I doubt it even budges anyone's recognition score.

Derlock and I have weightless sex often. I relish the envy for Satan's girlfriend in the other girls' eyes, but I go back to my own sleepsack for the night. Derlock likes morning sex, he likes to get himself going by talking about awful things he did to people, and the combination means waking up every morning to the guy whispering about someone he cheated, betrayed, beat up, or reduced to helpless tears. I'm thinking that the moment enough meeds are out there, I'll be de-declaring, and trying for the biggest closursation "since Nora slammed the door." (*Get out of my head, Pop!*)

UP-LEG
EARTHPASS
TO
MARSPASS

APRIL 23, 2129—AUGUST 27, 2129

POSITIONS OF THE EARTH, MARS, AND *VIRGO*— APRIL 23, 2129—AUGUST 27, 2129

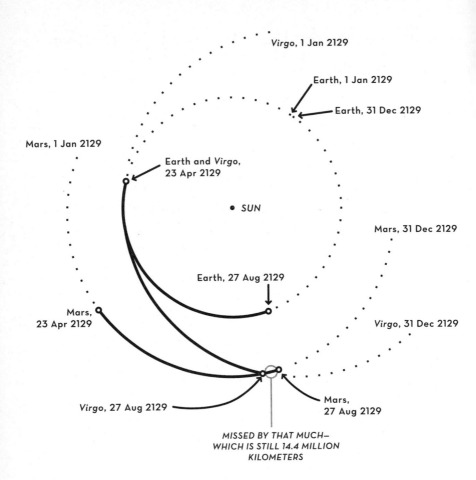

Virgo, 1 Jan 2129

Earth, 1 Jan 2129

Earth, 31 Dec 2129

Mars, 1 Jan 2129

Earth and *Virgo*, 23 Apr 2129

SUN

Mars, 31 Dec 2129

Earth, 27 Aug 2129

Mars, 23 Apr 2129

Virgo, 31 Dec 2129

Virgo, 27 Aug 2129

Mars, 27 Aug 2129

MISSED BY THAT MUCH— WHICH IS STILL 14.4 MILLION KILOMETERS

Again, the whole year of 2129 is shown for reference. The dark solid lines show the movement of Earth, Mars, and *Virgo*. The most interesting thing here is the gap, as represented by the small gray circle; because of what happens in this section, they are not able to get close enough to cross the gap, which is 14.4 million kilometers, 37.5 times as far as the Earth is from the moon.

Notes for the Interested, #7

The ride they're planning to take

Susan, Derlock, and the rest are planning to go up to Mars on *Virgo* and come back down on *Leo*; this will give them about three weeks on Mars. It's very different from travel on Earth, where locations at least stay in one place, and only the travelers move, and where the vehicle doesn't just keep going of its own accord after the traveler gets on and off. So the table below is a short guide to refer to if you start to get lost in the orbital process.

Of course, their plan is going to encounter the two absolute rules of travel, from the Stone Age to the Space Age, which are:

- Your Mileage May Vary
- Subject To Change

But for the moment, the chart on the following page will tell you what everybody thinks is going to happen.

You might notice that if everything goes well, they will be on *Virgo* for only four months (and Mars for a few weeks, and *Leo* for four months). But if they don't get off *Virgo*, the next time there's anywhere to get off is almost two years away. But, after all, what could go wrong?

TIME/PART OF ORBIT	EARTH	MARS	UP-CYCLER (VIRGO)	DOWN-CYCLER (LEO)
Next 4 months: Virgo's Earthpass to Marspass	Behind Mars in orbit and now overtaking it	Ahead of Earth in orbit and being overtaken	On the up-leg between Earth and Mars. Moes are on board Virgo	Downward leg, falling back toward sun and Mars
Both cyclers Marspass	Opposition (Earth passes Mars in orbit)		Passing Mars and continuing upward; Moes get off and spend a few weeks on Mars	Passing Mars and continuing downward; after a few weeks on Mars, moes get on board Leo
Next 4 months	Going ahead of Mars in orbit	Falling behind Earth in orbit	Still on up-leg, continuing up above Mars	Down-leg from Mars to Earth
Down-cycler Earthpass	Going ahead of Mars in orbit	Falling behind Earth in orbit	Still on up-leg, continuing far up above Mars	Earthpass, changing direction to go back up; moes get off back at Earth
Next 5 months	Going ahead of Mars in orbit	Falling behind Earth in orbit	Still on up-leg, continuing far up above Mars	Rising away from Earth on the empty up-leg, which never comes near Mars
Up-cycler aphelion	Going ahead of Mars in orbit	Falling behind Earth in orbit	Aphelion: Highest point above the sun, far up above Mars; from here on Virgo begins to fall back toward the sun	Rising away from Earth on the empty up-leg, which never comes near Mars
Next 4 months	Going ahead of Mars in orbit	Falling behind Earth in orbit	Falling back toward sun and Earth on the empty down-leg, which never comes near Mars	Rising away from Earth on the empty up-leg, which never comes near Mars
Conjunction	Earth and Mars are as far apart as they ever get, with the sun directly between them		Falling back toward sun and Earth on the empty down-leg, which never comes near Mars	Rising away from Earth on the empty up-leg, which never comes near Mars
Next 4 months	Behind Mars in orbit and now overtaking it (it's like lapping on a circular track; eventually you're so far ahead that you're behind again)	Ahead of Earth in orbit and being overtaken (it's like being lapped on a circular track; eventually your opponent is so far ahead that they're behind you again)	Falling back toward sun and Earth on the empty down-leg, which never comes near Mars	Rising away from Earth on the empty up-leg, which never comes near Mars
Down-cycler aphelion	Behind Mars in orbit and now overtaking it	Ahead of Earth in orbit and being overtaken	Falling back toward sun and Earth on the empty down-leg, which never comes near Mars	Aphelion: Highest point above the sun, far up above Mars's orbit (Mars is nowhere near); from here on Leo begins to fall back toward the sun
Next 5 months	Behind Mars in orbit and now overtaking it	Ahead of Earth in orbit and being overtaken	Falling back toward sun and Earth on the empty down-leg, which never comes near Mars	Downward leg, falling back toward sun and Mars
Up-cycler Earthpass	Behind Mars in orbit and now overtaking it	Ahead of Earth in orbit and being overtaken	Passing Earth (lowest point in orbit, will now head up)	Downward leg, falling back toward sun and Mars
Next 4 months: from Virgo Earthpass to Virgo Marspass (back to where we started, that's why it's a cycler!)	Behind Mars in orbit and now overtaking it	Ahead of Earth in orbit and being overtaken	On the up-leg between Earth and Mars	Downward leg, falling back toward sun and Mars

3

RENDEZVOUS WITH DESTINY

April 23, 2129. On *Virgo*, upbound from Earth to Mars. 149 million kilometers from the sun, 171 million kilometers from Mars, 2.5 million kilometers from Earth.

AUNT DESTINY'S ARMS grip me; we're laughing and babbling. The shape of her face is so much like mine, but she wasn't geneered for rich-cocoa skin, so she has a space crew tan: the goggle-and-resp triangle from her eyebrows to her upper lip is coffee-with-fresh-cream, about like Pop's color; her cheeks, chin, and lower forehead are deeper brown than mine, and freckled black, where the light comes in through her faceplate; and her neck, ears, and forehead are another band of warm light brown beneath her glistening black crew cut. Her face looks like a sepia-and-chocolate bull's-eye.

"Hey." She holds me at arm's length to look at me. We tumble like a slow-motion dumbbell, bouncing off the soft walls of the receiving area, laughing. "Hey. It's so good to see you again, kiddo." She thumps my back like she's afraid I'm choking. "I won't exclaim about how you've grown, but you do look older. And if you say 'so do you,' you're dead."

Derlock glares; the attention café is closed due to a private party.

The rest airswim away after Rojdeff, the crewman that Emerald has already started calling "Mr. Junior Spaceman." Emerald may not be exactly splycterbait, but she can turn on the cute, and I suspect Rojdeff is in for an *ultra* distracting day.

"So," Aunt Destiny says, "would the biowaste recycler, the star spotter array, or the medical bay interest you?"

"Um, not very much, but if *you* like them—"

She snorts. "Kiddo, I just wanted to make sure we don't skip anything you really want to see. Just trust me that most of the standard tour is boring. Now, shall we see the cockpit before the regular tour gets there, so we don't have to hang around respectfully at the back?"

Her enthusiasm is like a dance beat you can't resist. "Sure."

In the cockpit, the watch is just five people strapped into chairs, three of them reading and two playing Go on a screen, all "waiting for an alarm to tell them it's time to watch the machines take care of something automatically," Destiny explains cheerfully. Everyone nods solemnly, so I guess she's not exaggerating much. "Commander Kanegawa, permission to move between the cockpit crew and the screens?"

A small, heavyset woman looks away from the game of Go. "Sure, Destiny, but keep it short. If you're going over to the pod, maybe you can take a longer look in the auxiliary cockpit?"

"That's a great idea, thanks!" Destiny says. "Let's just look at the things that the main cockpit has but the auxiliary doesn't, then." She guides me to an all-wavelength hologram tank; inside it, what looks like a tiny model of *Virgo* floats at the center. The illusionary object is only the length of my index finger; almost all of it is a stumpy window-dotted cylinder, the pod, where all the cargo is stored. At the front end of the pod there's a small pointed structure, rings and slopes leading up to a little needle; that's the nose spire. At the back of the pod, like a blister or a wart, is a little cone half as wide as the pod, attached to it by the wide end: the crew bubble, where the crew live and everything is controlled and planned. The main cockpit, where we are now, is almost at the rear of the crew bubble.

"The ship is steered from the tail," I say. "I didn't think of that before now."

Commander Kanegawa nods. "Form follows function," she says. "Airplanes are steered from the front because they're mostly steered visually and the biggest concern is that you might run into something. Ships are steered from a high platform so you can see farther and in more directions. Down here at the bottom of our orbit, relative to the solar system as a whole, we're moving at about 35 kilometers per second, and we steer entirely by radar and instruments, so the best place to put the controls is in the best-protected place, which is back here, with the whole pod and crew bubble between us and trouble, nestled snug between four big iceballs so that radiation

VIRGO'S POD

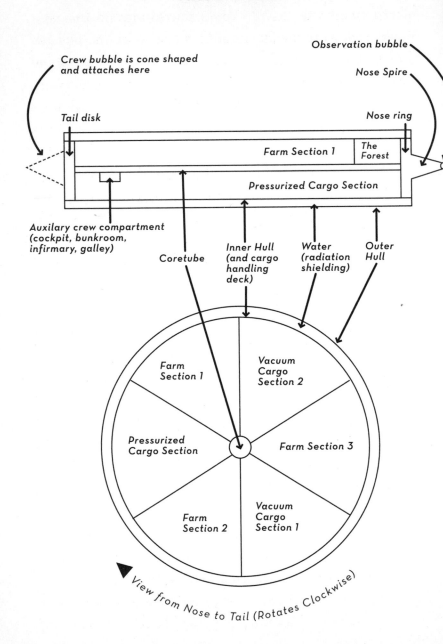

Crew bubble is cone shaped and attaches here

Observation bubble

Nose Spire

Tail disk

Nose ring

Farm Section 1

The Forest

Pressurized Cargo Section

Auxilary crew compartment (cockpit, bunkroom, infirmary, galley)

Coretube

Inner Hull (and cargo handling deck)

Water (radiation shielding)

Outer Hull

Farm Section 1

Vacuum Cargo Section 2

Pressurized Cargo Section

Farm Section 3

Farm Section 2

Vacuum Cargo Section 1

View from Nose to Tail (Rotates Clockwise)

and cosmic micrometeoroids can't nail us from the side."

She points to the three big spheres around the crew bubble; they are about the same diameter as the pod but attached at its edges, so that they meet in a central spandrel. Those are the iceballs; when all of them are in place, they will supply not just reaction mass, but also radiation shielding. Half of each iceball extends beyond the edge of the pod, so the four iceballs together, when everything is assembled a couple of days from now, will form by far the widest part of the ship, surrounding and guarding the crew bubble that huddles between them at the back of the pod.

Sticking up like a brush of long shiny bristles between the iceballs, Virgo's eleven engines wait to be summoned to action.

"It's so pretty," I say. "Like the best dollhouse you ever saw, if a dollhouse was an interplanetary ship."

"I shall take that as a compliment," Commander Kanegawa says.

There's a sound like distant thunder and a vibration in the air; I look back into the tank to see a tiny cap crawling away from the crew bubble.

Virgo is always at the center of the hologram tank, for quick reference. Now that I am looking for them, I see a small scattering of mostly cargo caps, coming in and going out. Iceball-4, still on its way, is a fingernail-sized white sphere far down in one corner of the tank.

"So even though you're only doing course corrections,"

I say, "you need almost, what, half the volume of the ship in water to do that?"

"It's not all reaction mass. A little bit of it also goes to the farm sections and life support, because we always lose some to leaks here and there."

"How long before the moon runs out of ice?"

Commander Kanegawa hesitates, and Destiny quickly jumps in. "At the rate we're using it, the conservative guess is we have 200 years of proven reserves, but most people who study it think it will be 1,000. It'll be a while before we're thirsty, and by that time there'll be plenty of other sources from comets or the gas giants." It sounds sort of memorized.

She flips the holotank display over to solar particle density scan, which shows the nanocurrents of ions surrounding the ship as a weave of yellow and blue flames ten times as long as the ship itself.

It's gorgeous, but I can't help noticing that I asked a bad question. Maybe the Moon of Our Ancestors League has been getting a lot of media coverage or something. (Pop always calls them "Save the Rocks.") "So let's go see the pod," I say. "Thanks for answering my questions, Commander!"

A little politeness will get you a smile and a wave, and I seem to have de-embarrassed Destiny.

We make our way noseward through the crew bubble. The corridors zig and zag to ensure that if they fire the engines when you're in midair you won't have far to fall. Doors open on all surfaces into all kinds of spaces. Destiny and I poke our heads in to visit an off-duty crew chief, who is also a sculptor, making ultra elaborate floating-string structures. In another workroom, we find the astrogator of the watch and chief economist discussing course corrections. They threaten to explain it; we flee onward, up one of the several entry corridors into the pod.

"You can always tell when you're crossing over into the pod," Destiny says, "because every corridor that goes into the pod's tail disk is interrupted by a double fast-close airlock, even though they have all four hatches open 99% of the time. If they ever have to, the pod and the bubble can be sealed off from each other in less than a tenth of a second. Of course if anyone's in the doorway at the time, one nasty job for the survivors might be matching up the pieces floating on each side of the door."

I shudder. "It seems like things are dull here, but you're always a meter away from something awful."

"Yeah. That's life: dullness that's a second, or a meter, from horror. In space, you're more aware of it. This way— I want to show you the Forest." I can hear the capital in Destiny's voice.

The walls inside the pod all have that odd sheen from being vacuum-plate-cast in a centrifuge. Where in the crew bubble the surfaces are covered with panels shipped up from Earth to look more "natural," inside the pod it's all *native*, stuff formed in space, glass, metal, and plastic salvaged from all the fuel tanks, engines, and scaffolding left over from putting *Virgo* into an Aldrin cycler orbit. I run my hand over it; the alclad surface is so smooth that it feels curiously soft to my touch.

Destiny says, "*Virgo* puts me in awe every time I look at her seriously. Can you imagine this ship once had fifty iceballs, instead of four, and a hundred fifty engines instead of eleven, and a factory where the crew bubble sits now? And the engines ran night and day, and they were still catching iceballs all the way to Mars? Do you remember our last Christmas together on Earth, kiddo?"

"Yeah." It's a sad memory; at age seven, I hadn't understood Anny Dezzy wasn't coming back, that she was going to be out there in the sky forever, while Fleeta and I watched the launch. I had cried for days, later, when I realized.

"Well, the shower I took Christmas night—remember we were all at the hotel in Singapore?—was the last bath I got that wasn't a sponge bath for more than a year, and that hotel room was the last time I had a room to myself till after the next Earthpass, a few months after your tenth birthday. When I first saw *Virgo* from the approaching capsule, the pod was still more than half open girderwork, the barracks was a big radiation shelter inside the finished part of the pod, and the factory was where the crew bubble is now.

"Year after year, trip after trip up into the far dark and back, we kept feeding junk engines and tanks into the factory, and pulling out plates and spars and everything else, till that last amazing three months when we fed the factory into itself, made the crew bubble, and then one bright day we all had quarters of our own instead of a bunk in a can. I remember floating slowly down onto *my* bed, after eating a huge meal I'd cooked in *my* kitchen, looking out *my* window, tears piling up on my face in pure happiness."

"You never put that in your messages," I said.

"I sort of did. That was why I wanted you to come up when you were eleven. My quarters in the crew bubble were only a couple months old; I wanted to show them off to family!"

"It sounds so primitive, like something out of a history book," I say, thinking that at about the same time I was running around with Fleeta, visiting all those weird scientist types, playing with my dog Stanley, and begging all the time for trips to the beach and to orbit, and having no idea that I was having the most fun I ever would. "I can't imagine how tough your life must have been."

"Oh, that was kind of my point. I didn't mean to make it sound like more than it was. Finishing the pod and building the bubble *was* a tough job, and it went on a long time, but it was duck soup, really, compared to what the first generation of evalists had already done. *Those* evalists, the guys who structured the steel and hung the first tanks and engines on the framework, all under constant acceleration, where if you lost your grip you'd fall away from the ship forever, or trail off into solar-temperature exhaust—years and years sharing a bunk with two other people and taking ten times the radiation anyone would be allowed to nowadays—*they* were evalists. They feared nothing, would try anything, and could do everything; I guess I'll always wonder if I'd've been up to their challenges, and be grateful I never found out. It was enough to have known men and women like them. The Senior Mentor on my shift when I first came up was old Charlie Tang, as in the Tang Rule."

"I've never heard of it," I say, slightly embarrassed.

"I suppose only evalists have, but we're all pretty grateful to Charlie for fighting for it in collective bargaining. Charlie had his pellor locked on the side of a LOX tank when it broke loose, and cracked the nozzle on his pellor to boot. He ended up working his way back to the ship because they didn't have any way to go get him. Took him nineteen days."

‖‖‖

Notes for the Interested, #8

Getting around outside

Pellor: a small, 1-to-4 person spacecraft with hooks, clamps, and manipulators, used by evalists to do assembly work outside. Compared to an evasuit, it provides more radiation protection (with lead-lined walls) and more comfort (bathroom, food locker, ability to take the suit off part of the time). Many important tasks can be performed with the pellor's mechanical arms. Except for the engine nozzle, practically the whole surface of a pellor consists of lead-shuttered windows; normally the operator only opens the shutters over a window to see to work for the briefest possible time, to minimize radiation exposure. The sills separating the windows are thick with mechanical arms, claws, magnetic clamps, smart cables, and other manipulators. (A *pellor*, in Latin, means "a thing that pushes," just as a *tractor* means "a thing that drags." Pellors usually push things into place rather than tow them.)

eva: pronounced ee-vuh. Any trip outside the main vessel, whether inside a pellor or in an evasuit. The term comes from EVA, a twentieth-century acronym for Extra Vehicular Activity. (In Latin *extra* means "outside.") Nobody at the time of this story remembers that, any more than you remember that *radar* once stood for RAdio Detection And Ranging or *scuba* stood for Self-Contained Underwater Breathing Apparatus. To them, an eva is just an eva.

LOX: liquid oxygen. A basic material in space operations since the very beginning of space travel.

Free fall: the condition of moving without resistance to gravity, going where the gravity takes you. Galileo's cannon-balls dropped from the tower of Pisa were free falling. So are objects in orbit. The path of *Virgo* in free fall is not a straight line but a very long curve around the sun; the engines don't so much speed it up, slow it down, or move it sideways as they change which curve around the sun it is riding on.

Similarly, Charlie Tang's pellor was also in orbit around the sun—unfortunately for him, not the same orbit as *Virgo*, which he was trying to return to. What Charlie had to figure out was which orbit he could get into with the fuel he had, such that his orbit would intercept the ship's orbit, at the same velocity as the ship, at exactly the same time the ship would be there.

All this as the ship changed its orbit constantly. It would be an interesting exercise for a third-year engineering student's semester project; Charlie Tang was solving it in a slowly tumbling closet-sized box.

███

"Nineteen *days* in a pellor? How did he *live*?"

"He was tied to a LOX tank, remember. So he had something to breathe if he could get to it. He hand-rigged a tap and hose, all out of parts in the general repair kit, in evasuit gloves, and got air flowing with about half an hour to spare. Then he rebuilt the damaged nozzle on the pellor's thruster, and hand-navigated back to the ship, which is a real good trick, because when one free-falling object is trying to catch another, the shortest path is *not* just to aim straight at it, and it's anything but intuitive."

"Wow. So what's Tang's Rule?"

"I was getting to that but I was enjoying the story first, kiddo. Charlie stretched his two days of rations out as long as he could, but he still ran out of food three days before he got back. He always said that first meal on return was the best he'd ever had. What all us evalists are grateful to him for is that he hammered out a deal with management so that every pellor always goes out with food, plus enough water and air-recycling capability, to last a month for a crew of four. Tang's Rule makes survival more skill and less luck, and I suppose it might save my life someday, and"—she grins, enjoying her bragging—"I used to bunk close enough to Tang to hear him snore."

‖‖‖

Notes for the Interested, #9

Virgo's pod—the reason for the ship

The pod is a double-hulled cylinder, 210 meters across by 1 kilometer long. Between the inner and outer hulls there is a 2-meter separation, filled with water to block radiation. Inside the inner hull, six **sections** run almost the length of the pod. Because the pod rotates on its long axis to supply artificial gravity, a person inside the pod experiences "down" hullward, and the apparent gravity varies inversely with distance from the center. Thus there is milligravity (if the object weighs 1 tonne on Earth it will weigh 1 kilogram on the inner hull) if you are standing on the inner hull, zero gravity if you are on the centerline of the coretube, and proportionate gravity in between: if you are 40 meters above the hull the gravity is 60% milligravity (1 kilogram weight on Earth=0.6 grams at that position).

If you sliced through the ship crosswise, you would see the sections forming a hex, looking like slices of a pie cut into six pieces. Thus each section is a little over 100 meters across on the "floor" (inner hull) and only about 5 meters across at the "ceiling," 100 meters above.

The six sections are:

- the Pressurized Cargo Section, which is filled with room-temperature air and used for transporting things that would be damaged by vacuum or extreme heat or cold
- Vacuum Cargo Sections 1 and 2, which are kept in vacuum and carry mostly bulk cargo like pre-built houses, shipping containers of flour, or specialty machine parts
- Farm Section 1, 2, and 3, which grow food for the ship and recycle its waste, air, and water.
- To keep the load balanced, cargo and farm sections alternate.

On the centerline of the pod, a 5-meter across coretube, nearly without gravity, runs the length of the ship. People use it as a shortcut, flying or jumping to the door nearest their work.

At the nose of the pod, the spire sticks about 40 meters into space, a tall thin tower where caps can dock and cargo can be loaded in directly; the tip of the nose spire is a small observation bubble. At the tail of the pod, the crew bubble attaches to a "tail disk," a disk-shaped whorl of corridors through which the crew go to and from duties in the pod. Just noseward of the tail disk, off the coretube, partly enclosed in the Pressurized Cargo Section, there is an auxiliary crew area, with cockpit, galley, bunk room, infirmary, restrooms, and everything that the crew of *Virgo* might need if some or all of them had to leave their quarters in the crew bubble and take shelter in the pod.

Most of Farm Section 1 is being prepared for planting. Old vegetable beds are being sterilized and filled with a mixture of sand and composted organic waste. We airswim past a lot of tanks and plumbing, and stacked bags of soil. It's like a low-grav gardening store.

The Forest is a hundred-meter-square grove of geneered trees at the nose end of Farm Section 1. The trees only have to support a thousandth of the weight they would on Earth, but their wood is as strong as it is anywhere, so they're geneered to grow into impossibly long and spindly spearheads whose tips all fit into the narrow upper space. Immense clusters of fruit and nuts—a dozen varieties on each tree—hang from every short branch of the hardwoods; a hedge of 5-meter-high conifers along the perimeter blocks the view of metal walls and doors, adding to the feeling of a clearing in the forest.

"The onboard kids *love* getting picking duty," Destiny says. "It means spending a day airswimming around from branch to branch, grabbing oranges and walnuts, apples and avocados, pecans and peaches, hanging out on the limbs, eating all they want, and being thanked for bringing so much back."

We stand on the hull, at the bottom of the Forest. The light is green and moist, with a glow like the sky overhead coming down through the dense branches. A fiber optic system captures sunlight from the hull and feeds it to light ports on the coretube overhead, sending down the light the trees need, mixing with beams from the windows below. The golden sun flashes up through glass-covered pools every other minute and a half, turning the space from twilight to bright day; a moment later it's back to twilight, and stars shine through the crystal clear water at your feet.

"I really hope the tour comes this way," I say. "Marioschke, our crazy hippie mystic girl, is ultra into plants and growing things."

Destiny grins and pulls out her wristcomp. (A wristcomp. Like Glisters and F.B. wear. Emblems of anti-fashion. I guess you have to forgive your favorite aunt, though, no matter what.) She makes me spell *Marioschke* and relays that suggestion. She probably thinks I'm a nice person for making it, instead of a sneak and a traitor.

I bombard Destiny with questions; Crazy Science Girl is ultra, ultra *back*. I can only hope no camera is watching, because the only hooks that could be splyctered out of this would be something like, *Self-Styled Sophisticated Bad Girl Susan Tervaille Is Brain-o Dork Inside!* Nothing is more splycterable than the humiliation of inconsistent styling.

But after a few minutes of exploring in the Forest, airswimming up to get fresh pears right off the tree, and eating them with our legs wrapped around the branches, somehow when I think about meeds and hooks and all that sheeyeffinit, the only thought that follows is, *So what?*

I lie on my back on the thick, soft carpet of grass, next to Destiny, looking up through the branches at the diffuse glow of the piped light, savoring the change from dim green to brilliant gold, turning in the dark times to watch the stars wheeling across the watery window beside me.

"Is it ever night here?" I ask.

"They opaque the windows for four hours of total dark; some of the trees have to have that. The Forest is a pretty complex piece of interactive design, but it was all dreamed up by one mind—Reggie, that sculptor we visited."

"It was a great idea."

"Absolutely great." A crew guy, in his black coverall, is stretched out a couple meters away from us, holding hands with a woman in a yellow coverall, and he has a little girl—his daughter, I guess—lying back with her head on his chest. "This is your niece, Destiny?"

"This is her. As you can see, every bit as bad as I said." She's beaming.

The crew guy lifts his daughter up without waking her—she's about six, but in the low gravity she weighs about what a dry bath towel does on Earth—and sets her to the side so he can comfortably turn over to face us. "Yeah, this place really preserves our sanity."

"If I lived here," I say, "I'd come here every day."

"Some of us do that," the crew guy says. "Right around shift change you'll see maybe ten or twelve people."

It's a good thing we didn't decide to stow away in the Forest.

Wow, I'm a good little spy.

Just like that I'm back to hating myself.

■ ■ ■

Bouncing through the maze of corridors in the tail disk, Destiny and I come to a ladder leading noseward. Via alternating ladders and corridors, we scramble to the aux cockpit. "Why is there a cockpit in the pod?" I ask.

"Well, two reasons," Destiny says. "First of all, the main server is here inside a superconducting Faraday cage. So if the connection to the main cockpit in the crew bubble ever goes down—say in a thousand-year solar storm or something—we can fly it from here if we have to. And also, it's not likely, but if the crew bubble ever separates from the pod, then we can call up the AIs in this cockpit, slave everything, and have it rendezvous with us."

"The pod has its own engines?"

"The pod has most of the engines on the ship—there are three on the tail end of the crew bubble, and eight on the pod. Really *Virgo* is like two docked spaceships that never undock. Both the crew bubble and the pod are designed so that in a worst-case scenario, we could ride them through an aerobrake into a low orbit around Earth or Mars, and wait to be rescued from there—which would be a lot easier for the Space Patrol than spending months or years chasing us, since an accident wouldn't make us stop moving and they don't fly any faster than we do.

"And of course it's always possible that a separation might happen while crews were over here working, and then they could use the cockpit to fly back to the crew bubble, which might take a few days. They wouldn't be very comfortable, but still, the pod by itself is a much more comfortable spaceship than the one Paulo Kfouri and his crew flew to Mars the first time." She swims forward to the console in front of the pilot's chair, and taps a few keys.

"You aren't, um, flying the ship—"

She laughs. "No, silly. It's slaved right now, the screens show everything that's going on in the main cockpit, but the only thing I can do locally is to select the display I want to see. I just want to see how they're coming with Iceball-4—ha! Right now! Follow me!"

Notes for the Interested, #10

The language of spaceship architecture

Because so many movies and novels imported their ideas about spaceships from our Earthly experience of sea ships, there has been a tendency to use nautical terms for the parts of science fictional spaceships, with the captain standing on the bridge and engines firing out the stern and so forth.

The reality is that spaceships are developing not from sea ships, but from airplanes, and the names of the parts of a spaceship are much more likely to be drawn from there. So you will not find *Virgo*'s captain standing on the bridge talking to the first mate; you will find the commander in the cockpit, talking to the pilot. *Virgo* has a nose and a tail, not a bow and a stern, and its working surfaces are three-dimensional, not two, so crew members move noseward or tailward, hullward or coreward—not fore, aft, port, or starboard.

In the almost-weightless coretube, Destiny says, "This part is fun. Watch yourself with all the handholds on the walls, don't jam a finger."

She crouches down at the tail end of the coretube, one hand holding a handhold between her feet, and I copy her. She lets go very carefully of the handhold, braces her hands by her feet, and springs forward like an awkward, lunatic frog, shooting noseward through the coretube. I do the same, but I'm not as accurate as she is, so where she only touches the sides twice in her kilometer-long flight, I touch five times, taking advantage each time of the chance to plant my feet and fling myself forward harder. I'm moving pretty fast when I catch up with Destiny at the nose hatch; she has to brace herself to catch me. "Careful about building up momentum, kiddo. Just because there's no gravity doesn't mean inertia doesn't matter."

She opens the hatch, and we climb into the nose spire, a 40-meter tall, narrowing cone that doesn't rotate, because "for docking a cap or maintaining an antenna on constant focus, it's nice not to have the rotation," Destiny explains. "Of course that means we have almost no gravity, except a whisper of attraction from the actual gravity of the rest of the ship. It's a regular school project for the kids to time how long it takes a marble to fall down the nose spire and calculate the mass of *Virgo* from that."

We pass through one more hatch into a pitch-black room; then Destiny says, "Open nose spire observation bubble."

Petals of steel peel back around us and fold under us;

at once I can see we're in a transparent bubble 5 meters across. "The tourist-brochure version of things is that this is a geodesic dome of synthetic sapphire facets," Destiny says, "connected and reinforced with carbon nanotube structural members that are about as thick as a human hair. The steel antimeteorite cover is in place whenever there's no one in here."

"What happens if a meteorite hits?" I ask.

"With most of them you get a bright flash of light and a scratch on the sapphire, like, oh, that one and that one." The scars are no more than a centimeter long, shallow oval pits. "A big one might punch a hole and leak air, so we'd have to replace the panel; that's why there's a shield. A really big one could kill us, I guess, but then a big enough one could vaporize the whole ship. No reason to worry about it, really. This wouldn't be a good place to live because of the radiation levels, but 20 hours here is like a dental X-ray, so some of us come here to enjoy it."

It's like floating in space without a suit. A black spot on the glass, where it opaques, tracks me so that it always blocks a direct view of the sun; I can see that Destiny has a similar spot keeping the sun off of her. Destiny shows me a couple of silly games with making the spots merge, cross each other, and so on, like artificially generated shadows on the wrong side of our bodies.

She says, "It's almost time. Now look back that way."

Beyond the immense reach of the pod, above the curve of one iceball and the towers of the engines reaching up beyond it, a sphere hangs. It looks like a perfectly smooth moon, mostly in dark blue shadow barely lighted by reflection from the ship, but with a brilliant white crescent in sunlight.

Then the dark side flashes into a cloud of glare; white flame billows in a sheet from the far, day side. When the surface rotates toward us again, a wispy red eye whirls past. "The laser from the moon?" I ask.

"Yep, that's it, from the moon," she says. "They're bringing Iceball-4 into range—the last one we need before we course-correct for Mars. They flare off a little surface ice to adjust the course."

"Uh, what would happen if one of those laser shots missed the iceball and hit *Virgo*?"

"The surface fiber optics would catch it, the same as they do all the sunlight, and shunt the excess power into the forward radiator, right down there." She points to a big ring around the nose spire. "The radiator's working fluid can go up to molten iron temperatures if it has to; it would gradually release the extra heat as infrared. Basically any extra energy—misdirected laser, solar flare, sudden nova from some nearby star, the death rays of the Booga Booga Space Invaders—would go *around* everything valuable, and come out the radiator here." She grins at me. "We're not about to be blown to pieces or cut in half."

I make a face. "I didn't mean to sound—"

"No shame. It scares me too. Every time I pilot a pellor out to an iceball, I remember how thin the wall is between warm little pressurized water-filled me and the cold, the radiation, and the vacuum. But I still plan to die of old age." She's peering at me like she sees something wrong.

I'm terrified she'll ask, *Is something bothering you?* Or maybe I hope she will, so I'll tell her, and Derlock be damned. But she doesn't ask.

- - -

The day goes by too fast. Back in the crew bubble, we play spherical handball. At one point in the window of her cabin, Iceball-4, Earth, and the moon all line up close together, and she gets a great picture of me with that in the background. (But even though she'll put it up, nobody will ever splycter it; it's got no interest, it just looks like me, happy.)

We catch up on old jokes and embarrassing stories about when Pop was a kid. I want it to go on forever.

We're just finishing our peanut butter pancakes and scrambled eggs—what I called an "Anny Dezzy Pangcake Sangwidge" when I was four. Pop swears it was the only breakfast I would eat voluntarily for a full year after she shipped up. A noise like a muffled siren interrupts. Destiny says, "Acknowledged."

"Destiny, Commander Kanegawa says there's some bad news the kids need to hear about, and Susan should join them in the noseward commons."

She glances at me. "Should I come along too?"

"The commander requested that specifically." Soft disconnect chime.

"Hmm. Susan, if the commander wants to break the news herself, it's big, and we need to move."

Obviously we've been caught. I airswim after Destiny, trying to think of what I'm going to say to her when she finds out.

At the lounge, all the moes are styling bored/annoyed. We're the last there; I'm still trying to think of how I will say I'm sorry when Commander Kanegawa says, "This is about two of your classmates. The headmaster of Excellence Shop radioed us with the news that Bari Sylbrith and King Tzieschkarin died last night."

Destiny's arm around me is strong and comforting. No moe reaches for anyone's hand or gives a hug. Everyone's in it by themselves—except me, folded in Destiny's arms.

I ask, "Was it a happistuf overdose?"

Kanegawa nods. "I take it you knew they had a problem."

My voice comes out as a squeak. "Bari used to be my boyfriend. We just de-declared a few days before we came up here. He was . . . he was planning to take the laughing dive. That's why he didn't come with us. That's why I de-declared."

The commander looks like she's making herself talk. "Apparently they took a very dangerous combination—happistuf and Torporin."

Everyone looks puzzled; Stack ventures, "I've never even heard of Torporin."

Kanegawa looks even more uncomfortable. "It's rarely used recreationally because it's just the first drug in the suspended animation sequence; it's a high-powered hibernifacient, it makes people sleep very deeply for a long period of time. Not a lot of fun, I gather, for the people who want a drug to be fun. But it interacts fatally with Fendrisol, the happistuf inhibitor."

"That's why they can't just put me in suspended animation till there's a cure," Fleeta says, looking down at the deck. "Besides that, happistuf keeps right on forming even when you're in suspended animation anyway." Destiny reaches out and puts a hand on her shoulder.

Commander Kanegawa continues. "Apparently the boys took a big dose of both, and the ambulance crew tested for happistuf and some other drugs, but not for Torporin. Trying to undo the damage as fast as they could, the medics gave them a big injection of Fendrisol; it killed them almost instantly."

Then everyone says a lot of polite things, until finally I can go back to Aunt Destiny's quarters.

She just holds me. "Oh, Susan, I'm so sorry. Everyone has some terrible things like this in their lives, eventually, but you're awfully young for it."

Me? *Awfully young?* Decadent, jaded, seen-it-all me? I haven't cried like this since my old Labrador, Stanley, died two years ago; maybe not since Mom told me that hearing about my life, after she got divorced, made her so jealous and angry that she never wanted to see me again.

It's so good to have Destiny with me. And I *do* feel way too young for this.

4

BREAKFAST WITH THE RIGHT HALF

Seventeen hours later. April 24, 2129. On *Virgo*, upbound Earth to Mars. 149 million kilometers from the sun, 169 million kilometers from Mars, 2.9 million kilometers from Earth.

DURING THAT WHOLE day of lies, the most uncomfortable lie I tell Aunt Destiny is that I'm afraid I'll burst into tears in front of my friends if she sees me off at the cap dock, so could we please just hug good-bye here in her cabin?

At the cap dock, all our carefully planned ruses are unnecessary—there are no crew there, only the moes, simmering-pissy and sneaking glares at Derlock. Figuring it's where I'll get the most accurate reporting, I squeeze over next to Emerald and mutter, "Why isn't any of the crew here?"

She mutters back, "One day of the moes was more than enough. Tell you later."

We pick up our concealed bags from the cap and slip back out. Derlock hits the red-yellow-green keys, close/seal/ready-for-launch, as he ducks out. The door thrums shut behind him.

We push off from the wall and float 25 meters to where

an airlock connects to the tail disk of the pod.

I'd have expected F.B., Marioschke, and Wychee to be awkward airswimmers, but I'm surprised at how awkwardly Derlock and Stack bounce around in milligravity. On the other hand, Emerald airswims like a natural. Maybe she went to space a lot as a kid, the way Glisters, Fleeta, and I did.

Glisters has our route memorized, so he glides ahead, graceful as a cat walking a roof ridge. Emerald and I, the unofficial rearguard/catchers, fly in comfortable tandem. In between, it's all awkward chaos.

We're still in the ring corridor when the catapult sends the moe-less cap out of the ship. It's only maybe a half-second of 5% gravity—like being tugged briefly by one-twentieth of your Earth weight—and Glisters, Emerald, and I glide slightly to the right, correct course, and continue, but the moes in the middle tumble and tangle with each other, even throwing Fleeta's good balance off. Derlock falls out of that aerial scrum and bumps against Glisters, who guides him back into airswimming position. Derlock thanks him with an elbow to the ribs and a very insincere "Sorry."

Glisters winces but doesn't say anything.

"Hey, Emerald," I whisper, "how did they get them around for the tour?"

"Me, Glisters, and Fleeta took the tour," she whispers back. "The rest were so pissy and nasty that the crew just stuffed them into a room to watch meeds and eat all day. And by the time they did that, Rojdeff had lost all patience and was barely civil. Do you think we'll have to nurse-maid them like this forever?"

"Stack will get his wings pretty quick."

"Unh hunh."

Neither of us says a word about the others. We find the path to the coretube that Glisters is looking for and begin a complicated, awkward group struggle through the corridors; I could do it by myself in three minutes.

Finally we drag Marioschke off the last ladder she's clinging to, pull Stack back to the railing after he over-swims, and climb into the coretube. We airswim 20 meters, open a hatch into the Pressurized Cargo Section, and emerge onto a narrow railed platform just below the coretube on Cargo Wall 98. On Cargo Wall 99, tailward across from us, a vast array of crates, barrels, cubes, and odd shapes like eggs, balls, and pie wedges, cling to the wall in a dozen different colors. Almost 100 meters below us, the window keeps flashing from harsh sunlight to dim starlight, every hundred seconds or so.

"How do we get down?" Marioschke asks, nervously, clinging to the rail and frantically pushing herself back down as her feet float off the platform.

Glisters says, "Basically, if we just step over the rail and let the section wall bump into us, we'll slide down and hit the bottom with about as much force as you'd get falling off a low stool on Earth." He adds, "However, it would take us most of an hour to fall to the bottom, so I suggest doing this." He grabs the railing with one hand, puts his feet on either side of his hand holding the railing, bends over the edge like a bat hanging from a rafter, and pushes off. I follow suit; it's more like flying than swimming, and it's great, zooming down to the window in maybe 20 seconds, plenty of time to turn around and land on our feet on the sunlit window, looking up.

Fleeta and Stack are coming down after us, Fleeta grinning because it's fun, Stack grimacing and flailing. As the windows darken again, I catch Stack. He overcorrects, almost knocking me down. "Sorry, I need practice."

Fleeta doesn't need catching, exactly, but Glisters helps her land. "You're practically a gentleman," I tell him.

"Don't tell the other guys."

Derlock is next, tumbling slowly, trying to airswim into the right position. None of us moves to catch him, so he bumps backward against the starlit window, bounces a couple of meters like a goon, and lands on all fours with a thud. Wychee comes down in a slow tumble, turning over twice, which she styles all huffy, impatient, and put-upon, but she lands on her feet, waving Glisters off; F.B. is the exact opposite, tumbling gracelessly in a bony jumble of arms and legs, landing in a silly-looking headstand and flopping onto his back on the window, but obviously having a great time, and thanking me too profusely as I push him back to keep him from bouncing.

That leaves two people. "Emerald," I call, "are you okay up there?"

"About to be." Far above us, Marioschke is suddenly tumbling end over end, sputtering and furious, barely descending at all, bouncing between the walls. Emerald shoots by her, pinging from one section wall to a blank spot on Cargo Wall 99 to the other section wall, repeating the cycle to build up speed, then to brake, till she zooms in for a perfect landing among us. "Slick," I say. "I'll have to try that myself."

"How are we going to get Marioschke down?" Glisters asks.

"I came down here to ask you. After trying to talk her into it, I gave up and just pried her hands off the railing and shoved her by the head," Em explains. "I think it pissed her off."

Above us, Marioschke bounces off the section wall, maybe two meters below the platform.

"Push off the wall," Glisters shouts. "Toward us."

She kicks hard but only tumbles faster. "I guess one of us could jump up and stabilize her, but I'd be afraid of having her grab on or hit me," I say.

"Let's gang up on her," Emerald suggests. "Glisters and Susan go up above. Stack jumps up and wraps her—just aim straight for her, you don't really have to swim or navigate. Glisters and Susan dive from the railing and grab Stack, so that their momentum starts everyone moving downward, and then bounce off some walls on the way down and pick up more speed. The rest of us, at this end, will pull you all in for your landing."

It semi-works. Marioschke flails so much that all Stack can do is convert the rapid tumble to a slow roll, and when Glisters and I dive on them, grab Stack's shirt, and carry them with us, we're only adding our own momentum, so they don't move fast, and we're centered so we don't get a chance to pick up momentum by bouncing.

Even though Marioschke won't hit the deck hard enough to break an egg, she's fighting like it'll kill her, so Emerald jumps up with a rope from her pack and ties it to Glisters's feet, and the rest reel us in.

Once Marioschke's feet are on the handling deck, she calms down, but she's pretty sullen as we bounce nose-ward to Cargo Wall 8, where we're planning to make our camp.

The empty ledge we're camping on is only 10 meters up. Marioschke whispers to me, "If I shut my eyes, will you catch me and pull me onto the ledge?"

I say yes, jump up, light on the ledge, and turn around. Marioschke shuts her eyes and jumps; I catch her and pull her over the edge, airswimming to steer her back onto the ledge. She bounces slowly over to where the ledge joins the cargo wall, right at about the midpoint of the section so the ledge floor curves up and away from us in both directions—the maximum distance from any place where she can see down. She unrolls her sleepsack, gets inside with all her clothes on, and turns to face the wall.

"Hey," I whisper. "If you need to be alone, that's fine, but before I leave you alone, are you all right?"

"Yeah." She sounds miserable. "I was so panicky in free fall, too scared to move, and I was crying and yelling about that, and I really wanted to see the farm section, Susan, thank you so much for telling them I'd want to. But

I acted up so much they just stuffed me away in a lounge with the other bad attitude people."

"When we come out of hiding there will be months and months on the way to Mars," I point out. "And in a couple days you'll have your space balance and you'll be fine getting around. You'll get to see the Forest, and the farm sections, and everything. Probably they'll even let you help. You'll see, it'll be okay."

"Yeah." She doesn't sound like she believes me. "Susan?"

"Yeah?"

"Thanks for being nice to me sometimes. I know I'm a pain in the ass."

"Good night, Marioschke."

She mutters "g'night" and curls deep down into her sleepsack, styling ultra DO NOT DISTURB.

The rest are already tying bags and sleepsacks off to brackets; the ledge is about 5 meters across and runs the width of the section, and stacked crates are scattered around on it. While I'm getting my stuff tied down, everyone else breaks out the drugs and music to give Glisters a party to shoot.

When I look up, Glisters is flying from "Look at this!" to "Get this shot!" as everyone acts like they're having crazy fun. He looks harried and exasperated.

All my practice and training says to dive in and grab focus, but instead I jump over a 10-meter stack of crates, grab a bracket to change direction, and touch down noiselessly out of sight of the others. I bounce along the ledge to the corner it makes with the section wall, pull my butt down onto the edge with my hands, and sit with my feet dangling over, watching the stars and sun alternate through the glass-covered water below.

I just want to think about Bari for a while.

I used to love his arm around me. Weird. His skin was pale, unhealthy-looking, damp, and cool. He had muscles as flaccid and squishy as an old woman's. Yet I loved to lay in his arms; he was an ultra good listener.

I sprawl with just my head off the ledge, looking hull-ward into the thick white band of the Milky Way. I wish Bari could see this.

Emerald floats in beside me. "Derlock wants Glisters to record him and me doing some naked dancing, all flirty and holding squeezebulbs of gin, with some grabs and gropes, like we're drunk."

I shrug. "Derlock and I are not declared yet."

"I'm trying to be sisterly."

I look sideways at her. "And you *are*. And it's appreciated. I'm just—you know, I don't want to party tonight. I don't feel real good about this, I'm going to get my aunt in a lot of trouble, and Bari . . ."

She nods. "You style that so well. Glisters ought to come over here and shoot you being sad; you look ultra more interesting than me bouncing my boobs at your boy-friend-to-be."

"Well, maybe to you or me," I say, "but the splycterage is in bouncing boobs."

"Yeah." She sits next to me. "Want company, or to be alone?"

I smile as much as I can. "I'm grateful for the company, but don't miss your chance for good meeds. You want to get shot before everyone's too blasted and while Glisters is still doing his best work, before he takes enough stuff to feel like a genius."

She laughs. "How'd you learn to airswim so well?"

I tell her a little about being Crazy Science Girl growing up, and it kind of slides over into some girl bonding stuff, about my mom, and Stanley the dog, and even why I call Destiny Anny Dezzy and a lot of other embarrassing, losery sheeyeffinit. Emerald counter shares: she was Crazy Space Gymnast Girl, and her cat was named Dog, which she thought was ultra original until it turns out it goes back almost two hundred years in meeds.

"We'd probably have been ultra friends if we'd met before Excellence Shop," she says, "and then we could have had betrayal and rivalry and reconciliations, and we'd've had a *great* story line for meeds."

I mean to smile but it comes out really sad. "Fleeta and I were like that. You'd have made a great addition to the team, Emerald, I'm sorry you weren't at our school."

"Your eyes get so sad when you look at Fleeta."

"You should get back to Derlock. Don't let him hog the camera."

"No risk with Glisters shooting; you'd think that guy never saw a girl naked before. Hey, we should redo this girl-bondosation in front of him sometime soon; seriously, great hooks in it."

"Yeah. Maybe when I'm more over Bari."

"Won't be as good then, you know. The shots where people really feel emotions intensely are the most splycterable hooks. Thanks for understanding about me and Derlock." She pushes up and airswims away.

I let my mind empty out and even doze for a bit; I wake up in a sun flash, rolling over till my eyes adjust and I can see stars through the window again. By now the little party is pretty loud; most bloodstreams must be loaded up.

I airswim up onto the stack of crates beside me and peek over the edge. Glisters is shooting Fleeta's boobs wobbling around in milligrav; she's goofing around, giggling at the funny ways she can make them move, and he's trying, without success, to make her be serious. "But *you're* smiling," she says.

"You're having so much fun," he says, "but the audience wants to see you act hot. Having fun doesn't get splyctered."

Wychee and Emerald are dancing naked with Stack, with a lot of feeling and making out. F.B. is kind of flapping around at the edge, maybe hoping Glisters will ask him to help with the camera.

I'm missing a chance for major exposure. I still think, *No. Not tonight.* I airswim to my sleepsack and crawl in.

Sometime after I doze off, I feel the sack opening, and Derlock says, "Hey."

"Hey." I try for the least-committal "hey" in the history of the universe.

"We haven't talked since hearing about Bari."

"What happened?"

"Susan, it's tearing me up inside, I dosed with the

hibernifacient like we talked about, so they'd go into coma, I thought that would get them caught and stop everything, I didn't know they'd give them a big shot of Fendrisol and anyway I didn't know about how it interacts with Torporin. I'm so sorry. I know Bari was special to you." He runs a hand along my neck, strokes my face and hair. "Anyway, I thought you might like me to hold you and comfort you."

Derlock's concept of "hold and comfort" has a 100% overlap with most people's concept of "sex." When he's done I tell him I want some time alone and that I'm too warm with him there. He goes back to his own sleepsack, and I close mine up tight and plummet into deep, dreamless sleep.

██

Notes for the Interested, #11

MILLIGRAVITY: *just enough but not too much*

The milligravity in the farm and cargo sections is strong enough so that work crews on the handling floors can put things where they'll stay put, spilled liquids eventually collect at low points instead of floating around in blobs forever, and plants in the farm sections grow in one direction. Yet it is still weak enough for people to airswim, push grand pianos around one-handed (as long as they watch out for inertia), and sleep on an alclad deck as comfortably as a featherbed.

On Earth, an object falls 5 meters, about the drop from the

roof of a one-storey house, in the first second. In milligrav, in that same first second, that object will fall only 5 millimeters, less than the width of your little finger. Objects gain speed as they fall; on Earth the 100-meter drop from the coretube to the handling floor would take 4.5 seconds and slam you into the floor at 162 kilometers per hour. The same 100 meters if it were all in milligrav would take an hour and fifteen minutes, and you would arrive moving at a good deal less than one kilometer per hour. (That's why they had such a struggle getting Marioschke down to the deck.)

But in fact it's not even milligrav all over the ship; only at the hull. In the rotating ship, gravity depends directly on distance from the center. Milligravity at the hull, a bit over 100 meters from the centerline, means less than 3% of milligravity up at the coretube.

Thus in this story, workers on the handling floors (along the inner hull) often push objects into place against the floor to save time, because it takes too long to let them fall. Up near the coretube, where gravity is only a small fraction of milligrav, tour guides often demonstrate all the familiar weightless effects, like water forming spheres in midair, tennis balls bouncing all the way down the tube and back, and (if the tour party includes any boys) fart propulsion.

||||||||||||||||||||||||||||||||||||||||||||||||||||||||||||||||||||

April 25, 2129. On _Virgo_, upbound Earth to Mars. 149 million kilometers from the sun, 166 million kilometers from Mars, 3.6 million kilometers from Earth.

I roll out of my sleepsack and dress quickly; Emerald is dressing beside me.

"You look surprisingly well for a girl that was dancing drunk all night," I say.

She grins. "Styling Party Hot is ultra demanding. I do a better job being an out-of-control drunk for the cam if I keep my squeezebulb filled with apple juice. I don't remember you ever coming out to join us; I guess you just went to bed?" she asks.

"Yeah. I felt too bad about Bari."

"Yeah. Welcome to the exclusive club of the un-hungover."

"Are there any members besides us? "

She nods. "Fleeta can't, almost everything interacts with Fendrisol. And Glisters was too busy with his camera."

"Yep," he says. We turn back to realize he's been shooting us. We pounce on him together; Emerald gets a hammerlock. "Erase," I say.

"Susan, I—"

"Erase," Emerald says. "And let us see you doing it."

"But it would be sure to make the meeds," he protests.

"You can shoot me," I tell him. "Even naked, if you're nice about it and I'm in a mood for it. But shoot me with bed-head, and you're gonna be dead-dead."

"Deader than that," Emerald says.

"Okay, but just look, first, okay? See how pretty that curve of Susan's thigh is? And Emerald, that expression is so you—"

"And so are those boobs," she says. "Yeah, we look

zoomed, if you like loser messes. Not splycterable. Erase."

He shrugs and does. "It's a stupid world," he says, "where people would rather see you glaring at the camera and sticking out the hot parts than looking like your authentic, beautiful, graceful selves—"

"Nice try," I say. "Not that we believe a word of it."

"I never know what to believe," Fleeta says, sliding from her sleepsack.

Glisters reaches for his camera.

"Ask," Emerald says.

Glisters nods. "Fleeta, can I shoot you while you dress?"

"I won't look hot."

"But you'll look beautiful."

"Why would you want a picture of *that*?"

"Because I spend most of my time looking at hot, so it bores me. Beautiful is interesting."

"Oh, okay, then."

So he shoots, and he has to keep telling her not to pose, just do what she'd naturally do, and when he's all done, Em and I take a look at his work. "You're right, she's beautiful, the way your camera caught her," I admit grudgingly.

"Totally unsplycterable, though," Emerald says.

"So you don't like it?" Fleeta asks, obviously scared.

"You're beautiful," I say, truthfully, "and Glisters's work is actually—um, superb, to tell the truth." He looks more embarrassed than she does, and he's not the one whose nipples we're studying. "It's just not going to make any money for either of you."

Fleeta takes a look, says, "It looks more like me than most pictures do, is that okay?"

"Ultra okay," Emerald says. "Zoomed."

Glisters says, "I'm hungry. Anyone else want to go do our first raid on the crates?"

"Does one of us have tools?" I ask.

"Right here," Glisters says, holding up a couple drivers. "Also, if we go now, we'll get firsties at the toilets before the rest start thinking about it."

Emerald says, "And those are—"

"There's one on Cargo Wall 9, up by the coretube. They put them all over; nobody wants to airswim half a kilometer to get to a bathroom."

After the bathroom stop, I say, "Do you suppose the others will figure out where the toilets are, as opposed to improvising something?"

"Eww," Emerald says. "Maybe we should tell them?"

"I mentioned it to Stack and F.B.," Glisters says, "and anyway you know Wychee and Marioschke will ask. It'll be okay."

So only about half the moes can be trusted not to crap on the floor, but at least I'm having breakfast with the right half. Glisters scans through the manifest through his wristcomp to find a crate of meals from Le Sully on Cargo Wall 88. With all of us proficient airswimmers, it takes only a couple minutes to descend to the handling floor, bound to 88, retrieve the crate, open it, and take a meal each.

We sit on the nearest window on the handling deck,

letting the warm sun flash against our butts every other minute and a half. I know that most mineys eat out of temptrol boxes all the time, but I've only used them now and then, for camping trips and take out.

The keypad on the temptrol box offers me USE SUGGESTED DEFAULTS or SPECIFY INDIVIDUAL ITEM TEMPERATURES. I figure the packager knows how warm things are supposed to be, so I select USE SUGGESTED DEFAULTS, press NOW, and open it. The ham and over-easy eggs are just hot, with a nice chilled vegetable salad, a pichet of red wine at room temperature, and scalding hot espresso.

"That's so weird when we fall," Fleeta says, "all at the same speed, even though we are different sizes. I used to know something about that."

Glisters's tone is gentle, earning ultra points with me. "Probably you're remembering that gravity does the same thing on Earth—Galileo's experiment?"

"But we don't fall fast like we would on Earth."

"No, but inside a gravity field—at least once you take air resistance out of it—everything falls at the same speed. That's what Galileo proved," Glisters says.

Fleeta nods. "I think I was trying to remember that. I used to love knowing things."

When someone pretty is happy, Emerald *has* to get sarcastic. "Then why did you take happistuf?"

Fleeta's face screws up with effort, but then her expression clears, like fog blowing off a beach. "Because knowing things only made me a little happy some of the time, but happistuf made me ultra happy all the time. So it's just like gravity. Different weights but we all fall at the same speed. Like Galileo." She is obviously delighted with herself.

"Jesus," I mutter, sick at heart.

"Like Galileo and Jesus," she agrees.

The silence stretches on till Emerald asks, "Anyone wonder what everyone else is up to?"

"Well," I say, "Derlock is thinking up a way to hurt someone, and Stack is helping. F.B. is talking about being a great astronomer, and no one is listening. Wychee is whining, and Marioschke is either still terrified or back to being all spiritual."

Emerald clutches her chest. "And we're missing it!"

We're all still laughing when painful, blinding light flashes through the window like a blow directly to my brain. The hull thunders like a drum, and I float off the deck, clutching my face, weightless and tumbling yet crushed. It's like being a bug slammed in a book and thrown from a plane.

We hit the window hard, all of us shouting in surprise and pain. We're sliding along the hull's inner wall, but down is in the wrong direction, along the hull toward the tail, and the gravity is way too high, as if some giant had just grabbed the ship and stood it on its tail on a planet.

5

SEPARATION

April 25, 2129. On *Virgo*'s pod. 149 million kilometers from the sun, 166 million kilometers from Mars, 3.7 million kilometers from Earth.

I STAGGER TO my feet, bumping into Emerald, almost falling across Glisters, who is on his hands and knees; we're standing on the tail-end bulkhead of the Pressurized Cargo Section, way down at the crew-bubble end of the pod. We slammed down hard; this sudden new gravity feels like more than the moon's.

My vision starts to come back through the red and orange blur; I see Fleeta, who is standing in front of me and moving her mouth. Sounds are muted; I'm deaf from that immense boom. After long seconds, her shouting, "What happened?" penetrates through the ringing in my ears. Emerald is shouting, "I don't know."

Glisters's voice starts to penetrate. "Grav is about one-fifth g and I think we're turning over in less than two minutes, so that makes it, um . . . um . . ." I realize he's talking the problem through, turn and see him punching away at his wristcomp. I join the shout fest: "Everyone shut up and listen to Glisters!"

I'm pretty sure no one has ever even thought that sentence before, let alone shouted it. Maybe that's why Glisters is standing there with his mouth hanging comically open.

I try to reassure him with a smile and a wink, styling Best Bud Chick; the way he looks back at me, I must be styling Crazy Spastic Zombie.

At least I can hear a little now. "Loudly and slowly, Glisters, and start from the beginning."

He takes a deep breath. "We must be tumbling end over end pretty fast. That's why the grav is toward the tail bulkhead. It would take something ultra huge at one end of the pod to make that happen this fast. That big flash and boom must have been either a huge explosion or a huge impact, maybe both—"

"*Aunt Destiny!*" I run to the nearest hatch into the tail disk, which was a swim-through wall hatch moments ago and is now in the floor. When I open it, it swings down away from me, then sways back and forth across the opening.

Beside me, Glisters pushes with flat hands against the hatch cover, steadying it. "Is there a way to climb down?" he asks, just before I jump.

I hit the tail disk bulkhead hard; the 10-meter drop isn't a gentle float anymore, more like dropping from my own height on Earth. *Gotta remember now falling means going splat.*

"Aren't we supposed to stay in hiding?" Fleeta asks.

"That's all changed," Emerald says. "We have to know what's going on, and Susan has to know about her aunt.

Go, Susan, we'll find a way to climb down and join you."

"Thanks." I stagger along a corridor at what seems to be a weird angle pulling me to the side. When I reach a sealed emergency airlock, nothing will let me open it. The next lock is also closed, also sealed. When I lift the emergency phone beside it, there's no sound.

"We're finding all the airlocks are slammed closed, too," Glisters says, behind me. Emerald puts her arms around me, hugging me from behind. "And the pressure indicators show nothing on the other side."

I hadn't thought to check those. The display is flashing red: EXT PRESS 0.00 MP.

I'm almost curious, but my mind won't say what that means.

Emerald explains, "Glisters found a hatch right by the hull, and we used the handholds on the hull to climb down."

Glisters adds, "There are windows in the outer edge of the tail disk. We should probably find one and try to see what's going on."

Every lock is slammed closed. Every emergency phone is dead. Every pressure indicator shows 0.00. Then about 30 meters beyond the crew bubble's attachment, we come to a big window. Through the 2 meters of water and the outer window, I see the stars wheel crazily like a formation-flying swarm of bees.

From way back in my brain, Crazy Science Girl kicks in. "We're spinning on an axis through about the center of Auriga."

Glisters says, "Yeah. Okay, there goes Pisces—36 seconds for the window edge to cut through Pisces, now—mark . . ." Lost in thought, he holds still, staring at his wristcomp. In a burst of ultra loserness, I wish I wore a wristcomp, too. He marks the moment. "39 seconds for Aries. Figure each constellation is 30 degrees—"

"What the sheeyeffinit are you babbling about?" Emerald says, "I don't even know what kind of astrology that is. I never heard of a sign called Oregon, either."

The sneer in her voice reminds me of the way my mother used to sound during my Crazy Science Girl days, so I style some *real* condescension to show her how it's done. "*Auriga.* Name of a constellation. The 12 signs are constellations all along the solar equator. They each take up about 30 degrees of a circle across the sky—there's 360 degrees in a circle—"

"All *right*, Susan, you're as bad as he is. What's all the babble about?"

"He's figuring out how fast we are spinning—"

"Seven and a half minutes per revolution, in the tumbling end-over-end rotation," he says. "Plus we're probably still rotating around the coretube too. So the total—"

"Oh, my god," Fleeta says.

We look out the window. At first it looks like a gigantic gray metal funnel with a piece ripped and twisted almost off with tin snips. It is rotating at about three times a minute, and surrounded by tiny shapes glinting in the sun on one side and lost in shadow against the black on the other. Less than 20 meters from our window, a toilet spins by;

not far beyond it, clothing swarms around a tennis racket.

"Oh sheeyeffinit, it's the crew bubble," Glisters says. "We've separated."

The tumbling of the pod takes the crew bubble out of sight. More stars streak by. Glisters points out that besides rotating, we're precessing; our axis of rotation is now running through the head of the Great Bear. I'm numb, but I can appreciate that he's trying to talk about anything except the obvious until we can see the crew bubble again, and I'm grateful for that.

When the bubble comes back into view, the distance between the main piece and the big broken-off piece around the narrow part has widened to what I guess to be a 100 meters, bridged by a tangled wad of pipes and cables. I see now that the engines on its tail end are now a cluster of twisted and melted stumps, warped into a lumpy braid.

Things are still tumbling out of the gap between the pieces, which are twisting the knot of pipes and cables in opposite directions, like two hands wrenching a paper chain apart. All in dead silence—no sound in vacuum.

To the right of the torn crew bubble, there is a warped, slanted pinwheel of white dots around a fuzzy sphere. "Iceball," I say. "Maybe something hot is buried inside it? Maybe something big enough to pierce a 200-meter ball of ice was still going fast enough to smash the crew bubble when it went through."

"If that's what happened, it cut through the crew bubble and kept going," Glisters said. "There's another iceball much farther away, down and to the right, see?" The tiny spiral cloud trails a braided contrail. "Spewing a lot more. But the farthest one away doesn't seem to be leaking—"

"They were still bringing that one in," I explain. "So it wasn't on the ship. It's intact, but it's not going to do us any good way out there. I suppose that must mean we have one iceball still left on the ship."

Fleeta says, "Shooting away like a little galaxy. I know it's ultra bad, but it's *pretty.*"

She's right, I think. The crew bubble has rolled out of view. "I was so busy watching the iceballs," I said, "that I didn't look at—"

"I wish I hadn't," Emerald said, "and I don't think you should. We should try to be somewhere else before it comes around again."

"But I need—"

"I saw *bodies*, Susan. Not in suits. Floating out through that big rip in the middle. I counted nine that I saw, but I'm sure there are a lot more still in the wreckage, or flung so hard they're already out of sight. I don't want *you* to look—"

A hairy thing the size of coffee table passes by the window, about ten meters away: a dog, legs splayed, body distorted by escaping gas and air, ruptured eyeballs and something bigger than its tongue hanging out of its mouth, it must have been *one of the pets for the onboard school, wonder if that little girl I saw yesterday*—as abruptly as a door slam I understand why Emerald is trying to get me away from the window before the crew bubble is visible again. "We should go to the auxiliary cockpit," I say. "We can send a distress call from there."

"How do we get there?" Emerald says. "Come on, let's go."

I still remember the way from yesterday, but it's a little confusing because the tail disk bulkhead is now the floor.

I bounce the way you do on the moon, careful not to bang my head. Glisters's little "ow!" as he hits the ceiling the first time gives me a smug feeling, considering he's the only other person here—

Who knows what he's doing. Hmm. Second thought, be nice to Glisters.

"In case *you* bash your head on the ceiling, Susan," Emerald says, "where are we going and what will we do when we get there?"

I tell her, but it's a maze of corridors and surfaces to explain, and I keep stopping and correcting myself because having the gravity be stronger and in a different direction makes it so much more complicated to explain. Halfway through I realize she's just giving me something to think about besides the obvious, and I'm grateful, but I give up, and she doesn't ask.

Glisters bounces a little too high again and catches himself on the ceiling with his hands. I avoid noticing; a few levels up with less of the new gravity, and more of the old fighting it out, it is like being on a carousel on the Moon with a bad ear infection.

"I sure hope when we get there, there is a big button that says STABILIZE SHIP for us to push," Emerald says.

Glisters says, "There probably *is* a STABILIZE SHIP button, or more likely a utility in the operations software. I would bet they designed the emergency systems with the thought that after an accidental jettison, tourists or little kids might be the only ones in here. So if there are still working thrusters and engines, we can probably just tell the control system to stabilize us."

"In that case I'm also going to wish for a screen saying LIVE HUMANS DETECTED IN POD—SPACE PATROL NOTIFIED AND WILL ARRIVE WITHIN 24 HOURS."

"Well, for sure there *will* be a way to call for help," Glisters says. "Unfortunately, the Space Patrol you're hoping for exists only in meeds. The *real* Space Patrol only has nine ships, which are parked in Earth, lunar, and Mars orbit, *not* patrolling. They don't fly five real missions in a decade, and besides they're like any other spaceships—they don't move much faster than the planets themselves do, so it takes months to get anywhere. Their real job is just to arrive wherever something happened a while ago, take some pictures, fill out the paperwork, and stand proudly behind the SecGen at the memorial service."

"You sound just like Aunt Destiny—" It hits me that she's gone. I can't breathe through the tears and mucus. Fleeta tackles me in a hard, tight hug that feels really good, and for a blessed moment it's like having my best friend back, till she says, "I wish I could cry with you, but mostly I just feel happy that I'm here to hold you when you need it."

That snaps the spell. "Thanks," I say, softly. "Now come on. We have to get to the cockpit."

Glisters awkwardly squeezes my arm; Emerald says, "Right with you."

The hardest part is opening doors in what are now ceilings. At every level we have to find a door we can climb or jump to. After a few levels, the tailward gravity is lower, but now the shifting ratio of hullward and tailward gravities throws us off balance constantly, so that we have to keep hands on grips all the time.

The auxiliary cockpit door is sideways, which is at least easier to climb in through than overhead.

Glisters climbs to the main seat, straps himself in, and plays on the keyboard. "Found it. Hold on."

I grab a handhold. The cockpit tilts and wobbles madly for less than a second, then settles, right side up, gently rocking, as if it were floating on the ocean or bouncing on the end of a spring.

"Was that the STABILIZE SHIP button?" Emerald asks.

"I wish. No, the pod is still tumbling. I just stabilized *this cockpit*—it moves on powered bearings, so it self-adjusts its floor toward wherever down is currently, except when someone pushes the button to open the door—then it swings the cockpit around to line up the internal door with the corridor door—so grab a handhold and keep it all the time." Glisters turns back to the screen. "All right, let's get some images up and see what's going on."

The main screen suddenly shows a view of the crew

bubble, much farther away than when we left the big window. It is now in four large pieces, surrounded by a cloud of debris.

I look away, wanting to see anything else. On the tail-end camera screen, Earth is about half the size of a full moon back home; the moon is two hand-widths away from it, a circular dot twice the size of a period on a printed page.

I check another screen. Finally some good news. "We still have an iceball and three engines."

"If they work," Emerald points out. "And if we can figure out how to fly with them."

"About that," Glisters says, "excuse my pointing this out, but I've spent a lot of time on spaceflight simulators and in hacking unfamiliar computer systems, so unless Susan wants to throw down in an experience contest, I'm claiming the conn seat here for myself."

"I was thinking you ought to be in charge, actually," Emerald said.

"Are you crazy?" Glisters asks, not even looking up from the screen where he's typing away frantically. "Why?"

"Process of elimination," Emerald says. "Look at who else we have: Derlock would run things entirely for his own advantage, plus he'd try to fake things he didn't know. Susan has to . . you know, deal with her aunt."

"I'm pretty numb," I say.

"It will wear off," Emerald says. "Let's not ask you to do anything this hard when Glisters can do it, and he hasn't had the shock you have."

Glisters nods at me; Emerald shrugs and finishes her

roster. "Stack? Wychee? Me? None of us know crap about anything. Everyone else is helpless as kittens. Who's left?"

Glisters says, "It's not about what a person knows. I know enough and Susan knows enough and we'll work for whoever needs us. The important thing is whether people will listen to the commander. Which they won't, to me. Stack and Derlock beat me up, all the time, for fun. I'm scared of them. I'll back the commander against them, but I won't *be* the commander and make myself a target. You need a commander that'll stand up to them and a pilot to back up the commander. Besides, you also need an engineer, which *is* the logical job for me, and I can't do that and be commander both. If I'm trying to restore the air system, you don't want me to have to stop work so I can order Derlock or Stack to behave."

I say, "I can't believe I'm actually saying *Glisters is right* so often, but well, he keeps being right."

"Then who's in charge?" Emerald says.

I say, "None of us is perfect commander material. Perfect would be one of those high-achiever scholarship mineys from Excellence Shop, or that kid Eric that's going to be a fifth-generation space explorer, Mr. Top of Every Class. But none of them is here because they would never have been a moe in the first place. If we're going to get home alive we need to do two things: keep the ship running till we're rescued—which is what Glisters is the best guy for—and keep all us misfits from killing each other, which means leadership, and Glisters just told you he can't do that. So if not Glisters—then *not* Derlock, *not* Stack, *not* F.B., *not* Fleeta—"

"I'm listening, Susan, and I don't like it but you're right. Not Marioschke, either. So that leaves you, me, or Wychee. Wychee's not exactly the leader type, you'd actually be the best, but you're a mess—"

"You got it, boss," I say. Glisters looks up and nods vigorously. "And at least we're with you all the way. I know none of us were friends before—"

"I thought we were all friends," Fleeta says. "But I think a lot of dumb things."

Emerald puts her arm around Fleeta. "Well, we were always all *your* friend."

Everything lurches; the cockpit whirls, but this time we're all holding on. I tighten my grip and grab another handhold with my other hand. The door to the cockpit slides open, and Derlock, Stack, Wychee, and F.B. come through.

"Oh, good, you found it." Derlock bounds toward Glisters like a cat after a parakeet. Stack is right with him; Wychee and F.B. grab handholds and stay close to the door.

I'm moving to Glisters's side. Derlock is saying "—have to do is figure out how to fly this—" when Glisters hits the cockpit stabilization, and there's a big lurch that throws Derlock and Stack to the suddenly right-side-up deck.

"We have it covered," Emerald says. "Don't disturb Glisters while he's working. But since you're finally here—"

Derlock says, "Out of the chair, Glisters, I need to see

what you've been doing." Glisters keeps right on working and Derlock goes for his arm. "I said—"

"Derlock." I had no idea I could even speak in that tone, but it sure works; he turns and stares at me. Looking back into those blue eyes I realize I'm never drowning again. *"Games are over.* You are not the leader here because we need a real leader, which is someone we can trust, and *that is ultra* not *you.* I'm not taking any extra risk just so you can turn meeds of all of us into botflog for your career. Don't try to pretend you're not doing that; I know you way too well." He's glaring. Well, good—he's listening, so I keep talking. "Now let me explain this so that even a shithead like you can get it. I *know* you. I *know* you are thinking that here is your big chance to set up your own little tyranny in a can and boost your recognition score. You'll do any stupid crazy thing that pops into your brain if it looks like splycterable meed to you. I'd rather get home alive. So Glisters is staying right where he is. And you're shutting up and cooperating."

"So what are you, the commander? Or is Big Head Pink-Skin Loser Boy here the commander?"

"No, the commander is Emerald. She doesn't need your petty sheeyeffinit; she has things to do. Glisters is the engineer, and he *really* has things to do. *I'm* taking care of you two losers because my time's not as valuable, so I can waste some of it on you." I say it cold and low and clear, no rise in my voice, no anger, just watching and seeing if I'm going to need the jiu-jutsu—*dear god, I'm styling*

Pop in that World War Two historical meed, Pop's steely-submarine-captain role.

And not too badly, *thanks for all the genes and training, Pop.* Derlock moves back a step, keeping his hands close to himself. He must remember the last time I showed him jiu-jutsu. Unconsciously matching my role, he styles whiny-shiftless-mutineer, visibly nerving himself up to keep from cringing. "Oh, so she *ordered you* to give *me* orders—"

Emerald speaks like a dog trainer. "My pilot does not need an order from me to use her authority."

I nearly look around before I realize that's me—and pilot is the second in command on any spaceship. I guess Emerald's avenging herself for our sticking her with commander.

6

NOTHING TO BUY AND NOWHERE TO DELIVER

April 25, 2129. On *Virgo*, upbound Earth to Mars. 149 million kilometers from the sun, 166 million kilometers from Mars, 3.7 million kilometers from Earth.

GLISTERS SAYS, "GRAB a handhold."

A stomach-flipping lurch interrupts the gentle sway of the cockpit. We all hold tight to our grips, except for Derlock, who goes sprawling. For five minutes or so the cockpit slams around madly, there's a deafening thunder, the grip vibrates in my hand so hard it's painful, and even above the roaring and booming we can hear groans and creaks of metal being bent and forced. Whatever's going on, this time it involves a lot more than just the cockpit.

The last boom dwindles; my handhold abruptly stops vibrating. Glisters says, "Hang on one more moment while the cockpit rights itself." As the world comes around to a sensible angle again, the shuddering moans and harsh squeals from the rest of the ship die away. "All clear."

Derlock stumbles and flails away from the chair he had grabbed to avoid being flung helplessly around the cockpit. "You did that on purpose." He sounds like a frustrated little boy.

"If he did, it was with my endorsement." Emerald makes a point of turning her back on Derlock. Much more nicely, she asks, "Glisters, what *was* that?"

"I was working through the process to stabilize the ship," Glisters says, "and I didn't realize that once I checked off all the approvals, it would start automatically. So I only just had time to tell you all to grab on. But in a few hours, we'll be back to normal, steady milligrav with 'down' toward the hull and 'up' toward the coretube. That'll make it much easier to do our course corrections, as much as we can, given that we've lost three-quarters of the reaction mass we should have had."

Derlock is styling outrage, trying to catch Stack's eye.

Stack looks away from him, directly at me, and shrugs. It's not exactly an oath of loyalty and I'll have to watch that Derlock doesn't work Stack around his way again. Just the same, for the moment, Derlock has no stooge, and without one, he won't try a mutiny.

▐▌▐▐▌▌▐▌▐▐▌▐▐▌▌▐▌▐▐▌▐▌▐▐▌▐▐▌▌▐▌▐▐▌▐▐▌▌▐▌▐▐▌▐▌▐▐▌▐▐▌

Notes for the Interested, #12

REACTION MASS: *the thing Glisters is worrying about that only Susan really understands right now*

Almost everyone has heard of Newton's Third Law, "For every reaction there is an equal and opposite reaction." Think about what that means for a moment; when you stand on the ground, your feet push *down* against the ground with exactly as much force as the ground pushes *up* against your feet. If Superman leaps a tall building at a single bound, he must kick a hole in the sidewalk. Wherever there's a force in a system, it pushes or pulls both ways.

When a rocket pushes its exhaust backward, the exhaust also pushes the rocket with equal force forward. But whatever was in the exhaust is now gone; it disperses into the air or space behind the rocket. To go anywhere, a rocket must throw mass away. The mass it carries to throw away is called **reaction mass**.

Virgo propels itself by heating water from the iceballs to a very high temperature in its fusion reactors, and then sending the white-hot steam out the nozzles of the engines. How much *Virgo* can change its course depends on how much water it can push out. With only one iceball instead of the four it needed, it cannot push nearly as much as it should.

How much change does *Virgo* need to make? They are 123 days, or 167 million kilometers, from Marspass. If they could do the full course correction *Virgo* was planning to do (about a two-degree bend in their path and speeding up by about 3300 km/hour), they would pass within 20,000 kilometers of Mars. But every thousandth of a degree, or every kilometer per hour, that they can't correct for now will widen the closest-point gap between them and Mars by 3,000 kilometers.

How can such small things make such a big difference? If you've studied trigonometry, you know the difference at the far end is equal to the tangent of the angle you are off by, times the distance you are covering. The tangent of 2 degrees is about .035, and .035 X 167 million kilometers = about 5,830,000 kilometers, or 15 times the distance from the Earth to the moon; so even if they were moving fast enough, they'd cross Mars's orbit 5.83 million kilometers behind Mars.

But they're *not* going fast enough.

Mars orbits the sun at 24 kilometers per second, so if you are aiming at the place where Mars is going to be when you get there, and you are late by an hour, one hour = 3,600 seconds X 24 km/sec = you miss by 86,400 kilometers *for every hour you are late.*

To be on time, they would need to average about 97,200 km/hour, but they're going 3300 km/hour too slow, which is 93,900 km/hour. Their trip time to the Mars rendezvous should be 123 days X 24 hours = 2952 hours, but at their slower speed they will take (97200/93900) X 2952 hours = 3056 hours. That's "only" 104 hours late—a little over 4 days—but as fast as Mars is moving, it widens the gap by another 9 million kilometers.

▮▮

Glisters says, "Commander, there's something you'd better look at here—I think you, too, Susan." He swings his chair out to reveal his screen, which shows a view of each of the six sections of the pod. "The good news," Glisters says, "is that none of the trees fell over, and Farm Sections 2 and 3 were inactive, so everything in them was locked down in bins and beds. But there's a lot of spilled dirt and water in Farm Section 1, and bad news in all three cargo sections." On the screen, hundreds of little shapes—spheres, blocks, pyramids—like a kid's building set, are scattered all over the cargo walls, bulkheads, and decks. Most are blue and arranged neatly; some are yellow, at funny angles but still in the general array; many red ones are heaped together or lying across the array. "Red means unhooked and out of place, which means 'going to fly around and do more damage while we correct our spin.' Yellow means the hook or attachment is saying it's not fully secure, like a hook is open or a line is broken or something. Blue means it's fine."

He touches a red cube; it lights up with a string of numbers, and the same numbers appear on a cargo wall in the same hold. "That's where it is, and that's where it should be. In this low gravity, usually you should be able to put them back onto the hook they came from, but if it's huge and you can't move it safely, just hook it *somewhere*. Anyway, I think probably we can have it all rehooked well before the ship is back on its proper spin—"

"But why should we?" Wychee returns to her basic approach to the universe.

"Good question," Glisters says; his eye contact with me is saying, *don't jump on her.* "We want all that stuff locked down because it will make it safer for us to correct our spin, which has an ultra, ultra lot to do with our comfort, but also we need the spin fixed so we can course-correct into a trajectory that gets us close enough to Mars—"

"I want to turn around and go back."

"Me, too, but for that we'd need about a hundred more engines and at least 400 iceballs, and we don't have them."

"Could we pool our allowances, get money from our families, and just buy all that? I bet my parents would chip in just to avoid the scandal—"

I wonder if she listened, back on Earth, or if she just didn't understand what it meant. Either way, we can't afford to have anyone thinking we're just being mean. "Wychee," I say, "we can't buy *anything* out here. There's no one to sell it to us, it doesn't exist, and there's no way to deliver it. The ship is going to pass close to Mars because it orbits that way. But if we don't correct the course, it won't pass close enough for a cap from Mars to rescue us. And before we can correct the course we have to straighten out our spin, back to what it should be, because—hunh. Glisters, why *can't* we just fly like this?"

"We could if we had enough spare reaction mass, Susan. With the ship tumbling, we'd need to fire off a lot more steam through the nozzles to get the same effect as we'll get with the ship corrected. It'll cost us some water to correct the ship, but not nearly as much as we'd lose by trying to fly while tumbling."

"And we're going to be on the ship for months, even if they launch a rescue mission tomorrow," Emerald adds. "It takes that long to reach us. So it would be nice to have up and down be where they're supposed to."

Wychee doesn't say anything, but she looks furious. I ask, "Does that make sense?"

"I don't like it."

"But do you understand it, and does it make sense?"

"Yeah," she says. "Yeah. I'm just now realizing how much this is like the time my stupid tutor ran out of fuel in the middle of the Pacific, on the field trip, and it didn't matter how many eenie kids with how many credit accounts were on board, we had to wait for the fuel to come from Hawaii. And this is, like, ultra bigger, right?"

"Ultra-ultra," Glisters says. "Remember the Columbus-and-the-Atlantic example from school? Same deal."

He's talking about a math problem everyone does sometime in grade school. You divide the total volume of Columbus's ships by the total volume of the North Atlantic and come up with about two quadrillionths; then you divide the total volume of all the spaceships patrolling or carrying cargo between Earth and Mars by the volume of the doughnut-shaped space that the Earth's orbit and Mars's orbit mark out around the sun, and get about one septillionth. You divide that out and you find out that the Atlantic, proportionately, contained a billion times more of Columbus's ships than Earth-Mars space contains spaceships, even today, when there are more than 50 regular cap launches and recoveries on Earth per day.

Wychee says, "I suppose I'm mad because they told me space was big and empty since I was little, but I feel like they never told me *how* big and *how* empty—there was that business about traveling thirty times as fast as a rifle bullet and taking four months to get to Mars, and that didn't really sink in, either, till just now. So we're all alone out here."

"And it's ultra not fair," Derlock says, "and I don't think we should have to—"

"Shut up," Stack says quietly. "Uh, if I'm allowed to tell him to shut up, Commander."

"I'm authorizing it immediately," Emerald says, "and thanks for your initiative."

Stack says, "Glisters, if I get it right, the deal is this: We can't get close enough to Mars without course correction. We can't do course correction while we're tumbling. We can't stop our tumbling—at least not safely—until the stuff is tacked down. Does that cover it?"

"Uh, brilliantly," Glisters says.

"Then let's tack the stuff down. We can figure the rest out later. I want to understand it, but I want to do what we have to get done first."

The short silence is broken by Emerald saying, "He's right. Show us what we need to do, Glisters."

He puts it up on the big screen. "Well, the red ones are unattached objects, which will fly around and could break things or hurt people, and the yellow stuff is loose objects that might come loose and turn into red stuff. So in between each burst from the thrusters, we need to go out and drag the red ones back into place and hook them down, and then re-fasten the hooks on the yellow ones. We've got seven more thruster bursts coming, the next one in—about forty minutes."

Stack nods. "Okay, I see that part. Why do we have to wait so long between firing thrusters and engines? Why not just fire them all at once and get this thing right-side-up right away?" Under his natural deep brown skin he's distinctly turning gray-green; maybe the swaying cockpit is making him motion sick.

Glisters says, "It's another problem with being on a broken ship. We'd do it that way if we had the whole ship to work with. But out of eight engines we should have, we've got two working. So the computer has to wait till it has a working thruster or engine in the right position to give us just the right size push in just the right direction. Then once it corrects it has to wait for another thruster to come into place, and so on. Actually it's more complicated than that because I asked it to figure out what would waste the least water, since we want to have as much as possible to do our course correction. As it is, we'll use up almost all the remaining ice just to put ourselves barely in range for caps coming up from Mars."

"But they *will* come and get us, won't they?" Fleeta asks. "They won't be mad at us, and just decide not to bother?"

"They might be mad, but they'll still come and get us," Glisters says. "What worries me is that I keep getting MESSAGE NOT SENT when I try to send out the distress call, either the automatic or the custom. And I think that's because the antenna on the nose spire is gone—the nose would have whipped around harder than anywhere else, the sensors aren't showing it's there, and I think the force just tore it off—and the one on the tail was dead, and in for repairs, at the time we were hit. It's apparently waiting in the tail airlock for installation—"

"Well, then, let's install it!" Stack says.

"Hold on. That means going outside in an evasuit and working on the extreme tail of the ship, and right now, while it's tumbling, whoever does it could fall away into space—and we don't have any way to rescue them if they do, the second they lose grip on ship, they're gone for good—or much worse, the antenna could accidentally fall away and be lost."

"Losing the antenna is worse than falling away and dying in space?" I ask.

"There's nine of us and only one antenna," he points out. "So there is an order we have to do things. First hook the cargo. Then straighten the spin. Those can overlap a little. As soon as we're done with that, fire the course correction, because the sooner we do it the more effective it will be. Next, with the ship spinning in its regular way, and after we practice and get it all figured out right because we only get one chance, we put the antenna out there and let them know we're on our way to Mars. No matter what, it will be four months before our closest approach, so they'll have time enough to prepare, even if we don't call in for a month. But to make it possible for them to rescue us at all, we need to do the course correction as soon as possible."

Emerald nods. "Everyone understand why we're doing this? Good. Wait—where's Marioschke?"

Wychee says, "The last I saw of her, she was sitting on her sleepsack in lotus with her hands wrapped in handholds so tight the knuckles were white, eyes tight shut, and om-ing like crazy. I think she was trying to pray her-self out of this. I tried to get her to come along, Em, I did, but the others were leaving and—"

Emerald says, "Oh, I believe you. Whoever sees her next can try again. She might cooperate more once she's hungry or needs to pee. Meanwhile, though, she's not hurt?"

"Not unless 'scared out of her mind' counts as hurt."

"If *that* counts, we're all totally disabled. All right, here's how we do it. Glisters, do our phones work locally?"

He clicks keys for a moment. "They do now."

"Good job," Emerald says. "Let's try one thing first." She tells her phone, "Marioschke."

Marioschke picks up, shouting, "Help, the ship is bro-ken and I don't know what to do!"

"This is Emerald—"

"Emerald is dead, everybody's dead, the ship is bro-ken, my dad will pay you whatever you want but come and get me!"

"Marioschke, we're—"

"Come and get me! The ship is broken!"

Emerald sighs and breaks the connection. "We don't have time for this right now, and she can't be any more upset than she is already, can she? All right, then, Glisters will stay here and text out to the crews, directing us to whatever needs to be fixed."

He says, "Set your phone to pop me up on voice—*loud*! If stuff is moving around I may need to tell you right then, and I want you to have enough time to grab a handhold before each thruster burst."

"What Glisters said," Emerald says. "Glisters, do we have pressure suits?"

"We must, but I'll have to locate them."

"Then we'll start in the Pressurized Cargo Section first. I'm going to put you into teams—"

"What makes you think I'm going to *follow* your orders?" Derlock says.

"Because you're going to be *my* teammate," I tell him, "and if you either fuck off or fuck up, I will lop off your worthless dangly little pink nadsies and make you eat them," trying to style like Pop in *Space Patrol to Saturn!*, but to judge by the way people are reacting, I'm styling more as insane psychobitch ex-girlfriend. *Good. That probably scares him more anyway.* "We have things to discuss while you are being a big useful collection of muscles, anyway."

"Thanks for volunteering," Em says, smiling at both of us.

"How about me, F.B., and Fleeta as a team?" Wychee says.

Emerald nods. "Good. Stack, you're with me."

Interesting, I think. Each group has at least one person from Em's core group and one from Derlock's late arrivals. Em and I have the two potential mutineers. And Wychee helped make it look spontaneous. *I hope Wychee wasn't just useful by accident.*

- - -

At the coretube we grab the recessed handholds and climb; it's 5 meters across, so there's plenty of room for all of us to climb side by side. As we go up the gravity decreases, up to the weightless spot at the center of mass, where I do a handstand, which is easy in the low gravity, and get my feet pointed the other way for the climb down into the nose end of the pod. All the others copy me, although F.B. has to try it twice before he figures it out.

As we climb down the gravity increases. Glisters speaks over all our phones. "All right, at Cargo Wall 44, Wychee's team peel off, and I'll text you your instructions."

Wychee opens a hatch into the space between the cargo walls and helps Fleeta and F.B. through it; we watch this above us as we keep climbing down. Glisters is sending Stack and Em all the way to the nose end, because they're the most muscular team, collectively, and that's where gravity will be highest and unhooked cargo most abundant. Derlock and I peel off at Cargo Wall 14, to work our way down and meet Em and Stack.

Derlock says, "See, that's not fair, Glisters gave the first team thirty cargo walls to cover, he gave us thirteen, and those guys are only doing Cargo Wall 1."

"He's looking at the amount of work, not the number of cargo walls. The farther out toward the nose, the bigger the change in gravity, and the more cargo shook loose. Besides, anything that went over the edge of any cargo wall between 1 and 49 fell noseward. Glisters worked it out so that we all have the same amount of cargo to shift."

Halfway down Cargo Wall 14, three tumbling containers have loosened two more. We reconnect the cargo hooks on the two that are showing yellow on Glisters's screen, then look over the situation on this wall—this floor, for the moment. A three-meter cube painted bright red has slid about ten meters hullward; it is leaning against a mud brown box, a meter and a half on a side and five and a half meters long. A dull yellow cylinder, half a meter across and a meter long, lies wedged hard between the other side of the red cube and the cargo wall.

"My executive decision as pilot and team leader," I say, "is that we try to move the little yellow one first, then the long thin leaner, and then the big red one."

"Yes, sir, Mister Pilot Sir!" He gives me a lame parody of a salute.

I give him the raspberry. "Come on."

There are cracks in the red cube where the yellow cylinder jammed into it. We push on the red cube and it lurches wildly; we jump back, and the cylinder rolls out from under it and heads hullward with a low, heavy rumble.

We bound after it; it slams into an anchored black crate and gets stuck there.

Lifting the cylinder, or even getting a hand under it, is impossible. We shove it hard to free it from the cube, and let the cube settle back with a thud.

We can't lift the cylinder, even in the low gravity, but it's easy enough to roll it to the place it fell from. After we rehook it, I ask Glisters, on voice, "How can anything be that heavy in such low gravity?"

"It was a solid-gold copy of a Louis Quinze ottoman encased in concrete to prevent dents. They do that for things like that; at the other end they just have nanos eat the concrete. So you made sure it's dogged down good? I don't want that smashing against a window, no matter how tough that window is supposed to be."

"It's back on its hook and the hook says it's fine, but who knows? It got loose before; is there going to be another lurch that big?"

"Not if I have anything to do with it."

"Then we'll be fine. What's in the other boxes?"

"The long brown box is handmade quilts and rugs," Glisters says. "The red cube is orange tree seedlings on a centrifuge—that's why it jumped like that."

"Why are they centrifuging the trees? Are they trying to pre-extract the juice or something?"

"They don't have suspended animation protocols for trees, so they put them into a centrifuge with a light at the center, to keep them growing straight on their way to Mars."

Despite the size, I can pass the big mud-colored box of quilts to Derlock like a really awkward beach ball, and he hooks it down right away.

The red crate bucks and turns at every shove, and walks itself across the floor whenever we let go of it; it's too heavy to lift, almost too heavy to shove, and since it's basically a huge gyroscope, whenever it finally settles down it wants to stay right where it is. With enough dragging and shoving, we wrestle it into place, only to find we have to turn it 90 degrees to get a hook where it needs to be. It kicks and shoves like a cat in a shoe box, and Derlock and I get a couple bruises and use some language Pop wouldn't have wanted me to use at a *Revive the Family!* rally, but at last we hook it down.

"Conservation of angular momentum is not our friend," I say to Glisters over the phone.

"It's not anybody's. We're using up a tenth of our only iceball just to get pointed in the right direction. Speaking of that, you might as well go to the coretube and grab a handhold; we're seven minutes from the next thruster burst. It'll be quite a lurch but not nearly as bad as that first one."

In the coretube, we see Wychee's group coming out above us, and Emerald and Stack below. I'm trying to think of some appropriate phrase to reassure everyone when the wall of the coretube jumps at us, then slides sideways. For one instant I'm trying to hold on to a wall with my body extending horizontally. Weight swings around noseward in the coretube again, tugging at my hands on the handholds, but with only maybe half the force it had before. "Keep your grips," Glisters warns over the speakers. "We're only halfway through."

Another swing and shake, and the handholds seem momentarily to pull in opposite directions; my body swings out from the wall and then slowly drifts back onto it. My head seems to float, as if I'd just gotten off a carnival ride. Glisters says, "That's it for this time, but according to the database you may experience vertigo or dizziness, which it says you should recover from in about three minutes at most."

"Time that off for us," Emerald says, from far below.

"Nobody let go or try to move around till Glisters says we've had our three minutes."

While we hang there, I hear sliding and thumping noises. "Glisters," I say, "I want you to tell me nothing more came loose during that lurch."

"I know you want me to tell you that, but it's not true," he says. "The bad news is that seven more things are all the way off the hook, and they're sliding around. And nine more hooks loosened to yellow. But most of what you're hearing moving was already off the hook, and you guys just hadn't gotten to it to rehook it. And our three crews got fourteen crates re-hooked on that first—"

"Fourteen?" Derlock demands, outraged. "But Susan and I only re-hooked three!"

"You had the two most awkward objects this round," Glisters points out, reasonably. "And Wychee's crew got eight because they had several lightweight ones that had landed on empty stretches of wall; they just hooked them where they were and were done."

"But we did a damn good job!" Wychee shouts from overhead. "And we'll hook the most this round, too!"

"Is that a bet?" Derlock says.

"It's one with us, at least," Emerald calls from down below. Stack is grinning, nodding, and socking one hand into the other; it's easier to gesture with a floor to stand on, but I wonder what it was like being shaken around down there during the thruster lurch.

"You're on!" Wychee says. Seeing Derlock's eager nod, I say, "Count us in, too!"

"All right," Glisters says, "and I'm your scorekeeper. Sounds like everyone is feeling basically okay? Your three minutes are up in fifteen seconds, so on my mark—texting your directions to you now . . . ready—go!"

I clamber into the hatch for Cargo Wall 13 and Derlock follows me. Gravity is now much lighter than lunar but the precession is worse, and it's just a touch harder to balance.

Our first little lost package is a meter-diameter sphere that seems to weigh nothing; it's a Renaissance painting packed in aerogel, and I just swing it onto the nearest hook and lock it. Meanwhile Derlock wrestles a big crate of pre-served pizzas from some place called Mario's; it doesn't weigh much but it has the same inertia it would anywhere, so it's big and awkward. It takes him a couple of swings to snug it in where he can fasten its hook. We relock eight yellow-marked hooks and we're done with Cargo Wall 13. "Need more to do, Glisters," I say, just before his text pops up, telling us to go back up to Cargo Wall 14.

"Sorry," he says, "some fresh stuff came loose up there. I'm keeping stats on relocking the hooks, too, by the way, and you're ahead on that."

"Just so we get our full score," I say. Derlock and I re-hook seventeen objects and make it down to Cargo Wall 8 before Glisters asks us to go to the coretube for the next thruster burst.

As we work back to the coretube, Derlock says, "If we do starve to death out here, at least we can dress beau-tifully for our last world-class meal on gorgeous furniture. Somehow this doesn't seem like my idea of 'pioneer supplies.'"

"Yeah," I say. "Like Pop says, even the real stuff is fake now. The Martians are supposed to be adventurous pioneers on a frontier world, but robots do everything hard or dangerous. Mostly Martians just drive between sites to watch the robots work, type messages to decide what the robots should do next, and change clothes and sex partners, and throw parties and snits, same as they would in California."

"And no beach." He opens the coretube hatch.

"Actually, they even have that. Great big wave tank under glass, where one-third g makes a great surfer out of anyone, the water's always just comfortable temperature, and there aren't any sharks or much of any other way to get hurt." We hang face-to-face in the coretube. "Aunt Destiny surfed there once and her note to Pop was hilarious. I'm really going to miss her." I say it quietly, styling dignified brave grief, watching for his reaction. Derlock watches me with all the emotional involvement of a python watching a rat.

A month ago that would have been so zoomed; a week ago it would have been so infuriating; now it's so irrelevant.

7

ALL THE GLORY WE CAN EAT

**April 25, 2129. On *Virgo*, upbound Earth to Mars.
149 million kilometers from the sun, 166 million
kilometers from Mars, 3.8 million kilometers from Earth.**

THE WORLD WHIRLS wildly, spins differently, arrests and restarts, in a flurry of thruster shots. With only a little difficulty, I hang on to the wall and my breakfast. In the next round, Derlock and I, working our way down, meet Emerald and Stack, working their way up, halfway through Cargo Wall 2.

They're contemplating a blue-gray suspended-animation container the size of a vacation cabin. Even with the wrong-way gravity now down to 7% of Earth's, we can only budge the monstrous box slightly once Wychee's crew finishes and joins us.

"According to the manifest," Glisters says over a local speaker station, "this is Category Y, Type 4. If they have to abandon ship, Category Y is the next thing they save after the passengers, crew, and ship's pets. According to the steward's notes, this is 'Pets in Suspended Animation.' With one footnote: 'Fwuffy.'"

"Fluffy?" Emerald asks.

"Fwuffy. With a *w*. And that's all I have. So it's someone's pet or pets—"

"Pets?" Emerald says. "Even if half the space in there is suspended animation machinery, that box still has room for a four-horse team, half a dozen bears, or a whole pack of Great Danes. A fwuffy must be some geneered pet species. Anyway, on the side I'm looking at, it says, upside down, THIS END UP, NO TOLERANCE, DO NOT SHAKE OR TEMPORARILY OR PARTLY INVERT right next to an arrow that is pointing straight *down*. N-nillion red lights are flashing, on two different panels on different sides; there's a few green, but it's mostly flashing red, and most what's not flashing red is yellow. One corner is smashed in."

"Okay," Glisters says. "I can't get very much info at this end, either. It looks like it fell from the cargo wall overhead and slid around; it's a miracle it didn't smash on the nose bulkhead. Too many required fields overwritten with blanks and N/A; a pro hacked this one into the system, I'd say, so for sure it's semi-contraband—not an atom bomb or a load of happistuf, but not quite in bounds legally."

"Great," Emerald says. "So it's criminal, undocumented, upside down, heavy, broken, showing flashing red lights, . . . can anything else be wrong with it?"

"Well, if it dies," Glisters points out, "with suspended animation failing, we will have tonnes of rotting fwuffies in the part of the ship where we mainly live."

"My next engineer is going to be an incurable optimist."

"And your ship is going to stink, Commander. I don't make the news, I just report it."

Emerald looks around at the group. "Well," she says, "sooner or later, as Glisters gets the ship stabilized—"

"The ship is doing that automatically," Derlock points out.

"Sooner or later, as *Glisters does the things that make the ship stabilize itself, which* most *of us couldn't do in n-nillion years and* some *of us insist on sniping at*," Emerald says, "the gravity will be along the cargo wall and out toward the hull again, and a few tonnes of dying fwuffies will smash into the window. Anyone care to bet that that will make things *better*? So at the least we need to stabilize it, somehow, before we're back to regular milligrav."

No one argues with her. I'm beginning to think that Glisters and I have great taste in commanders.

"All right, then." She looks around at all of us, then back at the speaker. "Glisters, before we go any further, can we just dog it down in place?"

"That will keep it from smashing anything else but otherwise it won't solve the problem. It's already had ultra too much acceleration in ultra too many bad directions. Besides, the control panel you need to fix the thing—if it *can* be fixed—is on the top, right where that arrow is pointing, so you need to turn it over. I think you'll have to turn it at least enough to access the top, unblock the front, and aim the bottom at the windows. Sorry, I realize that sucks."

"I hate not wringing your neck just because you're right." Emerald turns to me. "Okay, you took all that high-end math and topology and stuff. What's the minimum number of turns to get it upright?"

I've been standing here thinking about just that. "Two.

First we rotate it about 90 degrees to get FRONT pointed that way"—I point—"so there's empty space to tip it into. That won't be so bad. Then we do the real bastard, tip it 90 toward the hull. That will get TOP pointed toward the coretube and the bottom toward the windows."

With all of us pushing on corners, we just manage the first move.

Tipping requires much more effort. Glisters finds us a tool locker along the outside of the coretube where there are crowbars, pulleys, hooks, cable, and lengths of pipe. With Stack, Fleeta, and me on one corner pushing down on a crowbar, and Emerald, F.B., and Derlock at the other, we lift one side of the crate enough for Wychee to roll the pipe lengthwise under the gap. We sink hooks into the raised edge and run lines to them through two triple-advantage block and tackle rigs, attached to a bracket on the handling floor. Stack has a couple of scary moments getting that rigged, and then has to go down to the nose and climb back around to rejoin us.

With all of us pulling like two crazed tug-of-war teams next to each other, the crate slowly tips up, up, and over, crashing down on its side. TOP and FRONT are pointed the right way. Two cargo hooks are close enough to reach, and then we run cable from two of its attachment rings to two more cargo hooks. Nobody wants to have to do this job over.

Another two red lights are flashing when we're done.

On the now-exposed control screen, I touch AUTO-CHECK.

A clear, pleasant female voice says, "Severe damage to nine support systems. Specimen harmed on four fatal and eighteen non-fatal identifiables. Death delay system will prevent permanent death for two to six hours. Press AUTO-CHECK for options."

I push AUTOCHECK again.

"Currently workable options are, option 1, painless euthanasia"—a red button labeled PAINLESS EUTHANASIA NOT REVERSIBLE appears on the touch screen—"with three days of follow-on refrigeration to allow time for disposing of remains. Option 2, release specimen from suspended animation without restoration." The next button that appears is also red, and is more prosaic than the voice; it says IMMEDIATE DUMP. "Unrestored specimen cannot survive if released," the voice goes on to explain. "Option 3, commence restoration with full repair." The third button to appear on the screen is blue, not red, and it says RESTORE & REPAIR.

Em reaches past me and pushes it. Her even gaze meets my startled reaction. "Susan, that's the only one that doesn't kill it, and I *won't* kill someone's pet." I must still look dubious, because she says, "Just thinking about how I felt when I lost my cat named Dog. You told me last night you had a dog, too. I don't know about you, but . . ." She shrugs in a mute plea for understanding.

I do understand; I understand so well I'm having trouble putting the words together to tell her. Back when Pop started dragging me out on all the *Revive the Family!* tours, we started putting poor old Stanley into suspended animation all the time. He was afraid of it—I don't know why, it doesn't hurt—but every time, as soon as he saw that tank, he whined and yelped and tried to hide behind me. And then he always came out of it pathetically begging for attention, and just wasn't the same dog for weeks; sometimes he'd have to go back in before he was recovered from the last time.

He was so crazy and miserable, and besides they told me he was really old anyway, so I agreed to let them turn the suspended animation off and let him just die in his sleep in the tank. They did that while I was on the moon getting felt up on camera, and Fleeta was destroying her brain.

Emerald is looking at me expectantly, and repeats, "I just don't want to be the kind of people who kill other people's pets."

I think, *Yeah, we* don't *kill people's pets,* and that just feels right, down in my bones. I can feel my smile escaping onto my face. "Well, I sure hope it doesn't turn out that a fwuffy is a shark with wings."

The female voice from the container says, "Anticipated complete restoration in about thirty-five hours." The screen displays a countdown that starts down from 35:00:00, and a single button that says REVIEW SPECIMEN STATUS. When I push it, it puts up a screenful of tiny graphs, not one of which means anything to me.

Glisters's voice breaks in, "If you all are ready, I think I've been able to plan out rehooking the loose stuff in the tail end to go a lot faster," he says. "And it's still about forty minutes till the next thruster lurch. Emerald and Stack are ahead with twenty-eight hookups, then the other two teams are tied at twenty. Derlock and Susan are ahead for fixing yellows, with forty-four; then Wychee's team with thirty-eight, and Emerald and Stack at twenty-four. Shall we continue the race?"

It's unanimous, and soon we're all scrambling down to our start points on the tail side of the pod. He's given Derlock and me the tail bulkhead, sent Emerald and Stack to Cargo Wall 58, and put the others at Cargo Wall 88. Derlock and I drop swiftly down the coretube, slowing ourselves on the grips as we go, because at 7% of a g, falling 500 meters in one plunge still means you're going almost 100 kilometers an hour when you hit the floor.

"We're going to win this thing, Susan. No sense playing if you don't play to win."

We're done by the next thruster lurch, partly because Glisters has done a better job of planning and mostly because we've now all had enough practice to do things quickly. Even poor, awkward F.B. seems to have the hang of it, and the routine repositioning and rehooking that took me or Derlock a couple minutes is now something we do literally one-handed in seconds before bounding to the next container. Derlock and I come out the winners—we rehooked forty-one reds and reset fifty-two yellows. "All the glory we can eat," I say, smugly, as the group stands around waiting for Glisters to figure out what's next.

Fleeta says, "Uh, not to be all complainy or anything, but *could* we eat sometime?"

I'm hungry the moment she says it. Looking around, it looks like so is everyone else. Emerald says, "Okay, let's eat somewhere near the cockpit so we can make sure Glisters does, too, because I'm betting he'll be just as obsessed by running the ship as he was with splyctering porn, and we can't afford to have him forget to take care of himself. Do we have a volunteer for figuring out lunch or do we just all go looting?"

"I cook," Wychee says.

"Actually you're really good at it," Emerald says, "but I was hoping I wouldn't be forced to use my inside information to get you to do it."

"Well, I'd rather eat my own cooking than most other people's. I need two helpers—"

"I don't know anything," F.B. says, "but I'd like to learn, so I'll help, Wychee."

"Me, too," Fleeta says. "Besides you're nice to work for."

I make the note to myself that Wychee obviously has a gift for getting work out of the awkward squad, and raise her a couple more points on my usefulness scale.

Emerald nods with satisfaction. "All right, kitchen crew created and I didn't have to do anything. Everybody be sure to remember my brilliant leadership when Ed Teach is putting together the meed about us." Then a thought wipes the smile off her face. "Before I forget again, did anyone find Marioschke while we were rehooking?"

"About an hour ago she was sitting on the end of Cargo Wall 28, looking out at the stars and om-ing like a hive of hornets," Wychee says. "I got her to say about five sentences. She intoned like she was trying out for First Chair Oracle. She's trying to peacefully accept her oneness with the universe so she can actuate her potential and do whatever it is that a person with an actuated potential does on a wrecked spaceship."

I ask, "Has she . . . uh, cracked up?"

"I don't know. After the intoning she went back to oming. Maybe I should have stuck around, but it was getting pretty om-y and I had work to do."

Stack grunts. "She's not crazy."

Something about how sure he is, and how embarrassed he looks, makes me ask, "How do you know?"

"We had a secret sex thing going for a while," he admits.

A freezing silence descends.

Stack adds, defensively, "I gave it up. She liked it, it was fun, and she's smarter than she acts, and nice to talk to, too, except I just couldn't cope with all the be-doo-be-doo philospho-pillow talk; she'd go on forever about how everything is spirit and how in touch she felt with all those plants, and I'd get so bored."

He can see that Wychee, me, and Emerald are too angry to speak; if F.B. and Derlock have any common sense, they're afraid to. His eyes not meeting any of ours, he explains, "So, like, I know her pretty well, I know how she thinks and what she dreams about and all that sheeyef-finit. She'd *like* to crack up, because it would mean everyone would worry about her feelings and what was going on inside her. That's all she ever wants, really, to be the most time-consuming mental patient on the ward. But she's . . well, really going all the way insane would take more effort than she ever makes. She just wants a lot of attention." He's looking at the stares with shame in his eyes, and then suddenly he squares his shoulders. "You're right. That was a rotten way to treat her, because she's just like all of us. She wants to be a genius and important and a star without having to know anything or be anything special." More silence. "Can I stop now?"

I finally think of something to say. "Stack, I might not be thrilled with you, but I'm glad someone understands what's going on with her, and yeah, you're right, it's not that different from the way the rest of us are. So thanks, it helps to know it's really just interpersonal botflog." I guess I'm coming down with a bad case of pilot or something, because I ask Wychee, "Cargo Wall 28, right?"

"Right. I don't think she'll have moved."

Stack adds, "Just keep reminding her that she's hungry."

I consider baring my teeth at him, then realize my mouth is twitching trying not to laugh; bless her, Emerald does laugh, and then we all do. Finally Emerald says, "All right, bring her along, Susan. Try to be quick, because whether she needs to eat or not, you do."

"Right." I just shoot up the coretube; I'd rather not be late for lunch and this might be difficult.

- - -

Marioschke's face is red, her eyes are swollen, and there's a damp spot under her nose. She is still sitting on the edge of Cargo Wall 28, letting her feet dangle, and watching the much-slower rotation of the stars past the window. The wreckage of the crew bubble and the intact iceball are now lost in the stars; the two lost and shattered iceballs barely form disks, not much bigger, though a lot brighter, than the Andromeda Nebula. In a few hours they'll be entirely invisible.

She wipes her face. "The stars are all crazy. That has to be screwing up everything astrologically—"

This doesn't seem like the time to do any science educating, so I just say, "Come down to the cockpit area and eat. You must be hungry."

She drags one of her big flowy sleeves across her face and sighs; it must have been pretty tiring to play crazy to an empty cargo space for all this time. "How do we get there with the ship all wrecked, anyway?"

"We bounce along the cargo wall, then climb the core-tube. The gravity changes a lot along the way, but it's all very low, you won't weigh more than 2 kilos the whole way." (*Actually*, I think, *I won't weigh more than two, you won't weigh more than three.* I add to myself, *Meow.*) "You'll see. It takes practically no muscle, and your balance will get better if you try." I stand up, and when she follows me, she almost falls over the edge. I pull her back. "This way."

If it were just me I'd take the cargo wall in three big bounces, but I try not to run ahead of her, so I sort of patter along, using my ankles to rock from heel to toe. She trails after me in slow, chaotic bounces, like a balloon being dragged behind a little kid.

At the coretube, I open the hatch and say, "All right,

just kneel on the edge, facing out like this, lean back a little bit, grab a handhold, pull up, and grab the next one after." I demonstrate, pulling myself about 5 meters up inside.

She isn't following, so I go back. She's sniffling; rather than kicking her, I try gentleness again. "Come on," I say, climbing to be at the side of the hatch. "Sit down on the sill. You can do that."

She sits, gripping the doorframe like she's hanging her ass out of an airplane on Earth.

"Give me your hand. Turn it so your palm faces you." I reach down with my left and take a firm grip with my right.

She does, and I say, "Now let me just lift you up, and your body will come around to face the right way."

Marioschke shuts her eyes, and gasps when I pull her off her perch, so that she's just hanging by my grip on her wrist. Her elbow untwists the half turn, facing her the right way. "Reach out with your other hand," I say, "The handhold is right in front of you."

She grabs it and hangs on for dear life.

"Now just let go of my hand and feel how easy it is to hold yourself up." That takes a few seconds. "Now reach for the handhold above you and grab that." Awkwardly, slowly, making F.B. look like an Olympic gymnast, she begins to climb. By the time we're at the center of mass, she looks no worse than terrified.

She can't make herself try to turn over with a handstand and has to do it like a little kid, walking her feet through her hands and turning around hand over hand. She's almost there when she realizes that she can see half a kilometer in either direction, and could fall that far either way. She just freezes.

Talking her through climbing down is worse than talking her through climbing up, until there's enough gravity to keep her pulled against the wall; then it's easier. When we're at the level of the aux cockpit, I drag her in through the hatch; *works, but t'ain't elegant,* like Pop says in *Mighty Hard Row.*

By the time we're there, Wychee is making that food sing and dance, and it all smells way too good. The little kitchen, off the same corridor as the cockpit, has its own independent stabilizer setup, "Which is good, because I'd rather not face the challenge of cooking on a sideways stove," she explains.

Among the many crates, with Glisters's help, she located uncooked fresh fettuccine packed in helium, trout fillets pickled in white wine, a cubic-meter temptrol box embossed with *Laiterie de la Provence,* what appeared to be the stock of an entire spice store, and some self-heating mixed veg. Fleeta and F.B. are filling up the fridge and freezer with all the other food that was in the same crates; "We'll get more systematic later, right now I just want to get some food into people." She has just put the noodles into a boiling sphere, which is whirling up to speed in the stove's receptacle.

"Is it going to bother the sphere that there's so much

gravity?" F.B. asks—a surprisingly intelligent question. *Everyone* is surprising me lately.

"I don't think so," Wychee says. "I used one on the moon where the gravity was five times this." She puts cream, butter, and cheese into a stirring sphere to warm; after a while she has something going on in four of the eight receptacles. Somehow, it all comes out done at the same time, and we each get a squeezer, one of those heavy insulated plastic bags that you squeeze to put a bite-sized bit into a split bubble; when you bite down on the bubble, the slit opens, and the food pops into your mouth. It beats having it float all over.

We all enjoy a real meal; I hadn't thought about it, but the cargo rehooking was probably like four trips to the gym. *A few more days of this and all of us will be begging Glisters to make some recordings of our butts in something tight*, I think. *Splycterable for sure. I might yet end up as one of those loser celeb-chickies whose buttocks have a higher recognition index than her face.*

Strangely, I feel nothing about that thought. *I'm already beginning to not care how I look. And to not care that I don't care. Wonder if there's anything in the infirmary's database about recursive apathy?*

At the end of lunch, Emerald says, "Glisters, am I right that we have two hours till the next thruster fire, and then just two more after that, also about two hours apart?"

"That's right."

"Eight huge things to rehook in the vacuum cargo sections, and whatever shoveling we have to do in the one open farm section, right?"

"Also right. I have a feeling this is going somewhere."

"Are we all likely to die if something happens and you're away from the cockpit for a couple hours?"

"Probably not. I haven't actually done anything to operate the ship since I started the automated programs. Everything I've been doing is trying to get up on tutorials, and guiding you guys through rehooking the cargo."

"Perfect," she says. "You're coming with us."

"All right, where are we going?"

"The Forest," she says firmly. "This is mandatory. It gives us a chance to see how bad things are in Farm Section 1, but the main reason is I want everyone to unwind and take a nap. So far we've done a lot of hard work that could have caused some serious accidents, and nobody—knock on alclad—has been injured. Everyone is stressed and tired, even after this break, and probably a little sleepy with food coma as well. So let's go give everyone nap time."

Wychee grins. "Commander Em, would you like milk and cookies with that?"

"Some other time. I want *you* to rest and do nothing, too. Just like Glisters and Susan and everyone else. We're going for a nap in the Forest, people. You are all going to get de-stressed and rested. That's an order. Anyone that doesn't come along and chill is going to be flogged around the fleet."

"'Flogged around the fleet'?" I ask. "Have you been watching old meeds?"

"All my life. I'd've threatened keelhauling but we don't have the eva skills for that. Now, if all the squeezers have gone into the Phreshor for cleaning, let's get going. No goofing off when your commander orders you to rest."

Grumbling, but kind of liking her for it nonetheless, we clean the eating area and form up, making sure F.B. and Marioschke are in the middle in case they need help. Yesterday, when we learned Bari and King were dead, there wasn't one hand reached out to anyone; for better or worse, now we're a team.

8

THE EVIL ISSUE, THE IRREPLACEABLE ISSUE, AND THE SQUASHED-LIKE-A-BUG ISSUE

April 25, 2129. On *Virgo*, upbound Earth to Mars. 149 million kilometers from the sun, 166 million kilometers from Mars, 3.8 million kilometers from Earth.

WE OPEN THE hatch into Farm Section 1 with a utility stick, not knowing much about what might have gone where. Nothing comes at us, so we pull ourselves down the ladder past the big piped-light ports to the first growing deck, almost 15 meters down. Instead of vertical core-tube-to-hull walls, like the pressurized cargo section has, farm sections are divided into growing decks, with long narrow beds you walk between to do whatever it is you do with plants. (All I know about them is roots down, leaves up.) After the first big drop the growing decks are only about 4 meters apart; climbing down an enclosed ladder through several levels feels ultra confining.

The piped sunlight ports in the ceilings make every deck warm and bright. It's humid; wet soil and water have spilled from bins that didn't close fast enough, or jammed open. Looking toward the nose, I see mud, where soil beds and water tanks have dumped against the bulkheads.

There's a bigger mess on the bulkhead at the next level. I point it out to Glisters.

"Yeah, and that's not good. Mud *flows*, and when we fire the engine for the course correction, ugh. The tail end mud pile will just flatten out on the bulkhead without changing the center of mass much—but all that mud up near the nose will drop 850 meters at a tenth of a g or so."

"Now that you put it that way, I don't like it either," I say. "Emerald, have you been getting this?"

"Yeah. So the ship will boost at about a tenth of a g, and while that's going on, the gravity inside will be a tenth of a g, right? So falling 850 meters at a tenth of a g means . . . uh—"

"That mud will hit the tail-end bulkhead as hard as if it fell from 85 meters on Earth—like from the roof of a twenty-storey building. Of course some of it will hit stuff on the way down, but that's not necessarily good either."

Emerald shakes her head. "But that mud is only maybe 10 centimeters deep—not much more than up to our ankles; sure, it'll be going fast, but—"

That doesn't sound right to me. "But there's a lot of bulkhead—and mud is heavy. What's the total mass going to be like, that falls from there and hits the tail-end bulkhead?"

Glisters stops and punches his wristcomp. "Okay, 10 cm deep by . . . hmm, that's still 18 decks worth of it . . . okay, about 650 tonnes. If the density this thing is giving me for 'loose soft mud' is accurate. They don't define either *loose* or *soft* but that stuff is definitely mud."

"We can agree on *that*," Emerald says. Everyone has been gathering around us while we sorted it out. "Definitely mud. All mud, that mud. So 650 tonnes of it is going to come pile-driving down like it fell from a good-sized office building. I guess we have to get it someplace under control, then, before we can course correct."

Wychee says, "Em—I mean, Commander—"

"Wychee, we're on break. You have best buddy privileges—"

"Well, whatever. I have an idea. You don't need to put all the mud back in the *right* bins. You just need to keep it from moving around, right? So I was thinking, in normal operation—they must have to rearrange beds and move soil? Which means they must have power equipment for moving mud around and storage spaces to put it into. So shouldn't we look—"

Glisters is nodding. "Yeah. Yeah, you're right. All we really have to do is get the nose-end mud pile under control, and for sure they have gear to do it with. Thanks for thinking of that; I was drowning in the complications and you saw the real issue."

"What issue?" Fleeta asks, obviously having some trouble following this.

"Either the squashed-like-a-bug issue," I say, "or the giant-hole-knocked-in-the-tail issue."

She's scared but enthusiastically joyful, like she's

about to go on a really great roller coaster. "Are we gonna—"

"No, because Wychee's idea has taken care of it," I tell her.

She smiles the way a little kid will when something was scary but Mom says it's okay, and unselfconsciously takes my hand. I look into her eyes, and think about what she'd have thought of this adventure when we were ten or eleven, and how much we'd have *wanted* to be here together. Her expression is blankly ecstatic; she thinks nothing but she feels great. I'm afraid of crying, and I look away, but I don't let go of her hand.

There are no windows in the hull-level deck except in the Forest—the light is all piped to come down at the plants from above. It seems like a room with a warm sky-light.

As we move farther noseward, we are careful to come to a full stop and take a grip every 3 or 4 meters. Gravity shifts from hullward to noseward very quickly, and we don't want anyone to abruptly fly away and slug into one of those tree trunks.

Though most of it must have been trapped when the beds slammed shut, mud still oozes down the walkways, headed for the nose. Now and then a blob breaks off and flies on ahead of us, past the closed beds, spattering on the tree trunks down in the Forest.

"You know," I say, "I bet the Forest isn't as pretty as it was. Maybe we should give this up."

"Let's at least *look*," Emerald says.

By the time we're there, we're climbing, albeit easily, down the hull wall, and the mud drops on us in a constant drizzle that hits with enough force to sting an upturned face. The grass between the trees is all smeared with mud and water slowly dribbling toward the nose, and the lower trunks are a muddy mess. All but the least ripe fruit has shaken loose and plunged into the mud below.

It's nothing like it was when I was here with Destiny. And Destiny—

I'm crying. Hard. Really hard, as in, I sit down on a muddy trunk and just sob. Fleeta hangs on to me and keeps saying she's so sorry, she's so sorry, even though I can feel that she's stifling giggles. Then everyone's crying, and the place sounds like a big echoey funeral. The light from the windows flashes off and on, turning the green twilight white and highlighting the tear streaks in the dirty faces and the filthy misery of our clothes.

Fleeta does not cry, because she can't. Maybe that's why Derlock doesn't cry either; he sits staring, waiting for one of us to do something that matters to him.

After a while, Emerald says, "I guess that needed to come out."

Stack says, "I'm surprised we weren't all like that right after it happened."

Emerald shakes her head. "I'm just being reminded about something my mother said, and she's right. Meeds always show people running and screaming and freaking out when something big happens, everybody always acts like panic is the most common thing that happens, but you know . . . if you look at natural disasters, big accidents, terrorist attacks, any of that . . . mostly people get real calm and do what needs to be done. Everybody who ever planned to turn bombs loose on civilians was planning to start a panic, but that's exactly what *doesn't* happen. When my mom—Do you guys all know?"

It takes me a moment to realize that she means, *do you all know how my mother became a celeb-eenie?* and our real answer is *yes, but you're so embarrassed about it we never bring it up.* By then, slightly too quickly, Glisters has said, "Why don't you tell us, Emerald? I don't think all of us know, or know the whole story."

The gist of it is that her mother used to be a plain old talent-eenie, really about the plainest kind you can be— she was this really ultra-talented kindergarten teacher, like everybody wants their kids to have, one that every kid wishes was his or her real mommy. Then one of the nihilist-terrorist groups, the kind that want to ruin Perma-PaxPerity because they think people need to be scared and in pain, seized the school. Emerald's mom talked them into letting all the kids go, and just keeping her as a hostage. And then got them to all sit down to tell her what the matter was, putting them all on one side of the room, and abruptly dived under a desk. She'd guessed right, that the rescue team was already in place by then; they knocked down the door and killed all the terrorists within a couple of seconds.

"See, what Mom said was, if you'd asked her what

she'd do in advance, she'd have predicted she'd panic. She thought that because she'd always been told that it was what people do, and besides she was scared of weapons and hated the idea of violence and thought that if she saw any of her kids scared and crying and couldn't do something about it, it would just destroy her. Well, she just went all calm, took a deep breath, and was *there*. And much later on she made me read about what really happens in sudden crises. And you know, all the big accounts about whole cities panicking and people running around aimlessly screaming and all that? Mostly written by people who weren't there. Sometimes criminals take over and do awful things, but even they do the awful things in a pretty calm, organized way. There's more than two centuries of evidence; at least at first, right when things are going bad, people rise to the occasion."

Marioschke, looking down from the muddy branch where she's sitting, starts to cry harder. "I could have," she says. "I knew I could stop, and go find you all—"

Fleeta flees from me, clambers awkwardly out to her, and holds her.

I say, "I don't think any of us has to apologize about anything right now," *not* because I mean it—I'm actually pleased as all sheeyeffinit that Marioschke apologized. But now that she has, I want her to be a functioning member of the team, and it won't help for her to feel perpetually guilty.

Emerald nods, catching my eye, agreeing with me, and softly adds, "Anyway, we're a better-evolved species than our meeds give us credit for. We're usually okay during the worst; afterward we fall apart. Like we're doing now." She looks around, sniffling. "This place was so pretty yesterday."

The silence seems to stretch on forever until F.B. says, "If it's not true, why do we make so many meeds with people screaming and panicking and all?"

Glisters makes a strange little noise. "Visually more interesting. Ever notice that in all the panic scenes, there's a hot girl right where your eye goes?"

Stack snorts. "The panic act makes them scream and get intense expressions. And running makes skirts fly up and boobs bounce around."

There is a chorus of female raspberries. Abruptly, Glisters stands and walks along a tree trunk to the turf-covered hull. "Ha, they've built in a net that holds the sod in place. I guess they'd have to for thrusting. Okay, one avalanche hazard we don't have to worry about."

"Hey," Wychee says, from where she's been exploring up toward the coretube, "the trunks up here don't have much mud. And they're still big enough to stretch out on."

We follow her up there; she's right. We're still dirty, but it feels good to stretch out on a clean surface, without mud spatting down on us, and near the coretube, the damage to the Forest is not so apparent.

After a while, Glisters says. "Hey, Wychee, you're not just right, you're brilliant. I just did a search. All the farm sections are equipped with a suction system that we can configure to put all the mud into storage tanks. And every bulkhead and deck has suction drain inlets, and the ship has twenty robobarrows that can be told to just follow you around, take the dirt as you load it in, and go feed it into the nearest suction inlet. We'll all have to shovel but we won't have to haul."

"Attention, Engineer," Emerald says. "This is your commander speaking. Rest your damned brain, so it will be ready for me to exploit again."

"Yes, ma'am. I was resting it by working on Wychee's idea instead of on my own."

"All right, then, *both* of you stop thinking. This is some kind of conspiracy."

Everyone's quiet; I like the way the trunk feels against my back. I wish I could nap, or maybe cry some more.

"The sun feels good on my feet," Fleeta says. "Do you suppose it's okay to take my slippers off?"

Derlock makes a rude noise. "What, you think the Slipper Police might be hiding in the trees?"

"She probably can't remember whether there's anything dangerous," Emerald says in the quiet way that I am coming to realize means *you are ultra dead*. "Fleeta, you can take them off, but make sure you don't drop them, because they'll fall all the way down to the mud in the nose right now."

"Okay."

I notice that the warm flashes of sun do feel good on feet, and take my slippers off, too; I'm glad the crew bunk room has a shower and a Phreshor, because I'm going to need both pretty seriously when this long day is over.

"Well, I'm too bored to sleep," Derlock says. "Why don't all you super-genius goody-boys and goody-girls amuse me and talk about your fucked-up childhoods."

"Actually, I had a *great* childhood." Glisters stretches. He's on the trunk next to mine. For the first time since the accident I notice how small and short and pink he is, and what an enormous head he has relative to his body. I used to notice that every minute or so when I was around him, but I guess when a guy becomes your main hope of survival, it's not so important that he looks like something that would crawl out of a swamp in a fantasy meed (especially now that he's splattered with mud). "I *liked* being a kid. I did a *lot* of fun stuff."

"So you played with your little computer and your little lab and went on little nature hikes—" Derlock begins.

Crazy Science Girl inside me wakes up Psycho Ex-Girlfriend and they summon Pilot Susan. It's like a whole convention of us Derlock-haters in here. "And all those *little* skills and all that *little* knowledge that Glisters picked up might keep us alive all the way to Mars," I say. "Call me a sentimental chickie, but I don't consider staying alive to be *little*, at all." There's an awkward silence.

I re-break the ice that I just froze onto the conversation. "I had a *zoomed* childhood, too, I went a lot of places to see n-nillion things just 'cause I liked them."

"I remember," Fleeta says, beaming at me. Maybe I *will* cry some more.

Derlock grunts in exasperation. "I didn't want to hear about your childhoods. I was being sarcastic."

"We didn't feel like hearing your sarcasm, so we talked about our childhoods," I say.

Emerald is sitting up on one elbow; she raises an eyebrow, I shrug, and she says, "Derlock, if you have any ideas that are actually to our benefit—"

"Will you at least have the grace to admit my plan is paying off a lot bigger than anyone could have imagined? When we land on Mars we'll be celebs like nobody else! Our recognition numbers will break all records!"

A long silence. No one quite knows what to say. Back in Baker Lounge, he'd have hypnotized us with that; here and now, it's like trying to remember a foreign language you were never very good at.

"Can you play chess in your head?" Glisters asks me.

"No, and for the first time in my life I wish I could."

Wychee says, "D three."

Glisters replies with "E five."

"B D three."

"N F three."

In minutes, trying to follow their game sends me into deep slumber.

April 26, 2129. On *Virgo*, upbound Earth to Mars. 149 million kilometers from the sun, 165 million kilometers from Mars, 3.9 million kilometers from Earth.

Emerald decides that, since there are only a few huge containers in the vacuum holds, and Glisters says they don't need to be moved, just tied down, most hands will be more valuable on shovels. She says, "Glisters located pressure suit storage. Why don't you take Stack and Derlock up to the vacuum holds and dog the loose stuff down?" Our officer telepathy is getting pretty sharp; I hear that as: *Take these two whiny boys off my hands and make them do something useful.*

Vacuum Cargo Section 1 has cargo walls with a handling deck, and Vacuum Cargo Section 2 has decks and freight elevators. Each of them looks like a warehouse impersonating a submarine. The cargo in them is stored in boxes, cylinders, pyramids, and spheres, some as small as PersKabs, some the size of two-bedroom houses. For the moment walls work like decks and decks work like walls; we have to keep reminding each other of where down will be when it's all stabilized.

In soundless vacuum, we hear only the scrape of our own boots, and our pressure suit radios. Stack is uncharacteristically doing way more than his share of the work; Derlock predictably does much less. We only have to spin three crates around to match hooks with the floor. It goes fast.

When Glisters confirms it's all locked down in both vacuum cargo sections, we airlock out, strip out of the pressure suits, and go to share in the shoveling.

Derlock bounds on ahead and pops through a door, leaving Stack and me to climb down the coretube together. The moment we're alone, Stack says, "I know you won't completely trust me, but I'm with you guys. 100%. Derlock is crazy."

"You sound worried."

"Worried? Sheeyeffinit. I'm *scared*. I always knew he was evil, but I'm starting to think he's been crazy for a long time." Stack's face is usually flat and expressionless with an overlay of contempt, his attempt at styling Knowing Cynic, or maybe old-style Snotty Arrogant Punk, but this isn't his usual suppressed sneer; he looks really afraid. "Derlock was *not* in the lounge where the *Virgo* crew caged most of us," he says quietly. "Glisters, Emerald, and Fleeta went off to finish the tour, after Derlock steered the rest of us into being all rude and I-don't-care and like that, so we were all bottled up watching meeds and eating snacks. Then Derlock talked to the guy watching us, real quiet, and *bzzzp*, Derlock was gone for three hours." Stack works his way crosswise on the handholds toward the doors to the active farm section. "I'm sure he knew something was going to go wrong for Bari and King. I even think maybe he knew that something was going to go wrong for *Virgo*. Last night, before the accident, he talked privately to me about which girl I wanted to have, like he could just give one of you to me. Stuff like that."

"He thought he could *do* that?"

"It's so hard to know!" Frustration is choking him. "After being his bud for so long, I don't know how much is real and how much is Derlock's craziness. Sometimes he imagines having all this power, like it is just going to come to him. Mostly it's internal botflog, stuff he tells himself so often he believes it, he just expects things to work the way he wants them to. But the weird thing is sometimes they *do*. Maybe he was just ready for the accident to happen because he expects to have everything he wants all the time, or maybe he *knew* the accident was going to happen."

"You are suggesting," I point out, "that Derlock murdered a hundred and forty people."

"I'm *saying* I can't convince myself that he *didn't.* Maybe it's just that crazy way he just imagines things will work, because he wants them to, and then, if they do, he thinks he made them happen."

"You think it's just delusions?"

Stack stops climbing for a moment, hanging lightly by the handholds. "I'm not Derlock. If *I* was evil and planning to cause that accident and then take over, *I'd* study the ship till I could do ten times what Glisters is doing. But it's *him*, and *not* me, and the way *he* thinks, probably he knew there was a cockpit in the pod, and he just expected that whatever he did when he took it over would work. He really believes that once he wants a thing to happen, it happens. And, you know, well, the way things are now, with all of us caught here with him . . . that's all I wanted to tell you."

Embarrassed, or maybe afraid, Stack jumps down the coretube in big bounces, grabbing handholds like a crazed monkey. I climb after.

By the time we join shovel duty, they've finished with the mess on the Forest bulkhead and done about a quarter of the rest. Stack and I share a robobarrow; Derlock has partnered with Emerald, and I can hear his voice, constant, low, sounding reasonable, sounding affectionate, sounding sexy, sounding whatever he thinks will work. I remember it, of course—it's only been a couple of days—and I'm glad I'm too far away to hear what he's saying. I just hope she's far enough away, physically or mentally, not to listen.

- - -

When I come back to the cockpit after a fast run-over with my cleanstick, Derlock is sitting next to, and slathering the charm and admiration on, Glisters, who is reveling in having tech stuff to explain and a willing audience. "—the antenna is in the external storage bin just outside this tail-end airlock, not far from where we have to mount it. As soon as one of us is all the way up to speed in an evasuit, and has rehearsed the moves enough, we should be able to put the antenna up and yell for help. But we only get one shot with this antenna, and we can't afford to lose it, so whoever is doing it—"

"Dibs on that," Stack says. "I'll go. When do I start practice?"

"How about after *I've* had some sleep and some time to think through it all?" Glisters says. "So I don't overlook something or have you learn something wrong? A day or two won't matter at all, and like I said, we've got to get this right."

"Why does Stack get to do it?" Derlock says, like it's a trip to the ice cream store.

"He's strong, he volunteered first, and we know he can do it," I say, "Glisters, what's so precious about this antenna? I thought an antenna was just a long wire."

"You're about a hundred years out-of-date. This isn't

even really an antenna; it's a submillimeter-wave detector array."

"Do we have to waste time fussing about how we say it?" Derlock is fishing for a way for me to quarrel with Glisters.

Glisters and I exchange one glance and just bomb Derlock flat with tech talk for the next half hour.

|||||||||||||||||||||||||||||||||||||||||||||||||||||||||||||||||||||||||

Notes for the Interested, #13

Over time, waves get shorter, and frequencies get higher

Every form of communication that will work in space is some form of what physicists call electromagnetic radiation: radio, microwaves, light, X-rays, and other things. The wavelength is the distance between peaks of the electromagnetic waves that it is made of; the frequency is the number of waves that pass by in a second.

Small wavelengths mean big frequencies and vice versa. In 1906, Einstein figured out that in the vacuum of space, all electromagnetic radiation moves at one speed, c, the "speed of light" you've heard about. For any electromagnetic radiation, then, the wavelength times the frequency will be equal to c. (To see why this is so, think of it this way: the electromagnetic waves are like a train passing by. The wavelength is the length of the cars, and the frequency is the number of cars that go by in a given time. If all the trains move at the same speed, just as all electromagnetic waves do, then if a lot of cars go by, it's because they're all short; if the cars are long, fewer cars will go by in the same time.)

Ever since the first radios, people have been using shorter and shorter wavelengths (which means higher and higher frequencies):

Type	When First Used	Wavelengths	Frequencies	Current (2010s) Use
Radio	Pre-1910	Meters	Low 1000s	AM Radio
Microwaves	1940s	Centimeters	High millions, low billions	Radar, spacecraft communication, making popcorn
Submillimeter waves	2050s (in this future)	less than one millimeter	Trillions	Just barely being tried out in laboratories

Why do engineers keep moving toward short wavelengths/ high frequencies? Because of two things they explain in more detail in college physics:

1. **The shorter the wavelength, the tighter the beam can be.** The aperture—the hole the beam comes out of—determines the beam width, and no working aperture can be any smaller than half a wavelength. The tighter the beam, the farther it can reach for the same energy—think about how far a flashlight throws its big circular pool of light compared to how far a laser-pointer throws its tiny dot. At the huge distances between planets, when you're trying to put enough energy to be detected onto an antenna, this makes a huge difference in how much power you need to contact a ship from a station on Earth.

2. **Signal-to-noise ratio.** Signals are easier to pick out

from background noise (or "static") when they have more energy. The energy carried by a photon (particle of electromagnetic radiation) is directly proportionate to its frequency. (This was actually the very first thing discovered in the field of quantum physics). So higher frequencies are "louder" and easier to pick out of background noise, in exactly the same way a police whistle cuts through crowd noise.

In the 2060s of this future, as humans began to venture away from the Earth/moon system, higher frequencies and shorter wavelengths meant you could communicate with spaceships via a tight beam that could be more easily picked out from background noise.

This also meant a different kind of "antenna"—the word is in quote marks because it's not really an antenna at all as we use the term today. Technically an antenna is a conductor that resonates with some frequency of electronic radiation; when it resonates, an electric current forms in the antenna that we can detect and process into a signal.

Any big piece of metal will resonate with radio waves. But submillimeter waves need submillimeter antennae—tiny dots of semiconductor that resonate with their very short waves. Furthermore, to answer a tight-beam signal, it's necessary to know the exact direction it came from (the whole point is not to broadcast to the whole universe, as you did with radio).

So what you really need is two of those detector dots: When a signal shows up strongly in both dots, the line between them is pointing at the source. If you put one dot on the center of the glass covering of a dimple, and scatter dots all over the inside

CROSS SECTION OF A SUBMILLIMETER WAVE DETECTOR DIMPLE

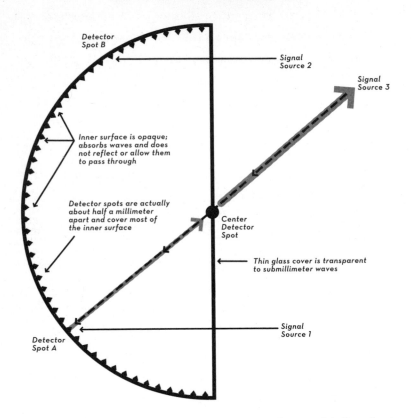

Detector Spot B

Signal Source 2

Signal Source 3

Inner surface is opaque; absorbs waves and does not reflect or allow them to pass through

Detector spots are actually about half a millimeter apart and cover most of the inner surface

Center Detector Spot

Thin glass cover is transparent to submillimeter waves

Signal Source 1

Detector Spot A

Actually, it's only half a centimeter across. Detector spots form a web half a millimeter apart all over the inside; there are 628 detectors on the surface of the dimple, and one in the center. Signal from Source 1 comes into Detector Spot A, but since it didn't also come through the center detector spot, the software ignores it, just like it does the signal from Source 2 coming into Detector Spot B. But signal from Source 3 (black dashed arrow)—which might be a spaceship, a space station, or a transmitter in orbit around one of the planets or the moon—comes in through the center spot *and* Detector Spot A, so the software reports the signal and its direction. To reply to it, a transmitter spot (not shown) next to Detector Spot A sends a signal back toward the center (smaller gray arrow), and the transmitter spot at the center reinforces it by sending the same signal exactly in phase, producing a very strong directional signal (large gray arrow) that goes straight back toward Source 3.

surface of the dimple, then when the center dot detects a sub-millimeter wave, one other dot will also detect it, and a computer can immediately calculate the direction from which dot on the dimple fired. In fact it can immediately return a signal and establish two-way communication just by going through those two dots.

Thus in this future, "antenna" is just the name still used for "the thing the signal goes out through," in much the same way that the front instrument panel on a car is still called the "dashboard," even though it no longer has the function of keeping mud from spraying up from the horses' hooves. The antenna is now a detector array—a surface covered with detector dimples.

It's not something Glisters or Susan could just knock together out of a spool of wire.

‖‖‖

"—can't knock one together out of a spool of wire," Glisters finishes explaining to Derlock, his enthusiasm undiminished. I think about suggesting that Glisters should make sure he's thorough about this, and show Derlock how to derive the frequency-energy relationship from the Heisenberg uncertainty principle, but Derlock glazed over a long time ago. Of course we could have had the same effect by telling him that just trailing a long wire off the tail would anger the antenna gods.

Glisters rides on. "Physically the antenna looks like a 4-meter-long post about 25 centimeters in diameter. But its surface is glass, and under the glass it's mottled with little half-centimeter dimples, and each dimple is lined with an array of receptor spots, connected to its own processor."

It's fun to watch Derlock sit there in shock from the volume of explanation, and I really am interested in what Glisters is saying, but there are other things to get on with, so I say, "All right, I understand now. All those dimples and all those little computers working together are needed to keep a signal focused on one station in a tight beam?"

"That's it," Glisters says. "The antenna can talk back and forth in tight beams to up to 10,000 different stations, or send one really loud-and-bright signal to just one station, but there are no general broadcast stations anymore, there haven't been since before PermaPaxPerity. We have to find stations we can link to in tight beam, ring their bells, and be invited in. The antenna was built to do that— and it would take a *lot* of study, time, and effort for us to build anything that could do it one-tenth as well."

"And *everything* is tightbeam submillimeter nowadays?"

"I don't think *anything* still uses the old longwave radio. Some things still use microwaves, like radar, toys—"

"And ovens," Derlock says, sneering. "Microwave ovens."

"Ovens don't listen," I say. "They just transmit in their own little space, like some people we know. So Glisters, that antenna can't be replaced, right?"

"If I had to build one, I'd try. No promises, but I think I'd be able to learn fast enough to get one built inside a year."

"So if we lose the antenna we have, or break it, we're ultra screwed, and there will be no rescue. This *has* to go right the first time."

He nods. "Exactly."

I look at Stack. "Still want to be the guy?"

Stack smiles—not like anything is fun, but like he likes being where he is, right now. "Oh, yeah, that job is all mine."

9

THE DARK SPACE SOMEWHERE BETWEEN GROUNDING AND FLOGGING

April 26, 2129. On *Virgo*, upbound Earth to Mars. 149 million kilometers from the sun, 165 million kilometers from Mars, 4.0 million kilometers from Earth.

FOR THE NEXT meal, Wychee takes command of the kitchen again, and F.B. and Marioschke absolutely insist on continuing to learn to cook. There's only room for one more helper, so I tell Commander Emerald to grab a nap in the bunk room or I'll mutiny, and put myself on kitchen duty. It's embarrassing that I can't make a sandwich without checking the directions.

Wychee speed-cooks a roast from a crate of raw Argentina beef, shakes up raw vegetables in vinaigrette, and makes a casserole from a couple kinds of fish and vegetables. I feel like a tolerated spy in the kitchen; I suspect they'd all enjoy their gossip and their grumbling more without me.

When dinner is over, Emerald says, "All right, the regulations say we have to hold a meeting—"

Marioschke says, "Oh, that's good. We need to get everybody's feelings out. Can we talk about how I ended up floating around by myself and crying? Because everyone thought what Glisters and Emerald were doing was so important?"

Emerald says, quietly, "Marioschke, it's supposed to be a business meeting. The Spacefarer's Code says we have to ratify articles, and officially elect a commander, pilot, engineer, and steward."

"Do we *have* to have a commander? Isn't that like saying one person is better than another?"

The room is really, really quiet.

F.B. says, "Commander, I guess this is where I bring in the stuff you asked me to look up. I found a set of model ship's articles, suggested by the Space Patrol for ships where the officers are dead. Should—"

Fleeta asks, "So those are like, articles about building model ships?"

"It's a list of things that the survivors in a ship's company agree to, until the company or the UN gets them a proper set of officers," F.B. says. "Should I just read them off?"

"We need to discuss," Marioschke says.

"That's what we're going to do," I say. "F.B. will read the suggested articles, and then we'll discuss whether we—"

"I mean a discussion," Marioschke says. "About our feelings. About my feelings. We need to get those out."

"Read the articles, F.B.," I say.

F.B. starts off with "'Article I, all conscious survivors

now on board shall be organized into a crew under a commander, whose authority shall be governed by the General Spacefaring Code. Article II, The surviving ship's company shall also elect a pilot who shall be second in command and command in the commander's absence or incapacity; an engineer who shall be third in command with primary responsibility for mechanical and informational operation of the ship; a steward who shall be fourth in command with primary responsibility for maintenance and dispensation of the ship's provisions, including air, water, heat, light, and food. These four officers shall serve at the pleasure of the general meeting.'"

"That means it matters how we feel about them," Marioschke says, "and everyone is making this big deal about all this space-law stuff and *not* considering my feelings."

F.B. looks at Emerald and me; we nod, he shrugs and reads on. "'Article III, All other officers shall be appointed and serve at the pleasure of the commander.'" It doesn't take F.B. much time to read through all eighteen of them; the most interesting is Article XVI, under which we're giving Emerald the power to execute us for mutiny if two other elected officers concur. With Derlock around, that's probably just prudent.

The election is fast: We ratify the articles, unmodified. We elect Emerald as commander with 7 votes, with Marioschke not voting on account of staring at the floor and wiping her eyes, and Derlock voting for himself. Then we quickly elect me pilot, Glisters engineer, and Wychee— who seems startled—steward. Each time there's one vote for Derlock and one abstention on grounds of sulking.

"Now," Emerald says, "we need to set watches, and then since everyone looks pretty tired I think we—"

Not looking up from the floor she's been staring at, Marioschke starts keening and sobbing. This chickie can *wail.*

Feeling stupid, I ask, "Marioschke, what is the matter?"

"This isn't a *meeting* at all," she says. "This is people talking business *and* doing deals *and* having their little elections—" She's working into a rhythm where each *and* is real deep gulp-snort of a sob. The sound of it is so much more interesting than what she's saying that I blur out for some sentences as the *and*s get louder and more gaspy. "—*and* setting up one person to be better than another one *and* all kinds of, *and, and, and*, sheeyeffinit, *and* it's all *bullshit!*" She screams the word. "I wanted a *meeting.* A meeting is where we talk about our *feelings.* Because people *have feelings*, you know, and I'm very empathetic and I need to be there to help people with their spiritual growth about their feelings and instead you all started deciding all this stuff, and there were not any feelings at all."

Pop always says if you need to look like you mean it, take a deep breath and let it out with your face relaxed, and it looks like you have thought everything through. I keep my face expressionless, wait for Marioschke to draw a long breath, and keep thinking at everyone, *Nobody else say a word.*

Finally Marioschke sighs and looks up.

I ask, "Marioschke, where are we? What's going on?"

"See, you don't even know or care—"

"I am trying to find out whether *you* know, because I'm starting to doubt it."

That stops her, for a second. She glares at me. Being treated like you're crazy really screws up acting crazy for attention.

Then I see the little wheels turn behind her eyes and think *Brace yourself! Poetry alert!*

She says, "We're right in the dark heart of secrets where authority crushes our spirits, and authority says our lives depend on this and that, but it doesn't matter if we live, if we can only live with crushed spirits—"

"Is your spirit crushed?" Derlock asks her.

"*Everyone* here's spirit is crushed, I'm just the only one who sees—"

"And because your spirit is crushed, you don't care if you live?"

She styles a real big-eyed teary expression. "That's exactly what I feel—"

He kicks against the bulkhead, flinging himself across the room like a missile, hands outstretched to pin her neck against the wall, and starts to squeeze her throat in one hand, using the other to knock her ineffectual, fluttering hands out of his way, driving his hip into her pelvis so she can't push him away with her legs. He slips into a cross grip on her collar and tightens it; she struggles frantically.

We all pile in, slapping and punching Derlock, pulling his hands away from her. Then I get a thumb-and-pinky combination on him, locking him up tight with an arm behind his back, and slip my free hand around to threaten his eyes with my fingers. "Limp now or blind forever," I murmur into his ear.

He says nothing, but he goes limp. Wychee helps me bind him in a hog-tie-noose combination. I mentally thank Sensei Kronstadt again.

Emerald is cradling Marioschke, who is gasping for air and sobbing, rubbing her throat.

Derlock's voice is calm and level, as if machine-generated. "See, Marioschke, for one second there you felt afraid of being killed. That's what *we're* all worried about. Because whether there's something Glisters doesn't know about or something just breaks, something could happen and we might all be dying any second, like you were afraid of dying right then. And if you won't accept that we're afraid of being killed and we don't have time for your philosophochickie sheeyeffinit—fuck you. Because no one, not even me, has time for you and your pwecious special wittle feewings." It creeps me out that his voice is not harsh or sarcastic, even when he puts on the baby talk; it is perfectly level and calm, despite the way his twitching legs threaten to tighten the line around his neck.

I see he's got a major case of tented pants. He sees me seeing that, and grins and winks at me. "Now, didn't that make the point so much more clearly than all that arguing?" Derlock says.

Marioschke is sobbing, still terrified, hanging on like Emerald is her teddy bear.

Wychee says, "I think I'd better take her to the bunk room for a while. If you need an officer's vote on anything about Derlock, count me yes to indict, yes to convict, max on the penalty." When she leads Marioschke out, the fear in the girl's face is unbearable just to see.

Derlock turns his chin quietly, trying to loosen his noose; I reach over and reposition his jaw with the knife edge of my hand, keeping him where he belongs.

"Well," I say, "good thing we voted in Article VI, we already need it. F.B., what does the General Spacefaring Code say about assault?"

"*Extra* fun for the kiddies," Derlock says, "playing policeman."

"We're not the ones who jumped a crewmate," Emerald reminds him. "And skip the part about how you had to do it. Eventually she'd've shut up and gone along—"

Derlock screams, *"Stack!"*

"No," Stack says. "I think these guys want to get home alive. I don't believe you do. I'm with them."

Article VI of the General Spacefaring Code gives many options, none of which actually looks like it'll work. There is a list of suggested electric shocks with volts and amps for each offense, and a force-of-impact, number, and location as an alternative if we want to flog him. It would be satisfying, but if we just inflict pain and then turn him loose he'll be a million times as dangerous.

It provides for locking him up for two months, but then he'll have escaped from work by being an asshole, not something we want him crowing about in front of everyone else.

We end up putting him on house arrest for a month—he can only work, eat, stay in his bunk, or sit where an officer can watch him—with a suspended-if-he-behaves sentence of a dozen shocks on the buttocks and confinement in a storage locker for a month. Obviously having inherited his father's lawyering genes, he argues that "like that" isn't a precise enough definition. I give him a more precise definition of "shut up or else" and we clip a monitor on his ankle and send him to his bunk.

Afterward, in the cockpit, we have a little officers' meeting. Emerald says, "I feel like a twentieth-century mommy in an old meed, telling him he's grounded, but it's better than letting him get away with it."

I say, "I still think we might have made a mistake in not flogging him."

She shrugs. "Hey, everything we do is a best guess based on imperfect knowledge."

Glisters makes a small uncomfortable inarticulate noise.

"Exactly," Emerald says. "Till today I had no idea why any human being might want to know astronomy, cooking, or jiu-jutsu. If I catch you all reading up on flogging, I promise I won't think you're a pervert."

Since neither Glisters nor I really wants to sleep, we're the first watch. "As a favor to me," Emerald says, "I want you to take Marioschke on your watch. She can just hang out or do tutorials or something, but she skipped half the work today, playing crazy-scared, and she even admits that's what she was doing, and then she pulled that sheeyeffinit at the meeting."

"She did okay shoveling mud," I point out. "And she looked pretty messed up after what Derlock did. He tried to kill her, you know."

Emerald shakes her head. "She likes dirt and plants. And we *all* almost got killed. I agree, she's not Derlock, we can get her to do her share, but *not* if we let her think that working is doing us a favor. So she has to stand a watch, right from the start. I'm taking Derlock, and that's enough problem; Wychee and F.B. will have their hands full just learning what they need to know. So guys, it's a favor but she has to be on *someone's* watch, and you two are the most likely ones to start her off right."

"Won't she be mad at me about the things I said?"

Glisters does a balancer with his outspread hand. "I think you win on comparison, Susan. You didn't pin her to the wall by the neck. Sure, Commander, we'll take her on. Make sure everyone fastens the acceleration nets on their bunks; we'll do the last accelerations and then fire off the course correction on this watch."

To our surprise, after the others have gone off to bed, and Marioschke joins us, she's almost contrite, sitting and working on tutorials about milligrav cooking and first aid.

Glisters runs two more thruster bursts, killing the last tumbling components in the pod's motion, with us hanging on in the cockpit. "At least now everything will be more or less pointed the way it was designed to be, milligrav outward along the hull, and near weightlessness in the coretube," he says. "That just leaves the course correction."

"How soon, and how long will it take?" I ask.

"The sooner we do it the more effect it has, and I'm all set up. We'll be done in two hours."

"And that just means one-tenth of a g toward the tail, right?"

"Less than that. That's what's normal for eleven engines running for ten hours, and they eat up three and three-quarters out of four iceballs. We only have two engines and one iceball, and we still need to save a quarter of it for maneuvering and to replace leakage. The calculation here is showing two hours of 4% g, and then we're done."

"Hunh, well, then I guess, what are we waiting for?"

"Well, the officer of the watch should give the order."

"The—oh, me. Sure. Do it."

It's one of the moments when I'm least like Pop in an old meed.

We don't really have to stay in our chairs in the cockpit. We were scrambling around in much higher and more irregular gravity earlier. Still, it's a good time for Glisters to walk me through all the things he's found out about *Virgo*, where all the tutorials are, and how to run the ship and find information in general. I'm tired, and Susan the Celeb-to-Be Bitch is shocked at how easily I relate to a big-headed pink pervo boy, but Crazy Science Girl has found a new best friend. I miss Fleeta yet again.

I must have drifted off from tiredness, because I seemed to hear Derlock saying, *till she got caught, her world was a paradise, and she'll still never be sad again,* and I say, "That makes me so sad and angry."

"I know," Glisters says, "when I read about real-time analysis software for submillimeter communication I'm constantly in tears of rage, myself."

I wake with a start. "How long was I out?"

"About half an hour. Marioschke and I were playing Go. We both thought you should sleep. I was going to wake you up for the end of boost, anyway, and that's coming up . . . now."

The distant rumble, the vibration of the engines passing through the ship, stops at once, and the chair is no longer pushing upward at me.

10

A GWEAT BIG BOX
OF FWUFFY

MARIOSCHKE SAYS, "WELL, um, guys, can I apologize for making myself such a pain? I mean, I still think we don't need all this hierarchy and bureaucracy, but I accept that you're just trying to get home, and if it makes you feel better to be all officers and things that's fine. I'll just try to be helpful and someone you can depend on."

I say, diplomatically I hope, "Well, we'll be glad to have your help."

"That's fair," she says. "Can I ask you for one very big favor, Susan?"

"You can always ask," I point out, "and I can always say no if I don't think it's something I should do."

"I—um—well, now that I can at least sort of fly, and I'm not nearly as scared, could you take me out to the windows? And be with me while I look out?" She looks away from me before miserably admitting, "I'm so tired of being so afraid of that."

My heart melts. "Sure. Glisters, you don't need us for anything?"

"As far as I can tell, the ship probably doesn't need any

of us right now," Glisters says. "Run along and have fun, kids."

On the way to the Pressurized Cargo Section, Marioschke flails, tumbles, loses grips, bumps into things, and rages at herself for being so awkward, but she mostly goes where she intends to; I can tell, another day and she'll be like anyone else.

At the window, she says, "Is it safe to stretch out on the window to look outside?"

"As safe as anything in space is," I say. "You're looking at space through 2 meters of water, which is enough to stop the radiation. Micrometeorites usually just bounce off the outer window—it's single-piece sapphire—you could jump on the windows all day in ice skates and never make a scratch. But even if there's a rare meteorite so big and fast it gets through, it loses so much speed going through the water that it can't penetrate the inner hull. Then the ice forming in the hole self-seals it, and one of the little crawlers comes by eventually and builds a patch. So the windows are not dangerous. Never, never, never."

"Okay," she says. "And thanks for over-doing the reassurance. I promise I'll try not to always need it."

She lays down on the window, putting her hands around her face to see better. I join her. We sit out one flash of bright sunlight, and then we've rotated into the shadow and stars.

She asks, "So the little blue ball is the Earth?"

"Yep, that's it. And that bright little white dot way over to the left of it? The moon."

"And can we see Mars ahead of us?"

"Actually it's more to the side than ahead. You know how when you're in a PersKab and it's going up to join express traffic, the way that the traffic you're going to join runs parallel to you while you're in the approach lane, till eventually you match speeds with it? It's more like that than like going to a place on the map."

"And it's—"

"Right over that way," I say. "Shut your eyes and roll." We roll onto our backs to escape the blast of brilliant sunlight. "When the stars come back, I'll show you. Mars is in Capricorn right now."

"I just looked it up and the almanac said it was in Aquarius."

"I mean Mars is in the same part of the sky as the constellation," I said. "Astrology is different. They haven't corrected their charts in two thousand years. Here, the sun's setting again, I'll show you."

I discover she's never actually learned any of the night sky, and didn't really know what a constellation was. She's surprised that Capricorn looks a lot more like bunched panties than a goat; Sagittarius looks at least as much like an open suitcase as a centaur shooting a bow; and Leo looks like a sick dog with a tiny head, not like a lion. I guess her world is rapidly becoming a wider place.

My phone zizzes. "Hey, Glisters. What's up?"

"The box of fwuffies just messaged the main life support computer that it's going to dump out the fwuffies in three hours if we don't do it first. I was going to go open the box, and see what comes out, just to have something to do. You guys want to come along?"

I glance at Marioschke. She gives me a thumbs-up; I detect some possible spirit of adventure, and grin back at her.

"We're on our way," I tell Glisters. "Wait to open it till we get there; let's all be surprised together."

"What's a fwuffy?" Marioschke asks as we bounce along the handling deck.

I explain about the huge suspended animation container, and that as far as we could figure it out, we had the choice of telling it to kill the fwuffies, or bringing the fwuffies out of suspended animation. "And Commander Em doesn't like to kill anyone's pet."

"I wouldn't want to either. Hey, this bouncing-along thing is *fun*."

"Yeah, watch your head—"

"Yike!" She barely catches herself before slamming into a cargo wall. "Yeah, I see what you mean." She bounces forward, manages to get her feet above her as she passes a cargo wall, and shoots back down onto the handling deck, catching herself with her hands and rolling forward into a rise, and bouncing between the bottom edges of the walls and the cargo decks the rest of the way to the nose, like an awkward, obese porpoise who has just discovered fun.

At Cargo Wall 2, we leap and airswim up to the suspended animation crate. Glisters is just arriving from above, having come through the coretube. He pulls the control panel open. "All the lights are green. I wish I knew what a fwuffy *is*."

"Me, too," I say. "I'd just as soon not turn a hundred intelligence-enhanced baby crocodiles loose in here."

"Hah," Glisters says, clicking through the info screens. "Here we are. *Care notes. Feed a mixture of whole fruits and vegetables with hay or other fiber-rich plant matter. Plenty of exercise in large spaces is essential and should be combined with free, vigorous play for optimal bonding with the child.* So whatever a fwuffy is, it's not carnivorous, and you can leave it in an open space with a little kid."

"Still doesn't say anything about how many of them there are," I point out, "and that's an awfully big box, so I supposed at worst there might be a lot of fwuffies. Well, here goes, I guess as officer of the watch, it's my job to be responsible." I reach forward and press the button that says RELEASE.

For a moment, nothing happens. Then the front half of that immense blue-gray cube shudders and shakes. The sides slide toward the gravity, then fall away. We're looking at its back end, so it takes a moment to perceive that it is something besides a wall of bright pink leather.

It's *massive*.

There's just one of it, perched on top of the lower part of the crate, which holds the suspended animation machinery. It would fit, maybe, into two big walk-in closets. My mind starts to get hold of it; that's a ropy pink tail longer than my arm, switching back and forth between two huge legs. I can't help noticing, too, that it's a male.

I'm about to say, *oh my god it's*—when he turns around and looks at us with big, pink, huge-eyelashed eyes, batting them at us. "Hewwo," he says, with a cartoon-character speech defect. "My name is Fwuffy. What's yaws?"

Yours, I translate mentally.

"Uh, I'm Susan, this is Marioschke—"

"It's a *horton*," Glisters says, "*Ultra* illegal –"

"I am pweezed to meet you, too, Hawton Iwegall."

"Um, no, my name is Glisters. I meant that you are a horton."

"Awwight, pweezed to meet you, *Gwistas*. But I am *Fwuffy*." He seems very offended.

"Of course you are," Marioschke says. "Of course you are." She airswims around him, lands in front of him, and rubs his face.

He rubs back, and she flies up against Cargo Wall 3. "Sowwy," he says. "Didn't huht?"

"Didn't hurt," Marioschke confirms. She bumps the wall, pushes off, and airswims back to him; now that she's not thinking about it, she's only a little awkward. "We just have to get used to each other."

Then he looks down. They design them to have such expressive faces that all three of us, seeing his sheer terror, fly to him, grabbing his feet and making sure he stays on his precarious perch.

His face goes blank. "Your horton unit," he says, in a completely different voice, a much deeper one with no speech problems, "is intensely afraid of falling, and must be safeguarded against it. If the fear has been triggered in a situation that is other than dangerous, the issue should be clarified to the horton."

Then Fwuffy seems to crumple. "I'm so *afwaid.*" It's his little kid voice again.

Glisters and I are looking at each other, with no idea what to do, but Marioschke says, "Listen closely, Fwuffy. We are in space. It feels like you're going to fall but it is not falling. It only feels like falling. It's actually flying, and flying is very nice."

"Fwying?"

"Flying. Yes, you can *fly* here in space. When we get to Mars, then you can't, but right here and now, you can fly, and it's not like falling as long as you are careful and fly the way we teach you to fly."

"I didn't know I could fwy."

"Only in space. Not on Mars."

"Okay."

"Now let us teach you how to fly."

"Awwight."

Glisters and I share a glance, reaching an instant decision that Marioschke is now the Technical Specialist for Pink Pachydermic Issues.

One big part of me is thinking *here's a really* massive *problem,* but another part is ultra glad we didn't kill him; if nothing else, he's definitely gotten Marioschke's mind off herself.

Fwuffy delivers a little canned speech that is probably the equivalent of a lost-and-found tag, explaining that he is supposed to go to Mars to be the best friend of "Wachel Webecca Wodwiguez, and she named me Fwuffy. Yi!" He has drifted a few centimeters above his narrow perch; in less than a thousandth of a g, he only has to shuffle his feet a little to do that. "Am I fwying?"

"You are," Marioschke says. "Let us teach you how to control it." She, Glisters, and I gently push his feet back down. "Now don't move your feet till we tell you to. We will be in space a long time before we get to Mars."

"That's sad. Wachel will be waiting for me."

I don't say anything to Fwuffy, of course, but I wonder. It takes a couple years to grow something like Fwuffy in a tank, and twice as long to load the personality. If Rachel named him, and her parents had to go through all the illegal back channels to get her a pink horton with a speech defect like her own, it might easily have taken most of a decade, and since kids who talk like that are maybe four to eight years old, usually, there's a good chance Rachel is now older than I am. More likely, she's barely aware he's coming.

I'm glad he and Marioschke found each other; everybody in the world, even pink elephants from test tubes, deserves to fall in love with something that will love them back.

For the second time today I feel like I might cry about poor old Stanley. Stupid old dog had such a big heart he didn't realize he was using it to love a celeb-to-be. "Fwuffy, we will get you to Rachel, I promise. But for right now you need to learn to fly."

"Absofuckinglutely," Glisters says.

In the same voice that explained the horton's fear of falling, Fwuffy says, "This horton unit is required to discourage the use of foul language. A record is being maintained." Then back in his little kid voice, "Gwistas, pwease don't talk that way."

It takes no time to teach Fwuffy to fly, or fwy, or really sort of paddle. He's hardwired so that when anyone with authority tells him he has nothing to be afraid of, he just stops being afraid, totally, completely, and right away.

We tell him to jump off and paddle down to the handling deck below, and that we'll straighten him out if he tumbles. We lift him and walk him forward, so that all he has to do is push once with his back legs; he spirals, in his aerial elephant-paddle, gently to the deck as we airswim around him, helping him stay upright and coaching him. It takes ten minutes or so, but we're not in a hurry.

Down on the deck, we lift him up, carrying him forward, to let him get the feel of flying forward. On the next bound he learns to take off; two more slow, gentle, elephant-paddling-in-air bounds, and he's most of the way to the tail-end bulkhead, and he has figured out flying about as well as any pink elephant ever has, saying "Whee!" and plainly having fun.

I swear, if I ever have kids, I'm buying them that fear-switch-off gene, even if it turns them pink and makes their ears grow as big as their heads. They can all date Glisters's kids, if necessary.

Aerodynamically, Fwuffy's sort of a canard design; the

ears and the trunk have more possibilities than his ass and tail, so he's always steering with a bow rudder, and therefore at risk of going into a flat spin, but that seems to be part of the fun. We go back and forth a few times; as his "graduation" into flying without help or spotting, he flies the length of the cargo handling deck in a single soaring triple roll, coming down as lightly as dandelion fluff.

"Just be careful whenever you're coming a long way in the direction of gravity," Glisters says. "Like coming down from the coretube up over our heads, or anything like that. Because if you're going too fast, you won't be able to control it."

"Okay, I'll watch out. Thanks, Gwistas." Fwuffy looks uncomfortable.

Marioschke asks, "Are you hungry? Thirsty? Need the bathroom?"

"I don't fit in a bathwoom but I'm housebwoken, so I need a pwace you say is okay to make poop."

There's a big washing cubicle on the cargo handling deck, one that seals on all sides, and we route the drain flow to the composting tanks in the farm.

While Fwuffy is in there, I ask Glisters, "Why *are* hortons so illegal, anyway?"

"Same reason there are no more upgrapes, at least not legal ones."

"Upgrapes—oh, the enhanced chimps. That's right, they were all over the news when we were little. What happened to *them*?" I ask.

Glisters shudders. "They were supposed to be like permanent affectionate five-year-olds."

"And they turned dangerous?"

"Not the way you mean. Something about the brain upgrades worked too well. They didn't stop at the five-year-old level, or even close; they were like fairly brainy people."

"Where did they go?"

He drops his voice to a murmur. "Hey, no reason for Fwuffy to hear this on his first day out. Some upgrapes were sterilized and sold to collectors, locked up away from the public somewhere. Some are in research labs, where they're trying to understand what went wrong. Jimbo, the one they were calling the spokesape, who applied to take the PotEvals? He's just gone, and the PermaPaxPerity authority is notified if you try too hard to search for news stories about him. Anyway, hortons turned out to be the same kind of smart, so now they're the same kind of illegal."

"What's so bad about being smart?"

"PermaPaxPerity authorities don't usually explain anything to anybody, it's part of avoiding having any kind of politics people could fight about. If you want my guess, it's two things: upgraded animals would set off some of the religious and political nuts among the mineys, and also, if there were enough technicians out there with access to the process, someone would be applying it to people. You want to compete for an eenie slot with somebody who has as big an advantage at language and math over you, as you have over an elephant or a chimp? We already have too many mineys who could've been talent-eenies, and the world can only consume so much work at the eenie, professional level. Smart, bored mineys already riot, sabotage, hack, prank, form cults, start weird movements, and rebel lots of ways the PermaPaxPerity Authority doesn't like. What if they were all twice as smart and therefore twice as bored?"

"I thought I remembered meeds that said that hortons turn killer at puberty."

"Susan, how much truth is there in meeds? Come on, you're a pro. Isn't that story too convenient to be—"

Fwuffy emerges from the cargo washing area, and Glisters nods and holds up a finger—*Later.*

After a moment of looking around, and perhaps trying to estimate how we feel about taking care of him, our new, big pink friend says, "I'm hungwy."

Through his wristcomp, Glisters finds several tonnes of argon-packed, enzyme-arrested Guatemalan bananas, which solves the problem for the moment. Fwuffy turns out to prefer them peels-on.

Once he has eaten his fill, he flies with us back to the cockpit. Since we don't need the back rows of seats, we fold them into the floor, which makes plenty of room for him to float; for convenience we give him a cargo net he can weave around through the handholds, so he won't drift into where we're working while he's asleep. Two minutes after we pull the net over him, which Marioschke tells

Fwuffy is "like us tucking you in," he's sound asleep and snoring. I guess he's had a big day.

"There's Prime Bitterroot Valley Hay in a big crate on Cargo Wall 19 in Vacuum Cargo Section 2—some Martians were bringing it in for their horses, god knows why—which should be enough to feed him for at least three months," Glisters says. "And if he's anything like his elephant an-cestors, he shouldn't have fruit all the time, hay should be the main thing he eats, at least till we get some fresh grass and bamboo growing in the farm sections. Emerald can put F.B. on hay-fetching duty when their watch comes on."

I giggle. "Wow, are *they* in for a surprise."

Fwuffy snores loudly, and rolls over slowly, waving his legs in the air in a dream. We all watch in awe.

Marioschke suddenly snorts with laughter. "The other watch was going to get up at the same time as the watch on duty, which I guess officially makes us the graveyard shift. So they'll be coming in here all together, Emerald and all—"

Glisters rests a hand on both our shoulders. "Well, if Fwuffy wakes up an hour before they do, that should be just enough rehearsal time."

11

THE BEST STEWARD WITHIN
TEN MILLION MILES

EMERALD AND WYCHEE swim in through the hatch together, and blurt, "What is *that*?"

All of us, including Fwuffy, simultaneously say,
"What's what?"

She gawps at us. Fwuffy says, "You must be Commanda Emewawd."

"It talks," F.B. says, from behind her.

"Why not? You do," Fwuffy says—another product of
our careful coaching.

Emerald's consternation dissolves into laughter. "And
I am guessing that this is Fwuffy. No offense, Fwuffy, but
I was expecting a larger number of something smaller."

So we explain that situation, and then Glisters
walks everybody through all the things that have to be
watched—I need the review, too!—and what to do about
the few things that we can do anything about. "So, if you
all feel like that's what you need to know, I guess it's time
to leave you to it."

"I'm ready," F.B. says. This must be the first time
anyone ever actually counted on him for anything, and

it looks like he's desperate not to screw it up.

"Whatever," Derlock says.

Emerald looks at me, and I almost say, *What? What?* before I realize I'm the ranking officer on the watch.

So I make something up, and say, "Commander Emerald, the cockpit is in good order, and I request that you relieve me of the watch."

She's smiling back at me; we both know it's silly and we both feel we ought to do it. "I relieve you of the watch, Pilot Susan. Go get some rest, you've sure earned it."

In the big bathing room, I throw my soggy-with-crud coverall into the Phreshor, then climb into a showersphere; I'm glad there are five of them, so no waiting. Showerspheres sense your body, and aim extra-hot extra-forceful jets at the big muscle groups and gentle sprays on your face, and balance out the force so you turn over slowly in the center of the sphere. All I have to do is remember to breathe and stay relaxed, and in about five minutes the showersphere has tumbled me around in a swirl of hot soapy water, pounded all the crud of a twenty-hour day off me, and massaged most of the tension out of my muscles, and, with bursts of warm, drying air, made me feel perfectly clean. When I airswim out I feel ready to sleep for a million years.

I hear Marioschke's showersphere releasing her, and Glisters's is shutting down, too.

"I sleep nude," I say, "and grew up in a family that was pretty casual about nudity, so a glance is okay, but stare and you're dead, and I decide what staring is."

"Same rules here," Marioschke said, "except I probably won't notice the staring."

Glisters chuckles, still not opening his sphere. "It's okay, you all go on ahead, and I'll just miss my chance for lookies. The truth is *I'm* shy—I sleep in PJs. So as much as I'd love to be out there shooting pictures, I'll wait till you all go and then change into my PJs in here. And I've already recorded you both more than once, I know that you're beautiful but I can control myself anyway."

As we airswim to the bunk room, Marioschke asks, "Would you say we've just been respected or insulted?"

"Respected," I say. "It's Glisters. What else would it be?"

"Yeah." She smiles a little. "We're lucky we have him."

"Yeah," I say, because it's true.

I'm just closing my faceshade when Glisters airswims in, wearing his pajamas.

It turns out I'm the one that stares. *"Ducks?!"*

"I also have clowns and teddy bears. Mom ordered the patterns when I was little, and being Mom, she made it a perpetual order and never rechecked it. So every year it messages me to ask for my size and sends me new clown, duck, and teddy bear jammies. It's okay, it reminds me I have a mom and she *wants* to care about me." He climbs up into his bunk, over mine, and turns around to face me for an instant. "When I travel on her account the hotel always brings me a pancake sandwich with a strawberry jam smiley face in the morning, and I've never changed that order either."

"Glisters, no wonder you're such a great ship's engineer."

"What? Why?"

"Because you're such a lousy pornographer."

"That doesn't make any sense," he grumbles. "I'll never understand girls." But he's smiling as he says it. I pull down my faceshade, and in the perfect darkness, I'm asleep instantly.

April 27, 2129. On *Virgo*, upbound Earth to Mars.
149 million kilometers from the sun, 164 million kilometers from Mars, 4.5 million kilometers from Earth.

I wake up at about one in the afternoon, totally arbitrary ship time. Digging out clean clothes from my scootsack, I look up to see Glisters's head just emerging from the face-shade. "Uh, sorry." He retreats like a turtle into its shell.

"Oh, no," I say. "Come out here and show me your ducks, jammie-slut."

Laughing, he rolls out of bed, grabs his scootsack, kicks off, and airswims into the bathroom. I take a minute to run my smartcomb around on my head, letting it put everything back to where the style template says it should go, and stroke my face with the coswand. Supposedly they're good for years without recharging or reloading; I wonder how soon I'll get tired of my face and hair? Or if anyone will care, including me?

Glisters returns, dressed. "Going up to the cockpit?"

"Probably the quickest way to find food," I say. "Let's go."

Wychee intercepts us just before we turn into the spur

corridor. "Come up to the kitchen. I just finished feeding Marioschke and Stack, so I have plenty of breakfast set up and ready to go for you guys."

"What are *they* doing?"

"They took off with that bizarre pink elephant to take inventory in the farm sections. My request. As your steward I want to know what we have growing and what we should maybe think about planting."

As we airswim in, I smell the eggs, cheese, and bacon. "This is wonderful. Do you really think we need to start things in the farm?"

Wychee shrugs. "Suppose we get rescued at Mars like we're planning to, and we've been farming all along. Then we leave behind a lot of food, and we've done some unnecessary work. Suppose we don't get rescued at Mars and we haven't been farming. My inventory of what's in cargo—that was the first thing I did on my watch, that steward thing, you know—shows us running out of food about a hundred days after Marspass, and as a couple of people once pointed out to me, we don't have anywhere to go shopping out here. And we can't change our minds and just grow a bunch of crops real fast if it turns out we were wrong. So I think it's better to do a little extra work, and have it turn out to be unnecessary, than save a little bit of work, and go hungry for more than a year."

"Wychee," I say, "I don't think we could have picked a better steward, and I'm so glad you took the job."

"Speaking as your superior officer," Glisters says, spreading jam thick on a warm biscuit, "you have just successfully bribed *me* into giving you one hell of a good performance review."

"Thanks," Wychee says, "but I'm going to pretend it's because I'm hot."

"Actually, as *Glisters's* superior officer," I say, "I'm going to overrule him and say it's because you've been doing a great amazing awesome wonderful job and we're so grateful to have you with us."

She looks a little stunned by the compliment, and does an abrupt change of subject. "So is it okay for officers to gossip?"

I say, "Mandatory. What do we have?"

Wychee shrugs. "Maybe just my overactive imagination?"

"Does it involve Derlock?" I ask.

"Um, yes, actually."

"Then if it's bad, you're not imagining it. He's good at making you think there's something wrong with you, but if something about him creeps you out, you're right."

"Well, the part I am sure I'm not imagining is that he's ultra cranking up a charm campaign on Emerald. Ultra ultra. I've seen him go after nice-looking girls and guys before, you know, I mean he—well, he'll say or do almost anything for almost anyone who can do something for him—" She looks like she's trying to find a way to say something; I realize that I'm the reason.

I explain, "You ultra don't have to worry about hurting my feelings. Yeah, I was about to declare with him before, and all that sheeyeffinit, but that's *over*. I stopped letting him fool me. Or I stopped fooling myself. Which might be the same thing." I squeeze a sip of warm coffee into my mouth. "The problem is I *do* understand the guy. We're alike, in a lot of ways. We both just have to be on top, any time we see people stacked up. Can't stand to finish anywhere except first, can't stand to be anywhere but first in line, top of the pyramid . . . if there's a game, we want to win. If there's a list, we want to be at the top of it. We're the horrible two-year-old that wants all the attention at the family reunion, and the horrible hundred-and-nine-year-old that still wants all the attention.

"You want to know what I saw in him? Somebody I could talk to about what really mattered to me, which was winning the whole big game. Realism here, I maybe could have been an okay *hobby* scientist or actor, but I didn't have the kind of talent that the talent-eenie actors and the talent-eenie scientists do. So the only ladder I could climb all the way was the celeb-eenie ladder." *Besides,* I think, but don't say, *what was there left to do? My best friend was turning herself into a vegetable, I let them talk me into killing my dog, my mom said she never wanted to see me again, and Pop only wanted me as a prop for his stupid* Revive the Family! *rallies.* "So I set out to hit just the right mix of scandal, sympathy, and interest about as soon as I turned hot. Derlock did the same thing—it's what most of our pillow talk was about. He was the first person I ever met, other than me, who had really analyzed what the pathway up to the top looked like.

"So I understand him, I feel what he's doing, ultra better than the rest of you do. Every move he makes, it's about pushing up his recognition score."

Glisters looks slightly ill and strongly disbelieving. "And you're telling us that *you're* like that?"

"You recorded some of my best meeds. Did they look spontaneous?"

"Yeah." He shakes his head. "Now I feel dumb."

"You are not dumb, and you know it. I'm just a good fake."

"I just thought the camera loved you. All right, so how soon are you going to stab us all in the back?"

"Well, that's what I *don't* get about Derlock. He called it right—we are already all going to be awesomely famous celeb-eenies as soon as we get home. So to me, that implies we should get home in one comfortable piece as quickly and safely as we can. But Derlock . . . he wants to be famous for . . . no, make that infamous. His father is famous for being a son of a bitch, and Derlock wants to be a bigger son of a bitch than his father ever was. Has Stack told you—"

As if his name had called him into existence, Stack appears. "Hey, Glisters, you're up! Would you have time to run over some of the antenna stuff with me before my watch starts? We'd have like half an hour?"

"Sure." The two of them are out of there like twin rockets.

"Poor Glisters. Afraid of what he might learn if he stays here." Wychee takes a sip of coffee. "Wow—look under the tree and find the apple, and it wants to grow into an even bigger tree. Your father is famous for playing likable people and telling us all to treat each other better. Derlock's father is famous for keeping really vile scum out of prison, turning them loose on us, and telling us all we ought to admire them. So here you both are, trying to outdo your crazy parents."

"You know, I wish I was nice like you."

"I don't. I have niced myself into second place for my entire life." Even though it's just a couple of seconds, the pause is so awkward that I am relieved when she says, "Look, I know something you don't."

"Lately everyone knows a lot of things I don't," I say. "It's that kind of adventure."

"I bet you and Derlock talked a lot about strategies for becoming famous, didn't you? And checked your recognition scores every six hours?"

I nod. It's embarrassing but true. "I studied those numbers like no numbers have ever been studied. At one point, no joke, I built a computer model to correlate my exposed cleavage area against my recognition score."

Wychee laughs; such a strangely happy sound after my glum self-accusation. "Hits per tits!" she says.

That derails the conversation until the giggles fade into an awkward silence. My turn to blurt. "How come you and I hardly ever talked one-on-one the whole time we were moes together, when you're so interesting?"

"I thought you were stuck-up, cold as a snake, and wouldn't want to be friends with a lesser mortal like me. Which, it turns out, I was right about, but things have changed. And if you had half a brain you noticed I was the worst case of loser mentality you ever saw, and always whining," she says. "And you were right about *that*. But now we have a spaceship to fly. We have ten minutes till my watch starts. Are you ready to hear my big secret?"

"Only if we get a fresh start on the friendship thing."

"What do you think this is?" She's smiling, and so am I. Suddenly serious, she adds, "So what do you call a person who is just as determined and obsessed as you and Derlock, but doesn't have the family connections, or the looks, or the charisma, or anything, for it? And hates everyone for having a better chance than she does, and it eats her alive?"

"I, uh—"

"Emerald." Wychee's mouth twitches. "You know, I was amazed when she reminded us of how her mother got to be famous. She's so ashamed of that story."

"Her mom was a hero."

"Exactly. She was incredibly brave and did exactly the right thing and saved all those lives. *But she was just a really good kindergarten teacher*. Still is. I've met her. Dumpy-looking like Emerald, and if you're not in kindergarten she doesn't know how to talk to you, dull as primer paint. Emerald is so ashamed. I have heard her say she wished her mom would just die."

"It sucks that she feels that way."

"Yeah. So . . . you know Derlock, I know Em, do you think he'd, um—?"

I think about that for a moment. "Derlock's capable of anything. What about Emerald?"

"Well, she really is a good person, I mean she does have a big chip on her shoulder and a lot of envy, but she's also got a big heart and common sense and . . . I don't know, Susan."

"I was thinking what a good job she's been doing as commander. Actually I think that about every hour."

"Me, too. And she's still my best friend. So I'm worried sick about her because . . . well, I know her and love her, but—"

"But I know Derlock and loathe him, and you're absolutely right to be worried," I say.

In the cockpit we put all our attention on making sure Wychee knows all the basic procedures cold, even though I can tell in half a minute she's already letter perfect.

THE ONLY DIFFERENCE BETWEEN US

May 5, 2129. On *Virgo*, upbound Earth to Mars. 149 million kilometers from the sun, 151 million kilometers from Mars, 12 million kilometers from Earth.

A FEW DAYS later, I'm up in the observation sphere at the tip of the nose spire. Wychee's watch just started, it's hours before mine will, and everyone else is either going to bed, busy with work, or playing some weird noisy game with Fwuffy in the Pressurized Cargo Section. There are plenty of things I could be doing, and I'll start doing them soon enough, but for right now, I need a little quiet approximation to sanity.

So here I am, with the steel shutters pulled back, in the center of my glass bubble in the stars, letting the universe look like it looks, letting the surrounding emptiness resonate with the emptiness inside me. Except, maybe, the emptiness inside me doesn't feature a big burning sun. Or anything like as many stars. Maybe I'm not resonating hard enough.

Space is so deep and empty. The red star of Mars on one side and the shielded glare of the sun on the other mark out where we are in our orbit; still whipping around at the bottom, ducking slightly inside Earth's orbit, we've barely begun to climb away from the sun, and at the moment the sky looks much as it does from home, except for the blue dot of Earth and its little star companion, the moon, now only three thumbnails apart.

My phone rings. Wychee says, "Susan, I've got something I need some *quiet* help with. Could you come to the cockpit?"

"I'm on my way."

I airswim back to the entrance—not starting by pushing off from a surface, it takes an extra few seconds till my hand closes on a handhold inside the access tube. "Close the steel shutters around the nose bubble."

"Closing," the mechanical voice says, and behind me the dark, starry night clanks into total blackness.

My few minutes of quiet have given me the urge to use my muscles. I go tailward through the spire in one big lunge, then ricochet through the coretube the way Emerald showed me, hitting the sides first to boost, then to slow down, flying the two-thirds of a kilometer to snag the auxiliary ops hatch in much less than a minute.

Wychee is alone in the cockpit. To my raised eyebrow, she says, "Stack is with Glisters and F.B. on the antenna project, and though Fleeta's technically on this watch, she's functionally useless. So I didn't want to leave the cockpit." She gestures at the screen. "I was doing my steward stuff and checking inventories everywhere. Look what I have in the infirmary."

The infirmary surveillance camera shows red rather than green lights over three doors in the pharmacy racks; they've been opened. "Those are the racks for painkillers, mood fixers, energizers, and anti-psychotics," Wychee says.

"In other words, anything with any recreational potential. And you can't tell from here if the drugs have been stolen or if someone was just nosing around them?"

"And I don't feel good about leaving the cockpit; I know *Virgo* flies itself but—"

"No, you're right. I'll go have a look."

The infirmary is another compartment in this little auxiliary-ship area around the cockpit, so I'm there in seconds. As soon as I open the red-lighted cabinets, I find what we were afraid of: empty racks, and their labels are the names of anything medical that people take for reasons that aren't medical.

Back in the cockpit, I tell Wychee, "You were right. And it's got to be Derlock. Where is he right now?"

We check phone locations; Derlock is in the bunk room, following the rules for his "house arrest"; I would guess he's asleep, since he doesn't read, or actually consume much entertainment at all. Emerald's phone is still in the bathroom; probably she's enjoying a long shower. "All right, then, you call Stack, and ask him to bring Glisters here. We need to do this with all the officers present."

"What are we going to do, Susan?"

"Whatever we figure out. Which might involve Stack's muscle for backup. I'll try to catch Emerald before she leaves the bathroom."

She is fresh from the showersphere, coverall neat from the Phreshor, and she was probably looking forward to bed until I turned up. "Sheeyeffinit," Emerald says. "Of *course* it's Derlock. *And* he's already under house arrest for assault." Her eyes widen and then narrow as she realizes. "He must have done it while he was standing his watch with me. And I swear I only let him out of my sight so he could go take a leak, but the infirmary is almost as close as the bathroom. Then he probably went and hid the drugs while I had him running errands, because I couldn't leave the cockpit. That *turd.* Right under my nose on my watch." Her jaw works as if she's chewing something nasty that she can't spit out. "I don't suppose you *did* look up anything about flogging?"

"Unfortunately not."

"It's so soon after the last time," Emerald says. "I mean, that makes it even *worse*, I guess, but . . . we aren't even sure we've managed to punish him, yet, for attacking Marioschke in front of all of us. We don't have very many options, do we?"

"Not many," I admit. "But we can't let him play 'too special to be just one of the crew,' and he's got to be shown that no matter how big a brat he acts like, he's never going to be too big to spank."

In the cockpit, Emerald brings Glisters, F.B., and Stack up-to-date with quick, brutal accuracy. She summarizes with, "So we've got more Derlock trouble, and we can't leave it alone."

Stack socks his fist into one hand, the only comment he's made so far.

Wychee shrugs. "It's not complicated, just hard. We wake him up and demand the drugs back. Either he gives them up or we search him, and find them. If he's hidden them somewhere we hit him till he tells us where. If he thinks that's unfair he can complain after we're all rescued. Then we give him the shocks that were suspended for his first offense, and sentence him for this one."

"And the sentence should be?" Emerald asks.

"When you consider what it could be like for one of us to be hurt or sick and having to 'buy' those drugs with favors or property, I say it's much worse than that assault. Just lock him up till we get to Mars and tell him he's lucky not to get another big round of shocks."

Emerald glances at Glisters and me; we say "Wychee's right" in unison.

After a moment, she says, "All right. Except I don't like him getting out of working for the whole voyage. We'll make the house arrest run to the end of the trip but we won't do the full lockup yet."

"Commander," I say, "I don't like 'yet.' If we know he's *going* to do something else—and we do—let's just lock him up and not give him the chance to do it."

She thinks, then shakes her head. "I see your point, but let's do it my way." Her voice is flat and neutral. "Okay, let's do this."

I notice that as we go into the bunk room, Stack,

still not speaking a word, positions himself beside me; looking scared, but not hesitating, F.B. moves to flank Emerald.

Em flips back the faceshade and shines a hand lamp at full power into Derlock's face. "Where are the drugs you took from the infirmary?"

His face and shoulders tense, then relax as he calms himself. "In storage locker 6 in the farm section near the Forest, floor 6, chamber 6. It just seemed kind of appropriate—"

"Wychee, would you?"

"On my way."

"I have Wychee's proxy for whatever we decide to do about you. You've already assaulted a crew member and now—"

"*I'm just doing what you're doing.* In fact I'm doing *less* than what you're doing. You took over the whole ship and everything on it, and all I've taken was some resources so I could develop some business and—"

"*Any of us could need any of those drugs, if something goes wrong!*" Emerald all but screams. "And you want to hold them to make someone trade for them—"

"There's no better customer than a desperate customer—"

"—or worse yet trade them away to people who take them for fun—"

"—they're exactly the same people you're so worried about protecting, why not let the individuals decide whether to use the drugs now or save them for later—"

"—and then when we have somebody with a severe burn or a psychotic breakdown—"

"Oh, sheeyeffinit," he says, in righteous disgust. "You can't predict the future, you can't say for sure that any of those things will happen, and if they don't, the drugs that could have been fun for everyone here would just go to waste. And just because I'm foresighted enough to take care that you have a place to buy those drugs, and see that they get allocated to the person who wants them most, you want to make it sound like I wouldn't help a friend in trouble. You grab the whole ship and everything that's on it, and then you won't let me just take some things to have a little business of my own, even when I do all the planning and all the work and put in all the effort. Both of us just took what we found and used it for our own advantage, and the only difference between us is I'm not saying it's for everybody's good—even though everyone *will* benefit."

"It's a very simple difference," I explain, styling Pop in some old adventure meed more than ever. "We're trying to save our lives and get home. You're a psychotic thug and you just like hurting people—"

"That is—*ugh*!"

He makes that noise because Stack has grasped Derlock's hair with one hand and punched him in the face with the other. "No evidence except we all know it," Stack says, and hits him again. "See, evidence isn't what this is about"—*thud!*—"because we're not doing your old man's stupid law"—*thud!*—"we're doing *justice*"—*thud!*—"and *justice* is about what's *true*."

I reach forward and touch Stack's elbow. "Stack, we don't want to be charged with abuse of a prisoner when—"

Derlock makes a disgusted noise. "Right, like you're going to care about the law when—"

"But I *do* care," Stack says, very softly. I don't know what it's doing to Derlock but his tone is ice on *my* spine. "You're right, Susan. Justice here, but law when we get home. If I didn't care about what the law is, I'd just keep hitting Derlock. Emerald, Susan, do you have to arrest me or charge me?"

"It's at our discretion, " I say. "Stopping when I asked you to was good enough for me. Look, Derlock, you can invent n-nillion reasons to act like your usual self, but out here with our lives at stake, none of us care what a big celeb you're going to be, or what principle you twist around to your own use, or that your father has gotten away with more murders and rapes than half his scummy clients—"

"*Don't you ever*—" He starts to sit up and Stack puts him down with a hammerfist to the forehead, then pins his neck to the bunk with one big hand.

"It's a little late for family honor," Stack says.

"Derlock," I say, "who you are, where you come from, and what you've done, is screaming so loud we'll never hear what you say. Do you understand that?"

"You don't trust me."

"You're right. We don't."

He shrugs off Stack's hand, rolls over to face the wall, and pulls his faceshade down, telling us all to go away. When Wychee comes back a few minutes later, saying that all the drugs are back in their rack in the infirmary, the four officers stand around Derlock's bunk and put him under house arrest until we make our pass by Mars, and declare that for the next offense, we will by god lock him up no matter how much trouble it is to guard him or how unfair it is that he gets out of all work. He pretends to be asleep but we know he hears.

Then we drag him down to the infirmary—sleep-sack and all since he won't come out—and after a certain amount of punching, kicking, and arm twisting that's probably worse than the punishment itself, we put him facedown naked on an operating table, and, referring to the manual, Stack uses the shockwand to put a dozen big welts on his ass. He's crying after the third one, it makes me a little sick, and everyone else looks kind of green, but we get it done. Stack looks flat-faced and dead; Emerald volunteers to put the ointment on his butt, and talks to him like she's his mommy.

By the time we all get to bed or back to our shifts, everyone is way off schedule, and for a day or so the ship functions, but none of us get along. Poor Fwuffy is beside himself with anxiety, because part of his programming is telling him to revere authority and another part is telling him to take care of poor, hurt Derlock. He gets over it after he tries to give Derlock a comforting hug and is rewarded with a kick in the trunk.

I add it to my list of reasons to kill Derlock some day.

13

ULTRA SERIOUS GIRL TALK

May 11, 2129. On *Virgo*, upbound Earth to Mars. 150 million kilometers from the sun, 141 million kilometers from Mars, 21 million kilometers from Earth.

A FEW DAYS later, when Glisters and I get up and find our way to the kitchen, there's a surprise: Wychee has packed a box brunch for her watch and mine to all eat together in the Forest. "I almost feel sorry for Emerald's watch," I say, sipping her crab bisque out of a squeezer as I sit on the warm ground cloth beside a glass pool.

"Well, don't. My special cockpit tiffin is even better, and that's what they got. Some evening when I feel like staying up I'll fix one for you and Glisters, or pretty soon Marioschke or F.B. will be able to do it. Sheeyeffinit, we've got months; I might teach you both to do a little fancy cooking for yourselves. I'm just glad my job involves making life pleasant for everyone else."

We look down into the stars wheeling by the windows, up into the trees, and around at the quickly recovering Forest. We eat the warm apple pastries, fresh quiche, hard-crusted bread, and crab bisque; there's not much to say otherwise, and after a while, Glisters and Stack volunteer to take the dirty containers back to the kitchen, on their way to the ongoing process of figuring out how to install the antenna. Wychee sends Fleeta to the farm with Marioschke again, and heads for the cockpit to take over the conn. I decide that as the concerned, dedicated pilot, devoted second in command, and ranking officer awake, I will go see how everyone is doing.

I had thought F.B. would be with the other two guys in the fabshop, but when they look up from the mostly finished mock antenna, they haven't seen him. "And that's strange," Stack says. "He's usually right here as soon as his watch is over."

Glisters nods. "He loves this stuff. Maybe he's sick or something came up?"

I speak Guyish well enough to know that they're telling me that they're worried.

In the cockpit, Wychee looks up to say, "Emerald and Derlock went out of here like two rockets; Em barely did a handover at all, and Derlock was practically tapping his foot while she did. I don't like that."

"Me either. Hey, can you check where F.B.'s phone is?"

"Hunh. Corridor outside the bunk room. Maybe he dropped it or something."

"Could be." I've got an entirely different hunch. "I'll check."

F.B. is floating by the bunk room door. He looks exhausted, stupefied, and sad.

"I was going to work with Glisters and Stack," he says. "But I'm so tired I can't focus."

Instinctively, I rub his neck and shoulders; he's as tight as if he'd been doing high-resistance shrugs on the weight machine. I squeeze and pull at his knotted muscles. "What got you so tired? This feels like you've been carrying the weight of the ship, F.B."

"I was the only one on the screens for almost the whole watch. I'm not good at it like Glisters is, I had to keep looking stuff up and then checking between what I looked up and what the screens were doing, and I was so afraid I would make a mistake and get it wrong—"

"You stood watch all by yourself?"

"Just for the middle seven hours."

I want to ask him what Emerald and Derlock were doing but he might know, and tell me, and I'm already about to explode. "F.B., if you wanted to go to bed early, why are you out here?"

"I can't go in," he says. "Do you think if I ask very politely they'll give me my sleepsack and I can sleep somewhere out here? Except I don't really know how to ask politely—"

"God's nuts on a red-hot skewer, F.B.," I say, grateful that Pop went through a phase of doing Jacobean drama; sometimes an ordinary oath just won't do. "That's *not* how it works. You are going to sleep in your *own* bunk *now*."

I throw the bunk room door open, turn on the lights, and with the brightest cheeriness I have ever sparkled at a fellow human, I bellow, "Is everything all right in here?"

This literally causes a flap—they both try to flap away from where they were doing a mid-air. Derlock pulls his feet up, pushes off Emerald, and shoots into his sleepsack like a sidewinder down a hole. That tumbles her; she flaps like a drunken condor, trying to pretend she just happened to be naked and flailing across the room into her own sleepsack.

"See, F.B., nothing going on," I say. "Hope I didn't wake anyone. Did you need to go down to the bathroom and fresh up before bed?"

"Already did," he says, and unselfconsciously shucks his coverall. He wipes tears from his face, whispering "Thank you" as he gets into his sleepsack.

"Emerald," I say, much too sweetly, "I think the commander and the pilot need to have a quick conference. I'll wait for you in the corridor."

I close the door before she thinks of anything to say; now she'll have to come out and talk.

Seconds later, the door opens. Her expression triggers my jiu-jutsu training; I'm flexing my hands and finding my balance as soon as I see her face. Before she opens her mouth I say, "That was amazingly shitty, Emerald. Making F.B. stand your watch for you. Then locking him out of his own damned bed. All so you could have sex with the boy toy—who happens to be the most dangerous major disaster of a problem we've got on board. What kind of a commander do you call yourself?"

"You have ultra violated my privacy!"

"What the sheeyeffinit are you thinking, Emerald? If we were on Earth or Mars or anywhere safe of course it wouldn't matter and it would be all your own affair, and if you weren't one of the people we count on most here I suppose somebody could look the other way, but this—"

"Shut up!" She really looks like she wants to attack me physically, but maybe she's remembering how she's seen me take Derlock down. "I know what he is and I know what he's like. I'm just having some fun. In case it hasn't occurred to you, this being the commander thing is ultra high stress, and sure, he's using me, but I'm using him and—"

"Emerald, I don't know what he's been saying to you, or what he's been trying to work into your head, but I can kind of guess. As far as the reason for stowing away in the first place is concerned, Mission Accomplished. You have celeb-eenie locked in—"

"Derlock has bigger dreams than that."

"He sure does," I say, remembering too much pillow talk. "But, Em, there's no place for anyone else in Derlock's big dream. At least no place you want to be in."

"That's easy for you to say. You've already had him—"

I nod. "True. And you've just had the only part worth having." The silence drags on for a second or two. "Aw, sheeyeffinit, Em, be careful, all right? If you have to do this, then the second you're done, drop him like a live cobra, understand? I'm worried sick about you."

Something about my expression seems to take the fight out of her. "I can take care of myself." She opens the bunk room hatch and goes back in.

Later, in the cockpit, I'm braced with my feet on the

floor, my back against the slumbering Fwuffy (he seems to like being used as furniture), and my hands free to gesture like a mad conductor. I'm venting to Wychee and Glisters. "I guess saying 'Commander, you're being an idiot' is on the pilot's list of job responsibilities."

Glisters grunts. "I went to StarPolish with Derlock before we came to Excellence Shop. So I've known him maybe five years. Ten minutes after he met me he had my lunch money in his account and my head in the toilet. But I *still* went along on this stowaway to Mars deal. He does have a knack—"

"Hey," Stack says, sticking his head in, "Glisters, are you awake enough to give me some coaching on this antenna issue? I'm trying but I'm noticing that maybe I should've started paying attention in school about ten years ago."

"Right with you." Glisters is up and airswimming out the door immediately.

I say to Wychee, "Glisters's been pretty amazing ever since the accident, but one way the guy hasn't changed, he's definitely better with antennas than with relationships, and right now we've got a relationship problem. So—girlfriend emergency meeting. How do we tell Emerald she has to stop this, especially without me looking like a jealous bitch?"

"You probably *are* a jealous bitch," Wychee points out. "Just one who happens to be completely right. Your passion is a little, um, engaged here, and that probably makes it hard for Em to listen to you. I'll try later on."

"Thanks. You guys have been close for a long time, and probably I should just leave it to you."

"Yeah, except I don't have any idea either, Susan. I mean, I understand, she's going to be the star of the story this way—the commander, the prisoner, the good girl who blossoms, the bad guy she redeems, this will so ultra splycter. We'll all be celebs, but Em will be a star. That's what she's wanted all her life."

"I just worry that he's going to present her with just one more little thing they can do that will make the whole story just a tiny bit better," I say. "Nothing that will do any harm, of course, or not any *real* harm, just a *little* thing they can do that will make the story so much better, kick their recognition scores up to stratospheric. He thinks about angles like that, all the time. And when he does . . . things happen."

"Yeah, I know, and I'm . . ." She stops; she's wiping her eyes.

"Emerald is still your best friend."

Wychee nods, miserably. "I'm scared. Derlock's just plain—I mean, he's . . ."

"He's a really good reason to be worried about your friend," I say. "But if she'll listen to anyone, it'll be you. So talk to her—soon—and level her off. She's still a great person, she's just falling for a load of crap from what's probably the most effective crap salesman in the universe."

"I just wish she had your experience, and poise, and a relationship to stabilize her like you have."

"Derlock can screw mummified goats as far as—"

"I meant Glisters." She sees that she's startled me. "Sorry. You guys seem so close."

"Just friends. Stupid old line, but in this case it's true."

"If I had a friend like that I wouldn't care shit about not having a boyfriend."

"You know, maybe that's *why* I don't. One more thing I owe Glisters for. But no, I hadn't even thought about that side of things with him." The silence that hangs in the cockpit is ripped to shreds by one of Fwuffy's great glorking, sputtering snores; something about that makes us both laugh, which feels good.

Wychee sighs. "Gaw. I think more than anything else, I hate Derlock for owning every conversation you and I have." She stares at the screens morosely. "We're already doing everything we've thought of."

"Except kill him," I say.

It hangs in the air until Wychee says, "Seriously?"

"Well . . . I mean, I told you what Stack told me. I've told you and Glisters what I think is going on inside Derlock. Or think about Clytie—"

"She was a pretty sick little girl *before* he got his claws into her—"

"Yeah, true. Derlock has an instinct for finding vulnerable people." I realize a second too late it's exactly the wrong thing to say, considering how much danger Emerald is flirting with.

But Wychee's way ahead of me. She says, "You said Stack thought he might even have had something to do with the big accident itself. Do *you* think so?"

"I wish I thought Stack was crazy."

She keeps watching the screens; I imagine she'd have an expression like that if she were trying to conceal having been kicked in the stomach. "This is frightening."

"Yeah. My question is, though—that idea we just mentioned—what if it's him or us?"

"I don't think I can exactly face that," Wychee says. "I don't think I can. I'm sorry, Susan."

"Don't be. I happen to like that you're not the murdering type."

"I don't know that I exactly like it, but I do feel safer knowing you *are*."

We don't talk for a while, and then Wychee remembers some silly, mean, nasty story about one of the miney girls at Excellence Shop—I think she wore something exactly wrong to exactly the wrong party—and we relish a few seconds of being our old rotten selves together.

14

DYING COULD SPOIL THE WHOLE TRIP

May 13, 2129. On *Virgo*, upbound Earth to Mars. 150 million kilometers from the sun, 137 million kilometers from Mars, 24 million kilometers from Earth.

GLISTERS AND STACK have finally finished all the tutorials about the antenna, outside space-rigging, and microgravity tools, and built the mock antenna. Next session, they're going to hang mock mountings in Vacuum Cargo Section 1. They're both incredibly proud as they show me all their work.

I make myself pay attention and ask questions. I extract three important points:

- almost nothing about putting the antenna on is intuitive
- almost everything about it is dangerous
- the same thing Glisters didn't want to say when we first talked about it is still true: if we screw it up, we'll be ultra screwed.

A couple of hours later, after Glisters and I go on watch, he re-babbles the whole thing to me, again, with even more enthusiasm. Everyone has their own idea of fun, I guess, and it's good to see Glisters so happy. Maybe his real problem, all along, has been that he's a natural workaholic in a world with almost no work.

When I delicately raise the question of what to do about Derlock if the situation gets worse, I find that after years of being bullied, tormented, and exploited by Derlock, Glisters doesn't really care whether there's a legal rationale, a just cause, or anything else—he'd be up for chucking Derlock out an airlock right now. "We could always tell them afterward that we got mixed up and we thought being an asshole in the first degree was a capital crime in the General Spacefaring Code," he says cheerfully. "Just let me know when you want to do it."

"You're thinking like an engineer," I tease him. "If it's dangerous and unnecessary, jettison it before it can hurt anything."

"I wish I was that rational. No, I just like the idea of pushing Derlock out the airlock in his underpants and standing at the window, watching what happens."

I realize I didn't half enjoy the antenna convo as much as Glisters relishes the assassination convo.

By now everyone else is asleep; I settle in to study through the list of tutorials that Glisters has set up for Em, me, and Wychee. Crazy Science Girl has now not only come back, she's taken over; I find I'm running down all the digressions and supplementary material just because I like knowing it, pretending it's because I'll want to know it sooner or later.

I've been at it for hours when Glisters says, "Dinner-time." To me it seems instantaneous when he returns with four temptrol boxes. "Wychee left us ready-to-activate meals: burgers, fries, and shakes, with pie and coffee in a second container. If you can tear yourself away from your studies, I think this deserves appreciation."

"Agreed." Wow, when did my back get so stiff? I stretch, strap in, accept the main and dessert containers, and lock them down in front of me. I answer the questions on the main container, wait 30 seconds, and lift off the top. The burger is juicy and medium-rare; the fries are thick, soft in the middle and crisp outside; and the shake is almond-coffee and frothy, all exactly as I ordered. I dive in and enjoy every second of it; beside me, Glisters is making it disappear even faster.

The pie requires similar concentration, but once we're each into our second squeezebulb of coffee, it seems like a good time to talk. "What do you think is going to happen with Emerald and Derlock?" he asks.

"Nothing good. But I'm hoping he'll do or say something to piss her off soon. Then once F.B. and Marioschke are up to speed at watch-standing, we can just keep him locked up and under guard."

"Yeah." Glisters stares into space, thinking. "How does Derlock *do* that to girls?"

I shrug. "That dangerous-smart-boy thing. For some reason slick, smart, mean bastards cause some hearts to flip over and knock all the available brains onto the floor." *Like mine. Change the subject.* "So suppose the worst—we break the antenna or it floats off into space. What do we do?"

"Try to make another one. I'm pretty sure it could be done in the shop, but it would take me some weeks, at least, to learn how."

"What happens if we lose the antenna and can't make another one?"

"Well, out of four iceballs we needed, we lost two, never got another one, and used up some of the last one stopping our tumbling and had to reserve some of it to supplement life support. All that meant we didn't have nearly the reaction mass we needed to do a full course correction; instead of having a three-day-long window when we could all take our lifeboat cap down to Mars and get there in about eight days, at our closest approach, we'll have only about ten hours of a window for a sixty-five-day trip down to Mars. The caps aren't designed to go longer than forty-five days with a full crew, and at that point the recycling will be run out."

"I always thought recycling, plus the fusion power source, meant everything could go forever."

"Me, too. I was never into life support systems—that's like managing a tank of tropical fish except with people. *Bo*-ring."

"Yeah," I agreed. "Rockets and ballistics, *that's* sexy."

"Unh hunh. But, unfortunately, recycling has a lot to do with breathing, so sexy or not, I've been crash-studying it. Here's the deal. Because they never planned on having a cap last for much beyond the forty-day flight time that's already pushing your luck with radiation, they don't worry about efficient recycling. With a full load of ten people on a cap, they do a complete recycle every forty hours, and on every recycle they lose a couple percent of accessible oxygen from the combined tanks and living space."

"All right, I know I could set that up as a differential equation and solve it myself, but I also know you already did it. What's it come to?"

"Oxygen gets below breathable at fifty days, with all of us on board."

"Where's it go, though? Does it leak away or does it go somewhere it could be recovered from?"

"Neither. It's still there on board but it's all tied up in the big waste molecules that the system can't break down. So it's part of the sludge in the recycling tanks, and there's no gear on the cap to take it back out of the sludge. Only a little bit of it turns to permanent sludge each time, but it's like having a tiny hole in a water tank that never adds more, or a little bitty fee in a bank account you never put cash in; after enough time, it's gone."

I push up and bounce against the opposite bulkhead, causing Fwuffy to roll over and whine. One problem with the cockpit, you can't pace. I'm trying to think of a way around this. He's right, ballistics was way more fun. "What if we take along spare oxygen?"

"I did the numbers on that, too, and I want you to check me, but it looks like you'd need a few tonnes of liquid oxygen. There's not any regular way to handle that on the cap, so we'd have to hand-move temp storage tanks that aren't meant to be used for such a long period of time, then improvise the tie downs, the venting, everything, and if we had an oopsie—and caps aerobrake *hard* and land *really hard* out at the operating limits like this would be—you'd incinerate everything in the cap."

"Why don't the pod or the crew bubble run out of oxygen? What do they do that a cap doesn't?"

"The farms. Bacteria break down those complex organics out of the air into plant food and put oxygen back into the air, and heat-sterilizing all the soil every few months recovers the oxygen that's really locked up tight. We replace the leakage loss by electolyzing water from the iceball. There isn't room enough to farm on the cap—the farm volume is like three hundred times the volume of the crew bubble, and it has to be, and you couldn't make a cap like that. No, I don't see any way around it; you run out of breathing at fifty days, if you have ten people, and if you die on the way, it spoils the whole trip.

"Now, theoretically, we could send two people down with a message that the rest of us're here and alive."

"How does reducing the crew by seven-ninths only expand the range by 40%?"

"It's not linear," he says. "I'd have to show you the differential equations."

"Maybe later in the bunk room, when we can enjoy them all alone, you sly devil."

He grins. "I know a woman who falls for a partial derivative when I see one. Look, it's just, if the two people in the cap are the first notice that the authorities on Mars get about survivors on *Virgo*, the rescue for the people back here on the ship will be a long time coming. The cap will only arrive about the same time we're passing Mars, and a Space Patrol cruiser doesn't move much faster than we do or Mars does. They won't be able to chase us down before we'll already be back on a close approach to Earth. So if that's how we get rescued, we'll be stuck riding around to Earthpass, twenty-two months later.

"But that's all worst-case thinking, Susan. Stack's going to put that antenna in place, I'll power it up and make it work, and we'll call Mars with plenty of time for them to send out a real rescue."

"How's that going?"

"All right, I think. Now that we've got a mock antenna for Stack to play with, it's just a matter of his putting in the practice time."

He's nodding like he's just finished an argument, and he's looking at the screen, not at me. "There's something you're not saying."

"He was great while we were building the mock antenna and he's only had one practice round so far. I think he was tired when we started the practice runs today, though."

"Glisters, *what's happening with Stack*? There is something on your mind and I want to hear it. Isn't Stack practicing?"

"Well, he *thinks* he is. He put on the pressure suit and pushed the mockup antenna around, and sort of worked through it, but he skipped things, he doesn't pay attention, he thinks if he saw it once, he'll remember it. Kind of like F.B. used to be about being an astronomer—mostly he's watching himself in a movie inside his head."

"You're sure it's not like visualization or anything?"

"No. More like he's imagining himself at the victory party, and what he's going to brag about and how people will talk to him, before he ever plays the game."

"Are you guys going to practice tomorrow?"

"We're planning to."

"Why don't I drop in and see for myself? Maybe I'll come up with an idea."

"If you do, that'll be one more than I've got," Glisters says.

I could voice my guess that he's really worried about his friend, but most guys would rather let me extract a tooth than answer a question about something like that. I could change the subject but—

"Hey," he says, "since Fwuffy seems to be pretty solidly asleep"—he waits a second, and all we hear is a long, soft snore—"and Marioschke is off doing her tutorial, I wanted to tell you, I did check out that story about hortons 'turning violent at adolescence.' It has all the marks of a planted story. The original report was obviously designed to confuse the reporting system, and by the time it had been out on the net for a few iterations, it had turned into the crazy killer horton story. But the reality is a lot less scary and—kind of sad, really. The one tiny grain of fact under it all is that a male like Fwuffy, when he goes through puberty in a few years, often becomes sexually fixated on some human woman, because the hortons' designers designed them to like human pheromones." Glisters makes a face. "It's distantly related to the condition they call musth in his elephant ancestors, but it has at least as much in common with that withdrawn, moony phase in human puberty."

"Ugh. So he's going to suffer impossible depression, longing, loneliness, and frustration?"

"Yeah, like anyone else in puberty, but more extreme." Glisters grimaces. "Hortons feel only marginal attraction to other hortons and none at all to elephants. So the impossible romantic longings really are impossible. It's pretty hard to find a pachysexual human girl."

"You just liked making up the word *pachysexual*."

"You're jealous because you didn't think of it first."

"Guilty," I admit. "On the other hand, if there is such a thing as a pachysexual, I suspect we have one on board. So the good news, if I'm understanding you, is that we can probably stop worrying about Fwuffy?"

"No, it's that we can stop worrying about us. He's not going to hurt us, because he's engineered not to be dangerous. We still have to worry about him, because he doesn't have any more engineering than the rest of us against being miserable."

"I guess if they come up with a shot for that, we'll all get in line."

He shudders. "What do you think happistuf is?"

"Any more cheerful thoughts?" I ask.

15

ONE BIG JUMP INTO THE DARK, WITH FRIENDS

May 22, 2129. On *Virgo*, upbound Earth to Mars. 153 million kilometers from the sun, 122 million kilometers from Mars, 29 million kilometers from Earth.

WHEN I GET up, I find that Emerald has been yelling at everyone, mostly about their not giving her enough deference, with responses ranging from cowering (F.B.) to raging (Stack). I let Wychee know I'll have to be a little late for our usual breakfast together, and track everyone down to make sure they're okay; the last one on my rounds is Marioschke, who I find in Farm Section 1 with Fwuffy, showing him how to check tomato plants for some weird space blight. The tip of his trunk is as delicate and flexible as her hand, and she frankly admits he has more patience about running the scanner over every surface of every leaf.

"How does blight get up here, anyway?" I ask.

Marioschke shrugs. "It starts here," she says. "We circulate water through the shielding and back here, and sterilization is good but not perfect. Millions of different kinds of microbes grow on every different kind of plant, and every so often one of them makes it all the way around the loop, takes just enough radiation to mutate it without killing it, and turns into a pathogen."

"Are we going to be able to grow food?"

"Oh, sure. Every twenty-six-month orbit produces an average of—how many, Fwuffy?"

"Seven new pathogens, but on avewage onwy thwee out of a hundwed awe sewious."

His gift for startling me persists. "How did you learn that?"

"I read the tech notes to him," Marioschke says. "We stop at everything one of us doesn't understand, and look that up. I wish I'd taken a lot more biology back at school; I had no idea how interesting botany and microbiology can be if you pay enough attention and try to learn it instead of trying to get done."

I ask her about Emerald's ship-wide tantrum that morning, and Marioschke's smile is shy but real. "She doesn't like it down here in the lower levels. Says there's too much mud and her hair gets frizzy from the humidity. So she called me up on my phone and yelled, and I put the phone down on the table, on speaker, and did some re-potting, and just said I was sorry and I'd try to do better whenever she took a breath."

Fwuffy finds something, and the two of them are suddenly all over one little tomato plant, extracting samples to culture and examine under the microscope. I'm not sure they notice when I go.

I call Wychee and she meets me in our usual spot to have her-lunch/my-breakfast together, sitting on a window near the tail end of the Pressurized Cargo Section, to catch up on the human side of things. This morning she's a little out of sorts because she had to hold the food past its point of perfection while I made my emergency rounds. "On the other hand," I say, "I just came from talking to the only two really happy people on board."

"Fleeta and who else?"

"I guess that makes three. I meant Fwuffy and Marioschke. I have to visit the farm more often; it won't make any difference to them, but it's good for me."

"Tell me about it. I try to get down there every day to visit my future salads. I hope Em is at least staying off of them."

I explain about the mud and frizzies.

"Like her hair matters up here," Wychee says, gloomily. "She's spending more and more time alone with Derlock. In the churn of our little society, the cream and the scum have both risen to the top."

"I don't like it either." I always try to be fairly gentle and neutral around Wychee, because she's not just angry at Emerald like the others; she's feeling deserted, and hurt, and rightly so. "I wish there were something obvious I could have a confrontation with Em about. As it is, she's functioning as commander—"

"Sheeyeffinit, Susan, she's functioning because *we're* functioning. Mostly we solve problems, tell her we solved them, and she says 'good, keep doing that.'"

"Well, you and Glisters had your argument about how much water to reserve for the farm versus the thrusters—"

"And *you* worked out a compromise, Susan, and took it to Em and she made it an order. It's so frustrating. She was great right after the accident, but now it's like she's just waiting around for things to happen and make her famous." She catches herself and looks at me sheepishly. "I'm reverting to whining, aren't I?"

"I don't think *talking about problems* is the same thing as *whining*. According to the Susan rules, you're not whining if you're trying to figure out what's wrong and fix it."

"I like the Susan rules. Are you going to go over to Vacuum Cargo Section 1 and be the referee again?"

I shrug. "Why should today be any different? I guess I should get on with it."

"Don't let me chase you off with my rotten mood, Susan."

"It's not *your* rotten mood, you borrowed it from Emerald. And probably the boys have it much worse, so I better go deal with that. Thanks for breakfast and being fairly sane company."

- - -

When I come through the airlock into Vacuum Cargo Section 1, I'm amazed, as always, that although you can only see faces poorly in a pressure suit visor, the boys manage to be so expressive with their bodies. Glisters is sitting cross-legged on the outer hull, looking upward like he wants something to happen, and it's not. Meanwhile, two-thirds of the way up to the coretube, Stack is hanging by one arm from their antenna model, one hand on his hip, plainly not happy with Glisters.

I wait while a couple breaths hiss in and out of my breathing tube. Neither one says a word. I finally say, "Why don't you just show me?"

Stack shrugs elaborately—if you want people to see you shrug in a pressure suit, you have to put some effort into that shrug.

He and Glisters disconnect the antenna mockup—that piece of pipe, about the length and width of the antenna, filled with jugs of water and equipped with clamps and bolt mountings in the right places, that they had so much fun building together. They move it up into a locker almost at the coretube-top; as far as Glisters can tell from the specs, that locker is identical to an outside equipment locker. "From the start?" Stack asks.

"Please. I need to understand the whole thing."

Stack climbs into the noseward airlock by the coretube. He climbs back out, works hand over hand to the locker, undoes the doors and pins them back, undoes the fastenings on the antenna, and tows it behind him to the mounting position. He does a bunch of things with the clamps, then fastens the bolts, unclips the antenna from himself, and proceeds back to the airlock door.

"How'd he do, Glisters?"

"Near perfect this time, a couple little things but nothing serious."

"Pretend I don't know anything, because I don't. What were the 'couple little things'?"

"He fastened the secondary clamp before the main one, then let it hold the antenna in place while he did the far side clamp, and then did the main clamp last. Ideally he should do the main clamp first, because if a thruster fired exactly while he had the secondary clamp, but not the main one, the antenna might break the secondary clamp and fall away."

"Won't we have the thrusters locked up?"

"Sure, but I could make a mistake in the way I lock things, or maybe there's something I don't understand correctly."

Stack says, "But the antenna went in just fine."

"It did," Glisters says, "and chances are if you went out there and did that right now, it would go in just fine and we'd have you back in here before your watch started, and be calling up Mars and arranging our rescue."

Stack starts to say, "Then why don't—" just as Glisters says, "But that's not the point—" and they both stop with their hands on their hips, facing each other, like a guy arguing with himself in a mirror. I am torn between wanting to laugh and wanting to beat their heads in, and would like to compromise by beating their heads in while laughing. "I'm starting to understand some problems," I said, "not necessarily about the antenna. Glisters, you said a couple of things? What's the other problem?"

"Well, it's something that's not that big, usually," Glisters says. "Just another one of those things where if at just the wrong moment—"

"Did I lose a grip?" Stack asks. He sounds scared and ashamed.

"About a tenth of a second." Suddenly Glisters sounds

soothing, not critical. I wish I could see their faces.

"Fill me in," I say.

"I keep letting go with one hand before I have a grip with the other. Glisters catches that by monitoring the pressure pads on my suit. Yesterday I was between grips just when a thruster fired, and me and the antenna fell away from the noseward wall, just like we'd fall off the back of the ship if it happened in real life. I had nightmares about it all last night. It's the thing I'm most scared of." He sounds close to crying. "It's making a mess out of my self-confidence."

"I had nightmares too, Stack," Glisters says, taking a step toward him. He turns to me quickly, as if he were ashamed of reaching for his friend. "If that happens outside, we won't have any way to get him back. He'll fall forever, and suffocate in his suit, probably with the ship still in sight."

"But won't Stack be on belay?"

"Most of the time. The trouble is, if he fastens the main clamp first, his belay line tends to tangle with the one on the antenna. And the antenna masses a tonne—if a thruster fires and the antenna starts to go, he won't be able to stop it. So it has to stay on belay, so he needs to unclip—or else do what he's doing, do the other clamps first, then unbelay the antenna, then do the main clamp. But like I said, that could make an even bigger mess of things."

"So when he's not belayed to the ship, have Stack belayed to the antenna. If the antenna gets away, he goes with it, climbs back to it hand over hand, then climbs the antenna belay. As long as he never unclips from something tied to the ship, he's fine."

"Unless the antenna is only on the secondary clamp—"

"So Stack now has an incentive to do the main clamp first, like you want him to, and he also has a safety line, because he's belayed to the antenna that's securely on the ship." I'm feeling fairly smug about having solved the problem. "Let's try it, anyway. Think how good it would feel to have a perfect run, guys."

At least they instantly stop quarreling, now that they have a new procedure to work through together. Stack climbs into the airlock. Glisters says "Go" in the headsets.

The airlock door opens and Stack climbs out, belays himself to the clip beside it, works hand over hand to the locker, works its fastenings. He belays the antenna to his belt, undoes its fastenings, tows it to the mounting position, belays the antenna to a bracket nearby, undoes his own direct belay to access the main clamp, leaves all the other belays in place while he fastens the main clamp, does the secondary and other clamps, reattaches himself to his direct belay, retrieves all the other belays, and brings them all back into the airlock with himself.

Two seconds later he's bouncing back out saying, "How'd I do?"

I can hear the smile in Glisters's voice. "Perfect. No errors."

"So now we've had a perfect practice," I say.

Stack says, with more enthusiasm than I've ever heard before, "Hey, if we hurry a little, I think I can get in four more runs before my watch starts."

Fifty-two minutes later, we're all checking out through the airlock. Stack's been working much harder than we have, and he heads for the shower.

As soon as he's gone, Glisters says softly, "I think he can do it, now. Wasn't that weird? One good run and he was willing to do five."

"Should we do it for real tomorrow?" I ask.

"Well, it'll frustrate him, but I'd rather ask him to do one more day of practice tomorrow, and then go the day after. But if he's really whiny or pushy when we ask, we can always just let him go tomorrow. Anyway, it will be good to have all this taken care of."

- - -

Wychee has just taken the conn; Glisters and I catch Emerald and Derlock rocketing out of the cockpit, on their way to wherever it is that they go to use each other since I told them they can't lock F.B. out of the bunk room. I do my best not to notice his glare, or the flush on her cheeks. "Okay," she says. "Can you just tell me here?"

"We're ready to put up the antenna, maybe tomorrow but ideally we'd like Stack to practice for one more day."

Derlock says, "Keep an eye on Glisters while Stack is out there. Stack used to cover Glisters's face with one hand, push him up against the wall, twist his nipples, and slap him in the balls to make him cry. I wouldn't trust Glisters with a chance for revenge like that."

I can feel Glisters tensing into a ball of rage beside me,

and I'm not much less angry myself, but I say, "I was talking to the commander, not the prisoner."

"Anything you have to say to me you can say to him," Emerald says.

"Nonetheless, it's your business as commander, and it's none of his." I'm feeling sick and furious inside, but only Derlock knows why: Derlock used to brag about things like that to me in bed—only he said he did it, not that Stack did—and truthfully, it was part of the charm of evil, back when he was the guy I was hot for, and Glisters was that creepy pink big-headed pervert. Derlock *knew* that talking like that, about hurting Glisters and some of the others, got me going; I know perfectly well he's reminding me now that he remembers it working on me.

Unless he's reminding Emerald that it works on her now.

Glisters says, "Stack and I are friends now," very softly.

"Now that's Stack being brave—or stupid," Derlock says.

I say, bluntly, "He wants to get home the same as all of us. In fact, Emerald, if we can get Stack to do one more day of practice, you should really come and see it."

"Whatever," she says. "If you say they're okay to go, they are. Don't delay anything just to show me. If that's all you had, we have things to get on with, and I'm sure you do, too."

Glisters says he wants to spend a few hours making sure he completely understands how to lock up the thrusters, spin adjustments, and anything else, and work though all the possible situations we might encounter. "It might sound dumb," he says, "but I'm worried about Stack."

"Taking care of your friend's life doesn't sound dumb to me," I say.

Not long after, when I'm up in the bubble at the nose spire, letting myself feel the quiet and the aloneness, Stack floats in. "Hey, if you don't mind, I'd like to have a private conversation about the antenna and stuff." He looks around. "Wow, I never looked at this before. I guess it's about like the view I'm going to have tomorrow."

"Glisters told you we wanted to wait one more day, didn't he?"

"Yeah, that's some of what I wanted to talk to you about. It's fine with me, actually, I'll be glad to let him have an extra day to tinker, and I don't mind running through it another ten times." Stack sculls with his hands to float up next to me. "You're the only person I can talk with about . . . well, crap, everything. I mean, there's Glisters, but he's worried enough about me already."

"Five perfect runs today," I said. "That's real good."

"Thanks. I've got to keep my nerve up."

After a little silence, I say, "I'm still listening," which is corny, but as Pop always says, corniness is what difficult situations demand.

"All right, the thing is, Susan, I'm such a screwup, and it's like I've never really wanted to succeed at anything in my life, and now all of a sudden there's *this* and it's *important.* I've always *felt* like I could do great stuff. I've told myself stories about being, you know, heroic and calm and up for anything and all that sheeyeffinit . . . but I've always been afraid if I really tried anything, I'd find out I was kidding myself. I mean maybe I'm just stronger and better coordinated than the losers I hang with. I think I always felt like it was better not to know for sure than to lose and know. And now I wish I knew I was good enough to do this job."

"You'll be fine," I say. "It's going to be just like all that practice."

"I haven't done *all that practice*!" He's clenched up, muscles tight everywhere, like he's furious. "I've screwed off most of the time because it was hard, because I was afraid I'd never get it right. Now I'm going to try to make up for it with one more day of good practice. Only one more day. I could have had two weeks. And what really kills me is that if I was any good *I wouldn't need to practice*!"

"Okay," I say, "hold it, time out, that's just stupid. I can see being afraid to try because you're afraid you'll lose. I can see not wanting to practice because you're too lazy. I can even see wasting all your practice time daydreaming about succeeding instead of practicing. But if you're telling me you're *ashamed of needing to practice*, well— monkey poop. Sheeyeffinit, that's like being ashamed of needing to breathe to get oxygen. I mean, Aunt Destiny, herself, was always telling me about all the simulations and practices she did to get ready for a major eva. For that matter, Pop practices two, three times what most actors do, it takes him *forever* to do that 'look natural' thing that they pay him to do."

He takes a deep breath. "I'm just so ashamed of it, Susan, because it's so childish and stupid. But I always felt like I was supposed to just be able to do stuff, do it brilliantly, you know? Like the way it was in meeds, the moves in dancing and sports that get splyctered into a hook, those people just *have* it—I want to be the guy that can just do it, that's great without having to do—"

"There never was any such guy," I say. "You can't be him 'cause he doesn't exist. Of course you're scared, silly, it's the first real thing in your life—most people don't have that even once. The eenies pretend we do stuff that matters, the mineys pretend they care what we do and that they're not just n-nillion contented pets, and the meanies pretend they're brave rebels or crazy badasses. But you're not pretending. You're real.

"Win or lose, do it or die, put up the antenna or lose it, no matter what, you're going to matter," I tell him, "and of course you're scared—who wouldn't rather live in that kid fantasy where Special Wonderful You gets all that attention and affection just for being Special Wonderful You? But you're going to *do* this." I think it may be the feeblest pep talk ever given, but Stack is nodding like it was just the right thing to say.

"Yeah." He bounds off the floor and we glide and air-swim together. "Hey, look at Earth in the window. It's almost just a star now."

"Another two weeks and it will be," I say. "Then just all those stars, till we're practically on top of Mars."

He looks around; I think, *To me this is just beautiful*

because it's always here, safe, quiet, and alone, when I need it. To him, it's what the world will look like, the last thing he'll ever see if anything goes wrong. Great idea, Susan, draw his attention to that.

But after a while, he says, "Inside the ship or outside, it's all just one big jump into the dark, isn't it?"

I put my hand between his shoulder blades, where I can see so much tension you'd think he'd twang like a guitar string, and rub gently. I feel him relax under my touch. "With friends," I say. "One big jump into the dark *with friends.*"

16

SO FAR FROM ANYTHING

May 24, 2129. On *Virgo*, upbound Earth to Mars. 153 million kilometers from the sun, 119 million kilometers from Mars, 30 million kilometers from Earth.

STACK ELECTS TO try the antenna installation during his watch, because he doesn't trust Emerald and Derlock in the cockpit, and Glisters and I don't go on watch until he's about ready for bed. Wychee insists on handing the conn over to Glisters for it; he's the only one we all trust with controlling the ship. He slaves the cockpit through his wristcomp; he wants to be right there with the rest of us while Stack is outside.

Emerald and Derlock don't even stick around; they head straight into the bunk room as soon as their watch is over. Everyone else gathers around the tail main dock, the group of airlocks near the center of the tail bulkhead, where the crew bubble used to attach.

Stack gets a hug from each of us, and Marioschke startles him with a kiss. Suit-up takes about ten minutes as each piece has to go on right and attach where it's supposed to, with all the backup seals and connections. "Do I have to hook up the, uh, you know, tube?" he asks Glisters.

"All the practice runs took less than eight minutes," Glisters points out, "but if anything goes wrong, and you're out there for hours, you won't be able to take a leak, and all the water for an evasuit comes out of the recycler. You could get pretty miserable out there."

"I don't like how that tube feels."

"Obviously it's your mission, your suit, and your dick," Glisters says. "But *I* wouldn't want to be stuck out there with no water and nowhere to pee."

Stack shrugs and closes up without putting the tube on. Part of me wants to order him to do it, but if he has to pee or gets thirsty while he's out there, I guess it'll teach him a lesson.

He runs through the checklist with Glisters in a quick, businesslike way, waves at all of us, and climbs into the airlock.

Over the radio he says, "On belay here, cycling air out." We feel the vibration in the tail dock; the air has been pumped out of the lock and released in here. "Going out. Handgrips right where we planned. I've got the locker visually, and I can see the whole pathway to it. Climbing to the locker."

"Acknowledged," Glisters says.

He goes smoothly down the checklist: opens the locker, belays the antenna there, unclips it, brings it out, attaches it to his belt, heads for the mounting point. He tests the main, secondary, and far side clamps; they open and close. "All right, checking the belay between me and the antenna. It's still good. Removing my belay to the airlock to clear access for—"

The tail end dock vibrates, there's a sensation of air flowing past us toward the tail and then back toward the rest of the ship like a bouncing ball, and all of us are tugged toward the tail bulkhead for just an instant. We're all shouting and yelling, but Glisters shouts over us, "Shut up! I can't hear Stack! Stack! Talk to me, I'm here, talk to me—"

I hear Stack keening through the headphones. "Stack, Glisters knows what to do, just listen to Glisters—"

Now he's sobbing. "You were going to have the thrusters locked. You weren't going to let a thruster fire."

Glisters says, "I swear I had them locked, and slaved to my wristcomp, but something in the cockpit overrode and fired that thruster. We'll take care of you, Stack, we will, just tell me what's going on. Did you lose the antenna?"

"Kind of. It pulled me off the ship, all that weight all of a sudden, and it was belayed to me—"

"You're still belayed to it, though, just climb back up the line to the antenna, then up the antenna line to the ship—"

"I can't!" I have never heard a voice so ashamed before. "When it pulled me off I panicked and I punched the clip release. I'm floating away from it, it's not even ten meters away, I can see every dimple on it, but I can't do anything to move toward it, I can't airswim in a vacuum—"

I yank one of the evasuit lockers open and start suiting up. I've been external three times on tours, and figuring

Glisters has to stay inside to keep things working, I've got to be the one to go.

"Glisters," I say, "find me line, *now*, something I can throw."

"I"—he stares at his wristcomp in horror—"the cockpit has me locked completely, I can't even change my screen—"

I keep suiting up. "Then go to the cockpit. Tell me where there's a line or a long cable in an external locker by the time I get through the airlock." I run suit check as fast as I can, everything by the book, following the directions posted on the bulkhead. The catheter feels like holy hell going in, and as I wince from the pain, I notice that there was a tube of lubricant in the same sealed package. Oh, well.

By the time I climb into the airlock, Glisters, Wychee, and F.B. have raced off toward the cockpit.

I click on my suit radio. "Stack, tell me real calmly, how fast are you drifting away?" My faceplate display shows I've taken seven minutes putting on the suit. I start the airlock cycle as my hands fumble, stab, and grope through the rest of suit-up.

He sighs. "I think I've gone about another ten meters. It's so slow and it just feels like if I could find a way to move—"

"Tools on your belt," I say. "Throw them away from the ship, for reaction. *Away*, that's important, not toward the ship, away from it. It'll slow you down and it might even help you catch up. Anything you can throw, throw it *away* from the ship—"

"Okay, I'm — sheeyeffinit!"

"What's the matter?"

"I threw and it helped, but now I'm tumbling—"

The airlock light and all the indicators on my faceplate display are green. I yank the inner door open, crawl in, speed cycle the lock. "I'm on my way out, now, as soon—"

"Susan, come back in here, you are under arrest." Emerald's voice cuts through my headphones.

I'm so startled to hear her voice that it takes me a moment to realize what she has said. "Under arrest for what? Never mind, we can talk after I bring Stack in. We only have a couple minutes till he drifts out of range."

"I'm charging you with gross negligence in letting this happen, and especially not watching Glisters—firing off that thruster burst is probably attempted murder. Now get back in here, that's an order."

I hit the OPEN button. The outer door swings open. I clip my belay into the slot at the head of the airlock and climb out toward the wheeling stars. "Commander, I'm not going to let Stack die while you play whatever stupid game Derlock told you to play."

The antenna is at the end of its stretched belay, slowly moving outward as the ship rotates. Less than 15 meters beyond it, Stack is tumbling like a top, spun faster with every tool he has managed to throw.

"Put Glisters on. I sent him to find a belay line," I say.

"He's under arrest. As soon as you come back in, Derlock will go out to get Stack."

"There isn't time," I say, and then realize Stack's voice

has echoed mine; *sheeyeffinit, it's open channel.*

There's a pause that I hope means she's understanding the situation, but then she says, "Come back in and we'll discuss it."

I look around; Stack's main belay, still clipped here by the airlock and clipped at the mounting post, will reach right now, so I go to private channel with Stack, locking out Em and the others, and say, "Stack, try to push things out from your center like passing a beach ball, that way it won't spin you. I'm going to try to get a line I can throw to you." I grab handholds and clamber as fast as I dare toward the mounting point.

Stack is keening, a low frustrated whine. I keep saying, soothingly, that I'm going to be there in just a second, I'm almost there—and then I am, and I undo the belay from where he had it temporarily clipped. Now all I have to do is get it to him, and hope it will reach.

There's no time at all. I start coiling the loose end of his belay on one arm; it pulls me back toward the airlock, where the other end is attached. I count on my own belay to hold me, letting myself swoop three meters out into space.

I just need enough of a coil to throw, but Stack is moving farther and farther away. I will have it in just another moment, I'm actually almost at the airlock and I'll plant my feet there and—

Midship thrusters fire. I see the flickering white streaks, bright as a welding torch, for a moment all the way around; Stack and I are safely inside the protected space at the tail, but the hot plasma flares around the antenna.

I only glimpse that; all my attention is on my own trajectory away from the ship and toward Stack. I toss the coil at him and shout, "Stack, grab it!"

But the ship has already accelerated, and Stack, not being attached to it, hasn't. The gap that almost, sort of, maybe, we could have bridged, has opened too wide, and his belaying line cracks like a whip, two meters too short. He's moving away much faster now, because of the thrust; the line that didn't quite reach drifts out toward the rim, as the antenna did.

He is close to me; if he weren't in an evasuit, I would be able to see his facial expressions easily. But he's tumbling fast, and now he whispers, softly, "Susan, it didn't reach. You don't have another one, do you? And now the ship's moving away faster—" He sighs. "I'm getting so dizzy, tumbling like this."

The open channel is full of noise from some mike in the cockpit. Derlock is screaming that the thrusters just fired themselves, Glisters is shouting and maybe crying, and Emerald wants everyone to arrest everyone else.

Beyond the rim, the antenna is a tiny dot; the thruster exhaust must have cut the line, and the antenna was very likely cooked anyway. It's gone.

I go back to private channel. "Stack?"

He's crying. "I'm scared. You can't do anything, can you?"

"No. I wish I could."

He's still a distance that, on Earth, I could run in seconds. Inside the ship, I could airswim it in less than a minute; but here in the vacuum, so far from anything, he might as well be circling Alpha Centauri for all the good I can do him.

"Can you stay on the radio with me for a while?"

"I will. As long as I can still hear you. The transmitters for the outside private channels aren't very powerful, so probably we'll fade out before"—I think *before you die*—"before our tanks are out of air." (*Which means the same thing as "before you die," you idiot!* I scream at myself in my head.)

"Okay." I watch him tumble slowly away. After a moment he says, "I wish I'd hooked that tube up. I'm starting to have to go, and I'm kind of thirsty."

"The moisture recovery system that picks up your sweat and tears and stuff will work on your urine," I tell him, "just not as fast as if you were putting urine directly into it. But it'll pick up the liquid from the inside of your suit, and dry you, and then after a while it will have some water for you. So you probably won't like it, but you should, um . . ."

"Just go in my pants?"

"Well, you sure can't take them off."

He starts laughing. "All right, I wish Glisters was still on the line. I'd like to report it to him like all the other steps in an eva. Now squeezing bladder . . . now thinking relaxing thoughts . . ."

Definitely TMI. "Hey, let's talk, okay? Any subject you

want. Just so you know you have a friend."

We talk about our favorite toys and stories when we were little, and music and meeds now. He says he's wet and cold in his suit, but it's better than holding it. "Susan?"

"Right here. I'll stay right here till I'm sure you're"—*Dead. Shut up!*—"out of radio range." He's so tiny now I can't quite make out his human shape; it's been an hour since he fell.

"Susan, this is important. You *know* it wasn't Glisters's fault. He'd never fuck up, and he'd never have done this to hurt me. Even though I used to beat him up. He's just not the type. He'd never do that, would he?"

"Never."

"And Emerald showed up as soon as the thruster fired the first time; so someone told her. It has to have been Derlock, doesn't it? Hey, you and Glisters, you watch out. He hates you, too. So you watch out. And don't let him get away with it. *Please* don't let him get away with it."

"I won't. I promise."

"I know." There's a long pause and I can hear brief interruptions as groups of packets fail to make it through the distance, leaving holes in the message. "Susan, I'm so scared. And I feel so stupid. I threw the first aid kit while I was trying to get back to the ship. I bet it had morphine. I could've used that to sleep through the end, or even go out with an OD. That's another stupid way I screwed up. I could've practiced swinging away with the antenna on belay, too, and then I'd've done the right thing when it went wrong. I could've done a lot of things."

"I'm here, Stack, listening. Say whatever you want. But I wish you wouldn't be so hard on yourself."

"I know. I'm afraid to go into the dark alone, but your signal is starting to have big—in it—can't—much longer, so thanks for—"

"Stack, if you can hear me, I'll never forget you, and you did great, and you tried so hard, and nobody could've done better." I don't believe it, but with all my heart I want him to be able to think that I believe it. "Stack?"

Nothing.

I stay outside hailing him for another twenty minutes. No reply.

In case he can hear me, I tell him he was my friend, and a great guy, and I'll never forget him. Then I start cranking that belay line around my arm. I feel n-nillion tonnes hanging from my heart, even though I'm weightless.

I wind up my belaying line; it pulls me into the airlock. I grasp the handholds, clamber to the manual controls, push the CLOSE OUTSIDE. The outside door shumps shut.

No click of vents opening.

No rush of air.

The pale red screen has one gray message:

LOCK SEALED FOR QUARANTINE. NO ACCESS.

17

"YOU'RE THE COMMANDER, COMMANDER"

May 24, 2129. On *Virgo*, upbound Earth to Mars. 153 million kilometers from the sun, 119 million kilometers from Mars, 30 million kilometers from Earth.

THE QUARANTINE SCREEN lets me get as far as requesting an override, but then it wants a password that I don't have and can't guess. With my suit radio on scan and autorequest, I should automatically connect to anyone with an open mike. Nothing.

Faceplate display shows fifty minutes of air left. Figuring I was about half an hour behind Stack, he has around twenty. He's out there by himself, just the spinning stars around him. Maybe by now his suit has recovered enough liquid so he can have a drink of water. When *Virgo* whirls through his field of view, it's probably still bigger than his hand at the end of his arm; it must seem so close.

Minutes creep by. I float back and forth in the metal can of the airlock; I can just reach across it with my outspread arms.

I think about Stack, crying, afraid, ashamed of his failure. It's getting close to the time when he'll run out of air and die; no, looking at my faceplate, it's past then. Probably he just passed out a little while ago, while I was feeling sorry for him.

I hope the recycler scavenged enough for him to drink, so he wasn't thirsty. As the CO_2 built up . . . I try not to imagine him hot and panting, gasping and miserable, before he passed out, but it's all I can think about.

I can't get the sound of his crying out of my mind.

Fifteen minutes left on my air. Stack's surely gone by now. Everything must have seemed close enough to touch, and everything was far enough away to die, when his eyes closed on the swiftly tumbling stars. I wish there'd been a hand for him to hold, or a voice for him to hear.

Meanwhile, I'm still alive, but the green bar indicating my air is down to ten minutes, and I am in this steel box.

Nothing to lose. I suppose it's just possible that there is someone in there who would help me if they could, but they don't know where I am. I flip over and kick both boots against the inner door, clutching a handhold above my head so that I impact harder.

I kick, I kick, I kick . . . nothing. I keep it up. I can do this till I run out of air, anyway.

Glisters's voice in my earphone is strangely mushy and slurred. "Susan, grab a handhold—"

After a month together on *Virgo*, it's so automatic to do what he says that I have a tight grip when the door pops under my feet and air slams into the lock, trying to fling me backward for an instant. Then the pressure equalizes and something huge and pink, a tentacle or a snake, wriggles into the airlock, wraps around my ankles, and pulls me off my handhold and into the ship.

Fwuffy's trunk. Of course. Wychee's here, now, fumbling at my locking collar, popping off my helmet.

I suck in fresh, clean air.

"I was afwaid fuh you, Susan!"

"I was afraid myself," I say to Fwuffy. I turn to Wychee; her face is swollen and red on one side and her hair looks like someone grabbed it and yanked a few times. "Stack?" she asks.

"The line almost reached him," I say, "then the thrusters fired—and—" The feelings and the sudden availability of all that air get to me, and I start to sob. Wychee and Marioschke converge on me, helping me out of the evasuit and back into the coverall I left on the floor. Now that I'm inside and safe—and Stack is gone—there's time for it to hit us all.

It's a while before any of us speaks, and we're all avoiding each other's eyes.

Wychee notices me staring at her bruised cheek and the little trickle of dried blood under her nose; I can see that some of the hair just above her forehead came out by the roots. She wipes her teary face. "We had a kind of major discussion with Emerald and Derlock," she says. "Derlock tried to tell us that he and Em only woke up when the thruster fired the first time, and rushed to the cockpit to discover that Glisters had screwed up and the ship's automatic systems had taken back over. Glisters was yelling about you and Stack being out there, and Emerald and Derlock were yelling that he had gone insane and was trying to kill both of you.

"Then F.B. popped up a screen in the cockpit—neither of them had paid any attention to him, so he just airswam over and did it. He shouted that the record showed that the commander's password had been used for the override that let them fire the thrusters and lock out Glisters. Not that there was any mystery, but there was the evidence.

"Everyone started pushing and yelling, and punching and kicking each other. Fwuffy decided that Em and Derlock were being very, very naughty—"

"They wuhn't wetting Gwistas wescue Stack," Fwuffy says, firmly. Then, suddenly, in the deep voice that doesn't have the *r* and *l* problem, with his face expressionless, he says, "This horton is suffering conflicts in its moral sense because it was forced to harm a human to prevent a greater harm. It must be reassured that it chose the right course of action."

"Exactly right," Marioschke says, her arms around his neck. "You were a very, very good horton and we are very pleased with you. You did everything right." We all loudly agree, emphatically.

Fwuffy shakes himself. "I'm feewing much betta."

After a pause, Wychee resumes. "Anyway, Fwuffy just grabbed Derlock, tossed him into a locker, and locked him in; then he did the same with Emerald. They're still in those lockers." She makes herself look me in the eye. "Could you talk with Stack—?"

"I could until he drifted out of range. The suit-to-suit

is very low power. He was still alive when he went out of range, but by now—" I start to cry again, and Wychee and I hang on to each other for a while, unable to do or think of much else.

In the cockpit I find that Glisters has had a real beating; he's just in process of applying that nasty-tasting nanogunk that fixes your teeth. That would stop any other person in the world from talking, but he sits down and begins to type onto the big screen:

3 loose teeth
2 cracked
Maybe swallowed 2ple pieces?
Derlock kicked me in mouth w/heel
Nanos supposed to reassemble, grow new tooth where needed.
Goop will hold in place till nanos done

"Are you in pain, Glisters?" I ask.
He shakes his head.

Painblocker working

Then he takes some extra time to type:

I have recorded, isolated, and undone everything Derlock did in
ship's computer systems
It will make sure nothing more wakes up
And be evidence for trial.

F.B., floating over by one of the instruction consoles, is even more battered than Glisters; he waves "hi" and I see that the protective nanoplaster completely fills his mouth.

"How long before you can talk and eat?" I ask.

He holds up four fingers.

"Four days?"

A nod. He floats forward and squeezes my arm, looking into my eyes; I know that's about Stack.

Fleeta says, "You said she'd say some words."

Everyone looks at everyone else.

Glisters types:

Fleeta is right.

She dimples and beams at having been right about something. I'm still bewildered. Glisters types:

Commander officiates at memorial service

We arrested commander

Pilot = next in line = you

You're the commander, Commander.

Everyone is watching me, silently.

"Let's go to the tail deck for this."

We do, and I manage a little memorial service for Stack. If anyone realizes that I'm using a bunch of phrases and ideas from Pop's old retro-movie-imitation meeds, especially the ones set back in twentieth- or nineteenth-century military, they're smart enough not to say anything.

I guess I do all right. Everyone cries at the right parts, except Fleeta, of course. Big tears are rolling down Fwuffy's face. I didn't know hortons could cry, but then there's a lot I didn't know they could do, like stand up to injustice, make a right decision instantly, or save all our lives.

After the service, while we're standing around, Wychee says, "Susan, officially we should hold another election to elect you our commander."

"Why would you do that?"

"Because you're the one we're going to elect. Emerald and Derlock won't be voting, and you'll have everyone's vote—"

"Except mine, I'm voting for Glisters—"

"Okay, you'll be elected seven to one," she says.

I feel punched in the gut.

Glisters sees by my expression that I think he's still counting Stack. He says, "No, considering all the work Fwuffy is doing in the farm sections, Marioschke suggested he should have a vote, and I agree."

Wychee and F.B. are both nodding vigorously, so it's already a majority; I know Fleeta will vote yes, too, if we can get her attention and she understands the question.

I look at Fwuffy, who is still wiping his eyes with his trunk; the memorial service was hard on him. "You're right," I say. "Let's be the first outpost of horton equality."

"It makes me vewy pwoud."

"I'm proud of *you*, Fwuffy." I look around at all of them. "Well, I think Glisters is the real best guy for the job. Doesn't anyone agree with me?"

No one does, and just like that, I'm commander.

Glisters is now officially the pilot, which makes a little bit of sense, since he's done more "flying the ship" than anyone else, but after all, most pilots haven't done much flying in the last hundred years, any more than most chamberlains have made a king's bed or most pursers carry around a bag of gold coins. So he'll keep right on being our engineer, but his title will be pilot.

Wychee will be the steward, but her title will be engineer. "At least," I point out, "if something breaks, it will be because the engineer is actually a cook, and if there's ever anything wrong with the food, we can say it was cooked by an engineer."

Wychee razzes, then winces because it hurts her face. Emerald punched her hard enough to crack a cheekbone, and the nanos are at work on it right now; I wonder how that's going to feel, a week or so of having her face ache from where her best friend hit her.

I set new watches—Glisters with Fleeta, because he can run the ship by himself anyway; me with Marioschke, because so can I and that way she can study or do her farm work; and Wychee with F.B. because they're who's left, and if they're not perfect on everything in ship's ops just yet, Wychee will be soon enough, and F.B. will be eventually, no matter how much time or effort it takes him. Fwuffy was geneered not to need much sleep—he had to accomodate a five-year-old's whims—so he'll part-time on everyone's watch as needed.

Wychee and F.B. volunteer to take the first new watch; I think that's because Wychee doesn't want to deal with Emerald right away, which is where I'm going next. Glisters and I huddle to work out what we should do.

"First thing, though, I'm going to miss having our watch together," I tell Glisters. "I wish I could have more time with my best friend."

"Nye cess job you gib tuh nigh." His words sound like they're coming through a mass of raw steak.

"Show me on your wristcomp."

He keys, and a flat mechanical voice says, "Nicest job you gave out tonight."

"What job?" I ask.

"Your best friend."

"Yeah. So now *you're* happy, too. It occurs to me that everyone on board is happy with their new job except the commander."

"Not Emerald and Derlock. Their new job equal-sign 'prisoner.'"

"That's why you're my best friend; you can always think of something to cheer me up. Here's what I've got in mind—"

I think he's disappointed that I'm not executing Derlock for murder; maybe I didn't realize how much Stack's friendship meant to a lonely guy like Glisters. Or maybe it's just that engineer/techie solve-it-once-and-for-all instinct coming through. Grudgingly, though, he agrees to do things my way.

May 25, 2129. On *Virgo*, upbound Earth to Mars. 153 million kilometers from the sun, 118 million kilometers from Mars, 30 million kilometers from Earth.

"You people have no vision," Derlock says, coming out of

the storage locker that Fwuffy stuffed him into. "Emerald was the only one with any vision at all and she—"

"We're giving you ten minutes on the toilet," I say, "with Glisters standing over you with a length of pipe. If there's any sound of struggle, Fwuffy will come in to back him up. And no matter what Glisters tells me happened in there, I'll believe him, so you probably don't want to antagonize him.

"After your time on the toilet, you get a bag of food, which Wychee has graciously prepared for you, a pump flask of water, and an empty flour container she's donating to be your chamber pot, which has sort of a spout you can use; if you aren't careful about keeping that closed, and end up spending your time in the locker with floating blobs of piss, well, that'll be your own fault, won't it? At each change of watches we'll let you out and feed you; that's when you can use the toilet, wash out your chamber pot, and refill your water. Every third watch or so you can take a shower, under supervision. We're giving Emerald the same deal, so hurry up in the bathroom because she's going next."

"We need to discuss—"

"No, we don't. Your ten minutes started forty seconds ago. If you use it up trying to argue, it will entertain me a lot when we put you back in the locker still needing to go."

Sullenly, he lets us conduct him to the bathroom; he emerges with two minutes left in his time, accepts the food, water, and chamber pot, and lets us lock him back in.

Emerald comes out screaming; it's not very coherent

but apparently we are all very bad, we prevented her from saving Stack and being a hero, and despite our sabotage, she is going to be more famous than all of us. So there. I watch her crap; she cries the whole time.

As we airswim back, I say, "If you cooperate for a while, maybe we could talk about some kind of parole."

She shrugs. "It's your ship now."

Afterward, neither Glisters nor I can sleep yet, so we join Wychee in the cockpit. "Glisters," I say, "I could do the research myself, but I know you'll do it ten times as fast as I can, and understand it better."

His wristcomp voice says, "Ask ampersand I get answer. Maybe right one."

"Well, first of all, what are our options for getting somebody to come out and rescue us? The antenna's gone, and the thrusters probably changed our course. Can the cap still get anyone all the way down to Mars, alive?"

He plays around on the keys, and eventually he puts up a picture on the main screen. It's not a very attractive one.

|||||||||||||||||||||||||||||||||||||||||||||||||||||||||||||||||||||||||

Notes for the Interested, #14

Recalculating after the accident

Mars, *Virgo*, and the cap will all be moving in orbits around the sun. The problem is to figure out the best time and place to launch the cap from *Virgo* so that it leaves *Virgo*'s orbit and goes into an orbit of its own which crosses Mars's orbit at a time when Mars will be there. The cap is limited by its engines and fuel tanks in how fast it can take off (about 4 hours of 10% g of acceleration), and by its recycling system for how long the crew inside will have air to breathe (67 days for a crew of 2).

The time during which a launch can get onto a trajectory that reaches a specified point at a specified time is called the **window**. The computer finds the window by calculating, for each future position of *Virgo* and Mars, what the flight time for the cap would be (if it can get there at all). Glisters is having the computer search, down to the minute, for the departure times in the future during which the travel time is the shortest, because having 67 days of air and having to be in the cap for 64 days means that if any little thing goes wrong—a very small leak, or accidentally deflecting into orbit rather than down to the surface, which might require a few days to correct—then the crew will suffocate.

Obviously they can't do anything to change Mars's orbit, they have already used up most of their reaction mass changing *Virgo*'s orbit before this, and the cap has a very limited ability to change its orbit. With such a small menu of possibilities, it is not surprising that the window turns out to be very "narrow"—it doesn't last long, and it is only "open" for a very short time.

▌▌▌

Wychee holds her hands up, smiling. "Threaten me with math and I'll agree to anything. I trust you both to figure out what will work best, though I suppose I'll have to learn to understand it myself in case anything happens to you. But what I am getting out of this right now is that this is the place for the hook, in the meed, where Susan's father would lean forward, slap his desk, and say, 'Dammit, just gimme the bottom line here!'"

"Sheeyeffinit!" I'm laughing ultra hard. "Why didn't you tell me you could imitate him like that? That's a real old style he uses for twentieth-century stuff—uh, Asner Irate, that's what it's called. He's used it when he's played Sheridan Whiteside and Walter Burns. We've *got* to make it back now, it would be too terrible if he never saw that."

Glisters, seeing a chance to explain something technical, ignores us and plunges like an otter into a fish hatch. "Bottom line: Best minimum trip time for the cap we can do is 64 days, with a 40-minute window for departure. Maximum of two passengers because they'll be pushing the limits of recycling their air by day 67."

"When is that window?" I ask.

"32 days from now."

"And how fast does that get us rescued?"

"The two people on the cap should be within hailing range of Mars at . . ." He types and looks at the screen. "20 days from Mars or 44 days after they leave us. So the Space Patrol is going to know 76 days from now, or 19 days before we're at our closest to Mars, and if they take off the minute they get the message, they could probably catch us in five or six months."

"Five or six *months*?"

"They're starting behind us and at an angle, and they

travel in a solar orbit the same as us, so they can only be at a slightly higher speed. Ever hear the expression, 'A stern chase is a long chase'?"

"Ever hear the expression 'This blows'?"

"Unfortunately both expressions apply. By the time they catch us it will be faster to take us to Earth—only about eight months compared to ten for Mars. That's the kind of thing that happens when everything moves in orbits."

Unfortunately Crazy Science Girl knows more than enough to know he's right. I wish I could tell her to shut up.

He holds up his hands, as if trying to placate us. "I hope I can build a submillimeter-wave antenna with supplies on board here. It will probably take a long difficult while. I doubt we'll have it working by the time we'll need to launch the cap, so my suggestion is we try both."

"If your antenna works—"

"If we have a working antenna anytime in the next month, *Gagarin* will be able to come out from Mars and meet us, and we'll probably all be arriving on Mars right on schedule. But honestly, Susan, chances are I can't. I'll get going on it and work hard, but I'm not exactly brilliant."

"You're good enough to fool us," I point out. "All right. We'll figure out which two people can go down in the cap, and start training them, and you'll get to work on the antenna as soon as you've had some rest."

We have a bad moment in the bunk room when we box up Stack's stuff to put away, but we manage. Glisters, with the third watch, takes a sleeping pill and passes out in the bunk above me; I try to sleep, but I don't even really doze before F.B. comes in to wake me, and I have to go to the cockpit and relieve Wychee. There are a couple thuds and a swallowed scream while she's letting Emerald have her break from the locker. My investigation goes as far as asking Wychee, "Are you okay?" and getting back, "I'm *great*."

May 28, 2129. On *Virgo*, upbound Earth to Mars. 155 million kilometers from the sun, 113 million kilometers from Mars, 31 million kilometers from Earth.

A few days later, on my way to relieve Glisters, I'm passing by the storage lockers where we're holding Emerald and Derlock. I hear soft thumps; when I stop and listen, it's groups of between one and five thumps, separated by a breath or so, and after a long chain of them from Derlock's locker, there's a long reply from Emerald's.

I quietly push off the floor and airswim out. In the cockpit, I find Glisters is poring over an advanced tutorial on submillimeter-wave communication.

"Hey, Glisters, did you ever happen to see a meed my dad made, way back, one of those revival things he was so popular in, called *White Heat*?"

"No, why?"

"Well, in it, there were these two prisoners sitting next to each other in cells, who communicated by tap code. And guess what I heard in the storage lockers in the corridor coming here?"

"Taps?"

"More like thumps. And you know a guy like Derlock might just be acquainted with tap code, either through his sleazy dad or through his sleazy interests. *And* it only takes about one minute to explain how it works out loud. So if he took a chance just once, and explained, and none of us heard him doing it—anyway, these thoughts occurred to me, because after listening a bit, either they're using tap code, or they're amusing each other with the world's slowest drum riffs. So when we do the potty break this time, I think we need to move Emerald, maybe to a container in the Pressurized Cargo Section. It'll take more time to tend them, but I think we have to."

Glisters nods. "Well, you might want to try to split them up anyway. We might want to parole Emerald for something important."

"I wouldn't trust her with anything."

"Have you had any time to think about which two people should start training to go on the cap? Not you, me, or Wychee; we've got to stay here to keep the others alive. That leaves F.B., who can be okay by the time we send him; he's brave enough, he doesn't learn fast but he learns, and maybe most of all he won't give up and he knows what's important. Fleeta couldn't do more than keep F.B. company. Marioschke flips out and gets all helpless."

"Besides, we need to consider poor Fwuffy," I say, grinning. "Let's not separate a cosmic hippie chick from her pink elephant. And Marioschke's pretty important from an eating-regular standpoint, since she's really running the farm—Wychee doesn't have time. All right, I see where you're going. We need to send two. F.B. can go, he'll be fine, and he should, and his most logical crewmate is Emerald."

Glisters nods. "I guess we *could* send Derlock—"

"Lock poor little F.B. into a cap with him? Sheeyeffinit. No, you're right. It's like the problem about the farmer taking the fox, the goose, and the basket of corn across the river when there's only room for two of them in the boat on each trip; the secret is to keep the goose with you at all times. Derlock's the goose. F.B. and Emerald are the most competent people we can spare."

May 28, 2129. On *Virgo*, upbound Earth to Mars. 155 million kilometers from the sun, 113 million kilometers from Mars, 31 million kilometers from Earth.

"Would you like to stay out for another two hours?" I ask Emerald after her bathroom break as I'm returning her to her storage container.

She looks back at me as if I'm crazy, and I suppose that really was a dumb question. "If you're offering that, of course I do. What are the rules?"

"For the moment, you and I are just going to go somewhere for a talk. We were almost friends for a little while, you know. You can get some exercise or take a more leisurely shower, or for that matter just have more time on the toilet, if you'd like. But whatever you choose to do, I'm going to stay with you the whole time, and I'm going to at least try to talk to you. We're experimenting with giving you more time and more freedom."

"Is Derlock getting this, too?"

"No." I hold my voice level and even. "He's dangerous, Emerald."

"I guess you'd think that," she says. "I want to go somewhere with a window."

"Would you like to go to the Forest? I had Wychee set us up box lunches—it can be kind of a picnic."

"Yeah, I'd like that very much."

I pretend not to notice that she sounds choked and is rubbing her face.

In the Forest, we sit on the new grass by a window to eat. Sunflashes alternate with pools of stars.

I can't think of any tactful way to ask, so I blurt, "Do you understand what Derlock did?"

"What about what Stack did? Did you even think about that? He didn't practice, so when something went wrong he made a really stupid mistake, and then he was all whiny crybaby and wanting us to rescue him. Did you even think that maybe Stack was not all that deserving?"

"He didn't deserve to die."

"And he wouldn't have if he'd just practiced enough and known what he was doing. It was just a little prank."

"The second thruster fire threw the antenna off the ship, and the exhaust cooked it, and cut its cable. If he'd been belayed to it and climbing back in—"

"He'd have been back where it was safe long before that happened. It was just a little prank, to teach him that he

needed to stop having all these hero fantasies about rescuing the ship and concentrate on his practicing. He'd have
been fine if he hadn't been such a fuckup, and it was just a
prank to teach him not to be such a fuckup." She's looking
down into the window and recoils when the sunlight hits,
sudden and hard.

I'm lost for a moment in the memory of Stack calling for
me as he drifted out of range and his air ran out. I tell her,
"I think Derlock gave Torporin to Bari and King on purpose, knowing it would kill them. I'm not sure the explosion that killed the crew and passengers was an accident;
the witness that it might not have been was Stack, and
now he happens to have conveniently died in just-a-little-
prank." She stares at me, flat-faced. "Derlock got excited in
bed whenever he talked about hurting someone—"

"You never loved him." She sounds like you'd imagine
a zombie would.

"No," I say. "I didn't. I never did. Back at Excellence
Shop, and when I was only thinking about how I could
get splyctered, it was zoomed to have a boyfriend that was
probably going to be splyctered into n-nillion hooks because of something weird and scary. The scariness was
ultra attractive, because I didn't know he was a full-on
sociopath who kills people. Out here, he's just scary. And
no, no, no, I never loved him." She's slumped over the window like a cyberpuppet that's lost its control. "Do *you*?"

"Can we just look at the stars, and enjoy the open
space?"

So we do; I help her find the Earth and Moon (back by

the tail, a tiny bright dot that you can just barely see is round, and almost on top of it, a dimmer little star), and then pick out Mars (a dimmish star halfway down our sky toward the nose).

"Would you like to do something like this again tomorrow?" I ask as we turn to airswim back to the storage container that is her prison.

"Well, I'll have to check my calendar, but I think I can fit it in," she says.

I laugh; she doesn't acknowledge that.

June 18, 2129. On Virgo, upbound Earth to Mars. 167 million kilometers from the sun, 87 million kilometers from Mars, 37 million kilometers from Earth.

For the next three weeks, nothing much changes. Every day Glisters gets up and works on how to build a submillimeter-wave detector array that he can plug into our communication system. Wychee and I take turns drilling F.B. and Emerald on what to do in the cap. Marioschke's crops grow in the farm sections, Fwuffy gets better and better at helping, Fleeta seems more lost, and Derlock makes no noise from his locker.

As we start preparing them for the cap trip, Wychee and I slowly realize F.B. is not the poor moron kid we thought he was. His enthusiasm and attention make it easy to forgive him as he muddles and misses and does everything wrong. That's on the first try—by the tenth, he'll sort of have it; by the twentieth, he'll be right more often than not; and he keeps going a hundred or maybe a thousand times, till the only way he can do it is the right way.

Emerald is ultra polite and quiet about doing everything we ask her to do and absolutely no more.

One time, after practice, Emerald says. "I've been thinking. I'm sorry about the things I said about Stack, because working on this with F.B., I've started to understand how Stack felt, about practice and all. That's the sweetest thing about F.B., he has to work for everything, everybody's a natural compared to him, but he doesn't seem to resent anyone."

"Would you like to talk about maybe moving out of the storage container and back into your regular bunk till you go? We'd have to set some conditions—"

She shrugs. "Wear a tracker and don't go near where Derlock's locked up?"

"That's it. Thanks for understanding."

She nods, not looking at me. "I can do a better job preparing for the trip and I'll feel better. I just hope the rest of them accept me as much as you do."

"That's out of my control."

"That's why I'm just hoping."

18

I GUESS YOU'LL NEVER UNDER-STAND ABOUT LOVE

June 24, 2129. On *Virgo*, upbound Earth to Mars. 171 million kilometers from the sun, 74 million kilometers from Mars, 39 million kilometers from Earth.

WE'VE TESTED THE emergency siren to find out what it sounds like, so when it rips me out of a sound sleep, I snap awake analyzing:

- No pressure alarm, so nothing has breached us.
- Lights are on, we have power.
- Gravity is almost weightless, normal in the bunk room.

Clock shows it's the first hour of F.B.'s and Wychee's watch—no wonder Glisters and Fleeta are staggering around half-lost, they must've just gotten to bed.

As I yank on my coverall, Glisters is struggling out of his ducky jammies in an aerial flurry of arms and legs; Fleeta is blinking and feeling for her clothes.

I bounce and airswim as fast as I can; behind me I can hear Glisters scrabbling along, bumping the corridor walls, almost at my feet as I shoot into the cockpit, to find Wychee frantically racing through screen after screen.

Without looking up she explains, "I think Derlock and Emerald have taken off in the lifeboat cap—the screen is showing an emergency ejection, that's what set off the siren. Looks like they dumped a little air and water, and did a hot takeoff, so there may be rocket-exhaust damage up toward the nose."

"*Idiots!*" Glisters says. He's awake now. "It's four full days before the window! They don't have enough air and water to survive for their flight time. They—"

Wychee holds up her hand to quiet him, and gestures to the screen in front of her. "I'm trying to find F.B. I think he's locked in Derlock's cell, but I don't dare leave here in case they're still on board—we can't let them take over the cockpit—"

"Exactly right," I say. "Lock yourself in. Confirm before letting anyone in, call Fleeta and tell her to come here right away, then lock her in here with you—let's not have any hostages available. I'll check Derlock's cell and see if F.B.'s there. Glisters, go to the tailward entrance of Vacuum Cargo Section 2, and put on a pressure suit. Don't close the breathing loop unless you have to, but be ready to. Then take a crowbar, go up the coretube to the cap dock where the lifeboat was, and see what's going on. Look for pressure leaks or any other damage—"

"What's the crowbar for?" Glisters asks.

"Derlock," I say. "If you do find him, try to hit him before he sees you. Don't stop hitting him till you're sure he's helpless. If you find Emerald, same procedure. *No conversation till they're helpless.* Got it?"

He says "got it" over his shoulder as he shoots out the door.

At the locker where we'd been holding Derlock, I work the combination and the door pops open; F.B. is in there, all right, floating in the middle of the space, waving his hands in a little ineffectual flutter, crying. I pull him out. Derlock's and Emerald's ankle bracelets are in there with him.

"Wychee, I've got F.B., he was in the locker." I'm turning him to better see his swollen, puffy face. It's silly but I think, *But that's not fair, we've rebuilt his teeth once already!* He tries to say something but bubbles out blood.

Marioschke airswims in, takes one look, and barks, "Fwuffy! General Injury Kit from the pharmacy!"

"Wight!" There's a thundering boom out in the corridor.

At my glance, Marioschke says, "He's learning to read. The voice actuated software recognizes his speech. And when he's in a hurry he jumps down long open corridors, ultra faster than—"

F.B. bubbles. I pull out a clean utility rag to blot blood from around his mouth. "I can do that," Marioschke says, "and I'll be safe as soon as Fwuffy gets back. Wychee wanted me to relieve you so you could back up Glisters—"

Wychee comes online. "Marioschke, Fwuffy got the kit and he's on his way back. He says he thinks the infirmary has been looted. He's—"

A *whoosh* and a *boom* out in the corridor; a horton going full speed into a four-footed landing makes some noise. Fwuffy's trunk reaches into the locker and hands Marioschke the kit. "Hold F.B. steady for me for a minute," she says. "Firmly but gently."

Marioschke applies sensors to find the contusions, air-injects nanos to seal up the damaged capillaries, and checks for fractures. "You've got a bunch of little cracks in your cheekbones and one just below your eyebrow," she tells him, swabbing his face gently, "so I'm putting in some addressable nanos that will glue that and make it secure again. Your mouth is a mess, I'm afraid you weren't all the way healed and then he hit you again. Poor guy. I'm going to put in stabilizing foam, slap my arm if you have any trouble breathing."

She puts the nozzle of a can that looks like cake frosting between F.B.'s lips, carefully in the least-bruised place, and squeezes the button. He jerks and she asks, "Did it hurt?"

He nods with a shrug; I guess he expected it to.

She's calling for a robot stretcher from the infirmary as I bound away to join Glisters. "Where are you and what have you found?" I say into my phone as I fly along the coretube.

"I'm in the nose spire at the cap dock. The cap is gone, all right. No sign of them. There's heat-scarring on the metal outside the cap dock, and the shielding water near the nose is 20 kelvins hotter than it should be. Looks like they blew the door on the airlock, so *that's* permanent damage, but we've got seven more airlocks."

Wychee breaks in. "I'm running the body-heat and moving-mass detection programs they use in case a cargo animal gets loose, and all I'm finding is us. I was pretty sure they were gone anyway."

Glisters and I spend twenty more minutes scouting just to be sure, but "We knew they were gone from the first second," I point out to Glisters. "You might as well get out of that pressure suit."

"Yeah. See you at the infirmary; is F.B. bad?"

"Pretty bad, I think, but Marioschke's done all the first aid tutorials, and she's got a touch. After we look in on F.B., we probably need to have a meeting for everyone in the cockpit."

The infirmary recommends knocking F.B. out for ten days in a suspended animation tank; that way, he'll get up healthy and functional, but if we try to let him heal while doing ship's duties, it could be a month, and he'd be in pain for most of it. He indicates that he wants to do his duties and I override him and order him to get all the way well, quickly.

We roll out a suspended animation tank from the recessed storage in the wall. Very gently, Marioschke tucks him in, smoothing creases and wrinkles in the smartfiber cocoon so that he won't wake up stiff or with sore spots. Just before we close the cover she strokes his face and I see him try to smile.

We've been so busy that it's only then that I notice all the drawers in the infirmary hanging empty. Wychee runs an inventory from the cockpit. When we've all joined her there, including Fwuffy, Marioschke asks, "Why do people hurt F.B. all the time?"

"Well, I don't, or at least I try not to," I say. "I don't think Glisters ever did, or you."

"I didn't say *all* people," she points out. "I was just wondering why it is that when some people are struggling and doing their best, something about that just invites everyone else to stomp on them."

"I don't think anyone who is left on the ship will act like that," I say.

"Yeah. And we're going to be here for weeks or months, aren't we?"

"I'm afraid so," Glisters says. "Could be years, truthfully. Your farming work is probably going to save us all."

"At least F.B. will get some time without being picked on for being himself." Marioschke sounds oddly satisfied.

I say, "All right, let's talk damage, everyone. They looted the infirmary. Wychee, what do we know about that?"

"Still working on—hey. The system just popped up a note: PLEASE RELAY TO SUSAN, WHOEVER IS TAKING INFIRMARY INVENTORY."

"Of course," Glisters says. "They didn't want to send a note that might arrive and alert you before their getaway, so they tied it to something you were bound to do after they had already left."

We all lean over Wychee's shoulders and read the words scrolling down the screen:

Susan,

I'm sorry, I guess you'll never understand about love. The first
thing we'll do on Mars is tell them you're back on *Virgo* and need
rescuing. I made Derlock promise that. And don't worry that we
won't make it, I know Glisters said we had to go in a very narrow window, but Derlock said Glisters's numbers are wrong and
he'd checked them out, and besides if we have to he's loaded
in a bunch of oxygen tanks, and anyway if we have to we'll just
make more oxygen out of the water on board. So we're fine and
we'll send help.

I wish we could have been friends,
Emerald

P.S. Really sorry about how hard Derlock had to hit poor F.B. but
we had to do it, he was going to rat on us. We couldn't let anything keep us apart. Someday maybe you'll understand; you
seem like a nice person.

"Shee*yeffin*it." Glisters drags the syllables out till that
expression is a paragraph.

He clatters at a keyboard, pulling something up on one
of the side screens. In a minute or so, he says, "This makes
no sense. Derlock took the time and effort to load in a quarter of a tonne of drugs, which couldn't possibly have done
him any good, but I'm not seeing that he did what Emerald
said he did, at all. I mean, what he said could almost have

been true. *If* they rode down as far as they could on the air recycling system, then bled oxygen into the system from LOX tanks, they could extend their range enough to get them to Mars alive. Or just barely maybe they could do that with an electrolysis rig running their whole flight, if they bled off the hydrogen and released the oxygen, though they'd be nearly out of drinking water by the end. But she mentions both, and the inventory isn't showing any LOX tank or any electrolysis rig is missing. So instead of the things they needed to survive, they took—"

"That son of a bitch!" Wychee looks up from her inventory of the infirmary's drug supply. "Fleeta, how much Fendrisol do you have left?"

She looks confused. "I never have *any*. I take it whenever the infirmary calls me and tells me to come and take it."

"He took the *Fendrisol*?" I ask. Without Fendrisol, happistuf replicates in the brain like yeast in bread dough, and you spiral into the laughing dive very quickly.

Wychee gestures at the screen. "All of it."

Fleeta's confusion deepens, but she never loses that joyful expression. "But I *have* to take it. Every other day, nowadays. I'm close to the margin. If I don't take it, full terminal degeneration will start almost right away."

Wychee's fingers pound the keyboard as if she thought she could force it to give her the answer she wanted. "We can synthesize most of the other stuff he stole, like morphine, and the antidepressants and antipsychotics. But Fendrisol is extracted from farmed orcas."

Fleeta giggles in sheer glee. "It's okay. I'll miss you all, and everything, but I'm going to feel happier and happier."

"We're *all* going to get home, alive," I say, trying to style Resolute Will of Iron, which I used to be good at.

I guess not anymore. Fleeta's hysterical peals of laughter spoil the effect. She goes giggling off to the bunk room.

Wychee breaks the silence. "What can Derlock be doing? Fendrisol isn't something anyone would ever take recreationally; it slows down the effects of happistuf, and at high doses it's toxic enough so you can use it to kill yourself. That's all. Everything else he took had recreational potential and was something someone might deal. Fendrisol was the only purely medical drug he stole."

Glisters sighs. "Besides, how does he expect to get off the cap with what amount to four or five sizable crates of drugs, keep them all concealed, and then sell them? It feels like he's doing something on purpose and I can't see what."

I think about that. "Knowing Derlock, there's some reason for stealing that Fendrisol. I don't think it was to kill Fleeta, because he didn't care about her one way or another."

Wychee says, "You know, there's the old story about the guy who crosses the border in a big shiny new car every day for a year; the border patrol always searches, never finds anything, until they realize he's smuggling cars. Maybe Derlock stole the stuff with recreational potential because he hoped we'd just figure the Fendrisol was one more drug in a long list of what he was stealing. Neither he nor Emerald has ever used any of the recreational drugs much, and you're right, he couldn't have hoped to sell it. I think he stole the plain old drug-drugs to hide his real objective—which was the Fendrisol, not anything else."

"He took extra minutes to grab Fendrisol," Glisters says, "but he didn't take oxygen tanks or an electrolysis rig—so somehow, getting the Fendrisol was more important than air. And he didn't tell Emerald about it. He wants her to think they're okay for air when they're not." He glances from one to the other of us. "I think the worst part of this story is yet to come, and maybe I should be happy not to know it yet."

June 28, 2129. On *Virgo*, upbound Earth to Mars. 174 million kilometers from the sun, 69 million kilometers from Mars, 40 million kilometers from Earth.

Glisters finishes building his antenna when F.B. still has six days to go in the tank. He seems more sad than happy; when I ask him about it, he says he's just thinking how much F.B. and Stack would have enjoyed working on this project with him, and how it's exactly the day when F.B. was supposed to leave on the cap. "It would have been the biggest adventure of his life," Glisters says. "He'd've been so proud."

Then *I'm* sad.

Glisters's device is a weird-looking contraption, a post about as tall as himself with three crosspieces at 60 degrees from each other so that the points form a hexagon or a Mogen David. It's pitted with half-centimeter–half-spherical holes, each capped with a glass lid covered by a tiny gold dot. Underneath each of them is a fast processor so that each of them is constantly, independently reporting the direction from which any signal is coming, and all of those hundreds of feeds then come in over a big quantum-optic bus to the processors on board the ship, which sort out and decode signals and pick spots we can try sending to. And every bit of it, Glisters built by hand.

"For a guy who spent all his time in class farting off and sketching sequences of titty shots, you've come a long way," I tell Glisters.

"You're not a bad commander for somebody who used to be a drunken sex kitten, yourself," he says. "Wanna go find somewhere where we can play with my antenna? I want to erect it as soon as we can, but I want it to be working right first, and I trust you with it more than anyone else."

"Hi-effin-larious. I'm glad you found a career outside pornography."

We test it in the Pressurized Cargo Section; it transmits and receives along the cargo handling deck beautifully. We try along the floors in Vacuum Cargo Section 2, and it's still good. Glisters leaves it set up there so he can experiment with controlling it with software from the cockpit; there are a couple of days of fussing. At last he says it's about as ready as it will ever get.

Glisters built it to be easy to mount, so installing it outside won't be nearly as complicated.

He shows me how to do it; you're on belay the whole time, and there are just two clamps to fasten at the mounting position, which is farther out toward the edge than before, but it's a straight, easy climb. After he shows me, we take turns trying out his procedure in Vacuum Cargo Section 2.

Glisters does it with one minor error and I do it with two ("always one hand on a grip" sounds easy to remember but it's something else again in practice).

"Well," I say, "I'll just practice till I've had ten flawless run throughs in a row, and then do it."

Glisters shakes his head. "I'm going to practice and do it. Not you."

"Don't be silly, you're indispensable," I tell him. "The ship wouldn't run without you and if anything goes wrong—"

"You and Wychee have been through every tutorial that is actually important," he says. "The day after the accident, sure, you couldn't have gotten along without me, but nowadays, I'm not indispensable. You are. The ship can run without me, Susan, you have the people to run it with, but it can't run without you here to listen to everyone, find the thing everyone can agree on, keep everyone working together and not fighting, carry us all through our depression and loneliness—"

"Sheeyeffinit."

We agree to let Wychee settle it, as the ranking officer not involved. Besides, she's sensible enough to see things my way. (Strangely, Glisters seems to think she'll agree with *him*.)

Wychee listens to both of us. "You're both wrong. After F.B. comes out of the tank, and has a few days of practice, he'll be able to do this."

"Absolutely not—" I say, as Glisters begins, "He shouldn't—"

"Both of you shut up. You're both right about each other. The rest of us need you. And as for the rest, Marioschke is being braver and more competent than I would have believed possible, but to do something like this? She'd be scared out of her mind. Obviously Fleeta can't. I could pretend that you've all learned to run the supply system and the farm and keep everyone fed, and Marioschke could probably handle the farm, but you'd be living on raw vegetables for six months and considering how I have to nag you about not screwing up my inventory, I'm not getting killed and letting you make the mess you're going to die in. So it should be F.B. He'll do his best, and you know he can do it."

July 8, 2129. On *Virgo*, upbound Earth to Mars. 182 million kilometers from the sun, 57 million kilometers from Mars, 43 million kilometers from Earth.

When F.B. comes out of the tank, Wychee fixes fettucine alfredo, hummus on soft rolls, and tapioca pudding in deference to his still-sore mouth. Before he's had time to digest, he wants to go to the pressurized hold and get to work on learning how to put the antenna into place.

We insist that he take some time. He practices in almost every waking hour for six days—not just the way it's supposed to go, but every scenario we can think up for things going wrong. "My biggest fear right now," I mutter to Glisters, "is that he'll figure out how afraid I am for him."

Glisters shrugs. "Wychee was right, he'll do it perfectly no matter what, and it's great to see his confidence. But my heart will be in my throat the whole time he's out there."

We schedule it while Glisters has the conn. I'm standing by in a pressure suit, ready to go for a rescue or backup; Wychee helps F.B. do his suit checkout. At last he climbs into the airlock, gently pulling Glisters's homebuilt antenna after him.

F.B.'s voice is clear as a bell in my headphones. "Inside-the-lock checklist complete and verified, cycling the lock." I feel the shudder through my feet as the ship retrieves air from the closet-sized tunnel. "Opening the outer door. Antenna on belay and moving properly. I'm on belay and belay line is running free. Advancing through outer door. I have my first exterior handhold. Advancing along the line of handholds, no problem," F.B. says. "Approaching the mount point. Clipping my second belay into place. Glisters, the antenna is acting like it's wanting to fall off sideways, so I might not talk for a minute, kind of need to concentrate."

"Take your time," Glisters and I say, simultaneously.

"Plenty of time," F.B. concurs. "Positioning the antenna under way."

My helmet visor is up and I'm still breathing ship air, and can watch Wychee, who has her eyes shut and appears to be holding her breath; Marioschke, who looks like she's trying to twist all her fingers off against each other; and Fwuffy, placidly floating with a peaceful expression, trunk slowly stroking the sides of his face, occasionally tucking into his mouth. I've never seen him do that before.

After an eternity—I realize I've been holding my breath, too—F.B.'s voice makes us all jump. "Positioning the antenna complete. It's in the socket, first clamp fastened. Second clamp fastened. First clamp confirmed. Second clamp confirmed. Request power up and system check."

"Power up and system check starting now." Glisters's voice over the phones doesn't quite conceal his excitement. "Power on. All processors booting up. Receptors reporting as processors come on line. All processors booted up and running with full complement of processors. I have signal! We've got 400 faces from Mars, 9,000 faces from Earth and the moon. Come back in carefully, F.B., you did it."

Calmly, methodically, reporting each step, he unbelays the antenna, coils those lines, takes off his second belay, climbs back, makes sure his main belay has cleared the outer door, and starts the entry sequence. A few minutes later the vents pop, air rushes into the lock, and the door opens. He slides out, pulling up his visor.

"Time for a party," Wychee says. "F.B., I'm going to do

the best soft-food meal in history tonight. Then as soon as your teeth and jaw are all healed, we'll have an even bigger meal of whatever you like."

Fwuffy shakes his head, flapping his big ears, and blows a little air through his trunk. "And I saved you wots of fwesh bananas."

As we all airswim back to the cockpit—the celebration has to be there because now that his precious antenna is working, Glisters can't be pried out with a crowbar—I ask Fwuffy, "When we were all worried about F.B., why did you rub your trunk all over your cheeks like that? And put it in your mouth?"

"It's embawassing."

"You don't have to tell me."

"It's okay, it's just . . . childish. When I'm fwightened and anxious I want to twumpet wike my ewephant ancestas. But that's so woud and wude. So they twained me to do that instead of twumpet."

"Fwuffy," I say, "you can't imagine how much we all appreciate that."

"Actuwawy, I can. My heawing is maw sensitive than yaws. I didn't want to heah me twumpet eitha."

19

560 NEEDLES, 6,000,000,000 PIECES OF HAY

July 8, 2129. On *Virgo*, upbound Earth to Mars. 182 million kilometers from the sun, 57 million kilometers from Mars, 43 million kilometers from Earth.

FOR SOMETHING I wouldn't have recognized as a party a few months ago, it's a good party. Wychee outdoes herself on soups and blintzes; she says, "I'm just glad the people on Mars will already have resigned themselves to never getting this stuff."

Marioschke gives F.B. a major dose of shining eyes, completely undoing his newfound poise. It gives Wychee and me, the only gossips at the party, something to roll our eyes about. Fwuffy curls up like a gigantic contented cat, always happier when people get along. Fleeta rocks and giggles; her constant conspicuous happiness doesn't seem nearly so spooky today—it just sort of adds to the atmosphere.

"—change the key to the codes every few seconds," Glisters is saying to F.B. It sort of figures that F.B.'s hero would be supplying F.B. with the best girl-avoiding technique known; I decide to wade in and not let him.

"Submillimeter wave communication, always the way to a lady's heart," I say to them both. Marioschke is head to head with Wychee and not listening to us—probably getting some coaching.

"Lady?" F.B. says.

I nod in the direction of Marioschke; he freezes for a second, the way a guy does when you tell him someone he's interested in is interested in him. Particularly a guy who is scared to death of girls. "' . . . *front her, board her, woo her, assail her,*' if you remember that class."

F.B. gulps; I don't think he squared his shoulders half that hard when he went out to put the antenna on, but he pushes off and airswims over to her.

"What class?" Glisters asks me.

"That lit class all the kids with actor parents end up taking," I say. "It's from *Twelfth Night.*"

"I was going to read that but I was afraid I wouldn't understand it if I didn't read *First Night* up through *Eleventh Night.*"

I make a face at him; he nods toward where F.B. and Marioschke are sitting on a window, now, talking into each other's eyes, and we trade quiet thumbs-ups. "Actually," he says, "I was kind of thrashing out the communication problem and using F.B's ears to do it, before springing it on you."

"I thought putting up the antenna meant we had *solved* the communication problem."

"You might say it finally allows us to have one. It might be weeks before we're actually communicating with anyone out there, and that might use up any time they'd have to set up a rescue mission. We kind of have to prepare people for the possibility that we will be going home the long way round, and have to take the whole twenty-two months past Mars."

My first impulse is to be angry at him, and my next is to whine about it not being fair, but being commander, I swallow all that and say, "Okay, you'd better explain it to me."

||||||||||||||||||||||||||||||||||||||||||||||||||||||||||||||||||||||||||||||||||

Notes for the Interested, #15

Universal encryption, PermaPaxPerity, and why making sure that everyone gets a chance to be seen means Virgo can't be heard

There's only so much electromagnetic spectrum, and nothing can make there be more. In 2130, with regular communication among hundreds of spacecraft, dozens of space stations, millions of satellites, and three settled worlds, bandwidth (the available part of the spectrum for any one user) will be in short supply. It already is today; you run up against the bandwidth problem when it seems to take forever to download big files, when there are interruptions in your streaming video or audio, or when a multiplayer game "freezes." The pipe is only so wide (or there are only so many lanes of traffic), and only so much can go through at a time.

One way to solve this problem is **handshaking.** Using the

tight beams already mentioned, aim the signal only at antennas that say they want it, so everyone pings before talking, and beams information only to the antennas that agree to take it.

Another way is **packetization**: break the information into packets and put an "address" on each packet, so that the receiver only "unwraps" the packets addressed to it, and many receivers can share a single channel. This is how cell phones and the Internet share bandwidth today.

Finally, **unique encryption** puts every message in its own unique code, which makes the sorting simple at the other end: all the packets that can be decrypted with the same code are part of the same message. Right now in the 2010s, computers in high-security networks already encrypt and decrypt so fast that voice and even video can be transmitted in this way.

Long before this story began, as available bandwidth became scarcer and scarcer, handshaking, packetization, and unique encryption became universal. The PermaPaxPerity Authority immediately saw that this could be used to identify the source of every hook in every meed, and to keep tracking the parts of it no matter how often it was re-splyctered, which made it easy to track recognition scores. The UN began to require everyone to use the same standardized tight beams, packetization, and unique encryption. So that hackers cannot make themselves celeb-eenies by setting up bots to flood the system with counterfeit meeds carrying phony creator IDs and time stamps, the code keys are changed every few seconds on all the faces. There are about 1,000 faces (organized streams of messages, the equivalent of a 2010 radio station or website)

within a channel, and each channel corresponds to one physical beam of submillimeter waves.

This is great for all the regular, ordinary people in the solar
system. But it also means that to talk to anyone, *Virgo* must
ping billions of faces organized into millions of channels and
break their codes to find out whether that face accepts outside
signals. Almost all of them are simple one-way faces presenting
news or entertainment meeds.

▐▌

"So, cue up Wychee doing her imitation of Pop and pounding the table about bottom lines and all that, Glisters," I
say, trying not to panic, though the bleak frustration in his
face makes me want to shake him. "I understand enough
to see you're not making it up and can't do anything more
than you're already doing. How much time is this going
to take and how badly does that mess up our chances of
rescue?"

"Well, the Space Patrol maintains seven emergency
channels, which unfortunately look just like any other
submillimeter-wave channels before you decrypt them.
They carry 80 faces each, so we need to find any one of 560
emergency faces. Within the solar system there's about
6,000,000,000 faces. We just have to find the sending and
the receiving side of the same face out of all that."

"Well, how do we find them?"

"We're doing it right now. My antenna can only work

about one-ten thousandth as fast as the one we lost, but at least it's working. We spray the Earth, the moon, and Mars with submillimeter wave signal that says 'Hey, hit me with a face.' Any open transmitters that happen to get a fix on us—that takes a little time and luck, so not every antenna we light up will be able to get a fix—will send an encrypted signal back, which takes a few minutes because of the radio lag. Since we've been off-line so long, we don't have the keys, and we have to break the code to see what it is, which adds another 3 seconds per face."

My heart practically stops, and I say, "So if we have to try out 10 million faces to find one emergency face, and if it takes 5 minutes in radio lag to try it out, then that's 50 million minutes, which is—"

He looks a bit disgusted with me. "Commander, *chill*. Swallow the panic. Yes, if we were calling them all up one at a time and waiting for an answer, and if the emergency face was going to be the ten millionth one we tried, it would take 50 million minutes, and"—he punches his wrist comp—"that's about 95 years. But we don't have to wait for signal to come back; the real problem is just that it takes about one second for one of my homemade dimples to lock on a target and ping it, then it has to receive about two seconds when a signal comes back a few minutes later, and then it has to stay locked on a few more seconds till we decrypt and the computer decides whether it's an emergency face or not. Figure we can average a ping every 10 seconds from each of the 200 dimples on the antenna.

At that rate we'll have a fifty-fifty chance of finding an emergency face inside two weeks, and it'll be almost certain within a month."

"So we can call for help in two weeks, or a month at most?"

"Well, we'll be able to hear an emergency channel within that time. Then we have to handshake with it, which means hacking an access code for our outgoing message. That requires a lot of trial and error over a few minutes' time lag, though fortunately they were designed to be hacked, so it won't take impossibly long."

"You're kidding. Why would they design it to be hacked?"

"It's like a bicycle lock. It won't stop someone who really wants your bicycle but it makes anyone trying to steal it have to stay beside it, obviously doing something bad, for a long time. So hackers and crackers don't try to break in because they might get detected. Whereas, say, a spaceship that has been out of touch so long that it doesn't have any useful codes might even want to be detected."

"I get it. Okay, Glisters, one more try. What are the odds we'll contact them while they still have a chance to come out and get us?"

"Maybe 10% at best that we'll have it in time for them to come and get us during Marspass, but nearly certain that we'll have it for the next Earthpass."

"Two years away."

"Yeah."

"And it's been an hour since you got the antenna up and started cracking with it. How many incoming and outgoing faces have you cracked so far?"

"About thirty incoming and one outgoing," Glisters says. "Since F.B. put the antenna up—"

"F.B.!" Fleeta yells, raising her squeezebulb as if in a toast, and hugging the poor guy like she's going to hump his leg. Marioschke looks like she's been punched.

"So far the incoming faces," Glisters says, ignoring all that messy human stuff happenning around him, "are all botflog. Music, fashion, and celeb accumulators and re-posters, all of them."

"Can you get meeds?" Fleeta said.

"Yes, most of the faces carry meeds—"

"It would be so fun to see meeds again, I miss them."

"I can set up a viewing lounge, so people could do that if they want. Next off-watch awake time I have, I'll put that together—it shouldn't take long."

I'm about to raise the question of whether we want people to have a distraction to make them goof off. Then I see that everyone is nodding and looking eager; this is the most popular idea anyone has had in a long time. I decide I'd rather not trigger a mutiny just now. "So we have an outgoing face—"

"Yeah. It's a drop face."

Wychee asks, "What's a drop face?"

"A face that archives research material or bureaucratic reports. It's like if we were lost in the desert and we found an animal-research camera—we would wave at it and hold up signs, but chances would be it was just recording stuff that some scientist would look at in a few years. Almost all outgoing faces are drop faces."

"So you've sent a message to it—"

"I'm flooding it with messages. Maybe it will overflow its storage and attract attention that way. Maybe it actually logs distress calls and it's already notified the Space Patrol, but they haven't hacked in to our system to tell us yet. Lots of things are possible. But Emerald and Derlock, much as I hate to admit it, are still our best hope. They should be in hailing distance of Mars in a few days, and then it'll be all over the broadcast news faces, plus some smart guy in the Space Patrol or some news face will think to look in the drop face archives. Till then, well, we're pretty good at living shipboard, which is good, because even if they hear our call tomorrow, we'll still have to live here for at least two more months."

20

BEING DEAD IMPROVES OUR SOCIAL STANDING

July 23, 2129. On *Virgo*, upbound from Earth to Mars. 195 million kilometers from the sun, 40 million kilometers from Mars, 49 million kilometers from Earth.

WYCHEE CATCHES ME coming out of the shower. "Glisters says there's news from Mars."

I pull my coverall on quickly and use the smartcomb and coswand. The person floating in mid-air in the mirror looks professional, prepared—like a commander.

Seeing Glisters in the cockpit practically drops me out of the steely-eyed commander act right there. His expression is somewhere between "in shock" and "poisoned."

"Want to tell me now or shall we wait for the others?"

He glances at the screen. "Short summary: we're screwed, because—" He raises a finger in a discreet *shush!* at the noise coming from the corridor; in a moment the rest of the crew swims in, Wychee last, like they're her sheep and she's a border collie.

Glisters says, "I'll put it up on the front screen. We've got one minor news face open—"

"I still can't get *You Know You Wanna!*, even though—"

Fleeta begins, but Wychee gently rests a hand on her shoulder, and she's instantly quiet; apparently *those* brain cells are not gone yet.

Glisters nods to Wychee, just a slight *thanks*, and resumes. "So here it is."

A standard animated announcer says, "And again, on the incredible story that there is apparently a single survivor from *Virgo*, who was in the cargo pod at the time of the mysterious accident that destroyed the crew bubble—"

An image on the screen shows two big pieces of the crew bubble joined by a spaghetti of pipes and cables, with the caption *Missilecam, 148 hours post accident.*

"How come they can get that picture but they can't send a rescue ship for us?" F.B. asks.

Glisters hits pause. "One, they don't know we're here. Two, the camera that took that picture, from probably 50 kilometers away from the wreckage, weighed a couple of kilograms and was fired off on a one-shot missile; after it passed the wreckage it kept going and it's never coming back. A ship to rescue us would weigh at least a few hundred tonnes and have to carry enough reaction mass to rendezvous, match course, re-accelerate, and fly somewhere else. They have missilecams ready to go all the time, because something interesting might happen in space, but a real rescue mission will take them at least a couple months to assemble."

"They said sole survivor," Wychee says, "but we sent two people—"

"Two people *went*." Glisters's face is flat. "Here's the rest."

The image on the screen resolves again and starts to move; the sound slides out of a squeal. "—now on his way to Mars in a lifeboat cap. Contact was lost within twenty minutes of its being established three days ago, and we don't know what condition the survivor is in; authorities refused to speculate as to whether he's unable to answer because of equipment failure, or an injury situation, or something worse.

"Since his family has been contacted, we now can disclose that the survivor is Derlock Slabilis, formerly a student at Excellence Shop, an Earth-based prep school with an excellent reputation both for training students for PotEvals and for attracting high-level children of celeb-eenies to grace its social side. He is also the son of Sir Penn Slabilis, the noted trial lawyer and one of the best known celebrities on the law, crime, and politics circuit.

"Derlock Slabilis had been presumed dead after the mysterious loss of a cap returning his classmates from an Excellence Shop field trip to *Virgo* during Earthpass. The cap, inbound to Earth on a thirty-three day trajectory, failed to answer routine hails within a day of departing *Virgo*, did not deploy its main rocket to steer into a safe approach to aerobrake, and plunged into the atmosphere at an extremely steep angle over the South Pacific without jettisoning its rocket. Fuel tanks on the rocket exploded at an altitude of about 140 kilometers. Almost all debris vaporized during re-entry."

The screen shows a little cartoon of where the cap's engine should have fired and didn't. In the cartoon, the cap, with rocket still attached, plunges almost straight down into the atmosphere. The dashed blue line the cap was supposed to follow fades; the red solid line ends in an explosion image.

"During the full day between the departure of the cap and the accident that destroyed *Virgo* there were no communications from *Virgo* mentioning Derlock Stabilis, let alone why he might have stayed on board. Excellence Shop and his father expected him to return and take his PotEvals.

"What he was doing in *Virgo*'s pod, and how he survived for a period of several weeks before launching his cap toward Mars, is a question that can only be answered if he again answers a radio hail, or perhaps if, more than a month from now, the automated systems bring the cap safely through aerobrake, capture orbit, second aerobrake, re-entry, and descent—each operation fraught with deadly danger." Glisters rolls his eyes at me—typical media-speak. All those operations are *fraught with deadly danger* the same way that crossing a busy street or taking a shower are, i.e., people do die now and then.

The animated figure intones, "Perhaps not even then will we fully understand the remarkable events surrounding this remarkable young man.

"After the break we'll have a profile of the mysterious sole survivor, a young man of remarkable talent and charisma who now boasts one of the highest recognition scores of anyone of his generation—"

Glisters pauses it. "Everything after is PR and botflog.

You may be surprised to hear that us moes were the beloved social leaders of Excellence Shop, and that Derlock
was the leader of us beloved moes. Being dead apparently
really improved our social standing all the way to beloved.
If anyone would rather watch by yourselves, they do have
our families on there—"

"That's why I want my friends with me," Marioschke
says.

"I'm so sowwy, you must awe be so sad," Fwuffy says,
from where he's been watching at the back of the cockpit.

By common consent we pack into a ball of people all
leaning against Fwuffy; it occurs to me that it's a good
thing he's big enough to comfort all of us at once.

It's what Glisters said it would be. Excellence Shop's
PR company has changed and edited everything about
who we really are except our parents, and that's the worst
of it. Marioschke's father is training for the circumlunar
suit race and can't be bothered to say anything; her mother,
who's been bounced back to miney after the divorce, tries
to make her interview an audition. The principal of Excellence Shop lies his ass off about how wonderful and popular we all were. F.B.'s father threatens legal action when
they ask him why he named his son Fucking Bastard; his
mother's barred from ever appearing in media by the pa-
ternity agreement.

They move on to our math and science teacher, who is
too honest and too socially clueless to say that any of the
moes were any good at anything, except me and Glisters,
who didn't apply ourselves but could have been pretty

good if we'd wanted to, apparently. She finishes with a sad little, "I always thought if they just took on a challenge they might make me proud of them."

"If we get back I'm hugging her," Glisters says.

Fleeta's mother just can't stop crying; her beautiful genius with every advantage money could buy turned herself into a vegetable long before her purported death. She keeps repeating, *Oh, the waste.*

"She says that all the time," Fleeta says. "It makes me laugh she says it so much."

Stack's and Emerald's parents style Classic Meed, using Simple Grief. If you're not much of an actor it's at least a correct choice, the equivalent of a plain suit or black dress at a funeral. It works for Stack's dad, who is not very articulate, just a guy who can really ride a board, and it keeps Emerald's kindergarten teacher mom from breaking down and turning her grieving into some silly circus. It feels weird to see them doing that because they think their kids are dead—and their kids *are* dead.

Wychee's parents, who were one of those golden athlete-and-musician couples that splyctered into n-nillion hooks twenty years ago, and are now ultra retro, issue a quietly correct statement. Derlock's father tells us about how he's going to sue the whole universe and make sure his son gets everything he's entitled to.

Glisters glances at me and I know we're thinking the same thing: *we're next*—and they always put good hooks last. Then his mom, who is a famous talking-head explainer, comes on, and starts telling stories about things he did before he was eight. Then she says, "His last few years have been a disappointment, you know, we just haven't had the same closeness or enjoyed the same things together." Right then I know Glisters's whole story, because it's such a common one. He was a typical eenie-brat who turned an age his parents didn't like anymore, the way some people are always getting kittens and dumping cats.

Wychee floats over to bump a shoulder against him.

I'm so worried about Glisters that Pop surprises me when he appears on-screen. "Susan was always one of the best people I knew. Whether or not I liked what she was doing, I always knew a good person was doing it. I'm sure that if there was a spare fraction of a second before she died, she spent it trying to help someone else. I wish she could know how proud of her I always was."

I think I'm not going to cry, but then Fwuffy strokes my cheek with his trunk; he's been petting all of us as if we were upset puppies.

The announcers recap everything about heroic Derlock and mysterious cap journey and conclude the meed in a burst of "only time will tell" excitement.

It takes three hours of hot chocolate and hanging out to soothe Fleeta, Marioschke, and F.B. enough to send them back to bed or off to their duties. After they've gone, Glisters cocks his head toward Fwuffy, and raises an eyebrow.

"Fwuff," I say, "I think we're going to talk about things that require discretion."

He stretches, an impressive sight in a horton, and says, "If you need me to, I have bwoccowi I can tend. But you should know I nevah tell Mawioschke anything which I think might upset huh."

"Well, that's the discretion it requires," I say. "Stay if you want."

Wychee has wrapped herself up in her arms, and says, "That cap blowing up on its return to Earth . . . that was no accident."

Glisters nods. "It has to have been part of his Plan B. Maybe because if any of us had chickened out at the last minute, we'd have known about the stowaways. But we were planning to come out long before the cap would reach Earth—"

Wychee looks pale and sick. "If one of us had gotten down to Earth we'd have told them there might still be people alive in the pod. They'd have had time to send a cruiser to investigate. And we don't have to *guess* that there was something Derlock didn't want them to find: we *know* he didn't want them to find us alive."

I've listened enough. "We'll never know," I say. "No matter how deep you go into Derlock's convoluted evil mind and all you will find are more convolutions and deeper evil. Period. It's not worth digging into and it can't change anything we do. The point is, we're alive, and we're going to stay alive."

"And because we're going to stay alive," Glisters says, "we will ultra mess up Derlock's plan, whatever it is."

"That's just a side benefit," I say, "delightful as it might be. Glisters, the conn's all yours. I need a nap, and Wychee, you'd just gotten to bed when Glisters called us in, and you owe it to yourself to get some sleep."

She says, "I'll stick around a little while, if you need company to keep you awake, Glisters."

He looks a little baffled, but says, "Sure, if you want."

When I leave, she's sitting very close to him, and he's telling her about his mother.

August 27, 2129. On *Virgo*, at periareon (closest approach to Mars), 226 million kilometers from the sun, 14.4 million kilometers from Mars, 80 million kilometers from Earth.

I don't know why everyone wants to be in the Forest. But since *they* want to be, I *have* to. That said, it's pretty nice these days; months of work and re-growth have undone the damage from the mud and water. The tree trunks are clean again, and the grass is thick and soft. We lie around one window, averting our eyes for ten out of every ninety seconds as the sun flashes through in a fierce blaze, then peering again, watching the bright red star.

"It'll only be for a few hours," Glisters warns us again, unnecessarily. "And it's just going to be a really little red ball."

F.B. sighs. "I just want to see with my own eyes, even if we're never going there."

Marioschke says, "It kind of makes it real to me."

Like Mars wouldn't be real if she didn't see it as a disk, I guess. We're so far off the course that there will only be about eight hours when it looks like an orange circular dot instead of a bright red star.

There are half a million people down there on that tiny dot, scattered in the clusters of air-sealed mansions that the Martians call "petits-villes."

"Around today, we'd've been landing on Mars if Stack had been able to get our antenna out there and set up," Wychee says. "If Derlock hadn't wrecked the antenna and murdered him, *Gagarin* could've reached us about a month ago. We'd've been landing on Mars right about now." She hasn't sounded that whiny in months, but I don't feel like pointing that out to her.

Fwuffy sighs. "I'd be meeting Wachel. I wonda if she'd wike me."

There's a strange noise, a choked little keening sound, and I look sideways to see that Marioschke is crying, long wails that she's trying to fight down, like her heart is going to rip apart. F.B. drapes an arm around her waist, and she says, "Poor Stack, poor Stack."

Fleeta starts to laugh, long and hard and in the crazy, unable-to-stop way that now happens several times a day, shoving her hand into her mouth. At last she gasps out, "And I'd still have my drugs. And I'd still be me. And I'd still . . ." I don't know if it's my imagination, but around the edges of her gleeful giggling and whooping, I think I see pure terror. I take her hand, tug her away from there, steer her toward another little open spot in the Forest so that she can catch her breath, and she holds on to me, whispering, "Everything feels so good. The only feelings I have are happy . . . happy . . . what am I happy about? Susan, I don't remember what's making me happy right now. I don't remember what we just said."

I show her Mars through another window. She says it's silly and she loves it, and asks me if I think she's pretty. "I wish I could feel bad for making everyone cry."

"Heads up," Glisters calls. "The cockpit AI just called. Something new just came in from Mars."

"Derlock?" That's my first thought.

"Might be. He was in range to land."

We all airswim after Glisters as fast as we can, carefully leaving a clear path for Fwuffy because, as the saying goes, mass times velocity equals right of way.

In the cockpit, I notice that the ongoing face search is up on the big front screen that normally shows a visual range image from one of the ship cameras. Today, I guess, Glisters just wanted to fly the ship, and not watch Mars fade back from a tiny dot to a bright red star, as we crossed its orbit and kept going, higher and farther away from the sun and into the cold and dark.

Glisters clicks to the face that the AI found, and I feel like asking him to just turn it all off forever.

Derlock's lifeboat cap is arriving on Mars. We gather in the cockpit because it has more big screens than anywhere else. Systemwide News, which has become the all-Derlock all-the-time face, has exclusive rights to the live coverage, which they remind us of every few seconds. After a while they get around to telling us that it will be about forty minutes till touchdown.

Wychee snorts. "I'm going into the kitchen to make

caramel popcorn, cotton candy, and saltwater taffy," she says. "I assume you all want some."

"Sure," I say, "but why that?"

"What else do you serve for a circus? And besides, all the sugar will make us all feel better temporarily, then knock us out for a long nap, which is about the best we can hope for."

F.B. and Marioschke airswim after her to help. The rest of us hang out in the cockpit and wish Wychee needed more help.

On the screen, animated reporters scream about how exciting this is, interrupted by live reporters screaming that no, it's really, *really* exciting. Over and over, they re-show the last missilecam pictures of the cap's approach, a few frames of a white bulb-shape scarred black around the broad end by its first aerobraking pass through the Martian atmosphere.

At last Wychee returns with the snacks, just a couple of minutes before the big climax to the show.

Some flying camera spots the drogue, finds a great angle, and zooms an icon-shot: you see the steeply curved, close Martian horizon, a swath of red desert at sunrise under a very thin layer of pink, dusty air, and the rainbow-reflective, diffraction-shimmering dome of the drogue against the black-velvet sky.

For about twenty minutes we enjoy our junk food and make silly jokes while the screen shows progressively better pictures of the cap under the drogue.

At last the cap pops its main chutes—wafer-shaped inflated balloons to offer more resistance to the thin Martian air. Gently swinging under four city-block-sized bulging disks like giant pancakes made out of circus tents, the cap settles onto the red-grit desert, with Systemwide News chase aircraft landing all around it. The reception hopper, almost as large as the cap itself, lands on a pillar of jet fire, kicking up dust that momentarily blinds all the cameras; when that clears, we see it crawling the final hundred yards to the cap, where it attaches to the airlock.

Systemwide News's feed switches to the inside view. Four people are standing around the hatch: the mayor of Mars, crisp and sleek in her formal uniform; another woman in the light blue uniform of the UN Space Patrol, styling a taut lack of expression; Systemwide News's senior anchor for Mars; and a tall, thin young man in the traditional three-piece suit. Unnecessarily the subtitler tells us he is the senior person on Mars for Slabilis Celebrity Law.

In the foreground, there's a swarm of heads and bodies; Systemwide owns the story, but they're subletting permission to ask questions and record reactions back to the other news services.

The door opens on Derlock, who is doing his best to style ragged and tragic, but he's no thinner than he was, there are no lines on his face, and he doesn't actually look as much like a guy who's been through an ordeal as he looks like a teenage boy styling haggard-from-an-ordeal. Or maybe I'm just a really tough critic.

The man from Slabilis steps up, catches Derlock's elbow, introduces him to the other three dignitaries, and guides him to a rostrum.

When the single camera focuses on Derlock, a generated backdrop appears—a small crowd of people standing behind Derlock, probably pre-recorded actors from Systemwide's reaction file—and behind them there's a Martian sky, two rows of buildings at right angles to each other, and the distant, shadowy shape of Olympica. Now it looks absolutely impossible: Derlock and a crowd in a town square, outdoors on Mars without pressure suits. (Aside from very little air, Mars has no towns—no petitville is big enough to make a half-decent village, and if it were, it wouldn't have a square, and if it did, the square would be underground.)

"For the Earth audience that never bothered to learn anything," Glisters mutters.

"And for the Mars audience that likes their Mars fake," I add. "There's a lot of them who don't want to be reminded very often that they live in a big fancy basement under a near-vacuum desert—"

"Quiet," Wychee says, "the son of a bitch is about to start lying."

In one of those happy camera accidents, Derlock seems to look out of the screen right at her. "Let me begin," he says, "by thanking everyone for welcoming me here. I suppose my turning up at like this must seem very strange to all of you. To me, of course, it seems perfectly normal; after all, I always knew where I was."

The crowd does little what-a-guy chortles. *Aha. They must be supplied by Slabilis rather than Systemwide. His daddy already has the story locked up tight. Wonder if they had any way to coordinate with Derlock before this, or it's all improv?*

"I guess people will say I'm too young to really know what this means, so I'll just say, *you're wrong*, and to all the people who are as young as I am, I'll add, *we all know how wrong adults can be about something like this.* What I mean to say is, the love of my life, now and I'm sure forever, was Emerald Azhan. Oh, we were very different, no doubt about that. I was, you know, used to the glitter and glamour; she was the daughter of a celeb-eenie, but I guess you just have to say, she never forgot where she came from. Intellectually she was way ahead of me; socially I was way ahead of her; I was all looks, she was all brains, but we found a way to forgive and cherish each other, and even though I've had some of the hottest matchups in the underage celeb market, I fell pretty hard for my wonderful, funny-looking smart girl—"

"I wish she'd lived to kill him," Wychee mutters. It's not a joke.

"Shh," Marioschke says.

" . . . we grew close, but there was a cloud over me because of some bad things I had done earlier in my life, and it just never seemed like time to declare; and then, truthfully, too, I was working pretty hard on getting my recognition score up, and there were other girls who could help me a lot more with that. Other girls that I didn't love nearly as much as I loved Emerald."

Glisters makes a gagging noise and everyone joins in.

"But," Derlock says, and pauses to make the *but* more significant. Pop always says when an actor throws his big *But* in, he's planning to sit down and stay a while. "I didn't understand how being my don't-tell lover was affecting Emerald until it was too late—when she started to be so accepting, and so easy to get along with . . . so . . . happy."

The crowd behind him styles the Classic Meed version of Dawning Wince so uniformly that I know at once they were all pulled out of the same acting school class.

Derlock looks down, composes himself, looks up, loses it, has to compose himself again. *Virgo* erupts with rude noises; it's a pity we're 14.4 million kilometers from Mars and our distance is increasing, so they can't hear us. "Emerald had become addicted to happistuf," he says. "She was planning to take the laughing dive with Bari and King, two guys in our little group we called the moes, at Excellence Shop. I talked her into coming along with some of us on a field trip to *Virgo*, because I knew she wouldn't be able to get any more happistuf on the trip.

"But as everyone knows, you don't quit happistuf; you just stop it and control it with Fendrisol. At least Emerald had only taken it for a few weeks. I had to get her onto Fendrisol, and keep her away from happistuf. I had heard from the news meeds, especially the excellent ones produced by Systemwide News—" Everyone applauds. He must've had a chance to review the contract with some Slabilis Celebrity Law flacks during the approach and descent. "—that Mars had been kept very clean by the customs and immigration people, and so I persuaded her to stow away with me in the cargo pod, and though I knew it was wrong, I also broke into the infirmary in the pod's auxiliary living and control center, which had a supply of Fendrisol. It was honestly a struggle to get it into her—she had become so devoted to happistuf in the short time she had been gasping—but it had to be done.

"I had planned to come out of hiding and let the *Virgo* crew know I was there on the fifth day after the cap with my classmates went back to Earth; I calculated that that would put us forty-eight hours beyond when they would be able to safely send us back. I thought if I just took the blame for everything, perhaps they would let me take Emerald to Mars, where she'd be safer from happistuf, and where there'd be a chance for the Fendrisol to keep her from deteriorating further.

"But we awoke one morning to the sound of a terrible explosion. The pod was tumbling helplessly. It wasn't easy, and I'll explain a great deal more about it later, for the technical nerds out there—"

Again the crowd behind him styles What-a-Guy slightly too uniformly and simultaneously, but probably not enough for any but a suspicious pro to notice. We all make more rude noises.

"—almost all the rest of the story. We stabilized and

flew the pod till we were within cap range of Mars, got on the lifeboat cap, and set out for Mars.

"I honestly don't know what happened. Forty-one days ago, on a morning just like every other morning of the trip, when we should have both awakened, Emerald was dead beside me. I had been keeping her doses of Fendrisol up, and watching her to see that she didn't get confused and take more of it on her own, and she was at a safe dosage, the ship's computer will clearly show that. But she . . . she was . . ."

I see Glisters's mouth form a *wow* and realize I'm doing the same thing. It's awe-inspiring, in a horrible kind of way. "Probably he held her down and forced doses of happistuf into her right after they left, then built up Fendrisol in her blood till one dose too many would kill her," Glisters says. "And those little computer systems on something like the cap aren't very well defended. He'll have hidden his tracks *deep*."

A Systemwide News reporter says, "That's astonishing."

"Meed talk for botflog," Wychee says.

"Let me just ask because I know a lot of people will— why didn't you contact us between the initial distress call and now?"

Derlock nods. "I knew you would ask that. The truth is, I recorded that distress call the day that Emerald died; I didn't know what to do, and I felt so awful, and I just screamed for help. Then, well, I'd taken a supply of pain-killers and sleeping pills from the infirmary, as well, because they were the only drugs I thought we might need beside Fendrisol, and . . . so I set the distress call to call twice a day till it got a reply, and then shut down once it did. I know this sounds dumb but I didn't want it to be a nuisance, and I didn't want to have to answer myself be—cause—well, there I was, stranded in the cap, which was flying its own way to Mars, with . . . with the girl I really, truly, ultra *loved*—in a *freezer compartment*—I mean, I didn't know what else to do—"

He begins to cry. "After I recorded the distress call and put Em-Em-Emerald's b-body into . . . I mean, put her . . . I—well, I had drugs to make me sleep and drugs to make me feel better and I didn't want to-to-to . . . I just started cleaning up yesterday, just before the first aerobrake. I'm kind of going into withdrawal even now, I was cutting back, trying to get ready for the landing, and uh, uh, um, I guess I'll be pretty sick for a few days. But Emerald is in Freezer Compartment G inside, and I guess if anyone doubts what happened, they'll be able to analyze her body, they'll find a tonne of happistuf and Fendrisol. Or you can just ask any of the moes back on Earth, I mean, we were all close friends and they all knew—"

For the first time the camera goes all the way around Derlock to focus on the media people. A guy dressed as a reporter, looking just a little more like a reporter than any real life reporter I have ever seen, elbows rudely past the Systemwide guy, who doesn't put up any fight.

"Plant!" I say. Everyone nods; it's obvious.

Taking advantage of his moment of exposure, the plant straightens his tie and pushes his hat back on his head. "Uh, Mr. Slabilis, uh, Derlock, um, I think we have to tell you that the cap carrying your friends burned up on re-entry—"

And another guy shouts, "They're alive and they have contacted BOOOP—"

The screen is a very pretty cyan plunged into deep silence.

UP-LEG: MARSPASS TO APHELION

AUGUST 27, 2129—MAY 25, 2130

POSITIONS OF THE EARTH, MARS, AND *VIRGO*— AUGUST 27, 2129 TO MAY 25, 2130

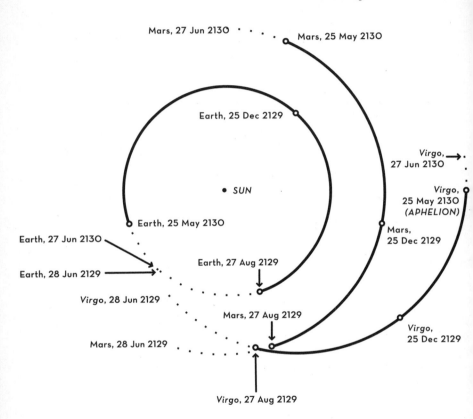

To Jupiter (more than twice as far as *Virgo* is from the sun) ▶

Mars, 27 Jun 2130 · · · ·   Mars, 25 May 2130

Earth, 25 Dec 2129

Virgo, →·
27 Jun 2130

Virgo,
25 May 2130
(APHELION)

• *SUN*

Earth, 25 May 2130

Mars,
25 Dec 2129

Earth, 27 Jun 2130

Earth, 28 Jun 2129   Earth, 27 Aug 2129

Virgo, 28 Jun 2129

Mars, 27 Aug 2129

Virgo,
25 Dec 2129

Mars, 28 Jun 2129

Virgo, 27 Aug 2129

For reference, dots extend the curves to show one full Earth year of motion, from June 28, 2129 to June 27, 2130. (Why June 27/28? Because it's exactly half a year before or after January 1.) The dark solid lines show the movement of Earth, Mars, and *Virgo*.

Ap- and apo- are Greek prefixes that mean "far from"; peri- is the Greek prefix for "near to." The Greek roots in English for sun, Mars, and Earth are -helion, -areon, and –ge(o) respectively, so in Part III, *Virgo* is moving from its periareon (closest approach to Mars) to aphelion (farthest separation from the sun).

21

POP MAKES A PLAY FOR THE PIRATES

August 27, 2129. On *Virgo*, at periareon (closest approach to Mars), 226 million kilometers from the sun, 14.4 million kilometers from Mars, 80 million kilometers from Earth.

AFTER ABOUT A minute and a half, the face starts again, a few seconds back, except the shouted interruption isn't there, and neither is the BOOOP. Instead it cuts straight from the burned-up-on-re-entry line to Derlock fainting.

"That fainting is much more real than he'd been up till now," I say as we watch them try to revive him.

Glisters adds, "Most convincing thing he's done."

"He had more to work with," Wychee says, and we're grinning at each other.

"You guys look like you know what's happening. What does all of that mean?" Marioschke asks.

"It means Pop is on the job," I say, blinking back tears and hugging myself. "And I'm sure some of your parents are in it with him, too, but that was my dad's sense of humor and the way he handled things. He found a way to let us know our distress calls are coming through and he's trying to break the censorship injunction. A surprise guy speaking up at Derlock's presentation—that's pure Pop. Something you'd see in a meed."

"Having a father like that must be . . ." F.B. looks for words, and Marioschke hugs him so hard that it's a miracle the boy doesn't pop.

"When I don't want to strangle him or he doesn't want to strangle me, yeah," I say. "Ultra yeah. It can be pretty zoomed."

"It'll probably give my mom a chance to try to cover it, too, and break the injunction another way," Glisters says.

"What injunction?" Wychee asks.

"I don't even pay enough attention in school to know what an injunction is," Marioschke adds.

"It's an order from a judge not to do or say something," I say, "and breaking it is a crime, called contempt of court, and the UN courts, especially the entertainment courts, get real serious about PermaPaxPerity issues, especially the ones about intellectual property," I explain. "Which you can bet anything are involved all over the place here. Here we have the son of one of the solar system's most important intellectual property lawyers, the guy who founded the whole field of media-interest defense. And that kid comes into Mars on a lifeboat, with his frozen tragic happistuf-victim girlfriend, the miraculous sole survivor et cetera and blah blah and all that crap. Right?"

"Right." I see Glisters is right with me. "Rights to that story would be worth astronomical amounts, wouldn't they? And Mom always says where there's money there's lawsuits—"

I see Wychee's light go on. "Oh, my god. My god. You're right. The first thing Derlock's dad did was file for an injunction arguing that Derlock has the rights to everything connected with the story. It's *Munshi versus Slabilis* but more so!"

All us girls are nodding; F.B. and Glisters both look like they've just awakened on a new planet where no one speaks their lnaguage.

Wychee says, "It's something any girl at a place like Excellence Shop has to be aware of, just for personal safety."

Glisters asks, "Personal safety?"

For a second I'm angry at him; it's so bizarre that boys don't have to know this, and so unfair that we do. But it's hardly his fault; if human males were all like Glisters and F.B., after all, there'd be no such issue. So I make myself explain as politely as I can, "If you hang around with celebrity boys it's one of those things you've got to always have in your mind. Sir Penn Slabilis was just your plain old garden-variety performing-bear celebrity lawyer till he celebrated winning a case for Carole Munshi—"

"At least that name is familiar, but I don't remember why. Was it in the celeb law class?"

"It's only one of the most important names in all of the history of special media interest law," Wychee puts in. "Gliss, Susan is maybe in danger of exploding, because she's having a hard time believing she's got to explain it;

it was one of the few things that all the girls stayed awake for in class."

"Even me," Marioschke says. "If you don't know about *Munshi versus Slabilis* . . . well, it just must be nice to not *have* to know. And most of us don't really like to talk about it, it's too—too—"

"Sad," Fleeta says, just as Wychee says, "Grim," and I say, "Infuriating." Sort of a bonding glance runs among us; then Wychee says, "All right, I guess it's my turn to explain."

||||||||||||||||||||||||||||||||||||||||||||||||||||||||||||||||||||||||

Notes for the Interested, #16

MUNSHI VERSUS SLABILIS: *guaranteed circuses to go with the guaranteed bread*

Very often the whole future of a nation, or even of the human race, will turn on a court case that establishes the way things will work from now on, for good or ill. Hardly anything else can change all of history so quickly; if you want to know what's going on in the world, you have to watch the courts. Our real history is replete with names and terms like Socrates, Cicero versus the Catiline Conspiracy, the Star Chamber, Dred Scott, the Dreyfus Affair, Sacco and Vanzetti, Nuremberg, *Brown versus Board of Education*, and *Miranda versus Arizona*. In this future history, one of the most important principles of PermaPaxPerity was established in the famous case of Munshi versus Slabilis.

Carole Munshi was a singer-songwriter with astronomical recognition scores and several major hits in the genre of

Bangala pop between 2089 and 2094. It later emerged, during her divorce suit in 2096, that her manager-boyfriend was taking all her earnings and holding her prisoner. Her attorney, Penn Slabilis, won a complete victory in court.

The day that the settlement was final, Slabilis took Carole Munshi out to celebrate, and raped her. He recorded this and distributed a meed of it in the pirate faces dedicated to violent porn. Hooks from that meed were among the most-splyctered Top 100 in that category for more than a decade afterward.

Brought to trial, Slabilis defended himself by arguing that because he had created the story by committing the rape, he owned the whole story. Therefore all the recorded material about the rape was his intellectual property, and the court could not use his recordings, any testimony from Munshi, or any part of the story, to convict him, including anything they learned if the recordings or her testimony were what had led them to look for it.

Although some social observers cited the old joke about the man who killed his parents and then demanded mercy because he was an orphan, and there were immense marches, protests, and demonstrations worldwide for more than a year, the PermaPaxPerity Authority declared the decision would stand.

The greater social good demanded it; the computer models clearly showed that some controllable, mostly peaceful unrest now would be better than widespread, unfocused social anomie and disaffection that might last for generations.

PermaPaxPerity, for the first time in human history, had abolished poverty and war and created universal security, and removed the dangerous, dull, and unpleasant aspects of labor (for the few people who still did any work). Earth was becoming less polluted, less overpopulated, a better planet every decade.

The one threat on the horizon to PermaPaxPerity was boredom, and for more than three centuries, since the theatrical fads, condemned-criminal cults, and musician manias of the late 1700s, one of the most effective, reliable antidotes to public boredom had been celebrity gossip. Penn Slabilis pioneered the concept of *overriding media interest*: If a story amused and fascinated enough people, they had a right to have it go on, and if conviction, imprisonment, or execution posed a significant risk of ending the story, then PermaPaxPerity required that conviction and sentence be suspended forever, or simply nullified.

For his services to society, in securing a vast stream of entertainment and ensuring that no one's favorite celebrity criminal would leave the media too soon, Penn Slabilis eventually received a UN Knighthood.

Carole Munshi's public self-immolation was one of the top media events of 2098, and the hooks of her struggling in the flames are still commonly splyctered even twenty years later. And, of course, every time one of those hooks is shown on any screen to anyone, Sir Penn Slabilis collects another microfee.

▮▮

As she has been explaining, Wychee has been realizing that Glisters and F.B. seem to be hearing this for the first time, despite our all having had it in a mandatory class two years before. "Sheeyeffinit, Susan and Em and I never studied anything if we could help it, and *we* did *all* the supplementary reading. Fleeta was already on happistuf and *she* studied it. When Susan was getting involved with Derlock, you can trust me, somewhere in her mind there was the thought that this guy could get rich by raping or mutilating her. Why do you think I was scared sick when Emerald got involved with him?"

F.B. is staring at her, and then suddenly he blurts out, "He's going to get away with it."

I say, "Yeah, *he's going to get away with it.*"

To my deep shock, F.B. bursts into tears. "Poor Emerald!"

Marioschke grabs him in a smothering hug. "Just keep listening, I don't know where Susan and Wychee are going with this, but it's important."

"So here's the thing," I say. "Derlock's dad has spent decades arguing, successfully, for this whole overriding media interest idea, which boils down to, people like stories about the psychos and the sickos and if we don't let them out to commit more crimes, we won't have enough stories to entertain the crime fans, and we need to incentivize our thugs to keep us all amused—and the incentive is that they get to own the story of their crimes. You know, historically it worked for novels and songs and meeds, why not for crimes?"

"And that's what Slabilis must be doing, right now, with this case," Wychee says. "Quite possibly he even put Derlock up to it in the first place. The whole thing *does* seem much more thought-through than I'd expect from Derlock. Anyway, every distress call they picked up from us is probably being archived and sealed under an injunction, as part of the forthcoming *Derlock Slabilis, Most Interesting Boy in the Solar System* documentary special. They're arguing that they own all the rights to it because if Derlock hadn't committed his crime, there wouldn't be any story."

"But it's not true!" Glisters seems to think this matters. "He *didn't* commit the crime they're using to get the injunction. It's just about the *only* crime he didn't commit."

I explain, "But truth isn't the issue. Being an accused criminal gives you the right to the story, whether it's true or not. Other people don't get to disrupt it, *especially* not with the truth, unless the truth becomes more popular and interesting, but of course there's no legitimate way for them to find it out, at least not while he's got an injunction, and whatever we do or say now, any message we get to anyone on Mars, will automatically be part of the story, and he'll own it."

Wychee is nodding vigorously. "*Help we are still alive and in trouble*, by us, is now Derlock's property."

"Except you can beat those cases by getting the truth out," I say. "Slabilis has lost more than once when a victim made himself or herself so popular on the pirate faces that the overriding media interest was in allowing that part of the story out. And the first step in getting out on the pirate faces is letting people know that they're not getting the whole story. So that was what Pop and probably your mom, too, Glisters, hired that actor to do. He jammed that revelation into the press conference so that a few million people watching the live feed would know there's an even better story being kept from them, which should get the pirates after the story.

"They were also letting *us* know they're on the case. And it knocked Derlock over because in his arrogant, Derlocky way, he fully expected that we would have screwed up and died out here by now."

"So what can we do to support the home team?" Wychee asks.

"Well, I have an idea," I say. "Let's pump out a fifteen-minutes-a-day slice-of-life program called, um, *Life on Virgo.* Just whatever happens for that day, but do our best to tell it as an interesting story. At first it will get some attention because it's contradicting Derlock, and that should get it onto the pirate faces—maybe even on one of the big ones like Ed Teach, at least as a novelty. It has a bunch of good hooks, you know: cover-up, kids stranded in space, people who are supposed to be dead are sending us a daily diary, officialdom is not telling the truth—that's going to play to the pirates. Of course, to do that means among other things we need a meed-maker with really major skills."

"If you say so," Glisters says.

"No modesty, Gliss," Wychee says. "That's what *you're* always telling *me.*"

"On the other hand, do *not* get all fancy and cut things into tiny little pieces and spoil the story telling aspect," I add. "Just remember, this will be the first time you've ever worked on something that really, really matters."

He sighs. "Everything comes with strings, doesn't it?"

22

CHRISTMAS ON THE WAY OUT

October 4, 2129. On board *Virgo*, upbound from periareon to aphelion (point in orbit farthest from the sun). 257 million kilometers from the sun, 42 million kilometers from Mars, 143 million kilometers from Earth.

"COMMANDER?"

I no longer have to think *that's me*. "Yeah, Glisters." I am squirming out of my sleepsack at his voice on the speakers.

"Something everyone should see. Big news in the cockpit. If you get here first I can show it to you before the others see it, so I'm not letting them know till you're here."

"Okay. Is it that bad?"

"That *good*. Hurry."

In the cockpit, he hands me a squeezebulb of coffee, and says, "Don't have any in your mouth while I run this meed, and strap in, okay?"

I suck welcome, warming coffee and strap in. "So are you going to call the others?"

"Soon as I've got you watching this." He's watching me strangely. "The answer to every question you're about to have is that all I know is what's in this meed, which I

watched three times before I called you. My search algo-
rithm found it on a pirate face that was shut down a few
seconds after I picked it up—naturally a onetimer."

"What's a onetimer?"

"Something that's costing Mom, and your father, a fortune, if they're behind it. A whole channel, not just some
faces but dedicated submillimeter-wave transmitter someplace in orbit, that pops up and runs till the UN Communication Control Center orders it to shut down. Only
intended to last a matter of hours, or even minutes, wildly
illegal because the software can't filter it—it can only be
turned off at the source."

"But the source is right there at the intersection of all
those submillimeter wave beams."

"You bet, and there are huge fines and all kinds of other
trouble for firing off a onetimer. But because the UN cops
have to get to it physically, during the few hours it's up,
nothing can stop the pirate community from download-
ing from it for later circulation—and once enough pirates
have it, it's impossible to keep it from leaking, over and
over, into all the other faces. Putting it out on a onetimer
makes sure a message gets out beyond recall. It costs plenty
because you have to bribe it onto a registered rocket launch,
or illegally push it off a space station, just to begin with, and
any kind of unauthorized launch is a high order UN felony."

"And you think our parents did that?"

"Somebody rich who wanted to make sure the whole
world knew something extremely relevant to our case did.
You know anyone other than our parents that could be?

So, the point is, anyway, at a guess, probably a hundred thousand pirates—say half of all the pirates there are—have recorded this and will distribute it to a few hundred million more locations within twenty-four hours, and it'll start being splyctered everywhere in a few days at most. The content is good news all by itself, but it's even better news that it came in through a onetimer, because this can't have been suppressed and somebody paid a lot to make sure it couldn't. Now you watch while I contact the others and bring them in here."

The screen image blips up abruptly; a lot of the pirates don't bother bringing you in or out, they just run the footage, wasting no millisecond of open face. It shows—for one instant, I think it's just some archived hooks of my Aunt Destiny and then I realize. *That's a Space Patrol cruiser and—*

The voice kicks in, "—the cruiser *Gagarin* on September 28, 2129."

Looking strangely bloated and half-dead, *Aunt Destiny, alive, just six days ago,* is airswimming feebly out of an airlock, between two guiding, supporting uniformed Space Patrolmen.

Cut to a pellor clinging to a mostly collapsed iceball.

Voice breaks in again over the pictures, and audio quality is poor, but it's my waves of emotion that block at least half of them: " . . . apparently stranded . . . explosion on *Virgo* . . . had the Tang Rule rations for four crew for one month in the lockers . . . crude electrolysis device made more oxygen . . . pellor engines can take ice from an aperture in an iceball surface membrane directly . . ."

I realize why she looks the way she does: She didn't have the anti-calcium-loss, anti-bloating, or muscle-maintenance drugs on board, because the longest they ever expected to be out in a pellor was a day or so. The voice explains some more " . . . Tang Rule, intended to ensure survival for stranded evalists . . . never intended to cover going to Mars in a pellor. Neither the necessary drugs nor the required radiation shielding . . ."

Oh, man, now that's the other reason she looks awful. For four months she was not behind two meters of water like we are, or half a meter of ferrocrete the way people were in the crew bubble; she's taken a pretty serious radiation bath. They'll be *pouring* preventive onco into her, they'll have to keep her in an almost abiotic environment for weeks, she's going to lose tonnes more blood cells, most of her hair, maybe some of her skin and intestinal cells . . .

And she's alive. *At least as of September 28, she was alive.* I'm crying too hard to listen well, but there will be months and months to rewatch the meed. *Destiny's alive.*

Voice again. " . . . cruiser *Gagarin* met the pellor approximately fifteen days out of Mars, in response to the distress call. Captain Khalidiya, in defiance of an injunction not to damage the commercial value of the the Derlock Slabilis survival story . . ."

Then the cockpit is filling up with my friends, summoned by Glisters, and I have to be calm and reassuring and all those commanderly things. I manage somehow, but I don't think I would convince myself. My brain is too busy with the thought that Destiny's alive, and Pop's on the job of getting us home. When the uproar has finally settled down to a happy buzz, F.B. asks, "Does this mean we'll get rescued sooner?"

"I hadn't even thought about that," I admit. "And I really don't know offhand. Let me think."

Now I see what a complicated mess Pop and the good guys must be dealing with. First Derlock called in, and Slabilis Celebrity Law got an injunction right then. Then Destiny turned up, and the Space Patrol (which I imagine likes Slabilis about as well as cops have ever liked lawyers) broke the ownership injunction by going out and rescuing Destiny; they'll probably do okay in court about that, because they can argue things about saving human life and being a government institution and so on, but they also had to keep the operation secret. Just about the same time that Destiny got close enough to Mars for her distress call to be heard, Glisters's transmitter-gadget started breaking into the drop-channels, starting an entirely separate pirate-versus-owner fight. And then Derlock finally landed, walked out of the cap, and under cover of that injunction, said several things that a few hundred thousand people knew were blatant lies.

I hope the judges on Mars enjoy complexity.

As we watch it the whole way through, with enough composure to be quiet and listen, I pick up the rest of the details; Destiny is alive, Pop is grateful, and they let him slip in a line about looking forward to having his whole family home and safe, but not mentioning me directly.

Probably the little sentence he was allowed to say cost a couple days of pricey lawyer-time, but if his results are measured in my gratitude, he got a bargain.

There's a last short shot of Destiny in a suspended animation tank. When it's down at the cellular level, as it is with radiation poisoning, precancer, advanced musculoatrophy, agravitic osteolysis, and who knows what else, it takes a lot more time than it did with the mere wounds and broken bones that Fwuffy or F.B. had; the voice says something about six months.

"F.B.," I say, "I think we're probably at a point in our orbit, relative to Earth and Mars, where they'll have to wait until we come back around into the lower part of the solar system, lined up with Earth, which is more than twenty months from now. There's just no physically possible orbit for any ship out of Earth or Mars to intercept us much before our perihelion. It's not that they don't want to, but—"

F.B. nods. "Sometimes life stinks," he says. "At least I'm with friends."

October 4 through December 5, 2129. On board *Virgo*, upbound from periareon to aphelion (point in orbit farthest from the sun). During these two months, Virgo climbs upward from 257 to 299 million kilometers from the sun. The distance from Mars widens from 42 million to 110 million kilometers, and the distance to Earth from 143 million to 280 million kilometers, as both planets, having passed Virgo in orbit, continue away from it,

**swinging back down toward the sun. Virgo, however,
still has a long way to go till aphelion.**

The news about Destiny, and its implication that the good
guys are working for us even if we cannot see or hear it,
bless us with about a week of morale boost. Our next few
meeds of *Life on Virgo* are upbeat, fun, and lively.

Weeks go by, and Marioschke and Fwuffy's work on the
farm pays off in fresh salad every day, and new vegetables
for Wychee to work with. The healthy diet, all the airswimming, and working in the farm takes flab off Marioschke
and puts muscle on F.B. Wychee slowly makes competent
cooks out of us all; Glisters and I keep pushing people
through tutorials until one day, he glances at me and says,
"You know, probably everybody on board except Fwuffy
and Fleeta could pass the science and math PotEvals now."

The whole crew spends a few days taking practice
math and science PotEvals, more for fun than anything
else. That's what life in space is like once things are working: every day like every other, everything routine, so dull
that doing math seems like a reasonable use of time.

We all ace our practice PotEvals, except for Fleeta, who
goes to the Forest to play. There's really no other word for
airswimming about haplessly and humming to herself.
She can no longer be safely left alone; Fwuffy watches her.
He says he doesn't mind—"I was bwed to be a babysitta"—
but we can all tell it depresses him, and Marioschke
spends some extra time reading to him. Now and then he
asks what Marioschke calls big-kid questions, like why

rotten people like Derlock get away with things, why nice people like Fleeta have to die, and why the world is just so unfair so much of the time. Once, after a long time batting philosophy around with Glisters, his adult "help text" voice kicks in to warn that we may be making him too grown-up and independent for his intended purpose. Glisters says it's deliberate, and we don't hear the adult voice on that subject again; Fwuffy is pathetically grateful, and asks if he can begin studying for the PotEvals.

That seems to motivate everyone. Now that we know we can all do the math and science, we plunge into preparing all the other subjects, with everyone taking turns at coaching Fwuffy. I find it slightly disturbing that he's better at math than F.B. and Marioschke, and that when he and Glisters study the more people-based subjects like literature, art, and history together, sometimes Fwuffy has to do the explaining.

For most of November, preparing for PotEvals keeps us going. There's always something to do every day, it lets some of us enjoy our newfound feeling that we really aren't dumb, and it's a good way to remind ourselves that we'll be going home eventually.

I find it a little hard to imagine that I used to think about which boys I wanted to be recorded making out with on which dance floor.

Glisters's homebuilt antenna only has about a fiftieth as many detectors as the real, regulation one we lost. Down close to Mars and Earth, where we started, we didn't even need that many to get clear signal. But as we rise away from the inhabited planets, the energy in a signal is inversely proportionate to the square root of the distance from the source; that's the fancy way of saying that if you're twice as far away you only get a quarter as much energy in the signal, and if you're 10 times as far away, you only have 1%. So where we needed only 20 detectors or so to pick up one face, down by Mars, we need more than 200 out here—and that's all we have, and as we go farther, we don't have enough. People back on Earth and Mars who are interested can buy more antenna space to compensate; they can still hear us, but we can no longer hear them.

Channels drop away, taking a thousand faces at a time with them, and there is less and less to see and hear outside the ship every day. Briefly, in the last week in November, there are a few seconds from *Life on Virgo*—not even in a story about us, but in a music meed for some song called "Everybody Shut Up and Agree." Just the same, "The pink flying elephant in it is unmistakably Fwuffy, and not some other pink flying elephant," Glisters says. "And that's a profile shot of Susan's butt. I've recorded pictures of it more than enough times to recognize it anywhere."

Every time things like that pop up on the pirate faces, we have a little celebration, and Glisters, Wychee, and I point out how clearly it means that someplace, somebody is fighting on our side. But each time the mood lift is smaller and briefer.

Meanwhile, the channels keep dropping, and we keep losing a thousand faces at a time, despite all the fussing and sweating Glisters does. The sun gets smaller, we drift farther away, and the better we become at living on *Virgo*, the less interesting *Life on Virgo* becomes. There's nothing duller than watching people do their jobs perfectly while nothing unexpected happens.

So day after day we record things growing in the farm, people learning new stuff, and little talks about how a spaceship works and navigates. "I see why there was never a legit 'life on a spaceship' show," Glisters says, looking at the latest *Life on Virgo* before sending it out. "If it weren't a PermaPaxPerity felony to watch, record, or circulate this, I don't think anyone would; all the excitement about *Life on Virgo* must be in risking arrest for having a copy of it."

Meanwhile the red star of Mars is dimming; the blue-green with white Earth-moon double star is now close to Mars in the sky, at about seven o'clock if the ship's nose is twelve. The little triple diadem of worlds with people creeps closer to going around behind the sun, which is now almost on our tail, as we continue up and away.

■ ■ ■

We're down to our last channel, a failed commercial venture mounted on a satellite in a wide-separation orbit from Mars that someone has left up and running. It only has about forty receiving faces—only six of news, and only two pirate. Well before the New Year, we'll have none.

Fleeta deteriorates. Now that she has no Fendrisol, the happistuf population explodes in her brain. Glisters documents it all: the strange, whooping, giggly orgasms that make it impossible for her to breathe, leaving her blue yet still ecstatic; the rapid loss of vocabulary as the prions invade her language center; the way Fleeta drifts out of talking at all for hours at a time, rocking, singing, shouting joyfully about "Mommy." *Virgo*'s onboard encyclopedia's long article about happistuf deaths says that that's a common behavior in the last few months. The leading hypothesis among neuroscientists is that the relatively normal dwindling remainder of the brain knows it is dying and wants its mommy, but its cries for help are all infused with the happistuf replacing it.

As November crawls into December, the sun has dwindled to half its width from Earth. The Earth-moon system, having whizzed on beyond us on its inside track, heads around the back of the sun, in retrograde relative to us, farther away from us than the sun itself. We see it only as a difficult morning star in our every-two-minutes morning, a momentary glimpse of a dim double star in the last second out of every 90, just before the sun flashes onto the window. Mars, though farther from the sun in the sky, is distant, dim, hard to pick out at all. On the inner, downward side, except the shrunken sun, it's all stars now.

On the outer, upward side, at about two o'clock, Jupiter blazes like a beacon. Though *Virgo* never approaches it closely enough for it to be a naked-eye disk, it's so big, so reflective, and so close to opposition that it's as breathtakingly brilliant as twenty Venuses, escorted by the little dim lights of its satellites, casting shadows through the windows in the floor of the Forest.

Of course, striking as the pictures of the Forest by jove-light are, it's still just some trees, grass, and pools—not that different from any park on Earth—and a hundred different research probes send out public-access pictures of Jupiter and its satellites from up close every day.

The farm is producing almost all our food now. We rely on the cargo section only for coffee, chocolate, tea, some spices, and the occasional meat dish whenever we are tired of fish. Theoretically we could take some dwarf pigs and rabbits out of hibernation, but at the suggestion that they raise animals and kill them so we can eat them, Marioschke, Wychee, and Fwuffy give us such a disgusted look that Glisters and I vow to each other that when we get home we will share a steak tartare the size of Nebraska.

December 5, 2129. On board *Virgo*, upbound from periareon to aphelion. 299 million kilometers from the sun, 110 million kilometers from Mars, and 280 million kilometers from Earth.

We lose our last channel. Glisters estimates that we will not pick up another one till about October of the coming year—eleven months of no new meeds.

Everyone seems so dejected that I ask for ideas about lifting the mood. Marioschke points out that it's only twenty days till Christmas, and there's a young conifer in the Forest, only four meters high, that we could decorate.

We all spend some days in the shop making all the things we can think of to hang on the tree, and Glisters shoots all sorts of great ultra-hookworthy ultra-splycter-ables of that, and of all of us decorating. Each of us takes a turn on camera at putting the star on the tree, including Fwuffy. "Think of it as an audition," Glisters says. "Star-putter that works best for the final cut becomes the person that finished it all off. You're going out with a star but you're coming back as the star."

After the decorating, we set about making and doing everything else Christmasy we can think of: rehearsing music, making special food, making and wrapping gifts, all the holiday botflog, which is just what we want it to be—if a hundred thousand hooks are splyctered out of this and end up in three million people's Christmas mes-sage, that will be perfect.

We're all second-generation celeb-eenies, so nobody wants any of that Jesus stuff that some of the miney kids used to insist on at Excellence Shop. That was always a mystery to me; to be a celeb-eenie you can't have any strong religion because anything you believed would make you unsplycterable to some part of the miney audi-ence; the mineys at Excellence Shop were in the place where they'd have their best chance ever to jump up to celeb-eenie; why would they stick to Jesus and Buddha and all that sheeyeffinit?

So we have to look a lot of it up, but we just do plain old Christmas. The most fun turns out to be working in the shop, making things for each other—everything from decorated ship's supplies like coveralls with titles lettered on them, to the individual milligravity cups that F.B. fires out of engine-nozzle repair ceramic. (They aren't nearly as easy to use as squeezebulbs but they have a simple, elegant shape and our names on them, and, well, I have a cup handmade from rocket-nozzle ceramic—do you?)

On Christmas Eve day, we do a whole-morning-long *Life on Virgo*. We read all the stock Christmas botflog—the Grinch, Dickens, *A Child's Christmas in Wales*, Yoshi Matamuro's *First Christmas on the Moon*, and *Prelude to a Divine Invasion*. In between we eat our feast (which does not include roast beast), open packages, sing all the songs we've been rehearsing, and put a big happy holiday wrap on it all, very traditional Las Vegas/London/Tokyo, and even drop in a little hint of Bethlehem because there's a niche miney audience that gets all happy, warm, and runny when they feel remembered and tolerated.

At the very end, we wave and say individual things to our families. I take the commander's privilege of going last and saying, "Pop, I miss you, and you don't have to worry about whether I know you're trying to get me rescued, because I know you've found out the truth by now, and I know you're working on it, and no one could do it better. So I'm just going to say Merry Christmas, and Happy New Year, and we'll see you at Earthpass, and I love you." We sign off singing "Santa's Night" over a slowly faded image of the glowing tree.

"I think we styled that perfectly," I say to Glisters.

He nods. "Well, you're the only critic within 150 million kilometers, and if you like it, I'm satisfied."

F.B. has taken the conn—that no longer makes me nervous, but it's still a big deal for him—and the rest of us are moving the leftovers back to the kitchen. We've just figured out how to get everything in so that it's possible to close the door on the main freezer when Marioschke says, "Wait, where's Fleeta?"

She was there for the whole Christmas celebration, though sometimes we had to work around things so it wouldn't be too obvious that she didn't know what was going on, and Glisters mostly used her for reaction shots, but she didn't have any of her Mommy-rocking attacks, she was genuinely excited at her gifts, and she even sang along with the rest of us a few times (and smiled while she was doing it, which is more than F.B. did).

"Fwuffy?" I ask. "Did you happen to notice—?"

"Oh, gowwy, she was wight behind me most of the way heah," he says, looking stricken; for the last few weeks, as she grew more confused and helpless, being her caretaker has become his default assignment.

"Not your fault," Marioschke says. "You were moving the big table and chairs box. I had her with me for a minute, but I stopped off to put the poinsettias back into the garden section—"

"And I had to check a couple of crate hooks on my way here, in the Pressurized Cargo Section," Glisters says, "and tell her not to follow me in there, but I don't know if she went back to the group. All right, we were all busy and excited, she wasn't officially anyone's job, and she slipped between us. No blame, but we better find her." He pulls out his phone and says, "F.B., do we have a position on Fleeta? She's not with us."

"She was following me and I sent her to the kitchen," F.B. says, over the speakers, "let's see if—her phone's in the bunk room, but she drops it there all the time."

I start to say, "Marioschke, could—"

"I'll check the bunk room, bathrooms, all of that," she says, and is gone.

"Thanks," I say to the air where she was. "F.B., thanks, that helps. Stay on line in case you have an idea, too. Okay, people, I'm guessing everyone was extra busy, and you know how Fleeta hates to feel she's being trouble, but if there's anything she can't do it's go off and sulk. So she'll have gone somewhere she really likes. Think of all the places we know are happy for her, everywhere between the Forest and here, look for any doors that might have been left open and would have had anything attractive through them." Weeks ago, we locked all the dangerous stuff so that Fleeta couldn't get into it, and my crew is way too good to go leaving doors open, but things happen.

Wychee says, "Gliss, let's you and me fly straight to the Forest. Probably she's just messing around there, she loves that Christmas tree, and the Forest has always been her favorite place. If she's not there we'll work our way forward."

"Good plan," I say. "Okay, Fwuffy, we're going to the Forest, slow and alert, taking our time, and we'll meet Glisters and Wychee wherever we do."

Fwuffy knows the usual way Fleeta goes to the Forest whenever he doesn't fly her down the coretube, holding her in his trunk. "She wikes that so much but sometimes, she wants to go awong Fahm Wevel Thwee, because the pea pwants awe bwossoming."

We descend to Farm Level 3 and split up to look along the two main parallel corridors between the beds. There's no sign of her there. "Any luck, Fwuff?" I call, figuring we should go to the next place he can think of.

"Nothing. I'm wowwied, I can't think of any pwace it makes sense faw huh to go. I was bwed to be able to un-dastand a wittle kid's mind, which is what Fweeta is, and she—"

My phone zizzes. It's Glisters. "Commander," he says, much too crisply.

"Oh, damn, Glisters." I know the whole story from his tone, and my heart sinks like a brick. "Where?"

"Right by the Christmas tree. I think she came back to just sit beside it; she had so much fun at the Christmas cel-ebration, and Fwuffy used to have to drag her to bed if she was sitting looking at the tree." I can hear him fighting the muscles in his throat. "I'll get everyone here ASAP; I've al-ready had F.B. slave the cockpit over to to his wristcomp."

"Right. Perfect. We all need to be there. I'll be there as soon as I can."

"Thanks, Commander."

I wish he'd called me Susan, but I guess it was easier to deal with the commander, for something like this. It's a substitute, but not a perfect one, that Fwuffy's trunk coils around my shoulders, the sensitive tip stroking my tears away. "You go ahead and be weady, Commanda," he says. "I'll go up to the cawtube and meet Mawioschke and F.B.—they aw going to need some comfutting."

I brush my face quickly and affectionately against his forehead, turn noseward, and airswim fast and hard, planting feet and kicking off every chance I get so that it's mostly a ballistic flight between the garden beds. At the first big downchute, I drop down to a big processing space against the hull, where I can bound and fly in a few more seconds to the Forest. Just before the entrance, I stop myself hard with my feet, and paddle gently in.

Almost under the Christmas tree, Wychee, crying hard, is holding Fleeta's body gently down on the turf, by the shoulders, so she won't float and tumble. Glisters is sitting on the grass a few feet away.

"You checked everything, I know," I say softly.

Wychee sniffles. "Yeah. She's, um, she's cooling off. The first aid gadgets detect no heartbeat, no breath, and the only brain activity is prion conversions. Even those are slowing down; not enough energy."

I take over holding her down; in the milligravity, there's always a risk that a thruster might fire for a second and set her floating in midair again, and I don't want any of the crew to see her flopping around lifelessly; somehow that would seem more dead than her being still.

It's much too soon for her to stiffen; her face is slack and blank—as it was the last few weeks anyway, when she wasn't smiling and giggling vacantly.

"I guess she came back here to take one more look at the Christmas tree, and some last critical brain cells died somewhere. She probably just turned off; even if it took a few seconds, all she could feel was happy."

"Good that it didn't happen during the Christmas show," Glisters says.

"Yeah."

Then F.B., Marioschke, and Fwuffy arrive, and we spend the rest of Christmas comforting each other. It's many hours before we resume our regular watches; meanwhile, we dress and clean Fleeta—*the body*—and seal it in a body bag in a freezer locker.

We use pretty much the same script that we did for Stack. Glisters shoots it for our next *Life on Virgo*.

I keep looking down at the body, and losing my place in the text on my pad. I'm not really seeing the body, or the pad; I'm seeing a brainy, beautiful little girl bouncing up and down on the acceleration couch next to mine as we get ready to go up to orbit. And I'm hearing her mother's voice: *oh, god, the waste, the waste, the waste.*

Later that night, when I'm on watch by myself, I remember Fleeta's young face on the screen of my wrist-comp; *Can you come over? Let's play! I've got all this ultra ultra zoomed stuff I have to show you!* It's a good thing the ship mostly runs itself, because I can't see any screen, tonight, through the wet blur.

23

THE WAY THINGS AWE

May 24, 2130. On board *Virgo*, upbound from periareon to aphelion. 347 million kilometers from the sun, 332 million kilometers from Mars, and 493 million kilometers from Earth.

WYCHEE AND I are sitting in the Forest, quietly; it's a habit that has developed in the long months since that awful Christmas, part of just being friends that can count on each other. I'm enjoying the brightness of Jupiter, and trying not to compare it with how small and dim the sun has grown; we're so far from home.

On breaks like this, I make it a rule to never think about ship's business, but that's no longer a difficult rule to follow. People know their jobs so well, and do them so well, that truly there hasn't been much to think about for the last five months.

After a while, Wychee says, "I have sort of an idea. I need to work it out, out loud, in front of you, Commander."

"Susan," I say. "Call me Susan. We're alone. I promise I won't take it as a sign of a mutiny."

"See, that's kind of what the matter is. I think maybe I've seen so much of the commander, since Fleeta died, that I keep wishing I could ask if Susan could come out and play."

I'm surprised at how good it is to hear her say that. "Well, I'm listening. What do you have in mind?"

She's looking at me closely. "Do you know what tomorrow is?"

"Uh, hum. Nobody's birthday, I kept track of that, no big holiday, hum . . . it's a little bit more than thirteen months since we got on the ship—"

"Almost there." Did she ever have that puckish little smile when we were moes back on Earth? Would I have noticed then, whether it was there or not? "You really *do* let Glisters do most of the flying, don't you? Where are we, Susan? Where are we?"

"We're—" Then I know, and I feel dumb. "We're at aphelion! Or we will be tomorrow!"

"And if that's not time for a party I don't know what is," she says. "Here's another thought for you: Gliss is only sending out an episode of *Life on Virgo* every couple of weeks, instead of daily like when we started. If he's right and the signal is still reaching Mars and the Earth-moon system, and we just can't hear anything back because no one's using a directional beam toward us, then I can't imagine anyone back home except our families are still watching *Life on Virgo*—and even them only out of loyalty. It must be dull as the drag races at the snail festival; it doesn't matter if Gliss is right and the big ground-based antennas are picking up everything we send, if what we send is too dull for anyone to pirate or sue about. Even if we had a huge fan base originally, after a few months where the most exciting things we did was routine maintenance, growing plants, and little nerd-education moments, we can't possibly have much of an audience left.

"So what I'm thinking, Susan, is that we need something to liven things up, for *Life on Virgo,* the meed, but also for life on *Virgo,* the painful reality.

"Here's the idea I've been working my way around. It's time to come out of mourning for all the terrible things that happened from July to December last year—it's nearly June, after all—and what better time than aphelion? We're turning around; we're all the way out at the highest, outermost, farthest point away from the sun in our orbit, starting to fall back around the sun, chasing down the Earth—it's something to celebrate, and maybe we can all quit acting so depressed about Fleeta, and about being stuck on the ship, and about Derlock getting away with murder."

"This sounds more like a prepared speech than like thinking aloud," I point out, but I'm grinning as I do.

Wychee nods. "I'm thinking aloud in a very well rehearsed kind of way, okay? Anyway, I want to celebrate, and I want to do it in a way that the media idiots, instead of 'still on their long journey outward' will start to say that we are 'inward bound at an ever-increasing speed,' because it will remind everyone that we're coming home and they'd better be ready to deal with us—and do something about Derlock. Now, come on, Susan, say yes, and let's have a party!"

I'm nodding. "You'd already won the argument when

you said *too much commander and too little Susan*. I really have been pretty grim and stuffy, haven't I?"

"Well, two murders, a death, and a psychopath trying to keep us from being rescued *is* grim, and that might entitle you to some stuffiness. But now it's time to throw a party, kick back a little, and feel more like life is worth living. Nobody's going to want to save us if we'd just depress them, you know?"

"I do know. Thanks, Wychee, you're right."

As soon as we announce the party, everyone gets behind the plan so quickly and eagerly that I suspect I was the last, rather than the first, person Wychee talked to.

May 25, 2130. On board *Virgo*, at aphelion. 347 million kilometers from the sun, 333 million kilometers from Mars, and 493 million kilometers from Earth.

Because of what happened at Christmas, no one wants to ever hold another party in the Forest. Instead, we set up on the cargo handling deck of the Pressurized Cargo Section. In celebration of our swinging back toward the sun, Marioschke doodles up a big bright sun with a sort of Tarot-card face, and Glisters machines a bas-relief of it out of some yellow plastic, two meters across. We hang that right at the center of the party space, from the lower edge of Cargo Wall 50.

By smearing paint in pastel bands on an empty foamed-cellulose liner from a spherical crate, we make a Jupiter-piñata, which we smash to celebrate our months out here passing close to it, if *close* can mean *several years away at our peak speed*. Still, the bright blaze of Jupiter has been the only visually distinct feature out here, and we are pulling away from it from now on, plunging ahead of it in orbit and dropping back down sunward.

And besides, inventing milligrav rules for piñatas is fun; everyone has to spot, so that when they miss, the people leaping blindfolded at the piñata don't bash the wall with their heads, or the spotters with the stick. After everyone's had a couple of tries, Wychee gets lucky; the piñata flies to bits and we chase all the little souvenirs and pieces of candy around in the air, catching most of them, we think, though I suspect we'll be finding them here and there around the Pressurized Cargo Section for months.

Glisters keeps trying to point out that perijove—the point where we were closest to Jupiter—was actually about a month ago. Fwuffy playfully gags him with his trunk, declaring, "Accuwacy is ova-wated, we'ah cwose enough to cewebwate," and everyone laughs, Glisters loudest and longest of all.

Sheer relief of tension, and release from mourning, has us all giddy. We sing silly songs. We give long roaming and rambling speeches that dissolve into giggles in honor of the sun. We put music on and do milligravity dancing. (We're only moderately impressive, but watching Fwuffy try to imitate us is splycterable if anything ever was.)

"Wychee," I say, "this was one of your most brilliant ideas ever, and I say that with the full knowledge that I'm speaking to the inventor of the spherical chocolate pie."

"Thanks, Susan." She sighs. "It was good that we toasted absent friends, too, and reminded everyone about the ones we lost—and about what Derlock did. Can we drink another toast to them?"

"Stack, Emerald, and Fleeta," I say, holding up my squeezebulb. "Never forgotten."

We all drink, and F.B. holds his squeezebulb up and says, "Derlock. Never forgiven." He's lost that hunted look he used to have, of fearing someone might hit him at any moment.

We drink again; I'm watching F.B. I'm not even sure he was ever really slow; so much of what we thought of as being dumb must have just been having no faith in his answers, even when they were right, or maybe especially when they were right.

We do a couple more milligravity dances, and some singing—Glisters has found us some songs about the long long trail a-winding along the long way homeward bound, and keeping the lights burning, and green grass and yellow ribbons and so endlessly sentimentally on until we're practically having to scrape sloppy sentiment off the windows.

I keep in mind Pop's injunction that for some shows there's no such thing as too corny, and try to style it big and fun, but even I choke up when we do a song from *Little Johnny Jones*—one of Pop's big revival roles. Of course it's all rebuilt, now, more than two hundred years later, and the actual place is now a seawater-filled crater, but "Give My Regards to Broadway" apparently still works on theatrical, or half-theatrical, blood. I'm not sure that more than a year is the same thing as "will soon be there," but still it feels disgracefully wonderful.

When we're tired of singing, five people and one horton subside around the window. It seems like a good time for a fade, so we all wave bye-bye to Glisters's camera, and force him to hand it to Wychee so we can show him waving bye-bye, and then sign off. Glisters says, "All right, it's a wrap, I'll edit all that into a special to send out tomorrow. At least we'll have a *Life on Virgo* ep that features something more exciting than the miracle of fresh carrots and the excitement of checking pressure seals."

The music goes soft and sentimental and we all stretch out on windows, alternately gazing down into the stars and enjoying the warm orange flash of sunlight through our closed eyelids. I'm about half awake when I notice Marioschke and F.B. slipping away together. Later, when I awake, Glisters and Wychee are gone, too, and Fwuffy is rolled over on his back on the window, stretching and enjoying the sun, like a two-tonne pink house cat with a trunk. I check the time. "Hunh. I guess I'll be an hour and a half early to my watch."

"Actuawawy I think Gwistas and Wychee would pwefuh you wate."

"They'd want me to wai—I mean, be late?"

"You being wate is the simpwest way faw them to have some pwivacy."

I kind of thought that vibe was in the air. "Thanks for the note, Fwuff." I look around. No party cleanup to be done; the area is spotless. "Gee, they picked up after themselves, too."

"They awe both the soul of wesponsibiwity."

"Your vocabulary's coming along so well since you've started reading all the time."

"Awso you gave puhmission faw me to devewop beyond smaw-child communication, which activated a wot of devewopment in my bwain."

"Is there a command or something we could use to turn your speech defect off? You really deserve more dignity than having to talk like that."

"I don't weawy know my own specifications. And I'm iwegal, so theah's no documentation."

"It seems kind of unfair. As far as anyone can tell you're at least as intelligent as a lot of human beings, and you've got better empathy and you're a nicer person. Glisters has been pushing that pretty hard in *Life on Virgo*, I know—"

"He's afwaid of what may happen when you awe wescued, so he wants to make sure I have a"—he slows down and speaks carefully—"a consti-tu-ency faw keeping me awive."

"Well, he's right. I don't know what we'd have done without you; you're a real part of the team."

He rolls on the window again, stretching and turning in pure pleasure. "Thank you, Commanda."

"You can call me Susan."

"I'd wather have compwiments fwom the Commanda; it seems gwanda."

I laugh, rub my face on his trunk, curl up against his

side, and pull out a tablet reader. I've been carrying it everywhere with me lately; there were a dozen of them in the ship's stores, and while it's not as convenient as the guys' wristcomps, it's way better than always looking for a terminal.

Lately I've developed a taste for South American poetry from the last pre-PermaPaxPerity generation, but today is not my day to read, because a thought pesters at me: after the voyage is over, since all of us humans have taken our calcium retention shots and our anti-dystrophy pills with religious regularity, we'll be able to go down and start Earth-retraining right away (though we'll have the standard couple weeks of bruises as we re-learn that you can't just park objects in the air, or slow down going downstairs by waving your hands). We'll ace our PotEvals, get talent-eenie training if we want it, do something or other with our lives.

But what about Fwuffy?

Probably right now he doesn't have the bones or the muscles for anything much more than milligravity, so he'll have to stay in space somewhere.

If they let him live.

After we're rescued, what if their media statement is just: *Horton? What horton?* They could just turn off the power and let out the air, and it might be years before they even had to issue the stock statement—*Oh, too bad, yes, it may have been unjust, but it's too late to undo it now.*

One of the principles of PermaPaxPerity is supposed to be "the discreet and efficient elimination of settled questions," but another principle is "a measure of tolerance for variance, especially in light of popularity." So which one will they apply to Fwuffy?

"Fwuff," I ask, "what would you like to do when the voyage is over?"

He rubs his forehead slowly with his trunk. "I don't weawy want it to be ovah, evah. I know it's what my fwiends need, but faw me, I wike it the way things awe. But I wike gwowing things, and I wike fwying. I think I would like anywheah with fwiends, miwwigwavity, and pwants."

I have no idea how to get that for him, but it doesn't seem at all unreasonable, so I leave the issue for later.

After I've read the same poem four times without remembering a word, Fwuffy asks, "Susan, what awe *you* gonna do when you get home?"

"Oh, take a long bath, hug Pop, work out, eat in restaurants, all that, at first. Take the PotEvals. After that . . . you know, Fwuffy, you've got more idea than I do."

"I think you should awways be commanda. Yaw vewwy good at it."

"Thanks," I say, slapping his thick pink hide hard; it's the only way he can feel it. I look back at the same poem and decide that today's not my day for reading.

DOWN-LEG: APHELION TOWARD EARTHPASS

MAY 25, 2130—JANUARY 9, 2131

POSITIONS OF THE EARTH, MARS, AND *VIRGO*—
MAY 25, 2030–JANUARY 9, 2031

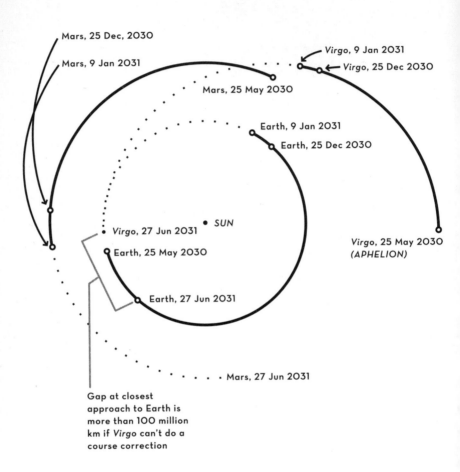

Mars, 25 Dec, 2030

Mars, 9 Jan 2031

Mars, 25 May 2030

Virgo, 9 Jan 2031

Virgo, 25 Dec 2030

Earth, 9 Jan 2031

Earth, 25 Dec 2030

• SUN

Virgo, 27 Jun 2031

Earth, 25 May 2030

Virgo, 25 May 2030
(APHELION)

Earth, 27 Jun 2031

• Mars, 27 Jun 2031

Gap at closest
approach to Earth is
more than 100 million
km if *Virgo* can't do a
course correction

Without course corrections (which require around 10 million cubic meters of water, or about three full iceballs, as reaction mass), *Virgo* gets more and more out of phase with Earth and Mars, so when they come back for Earthpass (also called perigee), they're going to be very, very far away from home (they'll cross Earth's orbit more than two whole months behind Earth—and the Earth moves through space at about 19 miles per second). And in future orbits, the situation will only get worse. If the *Virgo* survivors are going to solve their problem, they'd better do it soon.

24

BRILLIANT, WITH AN 80% CHANCE OF DEAD

May 25–November 29, 2130. On board *Virgo*, downbound from aphelion to perihelion. Descending from 347 million to 289 million kilometers above the sun. Mars begins at 333 million kilometers away and moves out to 449 million kilometers away as it continues around the far side of the sun. Earth begins at 493 kilometers, far behind the sun, but as it comes back around closes to within 165 million kilometers.

SO THEN, FOR about six months, we fall. So far away from the sun, we don't fall very fast, by space standards, which means we fall a lot faster than any bullet ever fired. Identical weeks crawl by, and Earth and Mars curve back, pass behind the sun, and pop out on the far side; we're still coming slowly down-system, well above what the ship's ephemeris tells us should be the orbit of Mars. Not that you can see an orbit, of course; it's an imaginary line in a vacuum that marks where the planet would be if this were some other time—you can't *be* more ephemeral.

We keep planting and harvesting in the farm section; fruits and nuts come in and out in brief seasons in the

Forest. Now that we've jailbroken his brain so that he can mature and learn, Fwuffy turns out to have a taste for adventure stories and mysteries, and loves most kinds of music, but math is a struggle. He sticks to it anyway, determined to pass at least a few practice PotEvals before we are rescued.

F.B and Marioschke are always in the same sleepsack now, and whenever they're awake and not working, they're leaning against each other. I haven't heard a word about astronomy from F.B. or metaphysics from Marioschke in ages; they talk about work, studying for PotEvals, recorded meeds they watch together, and food. They're the poster couple for letting people do something productive even if they're not out at the right tip of the bell curve; they've already decided that after our rescue, they'll apply to join a space crew or go to Mars, and take Fwuffy with them.

Wychee and Glisters are kind of a couple, I think, or at least they're tight with each other and sometimes in the same sleepsack. After a few months, at the ending of one session of running through checklists in the cockpit, I ask them, "Hey, I'm just wondering; why all this discretion about being all coupled up? If you dish on what all the secrecy's about, my solemn promise, I won't tell Fwuffy about it at lunch."

Wychee laughs and says, "Oh, I know I can trust my best girl buddy with our secret. We're being discreet for three reasons. One, Glisters is shy—you know he still wears pajamas."

Glisters looks up from the screen. "But I wear clowns

for Wychee. I could never wear ducks for someone else after all we shared, Susan."

I snort. "All right, I was afraid you might think I'd be jealous."

Wychee shakes her head. "Not really, we all know each other too well. But affection in front of you, when there's not really anyone here for you—"

"There's everyone," I say. "All four of you and one charming pink flying elephant. And I'm a lone wolf anyway, and besides something about being commander seems to mostly kill the sex drive. When I get lonely there's usually someone around to hang with and talk to, and that's what I really need. One of the best things about having ce-leb-eenie status pretty much guaranteed when we get back is that I'll never again have to think about my recognition score when I'm considering whether I think a guy or a girl is my type—and I think I'll usually decide they're not. Actually, when we get back, I'm thinking about a career as a hermit, as an alternative to living my life in meeds."

"Well, that's the third reason that Gliss and I have agreed to sneak around," Wychee says. "He's been careful not to include anything in *Life on Virgo* about me and him as a couple—so when we get home, with a little luck, we won't be splyctered into *Count Down to Break Up*."

"Wow, you're right. If you two are a couple in the minds of the fans, everybody will be waiting for the fights to start, so they can argue about whose fault it is and which stress was just too much." I laugh at a sudden thought. "F.B. and Marioschke are so happy with each other, hooks of them will be on *Count Down to Break Up* the first week we're back. But I wouldn't be surprised if they stuck together till one of them died, the way my grandparents did."

Wychee nods. "And they're the closest thing I've ever seen to a forever-couple—they just want a cozy little satellite where they can raise vegetables, babies, and hortons. That's okay, if they screw up *Count Down to Break Up* it'll just be one more thing to love them for."

Glisters chuckles. "Oh, yeah. Well, you know, when we all get rescued, let's make hash out of every media story about us. I think it's something we owe to ourselves."

That conversation seems to settle whatever small tension there was; they settle into being discreet rather than sneaky. *Virgo* falls on and on, month after month, gaining speed as, on the big oval track around the sun, we move down to the inside rail, lapping Mars (though it is still below us) and building up the speed we'll need to chase down the Earth just before it catches Mars again.

And far out in the cold and dark, our antenna still picks up nothing; we're too far out for broadcast and no one back home aims a beam at us. To some extent it feels like we could go on like this forever, and to some extent like we must, but mostly it feels like we already have.

November 30, 2130. On board *Virgo*, downbound from aphelion to perihelion. 288 million kilometers from the sun, 449 million kilometers from Mars, 163 million kilometers from Earth.

Glisters and I are hanging out in the cockpit, because it's his watch and I happen to be awake and it's time to do routine check-throughs of a bunch of minor things. The company is nice but the task is dull, and mostly we're talking about anything other than business.

We both jump when the distinctive *brawnk!* of his special alarm goes off; the antenna has managed to lock on to a beam from Earth long enough for the reception program to break the encryption on a face. We have our first readable signal since December 5, almost a year ago.

"That's so weird," Glisters says. "But maybe it will make more sense once we decrypt it."

"You weren't really expecting to get anything till February," I venture.

"Yeah, I thought that was the earliest we'd be in range to get a clear connection through that antenna, because I thought I knew what signal strength they use for signals to us. The weird part is that this signal is definitely coming from Earth and it's about 80% more power than it should be. Either they really want to talk to us or that's just a really hot station."

"Or they've upgraded the whole system," I suggest.

"Yeah. Or maybe it's the power level they use for live cyclers and they've reclassified us as live instead of derelict. It could be—"

The decrypted face pops up on the screen.

We both laugh. "No reason to wake anyone else up yet," he says.

It's a shopping face, selling quartz crystals specially blessed by the Polythete of Tashkent. "I'd forgotten how many faces Earth has," I say. "And what they use them for. Well, at least there will be new meeds. That has to be good for morale. Does this mean our face is open on Earth, for sure, now?"

"It's probably never been closed. And the power requirement to reach us would be no big deal; they could have opened a channel anytime, even when we were near aphelion and they were on the far side of the sun. The upper system probes out by Saturn and Uranus talk to home all the time, on the same gear, just at very short wavelengths and with a lot of juice."

"So probably, still, the reason they're not answering is the lawsuit? You think they're going to hear us and keep ignoring us?"

"You're the people person, Susan, what do you think?"

"It all turns on popularity," I say. "My guess is that the number of miney girls that wish Derlock was their boyfriend is ultra more than the number of mineys who can't wait to watch us grow broccoli in reprocessed sewage. And frankly, sex with Derlock *is* more exciting than running a smashed-up spaceship."

Glisters winces. "This unit's limits for information are being exceeded in category *icky*."

"Sorry. But if you're certain there's no physical problem—"

"For a little while back in early May, when Earth was all the way round on the backside, we were close to the sun in Earth's sky, which probably impaired reception, but now we're a good 40 degrees away. Really, Susan, I've checked everything ten million times. The problem isn't our antenna, it's Derlock's evil bastard daddy."

"Yeah."

Brawnk!

He checks. "News face! We can find out if anything happened in the last eleven months. I hope the Squid People from Tau Ceti haven't landed and taken over while we've been gone."

"If they have," I point out, "they've left at least one shopping face up and running. But I kind of hope they have, because I'll get to see Pop—he'll be the wily older advisor to the hero leading the Resistance."

"Yeah, and Mom will be doing the first in-depth interview with the charismatic, reform-minded Squid Person in Charge of Cultural Affairs."

He catches my eye as I catch his. Tiny shared headshake: *No more of this. Especially not in front of the others.* We've just made ourselves homesick, and everyone else is more susceptible than we are. We both bend to read the stream of information pouring out of the news feed, exclaiming to each other over some of the surprises, even though a year ago we'd have thought this was the dullest news day we'd ever seen.

But we don't get to read nearly as much news as we try to, because the world suddenly gets wonderfully, though inexplicably, busy. Faces pour into clarity, faster and faster; at first we're gaining a face every three minutes, then a face a minute, until finally it settles into gaining a face every ten seconds. Glisters flips off the horn so we don't go crazy being honked at constantly. "I just had that rigged up because I thought by the time we had signal again, people wouldn't be checking. Look at that data flood in. We have so much catching up to do."

Then the horn begins sounding again.

"I thought you turned that off."

"I did for faces. It's still on for channels. We must have already picked up another channel and—*look at that.*"

The screen is showing nine additional channels, a thousand faces each, have logged in within one minute.

"*Ten* channels have checked in?" Glisters says. "Ten? At this distance? Maybe your guess was right and the whole solar system is now just running at higher power. It'll be a few days to crack all those faces, but we're back in regular communication. Fifty million kilometers sooner than we have any business being, too."

"Maybe we should have the artificial intelligences hunt around and see if there's a related news story, maybe on one of the boring policy channels," I say. "Hey—are we just being egotistical?"

"Uh, clarify?"

"Maybe we're in line with some other ship, maybe an upper system expedition or something? And the beams trying to find them happened to rake across us, and because they're high powered, they were able to get a lock and keep sending?"

"It would be the biggest coincidence ever," Glisters

says. "I don't think there'd be any ship due back from Jupiter or Uranus, and those are the two where the trajectory might take them into our part of Earth's sky. But supposing there were, the whole point of using submillimeter-wave is that it's a tight beam so it carries farther with the same power. *Tight* means the beams they've got focused on us are only spread out to . . . uh . . ." He pounds on his wristcomp. "Wow. These channels are all at wavelengths around 0.14 mm, and the beam spread for that, out this far, with a standard aperture, should only be about 450,000 km."

"So that means it's hitting a disk that big? That's about the width of the moon's orbit, Glisters, it's not like it's a tiny target."

"At this distance it's a tiny, tiny target. For us to be in the beam of some ship behind us we'd have to be so lined up that a telescope on Earth would see them hiding behind us. There's a lot of other sky for them to be in and it's really a major coincidence." He raises his hands in surrender. "It's not that you didn't come up with a good explanation, just it's so improbable."

"Yeah, and it's still only ten channels"—*Brawnk! Brawnk!*—"uh, twelve, out of six million," I say. "I guess you can kill that horn."

"Yeah. There's still alarms set for a lot of other events, but I think this one has definitely happened, even if it didn't make much sense for it to happen now."

"I don't suppose diverting twelve channels—"

"It just went to fifteen—"

"Whatever, I'm guessing it's not enough to get us any attention."

"Not a prayer. There are porn-splyctering hobbyists in spacecrew who use up more bandwidth and energy, all by themselves, than we're plugging into right here. No one's going to notice a few diverted beams."

"Just hoping."

"I know. We all take a lot of long shots. F.B. spent ages writing a program to make the ship respond to a safety radar hit, and that's even less likely."

"Safety radar?"

"That radar system the idiots in the UN decided to require, the thing that's supposed to prevent collisions, because even though ships have been going through the asteroid belt for centuries, and the asteroids are so thin in the belt that most of the time none of them is even visible to the naked eye as a dim star, there's all those old meeds where the asteroid belt is a huge smear of floating rocks. And, you know, there could be up to fifty ships in space at once, more than enough for a traffic jam. Even though interplanetary ships usually never come within a hundred thousand kilometers of each other. But the UN insisted on installing those radars on everything in interplanetary space, and it's just possible we'll detect incoming radar sometime. And if we do, F.B.'s program will activate, and *Virgo* will fire three short thruster bursts, three long thruster bursts, and three short."

"SOS."

"Right. The anomaly would be reported to some AI,

and if we were very lucky, that AI might put up a public request for information, violate the injunction, and create more of a case for us. That might or might not do us any good, but probably the more ways we can violate it, the better."

"But we won't even be close enough to show up on safety radar during Earthpass?"

"We'll be 18 million kilometers from Earth at our perigee in June. On a normal Earthpass they come in to just inside a million kilometers. Even 18 million would be a reasonable trip for a Space Patrol cruiser, of course, with enough warning, and there should be three of those ready to go in Earth orbit and probably another one around the moon. We'd be duck soup to save, if they'd admit we were here, but since they won't, and we don't have a cap, we're screwed."

"So either we do something to force them to break the injunction, and answer a radio hail—or we're in for another two-year ride to nowhere?"

"More of a hundred-year ride to nowhere. Without course correction, after this one, we won't even come within cap range of Mars—not even the extreme one-way version Derlock did—and we'll be even farther from Earth on the Earthpass after, and so on. It'll be the early 2250s before the pattern of orbits carries *Virgo* back around to making any close passes. That's why I've sort of messed around with giving us another option."

"You think there's some way to force them to acknowledge the distress call?"

"No, there's a way we could maneuver into permanent Earth orbit; they wouldn't be able to ignore us when we were right there in their sky all the time." He pulls up a screen and shows me a thrust diagram and an orbital plot. "See, technically, we *could* extract most of the water from the farm sections—we're not using two of them anyway—and take all the water from the hull—"

"Our *radiation shielding*!?"

"Then we just run it all out through the remaining engines and thrusters, and steer into a close approach to Earth. The pod was made to be able to do a limited aerobrake; we could come in at a shallow angle, skip off Earth's atmosphere and lose some speed doing that, and fire the engines to push us back in again for a second bounce off the atmosphere. Of course, that's if the engines aren't torn off on the first aerobrake.

"Then we repeat that process one more time, and after the third aerobrake, we'd fall into an Earth orbit. Very high and elliptical, of course—our orbit would go out four times as far away as the moon, taking more than two months to do it, then shoot back in and tear across the sky in a matter of hours, but we wouldn't be going anywhere, they couldn't ignore us, and we'd be in easy reach for ships from the moon or Earth to intercept us, from then on."

"But with all our water thrown away, wouldn't we have radiation poisoning, early cancer, and genetic damage?"

"Everything has its drawbacks. We'd also be surviving on what's left of the stored food because Farm Section 1 wouldn't have enough water to feed us anymore. Not to mention that without the farm, our air supply would slowly become unbreathable."

"Those are *some* drawbacks, Glisters."

"I haven't even mentioned the *big* drawbacks yet. If we're even an eensy bit wrong coming in on the first aerobrake, or if we lose engines or thrusters from hitting at the wrong angle or debris flying off or just pure bad luck, we could go bouncing right off the atmosphere at way above Earth escape velocity. That would put us into a new orbit around the sun that would make it really hard for the Space Patrol to retrieve us, even if they were allowed to try. *Or* on any of the three aerobrakes, with no water supporting the space between the hulls, besides losing engines we might have a cave-in that would start breaking up the whole ship. And then, too, the accelerations in aerobraking are around four g. That's more than enough to kill Fwuffy—he wouldn't be able to open his lungs to breathe, and he'd probably rupture some internal organs. Cube square law and all that stuff."

"So the whole plan is utterly insane—"

"Well, I think it would have about a 15% chance of working—"

"That's about one chance in six for us, none for Fwuffy. Tell you what, I'll shoot Fwuffy and then roll a die; if it comes up anything except a three, I'll shoot you. Want to take that chance?" I'm trying to sound all even-voiced and reasonable about it, but I am itching to punch his idiot head—and then I see it. "How long will it take you to do some estimates about bringing us into Earth orbit—how we might do it, risks we'd have to run, chances of coming out okay?"

He looks a little puzzled at my sudden reversal, but he's always game and always prepared. "You know me, Susan, I've been working on it for weeks. I have all that already."

I pull my phone out of my pocket. "Did I hear Wychee in the kitchen?"

"These questions keep getting more random. Uh, yeah, she was going to—"

"Just wanted to make sure she wasn't still asleep." I put the phone to my ear. "Access Wychee voice."

A pause, then, "Yes, Susan?"

"If you can join Glisters and me in the cockpit, the officers need to hold a little meeting on the subject of how we're all getting rescued for Christmas."

"That's one of my favorite subjects. See you in one." She clicks off.

I turn back to Glisters. "All right, let's see that options list, and the grimmer the better."

"You're awfully cheerful. I suppose you'll explain all this sooner or later?"

"Oh, I thought I'd keep it all deeply secret. More melodramatic that way and we can all enjoy the confusion and accidents together. Of *course* I'm going to explain. Right away. I'm just waiting for Wychee—"

"No you're not, I'm here," she says, airswimming in.

"Here's the short version of the news," I say. "One, we're back in touch with Earth—or rather we're getting—

how many channels from them, now, Glisters?"

"Uh, forty-eight now."

"There's a huge backlog of decryption but basically we're getting them. They're probably still pretending not to get us, due to that injunction, but I've figured out a way to make them quit pretending. So—details to be worked out, which is what you're here for, but I know how we're getting rescued."

They stare. For one instant, I think they're about to sedate me and lock me up. Then they grin. *If they have that much faith in me, I'd better be right.*

"It's sort of an intersection of two ideas," I explain. "And I could have had it anytime, but after a year of no communication and now all this mystery flood of it, somehow that made me think a little differently. My idea might end up very badly, so we need to think about how exactly to do this. But here's the basics: Glisters, let's put together a special episode of *Life on Virgo* to describe your aerobraking plan for getting into Earth orbit."

Wychee says, "You hadn't told me about that yet," with a hint of whiny jealousy, so I bail Glisters out. "He just told me right now. Let's run through it."

Wychee is just as upset as I was, which tells me I'm on the right track.

Glisters finishes with, "I have maybe ten variants on the basic plan, but every single one of them will kill Fwuffy, risk putting us in an even worse solar orbit for being rescued, and no matter what, expose us all to a fairly bad dose of radiation. And the most we'll get out of it is that we'll keep making a low pass at Earth every couple months, so the few people on Earth who still look up at night will see us shoot across the sky a few times a year, and we'll be able to break into the pirate faces more often because of the long exposure and being constantly in range. But Fwuffy will be dead for sure and it's an 80-some-percent chance that so will all of us."

"*Beautiful.*"

Now they are *staring.* Maybe it's my big smile.

"That's *not* the word that comes to *my* mind," Wychee says.

I explain, "We are going to do a special episode of *Life on Virgo*, in which we explain that we have no other choice, because no one will answer our hails, and as far as we can tell no one cares, and obviously we're not important so we just have to save ourselves, even though poor old Fwuffy is going to die a horrible death—"

"Will anyone care?" Wychee asks. "Does anyone even still watch our meed?"

I shrug. "Well, until just now, I didn't see it myself. Suppose *Life on Virgo* is a flop, no one is watching, and nobody cares. What would hooks from it be worth?"

"Zip," Glisters says. "About as splycterable as all those miney prayer and folk song meeds, I suppose."

"And how much effort would the Slabilis family be putting into keeping our meeds off the net and out of faces?"

"Well, they still wouldn't want us to screw up Derlock's trial—"

"*That* won't be affected at all, no matter what we do. Derlock's *going* to be convicted, because the autopsy undoubtedly showed that Emerald got one huge dose of happistuf and then one huge dose of Fendrisol, *after* going up to *Virgo*. Probably they'll find bruises from where he forced the gasper over her face or tied her down to give her the dose. He's going to be obviously guilty as all sheeyeffinit, and he's certain to be convicted. He'll even *want* that, because it will enhance his value.

"Of course then he'll be let go because of overriding media interest—that's his father's specialty. At which point the Slabilis family will make a huge pile by selling the rights because they'll own *everything* connected with the story. That's always been the plan, and they're good at that; nothing is going to stop them. The reason we barely see anything splyctered out of *Life on Virgo* is because the Slabilis family owns all of it and they're holding it back for later resale.

"Now, to keep a major news story off of all the legal faces *and* buy off or shut down all the pirates—well, start adding up the costs: Sir Penn Slabilis has to buy the injunctions, rent the judge, keep a research staff on payroll to show that there's an overriding public interest in letting him own it, keep human lawyers standing by and AI monitors and enforcers watching all the time. Because this isn't something the court system does for free, you know, I mean it's way outside basic services. It's ten times what it would cost to just pay off our families, and us, to keep our mouths shut, especially since to get a rescue, our families would have paid a lot, and agreed to all kinds of things. They could have either rescued us, shut us up, or both, for a lot cheaper—unless. You see the unless?"

"Unless . . ." Wychee gets it. "Unless we own something they're trying to steal in court—and the only thing we own is *Life on Virgo*. Which means it *must* have n-nillion watchers." She gapes at me. "But how could it? I mean, we're not really interesting. Except for being out in space and a slight risk of being killed, we just aren't that different from *The Wang Family Daily Life*."

"I've never watched that," Glisters says.

"See?" Wychee winks at me.

I take pity and say, "That's Wychee's point. *The Wang Family Daily Life* is not a real show—well, probably it is, probably there are a couple thousand of it, because Wang is the most common name on Earth. There are n-nillion families, businesses, relationships, hobbyists, name what you want out there in miney-land, who have lives about as eventful as ours. Or as *un*eventful, more to the point.

"Yet back on Earth there are injunctions so tight, and bribes to law enforcement so extensive, that nobody is openly covering us. If our stuff wasn't worth anything, they'd leak it for free advertising—I mean, sheeyeffinit, think of the publicity of having Derlock maintain his preposterous story while all the time the supposedly dead people are on the air every day! Nothing could get more attention than barefaced villainy, you know? So why wouldn't they just use *Life on Virgo* for free publicity? *Because it's worth a fortune and they intend to steal the rights to it in the court settlement!*"

Glisters looks exasperated. "Okay, which side are you on? We either have the biggest meed in decades or we have *The Wang Family Daily Life*, in which Junior Wang learns the Pythagorean theorem and Papa Wang decides to plant marigolds this year. Which is it?"

"That was the problem I figured out," I said. "It comes back to something Pop pretty much taught me as soon as I could talk: *faith in your material.* It's like a moral principle for him; once you've decided something is worth putting in front of the public, never apologize for it, never wish it was something else, just do it as well as you possibly can—if it was a mistake to choose it, commit to it enough to go down in flames and at least make a pretty crash. He blows up about it when he sees a singer who keeps doing schtick to signal *I know this is corny,* or an actor smirking through a serious role where the writing's not up to standard, or a dancer who makes every step say *this is beneath me.* He always says, ask what the crowd came to see from you and make sure they get it—nobody comes to see you intone impressively, they want to see *Hamlet*; nobody cares whether this song was special to you and your boyfriend, they want to hear it the way you think it should sound. So what do people watch *Life on Virgo* for?"

Wychee's eyes roll back as she ticks off possibilities. "Not many explosions. No musical numbers. We're brave and all that but most of the time we're just doing our jobs.

There's danger but it's not really about the danger, it's about—well, at first it was probably Derlock plus the situation we were in, because betrayal and danger is a good mix for entertainment. But since then? We're weightless or in milligravity but so are hundreds of people on the other ships; we're a bunch of kids on our own, but there are n-nillion meeds about just that. I can't think of one thing that's individual enough or interesting enough—"

I feel so clever and sneaky. "Oh? How about the fact that one-sixth of our crew is a flying, talking pink elephant?"

Glisters looks like he just sat down on an open circuit; then he laughs. "Susan, do you think you could make Wychee the pilot so that I can just go back to being your poor dumb chief engineer, and not have to do all this hard human stuff?"

Wychee says, "Nothing doing—if she promotes me over you, your fragile masculine ego is going to collapse into a pile of rubble, and you'll be useless." She's nodding to me. "All right, I see the logic, Susan, people must be watching to see Fwuffy, so if we threaten to kill him, that'll rile up our side, but how are they going to do anything about it once they're riled? Sure, popular demand could save us, if the authorities are forced to pay attention to it, but how do we force them from here?"

"Well, it's an idea Glisters mentioned ages ago—way, way back when we first had the antenna problem. Sub-millimeter-wave cellular is complex and difficult to work with, and way out here it's all tight beams. That's why it took Glisters so long to figure out a working antenna. In fact, it's not even an antenna in the sense that the people who invented radio would have recognized it, is it?"

"Not really. It's a detector array. All the little detectors in all the dimples are the actual antennas."

"So here's the idea. Right up front, because the pirates and the hackers will just love it, we explain that we haven't heard anything back, and we say we don't know if it's because of the injunctions Sir Penn Slabilis is getting out of corrupt judges, or because no one is listening. If no one is listening then using up our water in the engines is the only way we can ever get home. But we *won't* do the aerobrake maneuver if we just know someone is listening and trying to get us home. So all they have to do is call us up and tell us—and then we tell them how to make an old-fashioned AM transmitter, what frequencies we're going to broadcast on and listen on—"

Glisters sits back, stares into space. After a moment he's nodding, like he's trying to pump his head off. "Yeah. Yeah."

"Would people do that?" Wychee asks. "I mean other than terminal nerds like Glisters?"

"Automated manufacturing—the same way everyone gets pirate meed gear or drug paraphenalia," Glisters says. "Send the instructions on another face simultaneous with the episode. As soon as they have the instructions, they can order their Call-*Virgo*-AM-Radio-Set from a hundred thousand no-questions-asked sources for delivery the next day. Then they just plug it in; I'll design it to use the neutral side of the power supply as an antenna. The cops would never be able to stop it if they tried—and the person asking them to try would be Sir Penn Slabilis, Friend to Crooks Everywhere. They wouldn't try. All of a sudden you'll have thousands or millions of people able to call *Virgo* directly, the pirates will argue that the security and rights management has been hopelessly cracked, and the whole story will be open access. At which point the judges lift all the injunctions—on grounds of overriding media interest, don't you love it?—and the Patrol is allowed to come and get us. It might be February before the rendezvous, but we'll be comfortable enough till they come."

"Is an AM radio hard to make?" Wychee asks.

"Well, I could make one in the shop in probably an hour," he says, "but to come up with something people can just hand to an automatic manufacturing company might take a couple weeks. That would give us time to test it and make sure it's perfect, if you'd like to make the whole thing the finale on the Christmas show."

"And Gliss says he's got no human skills." Wychee hugs him tight enough to make him squirm. I guess she, at least, is over this "discreet" thing.

25

THE SECOND AND LAST CHRISTMAS ON *VIRGO*

December 24, 2130. On board *Virgo*, downbound from aphelion to perihelion. 272 million kilometers from the sun, 444 million kilometers from Mars, 125 million kilometers from Earth.

"THAT'S AS READY as it's redding, people, everyone to places," Glisters says.

"We're *in* places, Gliss," Wychee points out. "We have been for fifteen minutes. You're the only one that's not."

"All right, all right, it's running," Glisters says, moving away from the small screen he's assigned to run his array of tracking cameras. He's moved those here to the Forest from all over *Virgo*, insisting since one way or another this is his last Christmas Extravaganza with us, it's going to be his best work to date.

He airswims to his place by Wychee, and says, "And . . . here I am, here we are . . . all the cam lights are green. Your show, Commander!"

This is no time for innovation. I style my smile warm-but-tired, in Classic Meed. "Hello, solar system, merry Christmas from all of us on *Virgo*, and I hope you're having a comfortable, joyful Christmas Eve with family."

We decided on Christmas Eve because it's when all the big events in the Christmas story happen—the Grinch's visit, Marley and the Three Ghosts, and so forth. Also this will leverage the media coverage payoff by making it happen early on Christmas Day—if there's any payoff.

F.B. takes his turn. For his minute or so, he really is the most-listened-to guy talking about astronomy in the solar system. He sits by the window with a camera floating over him; Glisters will intercut the hooks of F.B.'s narrating with outside cameras, to give a clearer view of the sun, still not even two-thirds of its size from Earth. He points out the Earth-moon system, now just to the right of *Virgo*'s nose, a bright blue and a dim white star almost touching— "the big sapphire and the little diamond," F.B. calls them, staying right on script. He shows them far distant Mars, a dim red star just coming around the sun behind us.

The next part is memorials. I talk about watching Fleeta slip away, as much as I can stand to because it will always be a raw subject. Glisters tells how, after years of bullying, Stack became his friend, and how he lost him so painfully, so soon afterward. Wychee has a whole montage from her personal files of images about her friendship with Emerald, and nobody has to fake tears for the reaction shots to that. We have Fwuffy go last, telling people that "out heah, in so much emptiness, we wearn how awe wife is pwecious," and some other conventional sentiments that Marioschke spent days drafting up, working harder at that than at anything else I've ever seen her do, including the farming. If anything will make him seem wise, human—deserving to live—that should do it.

Fwuffy's concluding uplift is just enough to let us move on to the gifts. They're just token things for each other, and I suppose I'd been thinking of them as sentimental props, but all our reactions surprise me by being so genuine. When Marioschke unwraps the farming coverall I'd had the fabricating machine make for her (heavyduty waterproof with numerous extra pockets) and hugs me hard enough to take my breath away; or when I see the cool, elegant pendant Glisters designed for me out of ultra-high-temperature steel and ruby drill tips; or how much F.B. is touched by the carefully worked out evalist undersuit Marioschke figured out for him, I realize that it wasn't just me—everyone was working on these things for months—and that we're all giving and getting the best gifts of our lives.

I improvise a little speech about that. Everyone's smiling, and I'm just about to wrap that up when the ship jerks hard, three times, then does sustained fire three more times, and then three more hard jerks; we all scrabble for grips and drift out of the view of the cameras we're facing.

"Sorry!" F.B. says, looking excruciatingly embarrassed. "That was my radar detection program. I'm sorry I screwed up, it shouldn't have fired—"

"It did everything right," I point out, "except it happened to have a false positive, since we know there's no radar within a hundred million kilometers. One little oopsie does not make it bad work."

"Yeah," Marioschke adds, hugging him.

Wychee asks, "Do you have it locked out now?"

F.B. nods, looking up from his wristcomp. "Yeah. It actually fired because it thought someone had lit us up with radar. So after making its one mistake it worked perfectly. I'm still kind of embarrassed."

"Don't be," Wychee tells him. "On with the show! And Gliss, don't even think of cutting this bit; we want people to know we're human, and see us reacting to the kind of surprises that are just part of life."

We talk of what we have learned about faith and courage on the journey. We remind them that we're 20% farther from the sun than Mars is, still out in the far cold and dark, and try to guide them to see us as an image of a tiny candle of love, faith, and hope flickering in the darkness so far away. I know all that sheeyeffinit would sell a lot of deodorant or beer; I just hope it's selling us.

The big moment arrives and I airswim into my place, lining up so that half the screen behind me is Christmas tree, and the other half is the group, including some of Fwuffy's face. Glisters, I know, will put a background of starry sky against that before we send it over. It's just as real as all the botflog from Mars and a whole lot prettier.

Strangely, I have no stage fright at all, not even the normal little twinge of this-will-be-good; I just begin to speak. "We'll go to the Christmas songs from the Forest, looking out into space, in just a couple of minutes, but I have to explain why this is going to be our last Christmas in space. As you all know, due to injunctions filed by the boy who murdered Stack, murdered Emerald, and arranged for Fleeta's horrible death—and may have killed many others—we've lived out here without rescue and without any news about any upcoming rescue. I want to thank the many pirates and hackers who have helped us get occasional bits of news, so that we at least knew that some of our signal was making it to Earth.

"We *don't* know whether our pleas for our rights and privileges as citizens under PermaPaxPerity, and the best efforts of our families, are actually leading to any sort of rescue. We *don't* know whether this is because the injunction prevents our receiving news of it, or prevents any rescue at all. But we have learned to rely on ourselves out here, and we *do* know that in six months we will make the last Earthpass close enough for us to perform our own rescue. To do that, we'll have to take several extremely dangerous steps."

Then I hand off to Glisters, who explains about the plan to sacrifice nearly all of our operating water through the engines, allowing us to do a very dangerous triple aerobrake maneuver that will kill Fwuffy for sure, and is highly likely to kill the rest of us, and certain to expose us to immense doses of radiation, but will make it more convenient for people on Earth to come and get us.

Among Fwuffy's many latent talents, he's not a bad actor. "Since I was cweated in an iwegal wabowatowy, the onwy otha people I have known have been the cwew of *Vuhgo*. They awe the best fwiends anyone could want. I cannot keep them away fwom theah homes and famiwies, stwanded in space foweva, just because I am onwy adapted to this habitat—"

The delivery is ultra perfect and if I'm right that *Life on Virgo* fans are mostly Fwuffy fans, that will close the deal or nothing will.

Then I'm back on camera for the finale. "This was obviously a very difficult and painful decision for me as commander, and I really did not want to make it. But it will be almost four months before we have to begin to carry it out, so perhaps something will turn up in that time. We would not even contemplate such a step, killing our beloved crewmate, risking all our lives, destroying the ship that is our home, and exposing ourselves to far more than a lifetime dose of deadly radiation, if we just knew that this is not our last chance. If we knew help was coming, we could and would be happy to take care of ourselves till it arrived, as we've been doing right along. And we realize that we can't ask people to violate injunctions, no matter how unjust, when they carry such severe penalties and are written and enforced by one of the slickest lawyers the solar system has ever seen."

I turn it over to Glisters, who tells them that he's uploaded information through thousands of pirate and hacker faces, and it will tell them how to make and use a simple AM radio. "And God bless the pirates, every one! Remember, all you have to do is download instructions and send them to wherever you have your technically illegal gear made—but if you want to let us know we're getting through and that someone is working for us, and if you want to help us build our case against that injunction, the time to do it is *now*. And as a further incentive, so you can prove to all your friends that you really built that radio and talked to us, we're reviving an old ham radio custom, the QSL card. Back when radio on Earth was a difficult thing for hobbyists to do, they used to mail each other cards that said, *Your transmitter reached me.* We have a nice-looking format for a QSL card that we will transmit through the first regular submillimeter-wave mail face we crack into, to anyone who asks for one via that AM radio. You can not only talk to us, and let us know not to give up, you can have that proof that you did. So don't forget to ask us for a QSL card, because these are probably the first ones in a hundred years, and they might be the last ones forever." He's grinning, but then he fades his grin—styling Thoughtful Irony just like I taught him. "Of course, there are a lot of things about this that might be the last time, forever."

Per the script, Fwuffy says, "Awwight, now, that we have depwessed the whole sowar system, can I finawy heah my favowite Chwistmas songs?"

He actually doesn't have any favorite Christmas songs; he likes music, but finds most Christmas songs cloying, sentimental, and excessively cute. I guess if you're an intelligent being condemned to be a five-year-old's idea of cute for life, you just don't need any extra cute in your life.

So we had to work up a list of which songs would do the show the most good, and then Fwuffy memorized how he'd ask for each one. We figure if it works out that he survives, and for the rest of his life he has to be subjected to childish, silly songs once a year, it's a price well worth paying. We all sing with deep enthusiasm, and Fwuffy, who wasn't geneered to have much in the way of pitch control, shakes a tambourine and manages to look like he's having the time of his life. He really *is* a natural actor.

Then we all troop down to the tail airlock to be there rooting for F.B. when he takes the wire AM antenna out to deploy. He doesn't have to go off belay at all, and he only has to go about 3 meters from the airlock hatch to the utility socket we're using. All he has to do is plug in one end of the big, coiled cable, check the connection, remove the clip from the coil, and throw the coil tailward into space. Still, it's an eva, and those are never without danger.

Of course he does it perfectly. As soon as he's back inside, with the hatch closed, Glisters fires a three-second burst from the thrusters, to stretch the cable out behind us.

In the kitchen, Wychee's hot chocolate is all the tastier because she warns us that she's starting to run low; we don't have any way to grow cacao on board. It's my watch, and everyone else turns in early, probably due to some half-remembered little-kid rule that Santa can't come till you're asleep.

Glisters's AM scanner remains silent. Fwuffy curls up in the back of the cockpit, and soon he is snoring gently. I read some tech specs and review some records; though it's dull, I don't worry about falling asleep on watch—that's just not something I do after more than a year as commander.

December 25, 2130. On board *Virgo*, downbound from aphelion to perihelion. 271 million kilometers from the sun, 444 million kilometers from Mars, 124 million kilometers from Earth.

My watch is almost over when a voice emerges from the scanner. "Um, hey, I don't know if this thing is working, but I think I followed the directions and it should be, and I just wanted to say I've been following you ever since Marspass and *please don't kill Fwuffy!*"

I am airswimming to the specialty screen, strapped in before the first sentence ends. I check the corner of the screen: radio lag to Earth is six minutes, fifty-six seconds, so the time between their speaking and my answering, for them, is going to be about fourteen minutes.

"Earth station, this is *Virgo*, go ahead. Glad to see the directions worked. This is Susan Tervaille, acting commander, *Virgo*. Please identify who you are and please broadcast, on the regular net, that you were able to reach *Virgo* via the AM transmission protocols. You know we don't want to kill Fwuffy, but we've got to get home, and without action from the UN and help from the Space Patrol, this is our last chance. If we can get Earth to listen to us, Fwuffy will be just fine. We love him, too, you know. This is Susan Tervaille, acting commander, again, sorry about the delay but we have a seven-minute time lag due to the distance. Please acknowledge; I'm keeping the channel open."

I click over to the speaker in the bunk room and say,

"All right, everyone, showtime in the cockpit. Get here as soon as you can, we've got at least one live one. I'll need—"

There's a hiss and pop and a different voice says, "*Virgo, Virgo*, hello, this is Dr. Mamadou N'diaye, director, calling from the Mascon Deep Drilling Project at the University of Selenopolis, Mare Smythii, Moon. The scientific staff here at MDDP took a vote and we have decided unanimously that the whole Slabilis family are assholes, that you should have a merry Christmas, and that *you should not hurt that horton!*" He sounds a wee bit drunk, which I suppose might be expected of a scientist at a frontier research post on a holiday; I went to Selenopolis during my Crazy Science Girl days, and it's really just a research station with an engineering school and a few stores and bars, located where there are a bunch of cool rocks but nothing much else.

I start to read our message to Dr. N'diaye, acknowledging that we've heard him, agree with him, and need him to pass word along, when the radio crackles again; he has one more thing to say. "Also, we're formally requesting a QSL card, which we intend to display on our face and in all the faces that relay our work."

I'm about to answer the QSL request when I hear, in the first voice, "Me, too, I mean, I meant to ask before, I want to get a QSL, this is Lee Chul Ho, I'm fourteen years old, in a corporate recreation apartment on Guam with nothing to do for the holidays. My parents are going to *kill* me when they found out I did this, it was all over the meeds how there's an injunction against it, and I bet the QSL is illegal too, but I want one anyway, and I'll put one up on my personal face, I swear I will. *Please* don't kill Fwuffy. He's my favorite. I always watch all the meeds he's in, and I use a hook of him for my personal logo!"

I realize that they can hear each other almost immediately—they're only about a second and a half apart by radio lag—so Lee Chul Ho was answering me when she heard Dr. N'diaye, but now they'll both be waiting fifteen minutes for the response. I'm about to ask for her address to send the QSL when she gives it, so I put her and MDDP onto the QSL list, and broadcast that I've done that. By the time I finish talking to them, there's a lineup of calls from Kuala Lumpur, Dubai, Honolulu, and Tashkent; cruise ships and yachts in the Andaman Sea, Bay of Bengal, South China Sea, Java Sea, and Weddell Sea; organizations that include the Natal Polyamory Intentional Community, Beijing School for the Extremely Talented, University of Asmara, Durban Extreme Surf Club, United Baha'i of Auckland, and the Maidan Hazzards Rugby Club. They all want us to save Fwuffy, they all announce they are going to defy the injunctions, and they all want a QSL, so that I'm hard put to record them all. Very luckily for me, the desk staff at the Sheraton on the island of Diego Garcia have been sitting out a hurricane that has left them with no guests and nothing to do. They go on the air and urge everyone to queue up and talk one at a time. They get most people listening in on their new, suddenly busy AM radios to contact the Sheraton's front desk via regular net and get a number, and to write out a message to read aloud, pointing out that we can't hold real conversations because of the time lag.

Once it settles into a rhythm of the Sheraton Diego Garcia saying, "All right, Number . . . your turn," with Fwuffy handling about half the calls, I can almost keep up, but still, I'm very grateful when the other four tumble in from the bunk room, all looking like rumpled shit on a crumpled napkin. Fwuffy is definitely the most popular, despite having some trouble making himself understood and needing to have Marioschke take down the QSL addresses for him; the Sheraton desk clerks start a separate queue for him.

Meanwhile the rest of my crew takes a screen each and gets to work at Glisters's direction. There are now separate queues for all of us; I think F.B. is probably the most flabbergasted I've ever seen a human being be when the fourth young girl in a row tells him he's her favorite and she thinks he's cute. Probably it would bother Marioschke if she weren't so busy answering calls from passionate gardeners, would-be poets, and creepy old guys who say they "like a girl with meat on her bones."

I have a moment to reflect that we're lucky that we got up and running when we did, so that the first radios were delivered and plugged in when we were facing the Pacific Ocean; there are going to be many more calls within a few hours as Earth's biggest cities, in West Africa and Central America, come over the horizon.

There's a little bit of a problem with jerks jumping the queue and calling each other names just to be rude, and some of the wealthy tech jocks on the moon are ungracious about waiting their turns, but still, with the help of the Sheraton, we're handling most of the traffic, and Sheraton corporate management, sensing that we're popular and the Slabilises are not, announces that several more Sheraton desks around the planet will help handle the traffic, and that the corporation is throwing its legal team in to fight the injunctions, filing in every UN district at once. Glisters shoots us giving a short group cheer for Sheraton; we figure they'll be able to use that in commercials for at least twenty years to come.

The lag deters most people from doing more than radioing in the basic message in their own words: they support us, they defy the Slabilis injunction, they beg us not to kill Fwuffy, and please send a QSL. But there are so many in total that the small minority who don't mind attempting actual conversation with fifteen-minute lags keep us busy; three-quarters of those want to talk to Fwuffy.

I'm still a bit surprised that we all have fan clubs, I guess you could call them, and quite a few people are willing to wait long enough to hear their favorite respond to them and directly say that we'll send a QSL.

"You seem to be the most popular human," Glisters says, while he and I take a fast water break.

"Yeah, and they all want to address me as 'Commander.' I can't believe how much it doesn't matter now; a couple of years ago all those fans would have been my biggest fantasy, and now they're just a job. But I admit, it's feeding my ego; the only thing keeping me humble is that all of us combined are not half as popular as Fwuffy. It's a good thing he was geneered to love attention and be polite to everyone. Did you hear that bratty kid ask what horton steak would taste like?"

"He handled it. You could hear the queued-up people laughing with Fwuffy, and at the jerk. Well, break's over."

We airswim back into the cockpit, which looks like an air defense center in one of Pop's silly old historical meeds, or maybe like the phone switchboard room in one hook I remember.

Before I can strap back in, Wychee says, "Top priority for you over here." She leans way back in her seat, reaches over her head, grabs my pant cuff, and literally drags me to her screen by the feet.

I say, "This is Acting Commander Susan Tervaille, *Virgo*—"

"Susan, it's me, your father, and I just wanted you to know I've been kicking desks and shaking bureaucrats all year—"

My eyes tear up and I think my chest is going to burst. "I know you have, Pop, I knew you must be—"

"—and the lawyers sitting here with me tell me you have just given us a brilliant opportunity. I've got word that all over Earth judges and lawyers are being called away from Christmas celebrations to sign off on counter injunctions against enforcing the Slabilis one; we're filing, Sheraton's filing, Ed Teach is filing, hundreds of faces are filing, and we're all winning. You've won, Susan, you've won! I'm so proud of you!"

"Oh, Pop, I don't know what to—wait a minute. *What happened to the radio lag?*"

Aunt Destiny's voice cuts in, and I notice for the first time that we're not on an AM channel—we're on ship-to-ship voice. "Kid, there's no radio lag you can hear across fourteen kilometers, which is currently our distance and closing. We're going to be there for lunch."

"How did you—I mean, but—so those accelerator bursts last night were your radar locking onto us! . . . what *ship* are you on?"

"Why, the good ship *Perdita*. And if you don't get the allusion, kid, your dad is going to turn around and dis-own you!" (I hear Pop, in the background, say "Damn straight!") "Bought with the pooled funds of a dozen ce-lebs, built practically overnight, and the first crewed ship in history to be designed for missions far above solar or-bital velocities. The technology has been around for sixty years and more, but you and your friends finally made us move it off the shelf. So I came out of the tank right about as *Perdita* moved into Martian orbit, on her shakedown cruise—imagine, this thing does Earth to Mars in just two months, right *after* an opposition—and, long story short, I found myself as the captain, with half a dozen ce-lebs that are your friends' families as passengers, and the best crew money could buy, which turns out to be a very good crew indeed. We got you on radar last night, from about 20,000 kilometers out, and we've been maneuver-ing in ever since. If you weren't all busy answering the AM radio, and you'd looked at a screen or out a window, you might've seen the flare of our exhaust."

Then I realize that while I've been lost in the conversation with Pop and Destiny, the room has fallen silent, except for the blessed desk clerks of Diego Garcia, telling everyone to queue up quietly and wait to see what happens, and everyone else talking to someone on regular channel; Glisters's face is streaked with tears as he babbles with his mom, Wychee and Marioschke are lost in confused, excited talk with their parents and steps, and even poor old F.B. is talking to his old nanny and his miney mother; I'm so relieved they found someone to bring along for him.

Just like that, I realize, we're rescued. I never thought about what it would be like, but one minute we're running Virgo *and the next we're going to be picked up and taken care of.*

I'm absorbing this when the AM channel crackles to life, as the news about the rendezvous with *Perdita* filters through the radio lag, and the response crawls at mere light-speed back to us: a huge, awesome roar of a couple of million people cheering into their radios.

Glisters catches my eye and whispers, "We did it, Commander." Wychee's hand touches my shoulder: "We're going home, Susan." And over it all, there's the joyful squeal of "Mewwy Chwistmas, I'm going to *wive*!"

26

THE GIRL I LEFT BEHIND ME

**January 9, 2131. On board *Perdita*, downbound to Earth.
240 million kilometers from the sun,
94 million kilometers from Earth.**

THEY DELAY THE big meeting while we all catch up on sleep and on our family connections. I'm a little shocked when Pop tells me I'm his hero, but not as shocked as Glisters is when his mother says, "I suppose it's been so silly of me, I've been putting you in the same snuggly little boy PJ's since you were four. How about some nice silk ones, suitable for a man of style and substance?"

"As long as they have ducks," he says.

Finally, at the big meeting, we find out how many different things our parents have been setting up, aside from just arranging for the first real advance in spaceship design in decades. The whole thing was so complicated that they brought along Courtland, Pop's main lawyer, who insisted on running most of the case from *Perdita*, "Because being a lawyer is the dullest job in the world that people still get paid for, and I'm not passing up the one real chance for an adventure I'll ever get." She's another funny-looking big-head pink person like Glisters, and like him she's obsessive and painfully smart and totally on our side, and has my love and gratitude forever. If I ever decide to get married I swear I'm taking out a personal ad, *extremely famous person seeks pink macrocephalic.*

As crew in possession of *Virgo* at the time another ship reached her, we have the salvage claim, and they think there's a way they can make money off our poor battered old ship, now lagging so far behind this fast modern one. "The best guess I can give you is that there might be three years of real profit in the theme park," Courtland is saying.

Right now she's explaining that Destiny has a huge claim against the UN Interplanetary Transportation Board, which owns *Virgo* and the five remaining Aldrin cyclers. She has a draft deal with the board that will let Destiny claim ownership for the "salvageable remainder of *Virgo*," by which they mean the pod, or *Virgo* as we've known her while we were her crew. There's more than enough left over to go partners with Pop and the consortium and have a robot pellor swarm, and a flock of iceballs, intercept *Virgo* as she approaches Earth, hook up into a workable configuration, and fly her to lunar orbit.

"The reason we think that orbiting the moon is the place for *Virgo*," Courtland says, "is that there will probably be about a three-year period during which we can operate her profitably as a theme park, something to visit and see for people taking a lunar vacation. After that, it'll be old news, but with the money we make on the theme park, we can then convert the two vacuum cargo sections into farms, put a Forest in each farm, and change most of the

Pressurized Cargo Section into luxury living quarters—living quarters for a small crew plus several bed-and-breakfast setups."

"I might like to live and work there," Marioschke said, "if I can apply."

F.B. nods. "It would be a fun place for little kids and families and all," he says. "And with us there—"

Courtland nods and says, "We're estimating that if you're there, and especially if Fwuffy is, it'll make quite a bit of additional money because it will be more 'authentically' *Virgo*."

"What else would it be?"

"Well, of course it'll be *Virgo* in the sense of the same ship, but for most of the solar system, what makes it *Virgo* is the crew, especially Fwuffy. So if you can imagine yourselves running a farm and a B&B, your presence there would make it 'really' *Virgo* to the tourists. And of course you would be good at it anyway—you have the skills and you're nice people. It would feel like such a warm, welcoming place; and of course even though there are farms on the moon, and with temptrol boxes, anyone anywhere can eat the best food from the best Earth restaurants, we *think* the cachet of 'fresh from *Virgo*' will mean premium pricing and another angle on more money. Maybe do some ag research there, get a few vegetables named after it—"

"I'd love to work on that," Marioschke says.

"As I said, the financial angles are endless, but what's more important, it's a place where we can keep Fwuffy alive and relatively free."

"Awive and wewativewy fwee is good."

"It's *very* good. And it's *not* easy. It is illegal in *depth* to have anything to do with hortons, upgrapes, and flipperwillies—that's an enhanced marine mammal, I didn't even know those *existed* till I tangled with PermaPaxPerity regulators and saw all the secret protocols, that's how systematic they are about the rules.

"Legally under PermaPaxPerity, no one can do *anything* connected to intelligence enhancement, *ever*, in *any* way. It's illegal to do any research into the process that creates them, illegal to perform any part of the process, illegal to hide the creation of one, illegal not to inform the police if you know about anyone doing it. However—luckily for Fwuffy—the first rule of PermaPaxPerity is *never turn off the entertainment*, and the second rule is *if you have to turn off the entertainment, don't let anyone see you turning it off.* They realize that Fwuffy's fan support is probably good for decades, so they're stuck—they can't kill him and they can't keep him.

"That's their dilemma. If they kill him they'll have global rioting, revenge murders of bureaucrats and revenge viruses all through the global net, decades of bad things; if they keep him, he's a magnet for all the people who like the idea of enhanced intelligence for any reason, from wanting a green dog that talks to wanting their kids to be Villanova-level geniuses.

"So, Fwuffy, officially, you're going to be a terribly nice but horribly shy and reclusive horton, unable to cope with all the publicity, who likes to meet people a few at a time, and too attached to *Virgo* to live anywhere else. We'll charge the B&B people extra to meet you—don't worry, they'll all pay it—but you're on the ship forever, and the conditions include that you won't do anything to secure legal rights for hortons."

Fwuffy nods. "I wike wuhking on the fawm, and *Vuhgo* is home. But I wish I could've twied faw my PotEvals, just faw the chawwenge."

"It might not have to be forever. Once we have you legally protected and in a safe place, and they've gotten used to the idea that your public existence isn't making the sun go out, we might find some ways to work out from under the restrictions, and maybe eventually overturn them. But till then . . . well, for the moment we have to play the game."

"But I'll be there with you," Marioschke says, reaching out and rubbing his face.

"And I will too," F.B. says.

Courtland checks a box on her tablet. "All right. Next issue. Incidentally, all of you, including Fwuffy, may change your minds about what you'll be doing, once you hear this offer. Destiny?"

Aunt Destiny says, "*Perdita* will reach Earth in about two months instead of the five it would take on an Aldrin cycler or four in a Space Patrol cruiser. After that we'll be re-outfitting her for the greatest crewed expedition in decades: a tour through six dwarf planets in the Kuiper Belt and out beyond it. We'll be doing about a 45° slice of it this first time, and going out a bit past 130 AU, which means we'll be out a bit over four times as far as the previous record holders, the Triton expedition. *And* we'll get home before they do, because by picking up ice out there from the various KBOs, we can spend a lot of time *way* up above orbital speeds.

"In point of fact we'll have to use gravity assists to slow down as we return, but we'll be back on Earth in just eleven years, after planting our footprints on six big worlds and maybe thirty small ones, and of course stomping a pathway through history that will never be forgotten. For what it's worth we'll also have *astronomical* recognition—"

"Boo," I say. We all spend a minute on making gagging noises.

When we're done, Destiny says, "All right, I'm an evalist, not a humorist. Anyway, the thing is, we'll be laying the groundwork for farther and deeper expeditions. Being blunt about this, I need crew that will do two things: try anything and never give up. Ideally, they should be young, because I want to try to get in four or five of these deep voyages before I'm too old. I'm putting up all my settlement money from the Interplanetary Transportation Board toward this, and Robert"—she nods at Pop—"has agreed to invest as well; we have half a dozen more investors lined up. So, fame, fortune, your name living forever . . . for a crew that follows the two basic rules, try anything and never give up. And in the whole solar system, where else can I find young people with exactly those attitudes?"

Glisters's and Wychee's heads have been pumping up and down like they're going to come off; they glance sideways, clearly expecting me to join in. And I float there in *Perdita*'s "conference bubble," the beautiful little starry room set up for everyone to talk, wondering what I will say, because perhaps when I say it, I'll know what I think.

Marioschke breaks the spell. "Well, when you come right down to it, I'm a space farmer—and the farmer part comes first. I'll want to visit some outdoor wilderness—with trees and grass and air I can breathe and no roof over it—a lot sooner than eleven years. I guess I'll stay with *Virgo*."

"Me, too," F.B. says, taking her hand.

"I'd miss pwants and fawming too much," Fwuffy says.

Destiny is shaking her head. "You won't *have* to miss that, Fwuffy; we'll be putting a farm module on *Perdita*; it's the only way we can travel that far over such a long time."

"Then I'd miss Mawioschke," he says.

"F.B., are you sure you want to miss the adventure?" Marioschke asks, anxiously. "I don't want to keep you home—"

"If I do, I'll go on the next one. We won't even be thirty when they come back, and that means probably sixty, maybe eighty, more good years in my life." He shrugs. "I just like the idea of being somewhere where people need me and want me, doing what I know I can do well."

It clicks, inside me, that *that's* what I want to do. Why did we ever, ever think that F.B. was dumb?

The problem is that for F.B. it's obvious that *being somewhere where people need me and want me, doing what I know I can do well* is working on *Virgo* for at least the next few years. For me . . . well, what is that?

"I think I want to think," I say, and try to convince myself that their smiles are supportive, rather than puzzled.

January 24, 2131. On board *Perdita*, downbound to Earth. 210 million kilometers from the sun, 68 million kilometers from Earth.

"If the world made any sense," I tell Destiny, "I would be trying to talk Pop out of going with you. But I'm reasonably willing to accept that my father is a grown-up."

"And I appreciate it," Pop says. "Many children never get that far with their parents."

The three of us are floating in the conference bubble together, just we three, watching the stars wheel slowly around us.

He tries again, tentatively, "It's just . . . well, a few months of travel in space, surrounded by all these stars, all the time. Just the peace of floating among them, feeling like the whole universe is there, you know?"

"I know that feeling, yeah, Pop."

"Meanwhile back home . . . there are a lot of roles for tired, jaded, old men. Some for evil, jaded, old men. Even a few for good, wise, old men. But nothing that I couldn't pass up. I've already done James Tyrone and Willy Loman, and King Lear can wait till I get back. So the more I thought about the last year when I mostly saw this"—he gestures, and I marvel that he's figured out a way to do a big sweep-

ing movement of the arm like that without tumbling himself—"the less need I felt to put my feet down onto a stage.
So it's hard for me to imagine someone wanting something
else. But I'll try, Susan, really I will, if you'll just reassure
me that this isn't some passing whim. I can't help but feel
that if *Perdita* leaves and you're not on it, you're going to
regret it, maybe—"

"'—not today, maybe not tomorrow, but soon, and for
the rest of your life,'" I say, finishing out the quote. "One of
your best revival roles, Pop, I'm glad you felt I was worthy
of the lines. Look, the reason why I won't regret it is that
I know if *Perdita* leaves and I *am* on it, I'll be wishing I
was home for the next eleven years. Really. Because here's
what I'm thinking. Three months after *Perdita* leaves, it
won't be even a blip in the media. A year after it leaves it'll
be part of a nostalgia quiz. When it does come back, eleven
years later, it'll be two months of excitement—if that, because all the images will have been transmitted home long
ahead of it, and the images are going to be mostly of you all
bouncing around on big fluffy snowballs, which is apparently what all those dwarf planets are."

"I . . ." Destiny looks sad—no, hurt.

"What's wrong, Aunt Destiny?"

"I just thought, if we can't even get you, Susan, to understand why we're doing it or what it's about . . . even
with all the experiences you've had, if you just want to go
back to your old life . . . that's *so* discouraging—"

She's breaking my heart, and I can tell Pop is thinking the same things she is, so I put an arm around each

of them, and squeeze tight, and say, "I know why it's important. I know why you're doing it. I know sometimes I'll wish I was with you, because I'll miss you, and because you'll be doing interesting things that I wish I could be there for. But it's not that I want to stay back here because I think I'll miss my chance for a higher recognition score. My recognition score is *already* mathematically indistinguishable from universal recognition; the only people who can't recognize my picture, my voice, or my name are hermits in suspended animation. It's not about that either.

"What I was trying to say was, if you do what you're planning to do, and I come along, it just means that every five or ten years there'll be an interesting exploration story on the meeds. And *only* that much. People back here won't be any different; there won't be any more ships like *Perdita* going out, there won't be any great decades-long exploration races like Scott against Amundsen, Korolev against Von Braun, or Santo against Nakamura. It'll be a twenty-days-out-of-a-decade media feature, like the Olympics without as many cute people."

"So what would you be doing staying back here?" Pop asks, quietly. "Running the space exploration fan club? Giving interviews to people who didn't care?"

"*Making* people care," I say. "What's Prince Henry the Navigator known for? This is a trick question, just answer it."

Crossly impatient to get to the point, Destiny says, "Well, he was the prince of—one of those countries back before the UN reorganized all the borders—in Europe, I'm pretty sure—Spain? Burgundy?"

"Portugal," I say. "And what was this navigating thing?"

Pop's gaze is far away as he sorts through a lifetime of memorized material. "Um, back in the Renaissance, he's the one who kept developing better and better ships, and sending them farther out on longer voyages, and kept records and maps of what they'd found, and I guess he was sort of European Exploration Central," Pop says. "This is all research from some role I was offered, not playing *him*, I don't think. It was a long time ago."

"Unh hunh. That's what we remember him for today. What was he known for in his own time?"

They look at each other, shrug. "No idea."

"Being rich, being a very eligible bachelor, being a guy who might get promoted to king any time, dressing beautifully, building beautiful houses . . ."

Pop starts to laugh. "I'm beginning to see this."

"The secret," I say, hugging them both tight, "is that Henry didn't get to be a prince because Navigator-ing was cool; his being one of Europe's hottest princes is what *made* exploration cool. It was the hobby of the most zoomed guy in the Western Christendom celeb circuit. So ultra cool that other kings and princes got into the exploration racket, too, and kept it going after his death; he was dead a generation before the caravels reached around Africa, and over to the New World, and circumnavigated the globe. But without Henry, voyages of exploration would have been occasional stunts. *With* Henry . . . you see?

"And one more reality, folks. You're old set-in-your-ways farts; you don't care if you ever set a fashion, or at least I hope you don't because I don't want to see sweaters like that one—"

"Hey!" Pop says.

"—or utility coveralls become fashion. I happen to be young, hot, recognizable, good-to-great at style and styling, and in six months I can own the media. What interests me and what I care about will *be* the fashion. You see? Somebody's got to sail the ship, but somebody has to stay home and teach people to care that it's sailing."

EARTH,
12
YEARS
LATER

APRIL 3, 2143

27

THE PRINCESS WHO STANDS ON THE SHORE

Wednesday, April 3, 2143. Headquarters of Tervaille Interstellar, Copenhagen, District of Scandinavia, Earth.

THE PERSKAB TURNS off the high-speed tracks and settles onto its wheels to glide up to my skyscraper. The first time I saw the plans for it, when they were building it for my nineteenth birthday back in '32, I thought I'd love it forever. Now that I'm turning thirty, it's just that damned building where I work—even if I do get the whole top floor to myself.

And I'm already busy enough tonight and I have to put in this silly appearance.

The front gate of Tervaille Interstellar appears beside my PersKab, which settles onto the walk. It's a big day, so I need to do my very best Susan Tervaille Awe-Inspiring Entrance for the robot cameras and whatever crowd has turned up besides the usual hundred or so tourists that come to gawk at me every morning.

Chrome stilettos with gyros and smart straps, set to cling to my feet and brace me up if I teeter, check. Deep cleavage surrounded by geneered self-grown silk lace, check. Skin as perfect as geneered resurfacers can make it. I run the coswand over my face to fix any stray issues in the makeup. I check myself in the mirror and style Devil May Care But Happy, that mix of sardonic upper-class eyebrows and common-touch grin that is ultra, ultra the style this year.

Checklist complete.

Showtime.

"PersKab, open door."

As it does, I stick one of those big pricey stilettos outside onto the pavement and rise through the door. There's an angle that minimizes the crotch flash and maximizes visible leg, and I hit the mark perfectly. Usually there's a few appreciative whistles or whoops; this time there's a roar like I just made a touchdown.

Wow. The crowd is bigger, all right. Ultra bigger. At least three thousand people, fifteen times the usual, singing "Happy Birthday to You."

Inside, I can kick off the ridiculous shoes, stretch out on the concentration sofa, and watch the screen on the ceiling while I talk my way through the business's affairs for the day. Everything is running perfectly, and there's fresh mail from *Perdita*, which is now only eight months away, almost home—sliding into the retrograde pass at Jupiter to gravity-break. I close my eyes, visualizing Glisters and Wychee, on watch together, just the big view screen with all its stars. In my imagination they're holding hands, and I smile about that.

Glisters's note is characteristically brief, dedicated to

the details of the ship's operation and urging me to pass it on to the design teams now building *Imogen*. Wychee runs a little longer, asking about this and that bit of gossip, clearly eager for some home time when she gets here. And Pop's note is more of that lyrical stuff he loves to do; he used to say there was nothing cornier than an actor writing his own material, so I really struggle not to quote that to him now.

I check the clock. More showtime ahead; notorious carnivore that I am, and this being my birthday, tonight I am expected, no, required, to be seen to dine upon fresh hot meat.

Wednesday, April 3, 2143. Club MockStop, Avignon, District of Provence, Earth.

He's twenty-one, an ultrazoomed star re-entry boarder, the first guy to manage a full hypersonic circumnavigation at the equator. His hair is what kids now call ultravery, which means something like stare-worthy, and his clothes must've been on a fashion meed ten minutes ago. Nothing wrong with the less trendy parts, either—his muscles and the big dark eyes are getting to me like they'd've gotten to Cleopatra.

He is the most fashionable accessory I can possibly wear in public on my birthday, or the most fashionable bit of meat I can possibly devour.

He's telling me stories about being very drunk and having fans fawn on him, interspersed with extremely technical stories of re-entry board rides he's taken. If it were possible to be literally bored out of my skull, my skull would still be here and I would be snuggled up in my apartment in Tunis, and grateful for it.

Still, even in disposing of a mistake, one must always think of exposure. I treat myself to a yawn, and his talk becomes a bit fast and nervous. Under the table I let the slit in my skirt open to flash more thigh for the cameras; he won't know about that till he sees the meeds, which I'm sure he'll do the instant he's away from me and in the PersKab by himself.

I press the rescue button that is discreetly under my belt at the hip, and a moment later my phone zizzes. I look at it, look concerned, say, "Yeah" and "On my way," and then to the beautiful doofus in front of me, I say, "Excuse me, have to go."

This has probably never happened around him before; he doesn't manage to say more than a sort of feeble "Yomph?" before I'm gone. I stride through MockStop, letting the maître d'hôtel flap after me like a pursuing chicken, out through the open front gates, directly into the crowd of celeb worshippers, and straight into the PersKab that the rescue button summoned. I suppose it's a chance for a very patient or very lucky terrorist to bag me, but the image of fearlessness it creates is worth something, too.

I fear I'm losing my touch; I was bored for about six minutes before I dumped Mr. Re-Entry Boarder. Though that's the wrong title for the man, he could not possibly have been bored-er than I.

In the PersKab I kick off the ridiculous shoes, loosen clothing, get comfy, and queue up the night's reading. The PersKab climbs onto a public line, and I hurtle through Italy, across the great bridge into Sicily, and down the trans-Med tunnel, writing a short friendly note to F.B. and Marioschke, and a longer letter to Fwuffy, who, I'm afraid, has definitely become the brains of that outfit.

Perhaps one night out in ten I meet someone whose eyes light up when I talk about the reports coming in from *Perdita*, plunging into the lower solar system at the highest speed human beings have yet achieved. Now and then one of my dates is so excited he or she brings up *Miranda* or *Rosalind*, now both outbound. There's a rumor that I bedded the captains of both; it's only true about one of them.

Perhaps three, perhaps four times a year, I find that one of my companions for the evening—it's always a celeb, I cannot afford obscurity—is not just a well-dressed ninny or a cunning and focused performer, but someone who really understands. When I do, there's at least enough of an affair to do us both some good, and he or she goes away with some enhanced recognition and fashion standing— along with some chances to play around with the great toys in the labs at Tervaille Interstellar, and it's from that, not from the affair, that a friendship usually blossoms.

I'm *so* disappointed that didn't happen tonight, especially on my thirtieth birthday. Mr. Re-entry Boarder had written me a couple of great letters and talked with me on net voice about things, and I thought he'd be fun; instead he was the classic handsome jock just waiting to be dragged off and used as a convenience, only able to talk about his jockly subjects. And it's been lonely lately. I didn't particularly want to use a partner but I could have used some company.

April 3, 2143. Tervaille Estate, Tunis, District of Sahara, Earth.

As my PersKab approaches my home, my phone zizzes. I pick it up even though I've checked and know it's my date; perhaps I want to take my disappointment out on him. "Hi," he says. "I happened to be in the neighborhood and wondered if the crisis was over yet. Ms. Courtland suggested I should see. I'm right by your front gate."

"You might as well come in, then," I say. "I'll meet you in my visitor's foyer in ten minutes; the gates will be authorized to guide your PersKab there."

Ms. Courtland suggested I should see. With no *you.* Code phrase. Suddenly my heart is pounding and I'm trying not to grin; someone was setting me up for a very happy birthday after all.

There's something different about his expression in the foyer; I realize he either took an alcohol-removing shot in his PersKab on the way here, or he was playing blurry-and-out on me before. He gets to the point. "Ms. Courtland told me to go out with you, bore you till you got rid of me, turn up like this, and then work that phrase into the first thing I said."

"Well, so far, you're following instructions, and I'm

sure she gave you some others. What did you do at the café after you bored me?"

"Oh, just ultra threw a tantrum. Also two wine bottles, more glasses than I can remember, and one chair, which hit the bottles behind the bar. I screamed that no bitch treats me that way. I think it is now clearly established that we are enemies."

"Very clearly."

"And next week I'm going to be doing a pro-am re-entry boarding event with Sir Penn Slabilis as my partner."

"Isn't he a little old—"

"He's old, but if you're strapped onto a hapless—you don't know boarding at all, do you?"

"Not a thing. And I'm afraid I wasn't paying attention before."

"Courtland said if I just kept talking about the dullest things I could think of about re-entry boarding, you'd be the rudest date I was ever dumped by."

"Was I?"

"Naw, Xera was worse. She's a lot dumber and more vulgar than you could ever be."

"I hate coming in second at anything," I say, and now I'm smiling, because I see where Courtland is going with this, and it's about as perfect as a thing can be. "So it is now well established that you and I hate each other. Penn Slabilis, only recently emerged from grieving for his son who died in that mysterious accident, is doing charity re-entry boarding—"

"Mainly because his fifth wife-to-be, who is nineteen, thinks boarding is hot," he says. "Which it will be for him. While we are flying in tandem, at the beginning of the run, 180 kilometers up, his detector will be curiously defective, which means it won't pick up the sudden, brief motion when I kick up the tail of my board, lifting his tail, and putting him into a roll. He will be on a hapless, which of course is designed to bring a mannequin down unharmed and to override anything stupid the rider might do. His hapless, like all of them, will have a built-in restabilizer, but this one will not have a built-in restabilizer *that works*. So he'll go into the atmosphere slowly rolling rather than board-to-the-air."

"And that's bad?"

"Bad sounds ultra judgmental. Bad in whose opinion?"

"Good point. What will happen?"

"In a roll, without a stabilizer, first the body leans backward—too much force to resist—and then the nose pitches the other way. You get lift in opposite directions, and the rotation gets faster and faster. Known as pinwheeling. Some of us do that as a stunt, on purpose. But we're young and strong enough to crouch down and stabilize before it goes through the point of no return. If, say, an older guy with weaker abs and back had that happen, he'd spin till his rotation became fast enough to black him out, or till his arms got away from him and extended above his head. Either way, a little further into the atmosphere, the force will be great enough to start plucking off extended parts of the body, such as hands and forearms. Then the plasma starts to form, only instead of a nice comfy envelope of it surrounding you, if you're rolling, you keep dipping into it. Eventually you get an effect rather like a match head."

I nod. "And you and I are known to be bitter enemies."

"We are."

I like his cockiness, his muscle . . . let's face it, there's something about the cold-blooded killer thing I like, too. I suppose some tastes are just incurable, even if we can learn to be more careful about them. *Maybe I can ask him to spend the night. Someday.*

I ask, "When someone does me a big favor, isn't there usually some reciprocal favor that comes with it?"

"Two," he says. "One's purely for satisfaction, something it would make me happy to know. Years ago, it happens, an older cousin of mine, who you might remember— a fellow named Stack—"

"Oh, my god. *That's* who you look like."

He nods. "Sometime—and it doesn't need to be now— you could tell me how Derlock Slabilis died. The meeds just said something about an out-of-control hopper?"

"Hmm. An athlete who works partly in space *would* find the details interesting," I say. "Well, Derlock was out on the moon in an open hopper, just taking the fast way to the other side of Armstrongia, up above the city dome. The engine fired a hot shot, sending him straight up at much more than escape velocity, and then the computer realized the mistake and brought the hopper back. Unfortunately, it was an open hopper, so when the restrain system failed, he flew out the top of the hopper at greater than escape velocity. So he left the moon and went into a very long, slow orbit around the Earth. Not that its being slow mattered much to Derlock; he wouldn't have finished one one-thousandth of his first orbit before his suit ran out of air. He's now an artificial satellite of Earth. Eventually he might impact the moon or Earth, or he might stabilize in a long-term orbit, but anyway, once he ran out of air and stopped shrieking, I would say the interesting part of the story was over."

And then he kisses me, and the boy can kiss. It's definite. I'll *never* lose the taste for cold-blooded killers. "We really shouldn't," I say, much as I am enjoying it. "We'll get tempted to get together on the sly, and that could be evidence, after Sir Penn's accident."

"Of course. Maybe we could think about resuming things when we're on our way."

"On our way where?"

"Can you figure out a way I can go on *Imogen* to Pandemonium? If it really does have a helium-II ocean, which means a *superconducting* ocean, then surfing on a magnetic board—since a magnet will levitate over a super-conductor—"

"Might be fatal, if anything goes wrong."

"Then I have to make sure nothing goes wrong." He shows me that grin again.

Maybe I *will* go on *Imogen*. I know I won't be able to, I have to keep things going here, but maybe I'll just decide I've been responsible long enough, by then. After all, *Imo-*

gen is just being built now; it will be six years before she departs.

He looks into my eyes and I see the expression that, nowadays, I seek constantly and find frequently. He's another one of us. He says, "An adventure no one else has ever had."

"I hope I can be there to watch you try it," I say.

Just before midnight. April 3, 2143. Tervaille Estate, Tunis, District of Sahara, Earth.

That evening, as I'm getting ready for bed, I'm considering. The Slabilises had to go, anyway; for what I'll be doing in the next few years, no one who has done me so much damage so publicly can be allowed to appear to have escaped. The fact that their fate makes me smile is charming but irrelevant, like enjoying the expensive lifestyle that is needed to maintain my aura of power; the power is crucial, and the aura is essential, but the clothes, girls, boys, and toys are merely fun.

Besides, I've played just as rough with people I didn't even know, if they didn't or couldn't understand what I needed them to do. That silly pop singer that recorded "Glad I Iz a Gurl & Glad Gurlz Iz Dumm" actually *was* too dumb, even after what happened to Derlock, to realize that she needed to take our money, and our orders, and find some new themes. And she could hardly have mattered less in and of herself, but pop stars have been cheap since her shocking accident, which could have been prevented if she'd ever paid attention in science class, as certain meeds immediately pointed out.

My privately commissioned studies of the mediasphere show that there's a definite trend for smart to be zoomed, ambitious to be zoomed, and dedicated to be zoomed, in the songs and meeds the kids like best.

It's a mildly dirty business and therefore an intensely exciting one.

Well. Glisters, Wychee, and F.B. will want to know. Marioschke and Fwuffy elected, long ago, to know nothing. For the three who choose to know I put, at the beginning of my enciphered letter, LUCIFER SHALL FALL. Then I tap out the usual, quick daily note about my life and how things are going; I try to say hi to them most nights.

There's another message from Glisters, one of the good ones he sends sometimes, with lots of pictures and recordings; this one is almost a half hour of life on *Perdita*. Pop looks great, younger than when he left; he and Glisters's mom have become an item, and we joke often about being brother and sister. They're doing the grav-brake trick across this week, a close pass at Jupiter in retrograde, bending around it and spilling speed; the pictures are awe inspiring, even if they're just the ones that probes have been showing for 150 years, and though it's corny, Wychee and Glisters posing, arms around each other, with Jupiter behind them, makes my heart leap up.

Perdita is returning to a world where deep space exploration hasn't been out of the news for three weeks at a time since they left; that took some doing. Along the way, though, I've reveled in luxury that Louis XIV couldn't have had, had experiences that Jezebel and Nero couldn't have dreamed of, and set an unbreakable record for recognition score.

I don't think that the forces I'm nurturing in the culture will sustain themselves, yet. If I go out on the next voyage of *Perdita*, or on *Imogen* after it—Glisters's first command and I won't be there—or the second voyage of *Miranda* . . . I keep thinking of later and later voyages. Truthfully I don't think the cultural changes I'm forcing will ever self-sustain, without constant celebrity leadership, and right now there's no other celebrity that can or will take the lead.

I wonder how many times captains said to Prince Henry the Navigator, *You ought to come with us,* and whether he ever said, *Maybe next time.*

I think about *Perdita* herself, a sweet, powerful, swift ship, and her even finer daughters; I think about what it would be like to welcome my new re-entry boarder friend back to the ship after he surfs Pandemonium's ocean of half-a-kelvin helium. I think of the long watches with no one else in the cockpit, just the instruments reaching far into the void, the stars on the screen, the sleeping ship around me.

And my heart aches.

ACKNOWLEDGMENTS

SOMETIME LONG AGO, just after the rocks stopped falling and the seas of magma began to skin over, I proposed this idea to Sharyn November, via Ashley Grayson, and pointed out that I really didn't know how it would end. This became one of the most accurate prophecies of my life.

I am grateful to both of them for their patience while I found my way to the ending, and deeply grateful at having been told, repeatedly, *Good is more important than soon.* Saying that to me was probably the height of commercial irresponsibility, but it was very much what the book needed.

Shelly Perron, the copy editor, greatly reduced the number of errors in this text (the remainder are all my fault, for those of you keeping track), and also asked a very large number of very smart questions that caused me to be much clearer about many different things.

Obviously this book would not exist without ideas that I learned about from Buzz Aldrin; the chance to work with him was one of the reasons why I wouldn't have wanted any other profession.

This book had a very large number of titles before someone realized that *Losers in Space* was what the title should be; none of us can remember who first said, "Why don't we just call it that?" So thanks and a shout-out to the Unknown Marketer.

Howard Davidson, lifetime promoter of the hard in hard SF, nitpicked, which was invaluable. I got more things right because of Howard; I'm quite sure I didn't get everything right, and that was because of me.

About the very ending: the last two paragraphs were inspired by and are deliberate *hommage* to the conclusion of John Steele Gordon's wonderful book *Overlanding*, a book which, when I was in my early twenties, held more romance than *Mutiny on the Bounty, The Merry Adventures of Robin Hood,* and *The Prisoner of Zenda*, combined, and which was indirectly responsible for some of the most treasured memories in my life. Sadly, much of the practical information in *Overlanding* is now hopelessly dated, most copies are long out of circulation, and it reflects a world that no longer exists. But since I myself am hopelessly dated, almost entirely out of circulation, and reflective of a world that no longer exists, I do hope someone, someday, will bring out a new edition. Meanwhile, if you see it, grab it.

This is **JOHN BARNES**'s thirtieth published book, including two books coauthored with astronaut Buzz Aldrin. Most of his work has been science fiction, but he has also written a number of nonfiction articles, including more than fifty in the *Oxford Encyclopedia of Theatre and Performance*. His (non-science fiction) novel *Tales of the Madman Underground* was a 2010 Michael L. Printz Honor Book.

At various times he has been paid to teach college classes in English, mathematics, theater, economics, speech, political science, and communications; design stage scenery and lighting; draw weather maps; work setups and tear-downs for a company that decorates building lobbies; write ad copy, political speeches, software reviews, blogs, and computer manuals; analyze poll data, employee satisfaction surveys, marketing research data, and social media metrics; copyedit a small city magazine; and travel a three-state territory as a sales rep. His parents always said he'd never be able to hold a steady job.

John Barnes lives in Colorado.